MORE ADVENTURES OF THE
SECRET SEVEN

Five exciting stories in one volume
by

Enid Blyton

CHANCELLOR
PRESS

The stories in this volume were first published
in Great Britain by Brockhampton Press Ltd
(now Hodder and Stoughton Children's Books).

Good Work, Secret Seven first appeared in 1954
Copyright © Darrell Waters Ltd
Illustrations copyright © Hodder and Stoughton Ltd

Secret Seven Win Through first appeared in 1955
Copyright © Darrell Waters Ltd
Illustrations copyright © 1970 Hodder and Stoughton Ltd

Puzzle for the Secret Seven first appeared in 1958
Copyright © Darrell Waters Ltd
Illustrations copyright © 1971 Hodder and Stoughton Ltd

Secret Seven Fireworks first appeared in 1959
Copyright © Darrell Waters Ltd
Illustrations copyright © 1972 Hodder and Stoughton Ltd

Good Old Secret Seven first appeared in 1960
Copyright © Darrell Waters Ltd
Illustrations copyright © 1960 Hodder and Stoughton Ltd

This collected edition published in 1989 by
Chancellor Press
Michelin House
81 Fulham Road
London
SW3 6RB

Arrangement and Design © 1989 Octopus Books Ltd

ISBN 1 85152 093 7

Printed in Czechoslovakia

50508

CONTENTS

GOOD WORK, SECRET SEVEN

CONTENTS

One

Secret Seven meeting

'WHEN are the Secret Seven going to have their next meeting?' said Susie to her brother Jack.

'That's nothing to do with *you*!' said Jack. 'You don't belong to it, and what's more, you never will!'

'Good gracious! *I* don't want to belong to it!' said Susie, putting on a very surprised voice. 'If I want to belong to a secret society I can always get one of my own. I did once before, and it was a better one than yours.'

'Don't be silly,' said Jack. 'Our Secret Seven is the best in the world. Why, just think of the things we've done and the adventures we've had! I bet we'll have another one soon.'

'I bet you won't,' said Susie, annoyingly. 'You've been meeting in that shed at the bottom of Peter and Janet's garden for weeks now, and there isn't even the *smell* of a mystery!'

'Well, mysteries don't grow on trees, nor do adventures,' said Jack. 'They just happen all in a minute. Anyway, I'm not going to talk about the Secret Seven any more, and you needn't think you'll get anything out of me, because you won't, Susie. And please go out of my room and let me get on with this book.'

'I know your latest password,' said Susie, half-way through the door.

'You do *not*!' said Jack, quite fiercely. 'I haven't mentioned it, and I haven't even written it down so that I won't forget it. You're a story-teller, Susie.'

'I'm not! I'm just telling you so as to warn you to choose a *new* password!' said Susie, and slid out of the door.

Jack stared after her. What an *annoying* sister she was! *Did* she know the password? No, she *couldn't* know it, possibly!

It was true what Susie had said. The Secret Seven had been meeting for weeks, and absolutely nothing had turned up. Certainly the seven had plenty of fun together, but after having so many exciting adventures it was a bit dull just to go on playing games and talking.

Jack looked in his note-book. When was the next meeting? Tomorrow night, in Peter's shed. Well, that would be quite exciting, because all the members had been told to bring any fireworks they had managed to buy for Bonfire Night. It would be fun looking through them all.

Bonfire Night was next week. Jack got up and rummaged in one of his drawers. Ah, there were his fireworks. And here was his big Humdinger. Jack was sure he was the only Secret Seven member who had got one of those.

'Fizzzzzzzz – WHOOOOOSH – BANG!' he said, and stamped on the floor. 'Fizzzzzzzzzz – WHOO . . .'

'Jack! What in the world are you doing? Are you ill?' called an anxious voice, and his mother's head came round the door.

'No, Mother. I'm all right,' said Jack. 'I was only thinking of this Humdinger and the noise it will make.'

'Humdinger? Whatever's that?' asked his mother. 'Oh, *Jack*! How untidy your bedroom is!'

'I was *just* tidying it, Mother,' said Jack. 'I say, could you let me have some of those chocolate biscuits out of the tin, Mother? We're having a Secret Seven meeting tomorrow night.'

'Very well. Take seven,' said his mother.

'Eight, you mean,' called Jack, as she went out of the room. '*Mother!* Eight, I want. You've forgotten Scamper.'

'Good gracious! Well, if you *must* waste good chocolate biscuits on a dog, take eight,' called his mother.

Good, thought Jack. We've all got to take something nice to eat tomorrow night, for the meeting. Choc biscuits will be fine! Now, what was the password? Guy Fawkes, wasn't it? Or was that last time's? No, that's the one. Guy Fawkes – and a jolly good password, seeing that Bonfire Night is soon coming! Why does Susie say she knows it? She doesn't!

The meeting was for half past five, in Peter's shed, and all the Secret Seven meant to be there. Just before the half-hour five children began to file in at Peter's gate and make their way down the garden to the shed where the meetings were held.

11

The shed door was shut, but a light shone from inside. On the door were the letters S.S., put there by Peter. It was dark, and one by one torches shone on the door as the members arrived.

Rat-tat!

'Password, please!' That was Peter's voice inside.

'Guy Fawkes!' answered the members one by one.

Pamela was first. Then came Jack, hurrying in case he was late. Then George, carrying a bag of rosy apples as his share of the food. Then Barbara, wondering if the password was Guy Fawkes or Bonfire Night. Oh dear!

Rat-tat! She knocked at the door.

'Password!'

'Er – Bonfire Night,' said Barbara.

The door remained shut, and there was a dead silence inside. Barbara gave a little giggle.

'All right. I know it! Guy Fawkes!'

The door opened and she went in. Everyone was there except Colin.

'He's late,' said Peter. 'Blow him! I say, what a spread we've got tonight!'

The shed was warm and cosy inside. It was lighted by two candles, and there was a small oil-stove at the back. On a table made of a box was spread the food the members had brought.

'Apples. Ginger buns. Doughnuts. Peppermint rock, and what's in this bag? Oh yes, hazel nuts from your garden, Pam. *And* you've remembered to bring nut-crackers too. Good. And I've brought orangeade. Jolly good feast!' said Peter.

'I wish Colin would buck up,' said Janet. 'Oh, here he is!'

There was the sound of running feet and somebody banged at the door. Rat-tat!

'Password!' yelled everyone.

'Guy Fawkes!' answered a voice, and Peter opened the door.

Well, would you believe it! It was *Susie* outside, grinning all over her cheeky face. *Susie!*

Two

That awful Susie!

'SUSIE!' cried Jack, springing up in a rage. 'How dare you! You – you – you . . .'

He caught hold of his sister and held her tight. She laughed at him.

'It's all right; I just wanted to give your high-and-mighty members a shock. Aha! I know your password, see?'

'How did you know it?' demanded Peter. 'Let her go, Jack. We'll turn her out in a minute. How did you know the password, Susie?'

'I got it from Jack, of course,' said Susie, most surprisingly.

Everyone stared at poor Jack, who went as red as a beetroot. He glared at Susie.

'You're a wicked story-teller! I never told you the password and I didn't even write it down, in case you found it. How *did* you know it? Were you listening in the bushes round the shed? Did you hear us say the password as we came in?'

'No. If I had, Scamper would have barked,' said Susie, which was quite true. 'I tell you, Jack, I heard you say it yourself. You were talking in your sleep last night and you kept yelling out "Guy Fawkes! Let me in! Guy Fawkes, I say!" So I guessed you were trying

14

to get into the meeting in your sleep and were yelling out the password.'

Jack groaned. 'I do talk in my sleep, but who would have thought I'd yell out the password? I'll keep my bedroom door shut in future. I'm sorry, Peter. What are we going to do with Susie? She ought to be punished for bursting in on our secret meeting like this!'

'Well, we've nothing important to discuss, so we'll make Susie sit in that corner over there, and we'll have our feast, and not offer her a single thing,' said Peter, firmly. 'I'm tired of Susie, always trying to upset our Society. Pam and Barbara, sit her down over there.'

Everyone was so very cross with Susie that she began to feel upset. 'It was only a joke,' she said. 'Anyway, your meetings are silly. You go on and on having them and nothing happens at all. Let me go.'

'Well, promise on your honour you'll never try to trick us again or upset our meetings?' said Peter, sternly.

'No. I won't promise,' said Susie. 'And I shan't sit still in this corner, and I shan't keep quiet. You're to let me go.'

'Certainly not,' began Peter. 'You forced yourself in, and you can jolly well stop and see us eating all . . .'

He stopped very suddenly as he heard the sound of panting breath, and running feet coming down the garden path.

15

'It's Colin!' said Janet.

There was a loud rat-tat at the door, and the pass-word. 'Guy Fawkes! Quick, open the door.'

The door was opened and Colin came in, blinking at the sudden light, after the darkness outside.

'I say, I've had an adventure! It might be something for the Secret Seven. Listen!'

'Wait! Turn Susie out first!' said Peter.

Colin stared in surprise at seeing Susie there. She gave a sudden giggle, and Jack scowled at her.

'What's she doing here, anyway?' asked Colin, most astonished, as he watched Susie being hustled out of the shed.

The door was slammed and locked. Scamper, the golden spaniel who belonged to Peter and Janet, barked loudly. He hadn't at all approved of Susie being in his shed. He knew she wasn't a member!

'Tell you about Susie later,' said Peter. 'Now, Colin, what's all this about? Why are you late, and what's happened? And for goodness' sake, let's all talk quietly, because Susie is sure to be listening at the door!'

'I'll jolly well see that she isn't,' said Jack, getting up, but Peter pulled him back.

'Sit down! Don't you know it's just what Susie would like, to be chased all over the garden in the dark, spoiling our feast and our meeting and every-thing! Let her listen at the door if she wants to. She won't hear a word if we whisper. Be quiet, Scamper! I can't hear myself speak with you barking at the top of your voice. Can't *you* whisper too?'

16

Scamper couldn't. He stopped barking and lay down with his back to Peter, looking rather hurt. But he soon turned himself round again when Colin began his tale.

'I was coming along to the meeting, shining my torch as I came, and when I got to the corner of Beeches Lane, I heard somebody in the clump of bushes there. You know there's quite a little thicket at that corner. There was a lot of whispering going on, and then suddenly I heard a yell and a groan . . .'

'Gracious!' said Janet, startled.

'And somebody fell heavily. I shone my torch at the bushes, but someone knocked it out of my hand,' went on Colin. 'Then I heard the sound of running feet. I went to pick up my torch, which was still shining brightly on the ground, but by the time I shone it into the bushes again, nobody was there!'

'You were jolly brave to pick it up and look into the bushes,' said Peter. 'What was going on, do you think?'

'I can't imagine, except that there was a quarrel of some sort,' said Colin. 'That isn't all, though. Look what I found in the bushes.'

The Secret Seven were now so excited that they had quite forgotten about whispering. They had raised their voices, and not one of them remembered that Susie might be outside. Scamper gave a little warning growl, but nobody paid any attention.

Colin was holding out a worn and battered note-book, with an elastic band round it. 'I've had a quick

17

look inside,' he said, 'and it might be important. A lot of it is in code, I can't read it, and there's a lot of nonsense too. At least it sounds like nonsense, but I expect it's part of a code. Look!'

They all looked. Everyone began to feel excited. Peter turned the pages and came to a list written down one page. 'I *say*!' he said. 'Here's a list that might be a record of stolen goods. Listen. .... Silver candle-sticks, three-branched, cigarette box with initials A.G.B., four silver cups, engraved ...'

Jack sprang up 'I know what all that is! My father read the list out at breakfast this morning. It was in the paper. It's a list of the things stolen from the famous cricketer, Bedwall, last night. Whew! Do you suppose we're on to something, Peter?'

Three

Exciting plans

THE Secret Seven were so thrilled that their excitement made Scamper begin to bark again. He just couldn't help it when he heard them all talking at once. He waved his plumy tail and pawed at Peter, who took no notice at all.

'It must be a note-book kept by one of the thieves, a list of things he stole!'

'What else does it say? I wish we could understand all this stuff in secret code. Wait, look, here's a note scribbled right across this page! See what it says?'

' "Gang meet in old workmen's shed, back of Lane's garage," ' read Peter. ' "5 p.m. Wednesday." Whew! That's tomorrow. I *say*, we *are* on to something.'

Everyone began to talk excitedly again, and Scamper thought it was a very good time to sample a chocolate biscuit and perhaps a ginger bun. Before he did so he ran to the door and sniffed.

Yes. Susie was outside. Scamper could smell her. He growled a little, but as no one took any notice, and he was afraid to bark again, he went back to the good things on the little box-table.

'What are we going to do about this? Tell the

police?' asked Colin, who felt most important at bringing all this exciting news to the Seven.

'No. I'll tell you what we'll do,' said Peter. 'We'll creep round to that old shed tomorrow night ourselves, and as soon as we see the gang is safely there, one of us can rush round to the police-station, while the rest keep guard on the shed.'

It was decided that that would be a good sensible and exciting thing to do. Pam gave a huge sigh.

'Excitement makes me feel jolly hungry. Can't we start on the buns and things? Oh, Scamper, you've been helping yourself! Thief-dog!'

'Scamper! Have you really been taking things?' said Peter, shocked. 'Go into the corner.'

'He's only taken a choc biscuit and a ginger bun,' said Jack, counting everything quickly. 'There should be eight of each thing, but there are only seven of the biscuits and the buns. So really he's only eaten what we brought for *him*, the eighth person.'

'Well, he shouldn't begin before we do,' said Peter. 'He ought to know his manners. Corner, Scamper!'

Poor Scamper retired to the corner, licking his lips for stray chocolate crumbs. He looked so woe-begone that everyone felt extremely sorry for him.

The fireworks brought by the Seven were quite forgotten. Jack's Humdinger lay on the top of the pile, but not even he remembered it – the evening's happenings were much too exciting even for fireworks to be examined. The Seven made their plans as they ate.

'I say, we forgot all about Susie!' said Peter, suddenly. 'We've been yelling out our plans at the tops of our voices. Blow! Scamper, see if Susie is at the door!'

Scamper obediently ran to the door and sniffed. No, Susie was no longer there. He came back and sat down by Peter, putting his lovely golden head on the boy's knee, hoping for a forgiving pat.

'Oh, so she's not there. You'd have growled if she had been, wouldn't you, Scamper?' said Peter, stroking the dog's silky head and fondling his long ears. 'Well, Susie will be most astonished to hear about our adventure when it's over – serve her right for laughing at us and trying to spoil our meeting!'

It was arranged that all the Seven should go quietly to Lane's garage the next night, after tea. Colin knew Larry, a boy who helped at the garage, and it would be quite easy for the Seven to talk to him and admire the cars until it was time to look about for the workmen's shed behind the garage. Then what would happen? A little thrill of excitement ran .all the way up Peter's back when he thought of it.

The Secret Seven are on the move again! he thought. What a good thing, after all these dull weeks when nothing happened!

It seemed a long time till the next afternoon. Everyone at the schools the Secret Seven went to was sure that something was up. The Seven wore their badges, and a lot of whispering went on. All the members looked important and serious.

Susie was very annoying. She kept looking at Pam, Janet and Barbara, who were in her class, and giggling. Whenever she passed them she whispered in their ear:

'Guy Fawkes! Guy Fawkes!'

This was very annoying because it was still the password of the Secret Seven! They had completely forgotten to change it the night before, in the excitement of making plans. Now Susie still knew it. They must change it as quickly as they could.

At four o'clock all the Secret Seven rushed home early to tea, so that they could be off again immediately to the garage. They were to meet Colin there at a quarter to five.

All their mothers were astonished to see how quickly the children gobbled their teas that afternoon, but luckily nobody was made to stop at home afterwards. One by one they made their way to the garage. Scamper was left behind, in case he barked at an awkward moment.

Everyone was at the garage at a quarter to five. Only fifteen minutes more! Now, where was Larry? They must talk to him for a little while, and then creep round to the shed at the back. How exciting!

Four

A dreadful shock

COLIN was already looking for Larry, the boy he knew who helped at the garage. Ah, there he was, washing a car over in the corner. Colin went over to him, and the other six followed.

'Good evening,' said Larry, grinning at the Seven. He had a shock of fair hair and a very dirty face and twinkling eyes. 'Come to help me?'

'I wish we were allowed to,' said Colin. 'I'd love to mess about with cars. Larry, can we have a look at the ones you've got in the garage now?'

'Yes, so long as you don't open the doors,' said the lad, splashing the water very near Colin's feet.

The Seven divided up and went to look at the cars near the doorway and wide windows, so that they could keep an eye on anyone passing. They might see the 'gang', whoever they were.

'Look! Doesn't *he* look as if he might be one of the gang?' whispered Barbara, nudging Jack as a man went by.

Jack glanced at him.

'Ass!' he said. 'That's my headmaster. Good thing he didn't hear you! Still, he does look a bit grim!'

'It's five to five,' said George in a low voice. 'I think we'd better go round to the shed soon, Peter.'

23

'Not yet,' said Peter. 'We don't want to be there when the men arrive. Seen anyone likely to belong to the gang?'

'Not really,' said George. 'Everybody looks rather *ordinary*. But then, the gang might look ordinary too! Gosh, I *am* beginning to feel excited!'

A little later, when the garage clock said a minute past five, Peter gave the signal to move. They all said goodnight to Larry, who playfully splashed hose-water round their ankles as they ran out.

'Blow him, my socks are soaked,' said Jack. 'Do we go down this alley-way, Peter?'

'Yes. I'll go first, and if all's clear I'll give a low whistle,' said Peter.

He went down the alley in the darkness, holding his torch, but not putting it on. He came to the yard behind the garage, where the workmen's shed was.

He stopped in delight. There was a light in it! The gang *were* in there, then! My word, if only they could catch the whole lot at once.

Peter gave a low whistle, and the others trooped down the alley to him. They all wore rubber-soled shoes, and made no noise at all. Their hearts beat fast, and Barbara felt out of breath, hers thumped so hard. They all stared at the little shed, with the dim light shining from its one small window.

'They must be there,' whispered Jack. 'Let's creep up and see if we can peep in at the window.'

They crept noiselessly up to the shed. The window was high up and Peter had to put a few bricks on top

24

of one another to stand on, so that he could reach the window.

He stepped down and whispered to the others: 'They're there. I can't see them, but I can hear them. Shall we get the police straight away, do you think?'

'Well, I'd like to be sure it isn't just *workmen* inside,' said Jack. 'They might be having their tea there or something, you know. Workmen do have a lot of meals, and that shed's pretty cosy, I should think.'

'What are we to do, then? We can't knock on the door and say, "Are you workmen or do you belong to the gang?"' said Peter.

A loud bang came suddenly from the shed and made everyone jump. Barbara clutched at George and made him jump again.

'Was that a gun?' she said. 'They're not shooting, are they?'

'*Don't* grab me like that!' said George, in a fierce whisper. 'You nearly made me yell out. How do I know if it's shooting?'

Another loud bang came, and the Seven once more jumped violently, Peter was puzzled. What was happening in that shed? He suddenly saw that there was a keyhole. Perhaps if he bent down and looked through that he would be able to see what was happening inside.

So he bent down and squinted through the keyhole, and sure enough, he got quite a view, though a narrow one, of the inside of the candle-lit shed.

What he saw filled him with such astonishment that he let out a loud exclamation. He couldn't believe his eyes. He simply couldn't!

'What is it, what is it?' cried Pam, quite forgetting to speak in a whisper. 'Are they shooting? Let *me* look!'

She dragged Peter away and put her eye to the keyhole, and she, too, gave a squeal. Then, to the amazement of all the others but Peter, she began to kick and bang at the locked door! She shouted loudly:

'It's *Susie* in there, Susie and some others! I can see her grinning like anything, and they've got big paper bags to pop. That's what made the bangs. It's Susie; it's all a trick; it's SUSIE!'

So it was. Susie, with Jim and Doris and Ronnie, and now they were rolling over the floor, squealing with laughter. Oh, what a *wonderful* trick they had played on the Secret Seven!

Five

A victory for Susie

THE Secret Seven were so angry that they hardly knew what to do. So it was Susie and her friends who had planned all this! While Susie had been boldly giving the password and forcing her way into their meeting the night before, her friends were pretending to scuffle in the bushes to stop Colin and make him think something really serious was going on!

'They took me in properly,' groaned Colin. 'I really thought it was men scuffling there, and I was so pleased to find that note-book when they had run off! It was too dark to spot that they weren't men, of course.'

'No wonder Susie giggled all the time she was in our shed, and laughed when Colin rushed in to tell us of his adventure!' said Janet. 'Horrid, tiresome girl!'

'She's the worst sister possible,' said Jack, gloomily. 'Fancy putting that list of stolen things in the note-book, of course, *she* had heard my father read them out at breakfast-time too. Blow Susie!'

George kicked at the shed door. From the inside came the sound of shrieks of delighted laughter, and some enormous guffaws from Jim, who, like Doris, was rolling about from side to side, holding his aching sides. Oh, what a joke! Oh, to think they had brought the stuck-up Secret Seven all the way to this shed, just to see *them*!

'You just wait till you unlock the door and come out!' called Jack. 'You just wait! I'll pull your hair till you squeal, Susie. I'm ashamed of you!'

More squeals of laughter, and a loud, 'Ho, ho, ho,' from Jim again. It really was maddening.

'There's seven of us, and only four of you,' cried Colin, warningly. 'And we'll wait here till you come out, see? You hadn't thought of that, had you?'

'Oh yes, we had,' called Susie. 'But you'll let us go free – you see if you don't.'

'We shan't!' said Jack, furiously. 'Unlock the door.'

'Listen, Jack,' said Susie. 'This is going to be a LOVELY tale to tell all the others at school. Won't the Secret Seven be laughed at? Silly old Secret Seven, tricked by a stupid note-book. They think themselves so grand and so clever, but they're sure that four children in a shed are a gang of robbers shooting at one another! And we only had paper bags to pop!'

The four inside popped paper bags again and roared with laughter. The Secret Seven felt gloomier and gloomier.

'You know, Susie will make everyone yell and hoot about this,' said Colin. 'We shan't be able to hold our heads up for ages. Susie's right. We'll have to let them go free, and not set on them when they come out.'

29

'No!' said Peter and Jack.

'Yes,' said Colin. 'We'll *have* to make a bargain with them, and Susie jolly well knows it. We'll have to let them go free in return for their keeping silent about this. It's no good, we've got to. *I* don't want all the silly kids in the first form hooting with laughter and popping paper bags at me whenever I go by. And they will. I know them!'

There was a silence. It dawned on everyone that Colin was right. Susie had got the best of them. They *couldn't* allow anyone to make a laughing-stock of their Secret Seven Society. They were so proud of it; it was the best Secret Society in the world.

Peter sighed. Susie *was* a pest. Somehow they must pay her back for this tiresome, aggravating trick. But for the moment she had won.

He banged on the door, and the squeals and shrieks from inside died down.

'Susie! You win, for the present!' said Peter. 'You can go free, and we won't even pull your hair, if you promise solemnly not to say a single word about this to anyone at school.'

'All right,' called Susie, triumphantly. 'I knew you'd have to make that bargain. What a swizz for you! Silly old Secret Seven! Meeting solemnly week after week with never a thing to do! Well, we're coming out, so mind you keep your word.'

The door was unlocked from inside and the four came out, laughing and grinning. They stalked through the Secret Seven, noses in the air, enjoying their triumph. Jack's fingers itched to grab at Susie's hair, but he kept them in his pockets.

'Goodbye. Thanks for a marvellous show,' said the irritating Susie. 'Let us know when you want another adventure, and we'll provide one for you. See you later, Jack!'

They went off down the alley-way, still laughing. It was a gloomy few minutes for the Seven, as they stood in the dark yard, hearing the footsteps going down the alley.

'We simply MUST find something really exciting

ourselves now, as soon as possible,' said Colin. 'That will stop Susie and the others jeering at us.'

'If only we could!' said Peter. 'But the more you look for an adventure the farther away it seems. Blow Susie! What a horrible evening we've had!'

But it wasn't quite the end of it. A lamp suddenly shone out nearby and a voice said:

'Now then! What are you doing here? Clear off, you kids, or I'll report you to your parents!'

It was the policeman! Well! To think they had been turned off by the police as if *they* were a gang of robbers, and they had had such high hopes of fetching this very policeman to capture a gang in that shed! It was all very, very sad.

In deep silence the Seven left the yard and went gloomily up the alley-way. They could hardly say goodnight to one another. Oh, for a real adventure, one that would make them important again, and fill their days with breathless excitement!

Be patient, Secret Seven. One may be just round the corner. You simply never know!

Six

A sudden adventure

NEXT day Peter and Janet talked and talked about Susie's clever trick. Why, oh why, had they allowed themselves to be so easily taken in? Scamper listened sympathetically to their gloomy voices, and went first to one, then to the other, wagging his tail.

'He's trying to tell us he's sorry about it!' said Janet, with a little laugh. 'Oh, Scamper, if only we'd taken you with us, you'd have known Susie was in that shed with her silly friends, and somehow you'd have found a way of telling us.'

Scamper gave a little whine, and then lay on his back, his legs working hard, as if he were pedalling a bicycle upside down. He always did this when he wanted to make the two children laugh.

They laughed now, and patted him. Good old Scamper!

Their mother popped her head in at the door. 'Don't forget you're to go to tea with old Mrs Penton this afternoon.'

'My bike's got a puncture, Mummy,' said Janet. 'It's *such* a long way to walk. Need I go?'

'Well, Daddy is going out in the car this afternoon. He can take you there, and fetch you back afterwards,' said Mummy. 'He'll call for you about six o'clock, so mind you don't keep him waiting.'

The car was waiting outside Janet's school for her that afternoon, with Daddy at the wheel. They picked Peter up at his school gates, and Daddy drove them to Mrs Penton's. She had been their mother's old nurse, and she was very fond of them.

They forgot all about their annoyance with Susie when they saw the magnificent tea that Mrs Penton had got ready.

'Goodness – cream buns! How delicious!' said Janet. 'And chocolate éclairs. Did Mummy like them when you were her nurse?'

'Oh yes, she ate far too many once, and I was up all night with her,' said Mrs Penton. 'Very naughty she was, that day, just wouldn't do what she was told, and finished up by over-eating. Dear, dear, what a night I had with her!'

It seemed impossible that their mother could ever have been naughty or have eaten too many cream buns and éclairs. Still, it would be a very easy thing to eat at least a dozen of them, Janet thought, looking at the lovely puffy cream oozing out of the big buns, and those éclairs! She felt very kindly towards the little girl who was now grown-up, and her own mother!

They played the big musical box after tea, and looked at Mrs Penton's funny old picture-books. Then the clock suddenly struck six.

'Goodness, Daddy said we were to be ready at six!' said Peter, jumping up. 'Buck up, Janet. Thank you very much, Mrs Penton, for such a smashing tea.'

34

Hoot – hoo – ! That was Daddy already outside waiting for them. Mrs Penton kissed them both.

'Thank you very, very much,' said Janet. 'I *have* enjoyed myself!'

They ran down the path and climbed into the car at the back. It was quite dark, and Daddy's headlights shed broad beams over the road.

'Good children,' he said. 'I only had to wait half a minute.' He put in the clutch and pressed down the accelerator; the car slid off down the road.

'I've just got to call at the station for some goods,' said Daddy. 'I'll leave the car in the yard with you in it. I shan't be a minute.'

They came to the station, and Daddy backed the car out of the way at one end of the station yard. He jumped out and disappeared into the lighted entrance of the station.

Peter and Janet lay back on the seat, beginning to feel that they *might* have over-eaten! Janet felt sleepy and shut her eyes. Peter began to think about the evening before, and Susie's clever trick.

He suddenly heard hurried footsteps, and thought it must be his father back again. The door was quickly opened and a man got in. Then the opposite door was opened and another man sat down in the seat beside the driver's.

Peter thought his father had brought a friend with him to give him a lift, and he wondered who it was. It was dark in the station yard, and he couldn't see the other man's face at all. Then the headlights

36

went on, and the car moved quickly out of the yard.

Peter got a really terrible shock as soon as the car passed a lamp-post. The man driving the car wasn't his father! It was somebody he didn't know at all, a man with a low-brimmed hat, and rather long hair down to his collar. Peter's father never had long hair. Whoever was this driving the car?

The boy sat quite still. He looked at the other man when they went by a lamp-post again. No, that wasn't his father either! It was a man he had never seen before. His head was bare and the hair was very short, quite different from his companion's.

A little cold feeling crept round Peter's heart. Who were these men? Were they stealing his father's car? What was he to do?

Janet stirred a little. Peter leaned over to her and put his lips right to her ear.

'Janet!' he whispered. 'Are you awake? Listen to me. I think Daddy's car is being stolen by two men, and they don't know we're at the back. Slip quietly down to the floor, so that if they happen to turn round they won't see us. Quick now, for goodness' sake!'

Seven

Something to work on

JANET was awake now, very much awake! She took one scared look at the heads of the two men in front, suddenly outlined by a street lamp, and slid quickly down to the floor. She began to tremble.

Peter slipped down beside her. 'Don't be frightened. I'll look after you. So long as the men don't know we're here, we're all right.'

'But where are they taking us?' whispered Janet, glad that the rattling of the car drowned her voice.

'I've no idea. They've gone down the main street, and now they're in a part of the town I don't know,' whispered Peter. 'Hallo, they're stopping. Keep down, Janet, and don't make a sound!'

The driver stopped the car and peered out of the open window. 'You're all right here,' he said to his companion. 'No one's about. Get in touch with Q8061 at once. Tell him Sid's place, five o'clock any evening. I'll be there.'

'Right,' said the other man and opened his door cautiously. Then he shut it again, and ducked his head down.

'What's up? Someone coming?' said the driver.

'No. I think I've dropped something,' said the other man, in a muffled voice. He appeared to be

38

groping over the floor. 'I'm sure I heard something drop.'

'For goodness' sake! Clear out now while the going's good!' said the driver impatiently. 'The police will be on the look-out for this car in a few minutes. I'm going to Sid's, and I don't know anything at all about you, see? Not a thing!'

The other man muttered something and opened his door again. He slid out into the dark road. The driver got out on his side; both doors were left open, as the men did not want to make the slightest noise that might call attention to them.

Peter sat up cautiously. He could not see or hear anything of the two men. The darkness had swallowed them completely. In this road the lamp-posts were few and far between, and the driver had been careful to stop in the darkest spot he could find. He had switched headlights and sidelights off as soon as he had stopped.

Peter reached over to the front of the car and switched them on. He didn't want anything to run into his father's car and smash it. He wished he could drive, but he couldn't, and anyway, he was much too young to have a licence. What should he do now?

Janet sat up, too, still trembling. 'Where are we?' she said. 'Have those men gone?'

'Yes. It's all right, Janet; I don't think they're coming back,' said Peter. 'My word, I wonder who they were and why they wanted to come here in the car? Talk about an adventure! We were moaning last

night because there wasn't even the smell of one, and
now here's one, right out of the blue!'

'Well, I don't much like an adventure in the dark,'
said Janet. 'What are we going to do?'

'We must get in touch with Daddy,' said Peter. 'He
must still be waiting at the station, unless he's gone
home! But we haven't been more than a few minutes.
I think I'll try to find a telephone box and telephone
the station to see if Daddy is still there.'

'I'm not going to wait in the car by myself,' said

Janet, at once. 'Oh dear, I wish we had Scamper with us. I should feel much better then.'

'The men wouldn't have taken the car if Scamper had been with us,' said Peter, getting out. 'He would have barked, and they would have run off to someone else's car. Come on, Janet, get out. I'll lock the doors in case there is anyone else who might take a fancy to Daddy's car!'

He locked all the doors, Janet holding his torch for him so that he could see what he was doing. Then they went down the street to see if they could find a telephone box anywhere.

They were lucky. One was at the corner of the very road where they were! Peter slipped inside and dialled the railway station.

'Station here,' said a voice at the other end.

'This is Peter, of Old Mill House,' said Peter. 'Is my father at the station still, by any chance?'

'Yes, he is,' said the voice. 'He's just collecting some goods. Do you want to speak to him? Right, I'll ask him to come to the phone.'

Half a minute later Peter heard his father's voice. 'Yes? Who is it? *You*, Peter! But – but aren't you still in the car, in the station yard? Where are you?'

Peter explained everything as clearly as he could, and his father listened to his tale in amazement. 'Well! Two car thieves going off with my car and not guessing you and Janet were in it. Where are you?'

'Janet's just asked somebody,' said Peter. 'We're in Jackson Street, not far from the Broadway. Can you get here, Dad, and fetch the car? We'll wait.'

'Yes. I'll get a taxi here in the yard,' said his father. 'Well, of all the things to happen!'

Janet and Peter went back to the car. Now that they knew their father would be along in a few minutes they no longer felt scared. Instead they began to feel rather pleased and important.

'We'll have to call a Secret Seven meeting about this *at once*,' said Peter. 'The police will be on to it, I expect, and *we'll* work on it too. What will Susie do *now*? Who cares about her silly tricks? Nobody at all!'

Eight

Another meeting

In a short time a taxi drew up beside the car and the children's father jumped out.

'Here we are!' called Janet, as her father paid the taxi-man.

He ran over, and got into the driver's seat. 'Well! Little did I think my car had been driven away while I was in the station,' he said. 'Are you sure you're all right?'

'Oh yes,' said Peter. 'We were half asleep at the back; the men didn't even spot us. They got in and drove straight to this place, then got out. They hardly said a word to one another.'

'Oh. Well, I suppose they weren't really car thieves,' said his father. 'Just a couple of young idiots who wanted to drive somewhere instead of walk. I shan't bother to inform the police. We'd never catch the fellows, and it would be waste of everyone's time. I've got the car back; that's all that matters.'

The two children felt a little flat to have their extraordinary adventure disposed of in this way.

'But aren't you *really* going to tell the police?' asked Peter, quite disappointed. 'The men may be real rogues.'

'They probably are. But I'm not going to waste *my*

time on them,' said his father. 'They'll be caught for something sooner or later! It's a good thing you had the sense to keep quiet in the back of the car!'

Their mother was a good deal more interested in the affair than Daddy, yet even she thought it was just a silly prank on the part of two young men. But it was different when Peter telephoned to Jack and told him what happened. Jack was absolutely thrilled.

'Gracious! Really! My word! I wish I'd been with you!' he shouted in excitement, clutching the telephone hard. 'Let's have a meeting about it. Tomorrow afternoon at three o'clock? We've all got a half-holiday tomorrow, haven't we? We'll tell the others at school there's a meeting on. I'll ... Sh. Sh!'

'What are you shushing about?' asked Peter. 'Oh, is that awful Susie about? All right, not a word more. See you tomorrow.'

Next afternoon, at three o'clock, all the Secret Seven were down in the shed, Scamper with them too, running from one to another excitedly. He could feel that something important was on foot!

The oil-stove was already lighted and the shed was nice and warm. Curtains were drawn across the windows in case anyone should peer in. Nobody had had time to bring things to eat, but fortunately George had had a present of a large bag of humbugs from his grandmother. He handed them round.

'I say, how super,' said Jack. 'Your granny does buy such ENORMOUS humbugs. They last for ages.

Now we shall all be comfortable for the rest of the afternoon, with one of these in our cheeks.'

They sat round on boxes or on old rugs, each with their cheeks bulging with a peppermint humbug. Scamper didn't like them, which was lucky. The children made him sit by the door and listen in case anyone came prying, that awful Susie, for instance, or one of her silly friends!

Peter related the whole happening, and everyone listened, thrilled.

'And do you mean to say your father isn't going to

the police?' said Colin. 'Well, that leaves the field free for us. Come along, Secret Seven, here's something right up our street!'

'It's very exciting,' said Pam. 'But what exactly are we going to work on? I mean, what is there to find out? I wouldn't even know where to *begin*!'

'Well, I'll tell you what *I* think,' said Peter, carefully moving his humbug to the other cheek. 'I think those men are up to something. I don't know what, but I think we ought to find out something about them.'

'But how can we?' asked Pam. 'I don't like the sound of them, anyway.'

'Well, if you don't want to be in on this, there's nothing to stop you from walking out,' said Peter, getting cross with Pam. 'The door's over there.'

Pam changed her mind in a hurry. 'Oh no, I *want* to be in on this; of course I do. You tell us what to do, Peter.'

'Well we don't *know* very much,' said Peter. 'Excuse me, all of you, but I'm going to take my humbug out for a minute or two, while I talk. There, that's better. No, Scamper, don't sniff at it; you don't *like* humbugs!'

With his sweet safely on a clean piece of paper beside him, Peter addressed the meeting.

'We haven't really much to go on, as I said,' he began. 'But we have a *few* clues. One is "Sid's Place". We ought to try and find where that is and watch it, to see if either of the men go there. Then we could shadow them. We'd have to watch it at five o'clock each day.'

'Go on,' said George.

'Then there's Q8061,' said Peter. 'That might be a telephone number. We could find out about that.'

'That's silly!' said Pam. 'It doesn't look a bit like a telephone number!'

Peter took no notice of Pam. 'One man had a low-brimmed hat and long hair down to his collar,' he said. 'And I *think* there was something wrong with one hand – it looked as if the tip of the middle finger was missing. I only *just* caught sight of it in the light of a lamp-post, but I'm fairly sure.'

'And the other man had very short hair,' said Janet, suddenly. 'I did notice that. Oh, and Peter, do you remember that he said he thought he'd dropped something? Do you think he had? We never looked to see! He didn't find whatever it was.'

'Gosh, yes, I forgot all about that,' said Peter. 'That's most important. We'll all go and look in the car at once. Bring your torches, please, Secret Seven!'

Nine

The Seven get going

SCAMPER darted out into the garden with the Seven. Jack looked about to see if Susie or any of her friends were in hiding, but as Scamper didn't run barking at any bush, he felt sure that Susie must be somewhere else!

They all went to the garage. Peter hoped that the car would be there. It was! The children opened the doors and looked inside.

'It's no good us looking in the back,' said Peter. 'The men were in front.'

He felt about everywhere, and shone his torch into every corner of the front of the car. The garage was rather dark, although it was only half-past three in the afternoon.

'Nothing!' he said disappointed.

'Let *me* see,' said Janet. 'I once dropped a pencil and couldn't find it, and it was down between the two front seats!'

She slid her fingers in between the two seats and felt about. She gave a cry and pulled something out. It was a spectacle case. She held it up in triumph.

'Look! That's it. He dropped his spectacle case!'

'But he didn't wear glasses,' said Peter.

'He could have reading glasses, couldn't he?' said Janet. 'Like Granny?'

She opened the case. It was empty. She gave another little squeal.

'Look, it's got his name inside! What do you think of *that*? And his telephone number! *Now* we're on to something!'

The Secret Seven crossed round to look. Janet pointed to a little label inside. On it neatly written was a name and number. 'Briggs. Renning 2150.'

'Renning – that's not far away!' said Peter. 'We can look up the name in the telephone directory and see his address. I say, what a find!'

Everyone was thrilled. Jack was just about to shut the door of the car when he suddenly remembered that no one had looked *under* the left-hand front seat, where the man who had dropped something had sat. He took a little stock from a bundle of garden bamboos standing in a nearby corner and poked under the seat with it, and out rolled a button!

'Look!' said Jack, holding it up.

Peter gave it a glance.

'Oh that's off my father's macintosh,' he said. 'It must have been there for ages.'

He put it into his pocket, and they all went back to the shed, feeling very excited.

'Well, first we find out Mr Briggs' address. Then we all ride over to see him,' said Peter. 'We'll make him admit he dropped it in the car, and then I'll pounce like anything and say, "And what were you doing in my father's car?" I'm sure the police would be interested if we could actually tell them the name and address of the man who went off in Dad's car like that, and probably they would make him give the name of the other man too!'

This long speech made Peter quite out of breath. The others gazed at him in admiration. It all sounded very bold.

'All right. What about now, this very minute, if we can find his address in Renning?' said Jack. 'Nothing like striking while the iron's hot. We could have tea in that little tea-shop in Renning. They have wonderful macaroons. I ate five last time I was there.'

'Then somebody else must have paid the bill,' said Colin. 'Yes, do let's go now. It *would* be fun, but you can jolly well do the talking, Peter!'

'Have you all got your bikes?' said Peter. 'Good. Let's just go in and take a look at the telephone directory, and get the address. Mr Briggs, we're coming after you!'

The telephone directory was very helpful. Mr H. E. J. Briggs lived at Little Hill, Raynes Road, Renning. Telephone number 2150. Peter copied it down carefully.

Got enough money for tea, everyone?' he asked.

Colin had only a penny or two, so Peter offered to lend him some. Now they were all ready to set off.

Peter told his mother they were going out to tea, and away they went, riding carefully in single line down the main road, as they had been taught to do.

Renning was about three miles away, and it didn't really take them long to get there.

'Shall we have tea first?' asked George, looking longingly at the tea-shop they were passing.

'No. Work first, pleasure afterwards,' said Peter, who was always very strict about things like that. They cycled on to Raynes Road.

It was only a little lane, set with pretty little cottages. Little Hill was at one end, a nice little place with a gay garden.

'Well it doesn't *look* like the home of a rogue,' said Jack. 'But you never know. See, there's someone in the garden, Peter. Come on, do your job. Let's see how you handle things of this sort. Make him admit he dropped that spectacle case in your father's car!'

'Right!' said Peter, and went in boldly at the garden gate. 'Er – good afternoon, sir. Are you Mr Briggs?'

Ten

Peter feels hot all over

As soon as Peter saw the man closely, he knew at once that he wasn't either of the men in the car. For one thing, this man had a big round head, and a face to match, and both the other men had had rather narrow heads, as far as he had been able to see.

The man looked a little surprised. 'No,' he said. 'I'm not Mr Briggs. I'm just a friend staying with him. Do you want him? I'll call him?'

Peter began to feel a little uncomfortable. Somehow this pretty garden and trim little cottage didn't seem the kind of place those men would live in!

'Henry! Henry, there's someone asking for you!' called the man.

Peter saw that the other Secret Seven members were watching eagerly. Would 'Henry' prove to be one of the men they were hunting for?

A man came strolling out, someone with trim, short hair and a narrow head. Yes, he *might* be the man who had sat in the left-hand seat of the car, except that he didn't in the least look as if he could possibly take someone else's car!

Still you never know! thought Peter.

The man looked inquiringly at him. 'What do you want?' he said.

'Er – is your name Mr H. E. J. Briggs, sir?' asked Peter, politely.

'It is,' said the man looking amused. 'Why?'

'Er – well, have you by any chance lost a spectacle case, sir?' asked Peter.

All the rest of the Seven outside the garden held their breath. What would he say?

'Yes. I *have* lost one,' said the man surprised. 'Have you found it? Where was it?'

'It was in the front of a car,' answered Peter, watching him closely.

Now if the man was one of the car-thieves, he would surely look embarrassed, or deny it. He would know that it was the case he had dropped the night before and would be afraid of saying 'Yes, I dropped it there.'

'What an extraordinary thing!' said the man. 'Whose car? You sound rather *mysterious*. Losing a spectacle case is quite an ordinary thing to do, you know!'

'It was dropped in my father's car last night,' said Peter, still watching the man.

'Oh no, it wasn't,' said Mr Briggs at once. 'I've lost this case for about a week. It can't be mine. I wasn't in anyone's car last night.

'It *is* the man we want, I bet it is! said Pam in a low voice to Janet. 'He's telling fibs!'

'The case has your name in it,' said Peter, 'so we know it's yours. And it *was* in my father's car last night.'

53

'Who *is* your father?' said the man, sounding puzzled. 'I can't quite follow what you're getting at. And where's the case?'

'My father lives at Old Mill House,' began Peter, 'and he's ...'

'Good gracious! He's not Jack, my farmer friend, surely?' said Mr Briggs. 'That explains everything! He very kindly gave me a lift one day last week, and I must have dropped my spectacle case in his car then. I hunted for it everywhere when I got back home. Never thought of the car, of course! Well, well, so you've brought it back?'

'Oh, are you the man my father speaks of as Harry?' said Peter, taken aback. 'Gracious! Well I suppose you *did* drop your case, then, and not last night, as I thought. Here it is, sir. It's got your name and telephone number in it. That's how we knew it was yours.'

He held it out, and the man took it, smiling. 'Thanks,' he said, 'and now perhaps you'll tell me what all the mystery was about, and why you insisted I had dropped it last night, and why you looked at me as if I were somebody Very Suspicious Indeed.'

Peter heard the others giggling, and he went red. He really didn't know *what* to say!

'Well,' he said, 'you see, two men took my father's car last night, and when we looked in it today we found this case, and we thought perhaps it belonged to one of the men.'

Mr Briggs laughed. 'I see, doing a little detective work. Well, it's very disappointing for you, but I don't happen to be a car-thief. Look, here's twenty pence for bringing back my case. Buy some chocolate and share it with those interested friends of yours watching over the hedge.'

'Oh no, thank you, sir,' said Peter, backing away. 'I don't want anything. I'm only too glad to bring your case back. Goodbye, sir!'

He went quickly out of the garden, most relieved to get away from the amused eyes of Mr Briggs. Goodness, what a mistake! He got on his bicycle and rode swiftly away, the other six following.

They all stopped outside the tea-shop.

'Whew!' said Peter, wiping his forehead. I DID feel awful when I found out he was a friend of my father's! Dad is always talking about a man called Harry, but I didn't know his surname before.'

'We thought we were so clever, but we weren't this time,' said Colin. 'Blow! The spectacle case was nothing to do with those two men in the car, but perhaps the button is?'

'Perhaps,' said Peter. 'But I'm not tackling anyone wearing macs with buttons that match the one we found, unless I'm jolly certain he's one of those men! I feel hot all over when I think of Mr Briggs. Suppose he goes and tells my father all about this?'

'Never mind,' said Jack, grinning. 'It was great fun watching you. Let's have tea. Look, they've got macaroons today.'

In they went and had a wonderful tea. And now, what next? Think hard, Secret Seven, and make some exciting plans!

Eleven

Jobs for every member

THE next day another Secret Seven meeting was held, but this time it was at Colin's, in his little summer-house. It wasn't such a good place as Peter's shed, because it had an open doorway with no door, and they were not allowed to have an oil-stove in it.

However, Colin's mother had asked all the Secret Seven to tea, so it was clear they would have to have their next meeting at his house, and the little summer-house was the only place where they could talk in secret.

'We'll bring all our fireworks and look through them,' said Peter. 'We haven't so much as *glanced* at them the last two meetings, and it's Bonfire Night in a few days. We simply MUST see what we've got and what we haven't got.'

So all the Secret Seven went laden with fireworks to Colin's house. They had a fine tea, the kind they all enjoyed most.

'Sardine sandwiches, honey sandwiches, a smashing cherry cake with cherries inside *and* on top, and an iced sponge cake. I say, Colin, your mother's a jolly good sort,' said Peter, approvingly. 'Isn't she going to have it with us? I'd like to thank her.'

'No, she's had to go out to a committee meeting or

something,' said Colin. 'All she said was that we've to behave ourselves, and if we go down to the summer-house this cold dark evening, we've GOT to put on our coats.'

'Right,' said Peter. 'Coats it will be. Mothers are always very keen on coats, aren't they? Personally, I think it's quite hot today.'

They finished up absolutely everything on the tea-table. There wasn't even a piece of the big cherry cake left! Scamper, who had also been asked to tea, had his own dish of dog-biscuits with shrimp paste on each. He was simply delighted, and crunched them up non-stop.

'Now we'll go to the summer-house. We'd better take a candle it's so dark already,' said Colin. 'And don't forget your coats, everyone!'

'And the fireworks,' said Peter.

So down they all went to the little wooden summer-house, carrying their fireworks. The house had a wooden bench running all round it, and smelt a bit damp. Nobody minded that. It was such a nice secret place to talk in, down at the bottom of the dark garden.

The candle was stuck in a bottle and lighted. There was no shelf to put it on, so Colin stood it in the middle of the floor.

'Have to be careful of Scamper knocking it over!' said Peter. 'Where is he?'

'He's gone into the kitchen to see our cook,' said Colin. 'She's cooking a stew or something, and Scamper smelt it. He'll be along soon. Now, stack the fireworks under the wooden bench for the time being. That's right. We'll go through them when we've had the meeting.'

'We'll begin it now,' said Peter. 'Owing to our silly mistake about the spectacle case, were not as far on with this adventure as we ought to be. We must do a little more work on it. First, has anyone any idea where "Sid's place" is?'

There was a silence.

'Never heard of it,' said Jack.

'Well, it must be some place that is used by men like those two in my father's car,' said Peter.

'Perhaps Larry at the garage would know?' said Colin, who had great faith in Larry. 'He knows a lot of lorry-drivers, and they're the kind who might go to some place called "Sid's" or "Jim's" or "Nick's".'

'Yes. That's a good idea,' said Peter. 'Colin, you and George go and find out from Larry tomorrow. Now, what else can we do? What about the number that one of the men had to get in touch with – what was it now?'

'Q8061,' said Pam, promptly. 'I think of it as the *letter* Q, but it might be spelt K-E-W, you know.'

'Yes, you're right. It might,' said Peter. 'That's really quite an idea, Pam. It might be a telephone number at Kew telephone exchange, Kew 8061. You and Barbara can make it your job to find out.'

'How do we set about it?' said Barbara.

'I really can't explain such easy things to you,' said

59

Peter, impatiently. 'You and Pam can quite well work out what to do yourselves. Now is there anything else we can work on?'

'Only the button we found in the car,' said Jack.

'I told you, it's sure to belong to my father's mac,' said Peter. 'It's just like the buttons on it.'

'But we ought to make *sure*,' argued Jack. 'You know you always say we never ought to leave anything to chance, Peter. There are hundreds of different coat buttons.'

'Well perhaps you're right,' said Peter. 'Yes, I think you are. Janet, will you see to that point, please, and look at Dad's mac. I know he's got a button missing, so I expect it belongs to his mac, but we *will* make sure.'

'You haven't given *me* anything to do,' said Jack.

'Well, if the button doesn't match the ones on Dad's mac, you can take charge of *that* point,' said Peter, with a sudden giggle, 'and you can march about looking for people wearing a mac with a missing button.'

'Don't be an ass,' said Jack. 'Still, if it *isn't* your father's button, it *will* be one dropped by one of those men, and one of us ought to take charge of it. So I will, if it's necessary.'

'Right,' said Peter. 'Well, that's the end of the meeting. Now we'll get out the fireworks!'

60

Twelve

Oh, what a pity!

COLIN and Jack took the bundles of fireworks out from under the wooden bench of the summer-house. The Seven then knelt down on the floor to undo the parcels and the boxes. What a lovely job!

'I wish we had a better light than just this flickering candle on the floor,' said Pam. 'It's difficult to read the names of the fireworks!'

As they all bent over the fireworks by the light of the candle, they heard the sound of a bark, and then scampering feet. Scamper had been let out of the kitchen door and was coming to find his friends. Where were they? Wuff! Wuff!

'Scamper!' called Janet from the summer-house. 'We're here!'

Scamper tore down the garden path, barking madly. Anyone would think he had been away from the seven children for a whole month, not just half an hour!

He rushed straight into the little summer-house and over went the bottle with the lighted candle in its neck! Crash!

'You idiot, Scamper,' said Peter and reached to set the bottle upright again. The candle was still alight.

61

But before he could take hold of it, the flame of the candle had licked against a bundle of fireworks. They were alight! And not only were they alight, but they were fizzing and spluttering!

'They're going off!' yelled Peter. 'Look out, Pam, look out, Barbara!'

Fizzzzzz! Pop-pop-pop! BANG!

Half a dozen fireworks went off together, and the seven children and Scamper tumbled hurried out of the little summer-house, trying to get out of the way.

The loose paper on the floor had now been set alight too, and in its turn it set fire to a pile of small fireworks, rather like squibs.

Bang-popbang-popbang-bang! They all went off too. The children clutched one another in dismay. Scamper, really terrified, had completely disappeared.

BANG! BANG! WHOOOOOOSH!

A rocket flew out of the summer-house, and Colin only just got back out of its way in time. Peter dragged everyone back, and Colin fell into a holly bush and yelled so loud that everyone thought the rocket must have hit him.

'Can't we save the rest of the fireworks?' cred Jack, dismayed at seeing all their precious bundles going up in smoke and flame and bangs.

'No. Not unless you want to be smothered in Rockets, and Squibs, and Blue-Flashes, and Whirligigs – and, oh my goodness, what was that?' yelled Peter.

'My Humdinger! My Humdinger!' wailed poor Jack, as something with a long fiery tail flew out of the summer-house with a loud roar. 'It cost me thirty pence!'

'I say, we'd better get some water,' said Colin, suddenly. 'The summer-house might get on fire. Look at that paper blazing up.'

They left the firework show and ran to get buckets. There was a little pond nearby, and they filled the buckets from it. Splash! Splash! Splash! The water was thrown all over the blazing fireworks, and there was a tremendous sizzling noise. Black smoke poured out of the little house and almost choked the Seven.

'Pooh!' said Jack, and coughed. 'What a horrible smell!'

'It's a good thing your mother's out,' panted Peter to Colin, coming up with another pail of water. 'She would be in a frightful way about this. There, I think we've about got the fire down now. Poooooh! That smoke!'

It was a very, very sad ending to the tea and meeting at Colin's. Barbara was in tears. She had saved up for weeks to buy fireworks, and now there was nothing left of them but smoke and smell and a nasty-looking black mess.

'It's bad luck,' said Peter, feeling as if he wouldn't mind howling himself. 'Blow Scamper! It's all his fault. Where is he?'

'Gone home at sixty miles an hour, I should think,' said Janet. 'It's a pity he hasn't got a post-office savings book like we have. I'd make him take a whole lot of money out and buy more fireworks for us. It's too bad. We shan't have any now!'

'Well we certainly shan't be able to buy enough to make a display,' said Jack, gloomily. 'Come on, let's go. Sorry, Colin, about making your summer-house in a mess. I'll come along tomorrow, when it's dried up a bit, and help you to clear it up.'

They were just about to go off to the front gate when Janet stopped them. 'We meant to choose a new password today,' she said. 'You know that Susie knows our last one, "Guy Fawkes", and we really *must* have a secret one. Susie has told everyone in our class.'

'Yes. I forgot about that,' said Peter. 'Well, I vote we have "Fireworks". It really does seem a very good password for tonight!'

'All right – Fireworks,' said Colin. 'I'm sorry its been such a disappointing evening. This is definitely *not* the kind of adventure I like! Goodbye, all of you. See you tomorrow!'

It was a gloomy company of children that made their way home. Blow Scamper, *why* did he have to do a silly thing like that?

Thirteen

Sid's Place

ALL the Secret Seven felt exceedingly gloomy next day, which was Sunday. They met at Sunday School, but none of them had much to say. They were all very subdued. It really was a dreadful thing to have seen weeks and weeks of savings going up in smoke in just a few minutes!

'Scamper *did* race home last night,' said Janet to the girls. 'He was behind the couch, trembling from head to foot. He is awfully frightened of fireworks, you know.'

'All dogs are,' said Pam. 'We always lock ours up indoors on Bonfire Night. Poor Scamper! Did you forgive him?'

'We simply had to,' said Janet. 'Anyway, he didn't mean to upset the candle, poor Scamper. We stroked him and patted him and loved him, and when he saw we weren't going to scold him, he crept out and sat as close to our legs as he could, and put his head on my knee.'

'He's a dear,' said Barbara. 'But all the same it's *dreadful* to have lost all our fireworks at one go.'

'It's quite put our adventure out of my mind,' said Pam. 'But I suppose we'd better think about it again tomorrow, Barbara. We've got to find out about that telephone number, Kew 8061. Though how we shall do it, I don't know.'

'Leave it till tomorrow,' said Barbara. 'I can't think of anything but our poor fireworks today.'

The next day was Monday, and the Seven were back at school. George and Colin went to call at the garage after morning school, to try and find out something about 'Sid's Place' from Larry. He was sitting in a corner with a newspaper, munching his lunch.

'Hallo, Larry,' said Colin. 'I wonder if you can help us. Do you know anywhere called "Sid's Place"?'

'No, I don't,' said Larry. 'Sounds like an eating-house or something. There's a lorry-driver coming in soon. If you like to wait, I'll ask him.'

The lorry drove in after three or four minutes, and the man got down, a big heavy fellow who called out cheerfully to Larry. 'Just off to get a bite of dinner. Be back in half an hour for my lorry.'

'Hey, Charlie, do you eat at "Sid's Place"?' called Larry. 'Do you know it?'

' "Sid's Place"? No, I eat at my sisters when I come through here,' said Charlie. 'Wait a minute now. "Sid's" you said. Yes I remember seeing a little café called "Sid's Café". Would that be the place you're meaning?'

'Could be,' said Larry, looking questioningly at Colin.

Colin nodded. 'Probably the one,' he said, feeling suddenly excited. 'Where is it?'

'You know Old Street? Well, it's at the corner of

Old Street and James Street, not a first-class place, and not the sort you boys want to go to. So long, Larry. See you in half an hour!'

'Thanks, Larry,' said Colin. 'Come on, George, let's go and have a look at this place. We've just about got time.'

They went to Old Street and walked down to James Street at the end. On the corner, sharing a bit of each street, was a rather dirty-looking eating-house. 'Sid's Café' was painted over the top of the very messy window.

The boys looked inside. Men were sitting at a long counter, eating sandwiches and drinking coffee or tea. There were one or two tables in the shop, too, at which slightly better-dressed men were having a hot meal served to them by a fat and cheerful girl.

'Oh so that's "Sid's Place",' said Colin, staring in. 'I wonder which is Sid?'

'Perhaps Sid is somewhere in the back quarters,' said George. 'There are only girls serving here. Well we know that one of those men comes here every day about five o'clock. One of us must watch, and we'll be bound to see the man.'

'It'll have to be Peter,' said Colin. 'We wouldn't know the fellow. He would probably recognize him at once.'

'Yes. It's going to be jolly difficult for him to hang about here, watching everyone,' said George. 'People will wonder what he's up to. Two of us would seem even *more* suspicious.'

69

'Well that's up to Peter!' said Colin. 'We've done *our* job and found Sid's place. Come on, we'll be awfully late for lunch.'

Peter was very pleased with Colin and George when he heard their news. 'Good work!' he said. 'I'll get along there at five o'clock this afternoon. How have Pam and Barbara got on?'

Janet told him while they had a quick tea together after afternoon school. 'They simply couldn't think *how* to do anything about KEW 8061,' said Janet. 'They simply couldn't.'

'Couple of idiots!' said Peter, munching a bun quickly. 'Buck up, I must go.'

'Well, Pam asked her mother how to find out if there *was* such a number, because she and Barbara really didn't feel they could wade all through the telephone directories,' said Janet. 'And her mother said, "Well, just ring up and see if there's an answer!" '

'Easy,' said Peter. 'Simple!'

'Yes – well, they rang up the number, feeling frightfully excited, because they thought they could ask whoever answered what his name and address were, but there was no reply,' said Janet. 'And the operator said it was because there was no telephone with that number at present! So Q8061 is *not* a telephone number, Peter. It must be something else.'

'Blow!' said Peter, getting up. 'It would have been marvellous if KEW 8061 *had* answered. We'd have been able to get the name and address and

70

everything. That clue isn't much good, I'm afraid. I must be off, Janet. Wouldn't it be wonderful if I spotted one of the men going into Sid's place?'

'It *would*,' said Janet. 'Oh, I DO hope you do, Peter!'

Fourteen

A wonderful idea

PETER went as quickly as he could to the corner of Old Street and James Street. Yes – there was 'Sid's Cafè, just as Colin had said. What was the time?

He glanced at his watch – six minutes to five. Well, if the man came at five o'clock, he ought just to catch him. Of course, he might come any time after that. That would be a nuisance, because then Peter would have to wait about a long time.

Peter lolled against the corner, watching everyone who came by, especially, of course, the men who went in and out of 'Sid's Café'. They were mostly men with barrows of fruit that they left outside, or drivers of vans, or shifty-looking men, unshaved and dirty.

He got a shock when someone came out of the café and spoke roughly to him.

'Now then, what are you doing here, lolling about? Don't you dare take fruit off my barrow! I've caught you boys doing it before, and I'll call the police if you do. Clear off!'

'I wouldn't *dream* of taking your fruit!' said Peter, indignantly, looking at the pile of cheap fruit on the nearby barrow.

'Ho, you wouldn't, would you? Well, then, what are you standing here for, looking about? Boys don't

72

stand at corners for nothing! We've been watching
you from inside the shop, me and my mates, and we
know you're after something!'

Peter was shocked. How dare this man say things
like that to him! Still, perhaps boys in this district did
steal from barrows or from fruit-stalls outside
shops.

'Go on, you tell me what you're standing about here for,' said the man again, putting his face close to Peter's.

As the boy couldn't tell him the reason why he was standing at that corner, he said nothing, but turned and went off, his face burning red. Horrible man! he thought. And I haven't seen anyone yet in the least like that fellow who went off in our car. Of course, all I've got to go on really is his hat and long hair, and possibly maimed finger on his right hand.

He ran back home, thinking hard. After all, that fellow might go to Sid's place each night and I'd *never* know him if he had a cap instead of a hat, and had cut his hair shorter. And most of these fellows slouch along with their hands in their pockets, so I wouldn't see his hand either. It's hopeless.

Peter went round to see Colin about it. Jack and George were there, doing their homework together.

'Hallo!' they said, in surprise. 'Aren't you watching at Sid's place?'

Peter told them what had happened. 'I don't see how I can go and watch there any more,' he said, rather gloomily. 'That fellow who spoke to me was really nasty. And how can I watch without being seen?'

'Can't be done,' said Colin. 'Give it up! This is something we just can't do. Come on out to the summer-house and see what I've made! We cleared away the firework mess, and I've got something else there now!'

They all went out to the summer-house, with their torches. Colin shone his on to something there, and Peter jumped in astonishment, not at first realizing what it was.

'Gosh! It's a guy!' he said, in admiration. 'What a beauty!'

The guy certainly was very fine. He was stuffed with straw, and wore one of Colin's very old suits. He had a mask, of course, and grinned happily at the three boys. He had a wig made of black strands of wool and an old hat on top. Colin had sat him in a garden barrow, and he really looked marvellous.

'I thought that as we shan't have many fireworks, worse luck, we would have a guy and burn him on a bonfire,' said Colin. 'I'm making the bonfire heap tomorrow. You can come and help if you like.'

The guy seemed to watch them as they talked, grinning away merrily.

'It's a pity *he* can't watch outside Sid's place!' said Jack. 'Nobody would suspect him or bother about *him*. He could watch for that fellow all evening!'

They all laughed. Then Peter stopped suddenly and gazed hard at the guy. An idea had come to him, a really WONDERFUL idea!

'I say! I SAY!' he said, clutching at Colin and making him jump. 'You've given me an idea! What about ME dressing up as a guy, and wearing a mask with eye-holes – and one of you taking me somewhere near Sid's Café? There are heaps of these guys about now, and nobody would think our guy was *real.*

75

I could watch for ages and nobody would guess.'

'Whew!' said the other three together, and stared at Peter in admiration.

Colin thumped him on the back. 'That's a wizard idea!' he said. 'Super! Smashing! When shall we do it?'

'Tomorrow,' said Peter. 'I can rush here and dress up easily enough, and one of you can wheel me off in the barrow – all of you, if you like! What a game!'

'But my mother doesn't like the idea of children taking guys and begging for money,' said Colin, remembering. 'She says that begging is wrong.'

'So it is,' said Peter. 'My mother says that too, but if we *did* get any money we could give it to a charity. We won't use it to buy fireworks for ourselves.'

'Oh well, that's all right, then!' said Colin. 'My word, this is grand! Mind you don't leap up out of the barrow if you see that fellow going into Sid's place, Peter!'

'I'll keep as still as a real guy!' said Peter, grinning. 'Well, so long. See you at school tomorrow.'

Fifteen

The peculiar guy

PETER raced home to tell Janet of the new idea. She was so thrilled that she couldn't say a word. What an idea! How super! She stared in admiration at her brother. He was truly a fine leader for the Secret Seven!

Scamper wuffed loudly, exactly as if he were saying, 'Grand, Peter, splendid idea!'

'*I've* got something to tell you, too,' said Janet, suddenly remembering. 'I looked on Daddy's macintosh and he *has* got a button missing; but it's a small one on his sleeve, not a large one like we found. And also it's not quite the same colour, Peter.'

'Ah, good! That means it probably *was* a button that dropped from that fellow's mac!' said Peter, pleased. 'Jack will have to take the button, Janet, and work on that clue, if he can! So give it to me, and I'll hand it to him tomorrow.'

'I wish we could find out about Q8061,' said Janet. 'I'm pretty sure it must be someone's telephone number, but it's very difficult to find out.'

'There's Mother calling,' said Peter. 'I bet it's to tell me to do my homework!'

It was of course, and poor Peter found it very difficult indeed to work out arithmetic problems when his head was full of dressing up as a guy!

All the Secret Seven were thrilled to hear of Peter's new plan, and next evening they were round at Colin's to see him dress up. He really did look remarkably good!

He wore an old pair of patched trousers, and a ragged jacket. He wore a pair of great big boots thrown out by Colin's father. He had a scarf round his neck, and a big old hat over a wig made of black wool.

'You look simply *frightful!*' said Janet, with a giggle. 'Put the mask on now.'

Peter put it on, and immediately became a grinning guy, like all the other guys that were appearing here and there in the streets of the town. Scamper took one look at Peter's suddenly changed face, and backed away, growling.

'It's all right, Scamper,' said Peter, laughing. 'It's me! Don't be afraid.'

'You look horrible,' said Pam. 'I really feel scared when I look at you, though I know you're really Peter. Nobody, *nobody* could possibly guess you were alive!'

Peter got into the barrow. 'Gosh, it's very hard and uncomfortable,' he said. 'Got any old cushions, Colin?'

Colin produced an old rug and three rather dirty garden cushions. These made the barrow much more comfortable. Peter got in and lolled on the cushions in the limp, floppy way of all guys. He really looked extremely guy-like!

The others shrieked with laughter to see him.

'Come on,' said Colin at last. 'We really must go, or we shan't be there till long past five. Not you girls. It's not a place for you, outside Sid's Café.'

The three boys set off, taking turns at wheeling Peter in the barrow. He kept making horrible groans and moans, and Jack laughed so much that he had to sit down on a bus-stop seat and hold his aching sides.

An old lady there peered at the guy. 'What a good one!' she said, and fumbled in her purse. I'll give you some money to buy fireworks.'

'Oh, any money we get is going to charity,' explained George quickly.

She gave him ten pence, and then, as the bus came up, waved to them and got on.

'How nice of her!' said George. 'Ten whole pence.'

They went on down the street, with Peter thoroughly enjoying himself! He lolled about, watching everything through the eye-slits of his mask, and made silly remarks in a hollow, guy-like voice that made the others laugh helplessly.

At last they came to Sid's Café. The barrow was neatly wedged into a little alcove near the door, from which Peter could see everyone who went in or out.

The boys stood nearby, waiting to see if Peter recognized anyone. If he did, he was to give a sign, and two of the Seven would shadow the man to see where he went, if he happened to come *out* of the café. If he went inside it they were to wait till he came out.

The men going in and out of the eating-house were amused with the guy. One prodded him hard with his stick, and gave Peter a terrible shock. 'Good guy you've got there!' said the man and threw five pence on to Peter's tummy.

'Colin! Jack! You're NOT to let people prod me like that,' said Peter, in a fierce whisper. 'It jolly well hurt.'

'Well, how are we to stop them?' said Colin, also in a whisper.

All went well till two young fellows came by and
saw the guy sitting there. 'Hallo! He's a good guy!'
said one. 'Nice pair of boots he's got. I've a good mind
to take them off him!'

And to Peter's horror, he felt the boots on his feet
being tugged hard. He gave a yell, and the young
fellows looked extremely startled. They disappeared
quickly.

'CAN'T you look after me better?' said Peter to the
others. 'Heave me up a bit on the cushions. Those
fellows pulled me off.'

Colin and George heaved him into a more comfortable position.

'Anyway, you've made quite a bit of money,' said George, in Peter's ear. 'People think you're jolly good, we've got quite a few pence, and some silver.'

Peter grunted. He was cross with the others. Why didn't they guard him from pokes and prods and pullings? Then, quite suddenly, he caught sight of somebody, and stiffened all over.

'Surely, SURELY, that was one of the men who had taken his father's car? Peter stared and stared. Was it? Oh, why didn't he stand a bit nearer so that he could see?

Sixteen

The two men

THE man was standing by the window of the café, as if he were waiting for someone. He had on a hat and his hair was rather long. Peter looked as closely at him as he could.

The fellow who drove the car had a low-brimmed hat, he thought and long hair. This man somehow *looks* like that man we saw in the car.

The man moved a little nearer, and coughed impatiently. He took a cigarette packet from his pocket and pulled out a cigarette. He turned away from the wind and towards Peter in order to light it, and then Peter knew for *certain* that it was the man he was looking for!

The top of his middle finger is missing! he thought. I saw it clearly in the flame of the match as he lighted his cigarette. It *must* be the fellow! Perhaps he's waiting for the other man.

Almost before he had finished thinking this, the second man came up! There was no mistaking that cap and the short, cropped hair, grown a little longer now. The cap was pulled down over his face exactly as it had been when he was in the car. He wore an old macintosh, and Peter tried to see if it had a button missing.

The two men said a word of greeting and then went into the café. They went right through the room to a door at the back, opened it, and disappeared.

'Colin! George! Jack! Those were the two men,' called Peter in a low voice full of excitement. 'One of them had half a finger missing. I saw it.'

'And the other had a button off his mac!' said Jack. 'I noticed that, though I didn't know he was one of the men we're after! But seeing that I'm in charge of the button now, I'm making a point of looking carefully at every macintosh I see! I believe our button matches his exactly.'

'Good work!' said Peter. 'Now listen. The next move is very, very important. Two of you must shadow these men. If they separate, you must separate too, and each go after one of them. Colin, you must wheel me home.'

'Right,' said the three, always willing to obey Peter's leadership. He really was very good at this kind of thing.

'Get as close to those men as you can and see if you can hear anything useful,' said Peter. 'And track them right to their homes if you can. Report to me at the Secret Seven shed as soon as you can.'

'Right,' said George and Jack, feeling as if they were first-class plain-clothes policemen!

The two men were not long in Sid's. They came out after about ten minutes, looking angry. They stood in the doorway, taking no notice of the guy and the boys.

'Sid's let us down,' said the man with the missing finger. 'He said he'd give us two hundred and now he's knocked it down to fifty. Better go back to Q's and tell him. He'll be wild.'

The boys listened intently, pretending to fiddle about with the guy.

'I'm not arguing with Sid again,' said the other man. 'I reckon I'm an idiot to come out of hiding, yet, till my hair's grown. Come on, let's go.'

They went off down the street, and George and Jack immediately set off behind them, leaving Colin with Peter.

'Did you hear that?' said Peter, in great excitement, forgetting he was a guy. 'They've stolen something and want to sell it to Sid, and he won't give them what he promised. So they're going back to Q, whoever he is, probably the chief, to report it. Well we know that Q is a man, now!'

'And did you hear what the other fellow said about his hair growing?' said Colin, bending over Peter. 'I bet he's just come out of prison, it's so short. They always shave it there, don't they? Or perhaps he's an *escaped* prisoner, in hiding. Gosh, Peter, this is super!'

'Wheel me to our shed,' commanded Peter, wishing he could get out and walk. 'Buck up. The girls will be there already, and George and Jack will join us as soon as they can. Do buck up! . . . I'm going to get out and walk,' announced Peter. 'It's a nice dark road we're in. Stop a minute, Colin, and I'll get out.'

Colin stopped, and Peter climbed out of the
barrow. Colin shone his torch to help him, and an old
man with a dog saw the guy stepping out of the
barrow. He stared as if he couldn't believe his eyes,
and then hurried off at top speed. Good gracious! A
guy coming alive. No, surely his eyes must have de-
ceived him!

It wasn't long before Colin and Peter were whispering the password outside the shed at the bottom of

Peter's garden. The barrow was shoved into some bushes, and Peter had taken off his mask.

'Fireworks!' said the boys, and the door opened at once. Pam gave a little scream as Peter came in, still looking very peculiar with a black wool wig, an old hat, and very ragged clothes.

'We've got news!' said Peter. 'Grand news. Just listen, all of you!'

Seventeen

Good work!

PETER quickly told the girls all that had happened, and they listened in silence, feeling very thrilled. Now they were really finding out something, and even that button had helped!

'I think the short-haired man has either just come out of prison or escaped from it,' said Peter. 'He may have committed a robbery before he went in, and have hidden what he stole, and it's these goods he and the other fellow are trying to sell to Sid.'

'Well, who's Q, then?' asked Janet. 'Where does *he* come in?'

'He's probably holding the stolen goods,' said Peter, working everything out in his mind. 'And I expect he's sheltering the thief, too. If only we could find out who Q is and where he lives. He's the missing link.'

The five of them talked and talked, and Scamper listened and joined in with a few wuffs now and again, thumping his tail on the ground when the chatter got very loud.

'When will George and Jack be back?' asked Pam. 'I ought not to be too late home, and it's a quarter past six now!'

'Here they are!' said Colin, hearing voices outside. A knock came at the door.

'Password!' shouted everyone.

'Fireworks!' said two voices, and in went George and Jack, beaming all over their faces, glad to be out of the cold, dark November night.

'What happened? Did you shadow them?' demanded Peter, as they sat down on boxes.

'Yes,' said George. 'We followed them all the way down the street, and away by the canal and up by Cole Square. We only once got near enough to hear them say anything.'

'What was that?' asked Peter.

'One of them said "Is that a policeman lying in wait for us over there? Come on, run for it!" ' said George. 'And just as a bobby came out of the shadows they ran round the corner, and the policeman never even noticed them! We shot after them, just in time to see them trying the handles of some cars parked there.'

'Then they slid quickly into one and drove off,' finished Jack. 'That was the end of our shadowing.'

'So they stole *another* car!' said Colin.

'You didn't take the number by any chance, did you?' asked Peter.

'Rather!' said Jack, and took out his notebook. 'Here it is, PLK 100. We didn't go back and tell the policeman. We thought we'd race back here and let you decide what we ought to do next.'

'Good work,' said Peter, pleased. 'If only we knew where Q lived, we'd know where the men were, and could tell the police to go and grab them there.

They'd get the stolen goods too. I bet they're being held by our mysterious Q!'

'I know! I know!' suddenly yelled Pam, making everyone jump. 'Why can't we look up all the names beginning with Q in our local telephone directory? If Q lives somewhere here, his name would be there, and his number.'

'Yes but there might be a lot of Q's, and we wouldn't know which was the right one,' objected Janet. 'Why, we ourselves know a Mrs Queen, a Mr Quigley and a Miss Quorn.'

'But don't you see what I *mean*!' said Pam, impatiently. 'We'll go down all the list of Q's, and the one with the telephone number of 8061 will be *our* Q! Don't you *see*?'

Everyone saw what she meant at once.

Peter looked at Pam admiringly. 'That's a very good idea, Pam,' he said. 'I've sometimes thought that you're not as good a Secret Seven member as the others are, but now I know you are. That's a Very Good Idea. Why didn't we think of it before instead of messing about with K.E.W.?'

'I'll get our telephone directory with all the numbers in,' said Janet and raced off.

She soon came back, gave the password and joined the others. She opened the book at the Q's, and everyone craned to look at them.

There were not very many. 'Quant,' read Pam, 'telephone number 6015. Queen, 6453, Quelling, 4322, Quentin, 8061. . . . ! That's it. Look, here it is,

Quentin, 8061, Barr's Warehouse East End. Why, that's only about two miles away, right at the other end of the town!'

'My WORD!' said Peter, delighted. 'That's given us JUST the information we wanted. A warehouse, too. A fine place for hiding stolen goods! My goodness, we've done some jolly good work. Pam, you deserve a pat on the back!'

She got plenty of pats, and sat back, beaming. 'What do we do now?' she said.

Before anyone could answer, there came the sound of footsteps down the path, and Peter's mother's voice called loudly: 'Peter! Janet! Are Colin and George there, and Pam? Their mothers have just telephoned to say they really must come home at once, it's getting late!'

'Right, Mummy!' called Peter. 'Wait for us. We've got a wonderful tale to tell you! Do wait!'

But his mother had gone scurrying back to the house, not liking the cold, damp evening. The seven children tore after her, with Scamper barking his head off.

Just as they went in at the back of the house, there came a knock at the front door.

'See who that is, Peter!' called his mother. 'I've got a cake in the oven I must look at.'

Peter went to the door, with the others close behind him. A big policeman stood there. He smiled at the surprised children.

'I've just been to Master Jack's house,' he said, 'and Miss Susie told me he might be here. I saw you tonight in Cole Square – you and this other boy here. Well, not long after that somebody reported to me that their car had been stolen near where you were, and I wondered if either of you had noticed anything suspicious going on.'

'Oh, come in, come in!' cried Peter, joyfully. 'We can tell you a whole lot about the thieves, and we can even tell you where you'll probably find the car. Come in, do!'

Eighteen

Don't worry, Secret Seven!

THE policeman went into the hall, looking extremely surprised. Peter's mother came from the kitchen and Peter's father looked out of his study.

'What's all this?' he said. 'Nobody has got into trouble, surely?'

'No,' said Peter. 'Oh, Daddy, you must just listen to our tale. It's really super!'

They all went into the study, the policeman looking more and more puzzled.

'I *think* you'll find that stolen car outside Barr's Warehouse, at the East End of the town,' said Peter. 'And in the warehouse you'll probably find a Mr Quentin, and quite a lot of stolen goods on the premises.'

'And you'll find a man with half a finger missing, and another whose hair is so short that he looks like an escaped prisoner,' put in Colin.

'Wait! Wait a minute! What's this about a man with a missing half-finger?' said the policeman, urgently. 'We're looking for him – Fingers, he's called, and he's a friend of a thief who's just been in prison. He escaped last week, and we thought he might go to Fingers for help, so we've been keeping an eye open for him too.'

'They met at Sid's Café,' said Peter, enjoying everyone's astonishment.

'WHAT?' said his father. 'Sid's Café? That horrible place! Don't dare to tell me you boys have been in there.'

'Not inside, only outside,' said Peter. 'It's all right, Daddy. We *really* haven't done anything wrong. It all began with that night when you left Janet and me in your car in the station yard, and two men got in and drove it away.'

'And we wanted you to go to the police, but you didn't think you'd bother,' said Janet. 'So we've been trying to trace the two men ourselves, and we have!'

Then the whole of the story came out how they found Sid's Café, how Peter dressed up as a guy to watch for the men, how they saw Fingers with his missing half-finger, and how George and Jack followed them and saw them steal the car near Cole Square.

'And we know where they've gone, because they have a friend called Q, a Mr Quentin,' said Peter. 'They mentioned his telephone number, it was 8061, and we looked up the number and found the address. We only did that a little while ago, actually. The address is Barr's Warehouse, as we said.'

'Amazing!' said the policeman, scribbling fast in his note-book. 'Incredible! Do these kids do this kind of thing often, sir?'

'Well, you're a fairly new man here,' said Peter's father, 'or you'd know how they keep poking their

noses into all sorts of things. I don't know that I really approve of it, but they certainly have done some good work.'

'We're the Secret Seven Society, you see,' explained Janet. 'And we really do like some kind of adventurous job to do.'

'Well, thanks very much,' said the policeman, getting up. 'I'll get a few men and ask the Sergeant to come along with us and see what we can find in Barr's Warehouse. You'll deserve a jolly good Bonfire Night tomorrow! I hope you've got a wonderful collection of fireworks, you deserve the best!'

'Well, actually we've hardly any,' said Peter. 'We collected masses, but they all went up in a fire last Saturday, quite by accident. It was dreadful.'

'That was very bad luck,' said the policeman, going to the door. 'I'm much obliged to you all. Good night, madam; good night, sir!'

'What a tale!' said Peter's mother. 'I never heard of such goings-on! Whatever will you Seven do next? To think of you dressing up as a guy, Peter, and watching outside Sid's Café! No wonder you look so DREADFUL! Take that black wig off, do!'

'Mummy, *can't* the others stay and have a bit of supper?' begged Peter. 'We've got such a lot to talk about. Do let them. Sandwiches will do. We'll all help to make them.'

'Very well,' said his mother, laughing at all the excited faces. 'Janet, go and telephone everybody's mothers and tell them where they are!'

The Seven were very pleased. In fifteen minutes' time they were all sitting down to potted meat sandwiches, oatmeal biscuits, apples and hot cocoa, talking nineteen to the dozen, with a very excited Scamper tearing round their legs under the table. What an unexpected party! thought Scamper, delighted, and what a wonderful selection of titbits!

The telephone suddenly rang, and Peter went to answer it. It proved to be a very exciting call indeed! He came racing back to the others.

'That was that policeman! He thought we'd like to know what happened.'

'What? Tell us!' cried everyone.

'Well, the police went to Barr's Warehouse and the first thing they saw in the yard was the stolen car!' said Peter. 'Then they forced their way in at a back door, and found Mr Quentin, scared stiff, in his office. When they told him they knew that Fingers and the escaped prisoner were somewhere in the warehouse, he just crumpled up!'

'Have they got the others?' asked Colin.

'Oh yes. Quentin showed the police where they were hiding,' said Peter. 'Down in a cellar, and the stolen goods were there too. It was a wonderful raid! By the way, the police want to know if we can identify the second man, the close-cropped man, and I said yes, if he was wearing a mac with a missing button, because we've got the button!'

Goody, goody!' said Barbara. 'So we have. We

forgot to tell the policeman about that! Where *is* the button?'

'Here,' said Jack, and spun it on the table. 'Good old button, you did your bit too! My word, this is one of the most exciting jobs the Secret Seven have ever done. I'm jolly sorry it's ended.'

So was everyone. They didn't want that exciting evening to come to a finish, but they had to say good-bye at last.

'There's only one thing that's spoilt this adventure,' said Peter to Janet, as they shut the front door on the others. 'That's the burning-up of our fireworks, and tomorrow is Bonfire Night. What a shame!'

But don't worry, Secret Seven, there's a parcel on the way to you, being brought by your friend the policeman. What's inside? Ah, you'll never guess!

It's a reward from the police for all your good work – two hundred wonderful fireworks of all kinds. Just wait till you see them, you'll hardly believe your eyes.

BANG! WHOOSH! BANG-BANG-BANG! What a lovely end to a most exciting story!

SECRET SEVEN
WIN THROUGH

CONTENTS

One

The holidays begin

'EASTER holidays at last!' said Peter. 'I thought they were never coming. Didn't you, Janet?'

'Yes. It was a frightfully long term,' said Janet, 'We've broken up now though, thank goodness. Don't you love the first day of the hols, Peter?'

'Rather! I get a lovely *free* sort of feeling,' said Peter, 'and the hols seem to stretch out in front of me for ages and ages. Let's have some fun, Janet!'

'Yes, let's! April's a lovely month – it's warm, and sunny too, and Mummy will let us off on picnics any day we like,' said Janet. 'Scamper, do you hear that? Picnics, I said – and that means rabbit-hunting for you, and long, long walks.'

'Woof! said Scamper at once, his tail thumping on the floor, and his eyes bright.

'You're the best and finest golden spaniel in the whole world!' said Janet, stroking his silky head. 'And I do so love your long, droopy ears, Scamper. You like it when we have holidays, don't you?'

'Woof!' said Scamper again, and thump-thump-thump went his tail.

'I vote we have a meeting of the Secret Seven as soon as ever we can,' said Peter. 'Tomorrow, if possible. Picnics and things are much more fun if we all go together.'

'Yes. Let's have a meeting,' said Janet. 'What with exams and one thing and another all the Secret Seven have forgotten about the Society. I haven't thought a word about it for at least three weeks. Golly – what's the password?'

'Oh, Janet – you haven't forgotten that *surely*?' said Peter.

'You tell me,' said Janet, but Peter wouldn't. 'You don't know it yourself!' said Janet. 'I bet you don't!'

'Don't be silly,' said Peter. 'You'll have to remember it by tomorrow, if we have a meeting! Where's your badge? I expect you've lost that.'

'I have *not*,' said Janet. 'But I bet some of the others will have lost theirs. Somebody always does when we don't have a meeting for some time.'

'Better write out short notes to the other five,' said Peter. 'And tell them to come along tomorrow. Got some note-paper, Janet?'

'Yes, I have. But I don't feel a bit like sitting down and writing the first day of the hols,' said Janet. 'You can jolly well help to write them.'

'No. I'll bike round to all the others and deliver the notes for you,' said Peter.

'Now it's *you* who are silly,' said Janet. 'If you're going to everyone's house, why not *tell* them about the meeting. All this note-writing! You just *tell* them.'

'All right. It just seems more *official* if we send out notes for a meeting, that's all,' said Peter. 'What time shall we have it?'

'Oh, half past ten, I should think,' said Janet. 'And just warn Jack that he's not to let his horrid sister Susie

know, or she'll come banging at the door, shouting out some silly password at the top of her voice.'

'Yes. I'll tell him,' said Peter. 'The worst of it is, Susie is so jolly sharp. She always seems to smell out anything to do with the Secret Seven.'

'She would be a better person to have *in* a club than out of it,' said Janet. 'But we'll never, never let her into ours.'

'Never,' said Peter. 'Anyway, we can't be more than seven, or we wouldn't be the Secret Seven.'

'Woof!' said Scamper.

'He says he belongs, even if we're seven and he makes the eighth!' said Janet. 'You're just a hanger-on, Scamper, but we simply couldn't do without you.'

'Well, I'm going to get my bike,' said Peter, getting up. 'I'll go round and tell all the others. See you later, Janet. Coming, Scamper?'

Off he went, and was soon cycling to one house after another. He went to Colin first, who was delighted to hear the news.

'Goodo!' he said. 'Half past ten? Right, I'll be there. I say – whatever's the password, Peter?'

'You've got all day to think of it!' said Peter, with a grin, and rode off to Jack's. Jack was in the garden, mending a puncture in the back wheel of his bicycle. He was very pleased to see Peter.

'Meeting of the Secret Seven tomorrow morning in the shed at the bottom of our garden,' said Peter. 'I hope you've got your badge, and that your awful sister Susie hasn't found it and taken it.'

'I've got it on,' said Jack, with a grin. 'And I wear

it on my pyjamas at night, so it's always safe. I say, Peter – what's the password?'

'*I* can tell you!' said a voice from up a near-by tree. The boys looked up to see Susie's laughing face looking down at them.

'You don't know it!' said Jack fiercely.

'I do, I do!' said the annoying Susie. 'But I shan't tell you, and you won't be allowed in at the meeting. What a joke!'

Peter rode off to the rest of the Seven. That Susie! She really was the most AGGRAVATING girl in the whole world!

Two

A dreadful blow

NEXT morning Peter and Janet began preparing for the meeting. Meetings weren't proper meetings, somehow, unless there was plenty to eat and drink while they talked. Their mother was always generous in giving cakes or biscuits and lemonade, and the two children went to find her.

'Hello,' she said, looking up from chopping parsley on a board. 'What are you two after now?'

'We're going to have a Secret Seven meeting,' explained Peter, 'and we wanted something to eat and drink.'

'Well now, let me see – you can have that tin of ginger biscuits – they've gone soft,' said Mummy smiling. 'And you can make yourself some real lemonade – there are plenty of lemons and sugar in the larder.'

'Ooh, good!' said Janet. 'I'll do that. I'll make it with hot water, and let it go cool. Anything else we can have?'

'Jam-tarts,' said Mummy, chopping away hard at the parsley. 'Only four though, I'm afraid. That's all that were left from supper last night.'

'Four – well, we'll halve them,' said Peter. There'll be one half over, so . . .'

'Woof! woof!' said Scamper, at once. The children laughed.

'All right, you shall have the half left over,' said Peter. 'You never miss a word of what we say, do you, Scamper?'

Janet made the lemonade, and Peter got the tin of biscuits and found the tarts. He cut them carefully into exact halves and put them on a plate.

'Come on, Janet,' he said. 'It's nearly half past ten.'

'Peter, please do tell me the password!' said Janet. 'I'm very, very sorry I've forgotten it.'

'No. I shan't tell you,' said Peter. 'You'll have to be in the shed, anyhow, and you can jolly well listen to the others coming along and saying the password, and feel ashamed of yourself.'

'You're mean!' said Janet. 'Isn't he mean, Scamper?'

Scamper didn't answer. 'There,' said Peter, 'he won't say I'm mean. He never will. Do come on, Janet. I'm not going to wait a minute longer.'

Janet was ready. She put the jug of lemonade and seven unbreakable mugs on an old tray and followed Peter out of the kitchen. 'Thanks, Mummy!' she said, as she went carefully down the steps outside the kitchen door.

Peter was ahead of her. He went along the path that wound between the bushes right down to the bottom of the garden, where the old shed stood that they used for their meetings. On the door was always pinned the sign 'SS'. How many, many times the Secret Seven had met there and made exciting plans!

Janet followed a little way behind, carrying her tray carefully. She suddenly heard Peter give a startled shout, and almost dropped the tray she held.

111

'What's the matter?' she called and tried to hurry. She came in sight of the shed – and stared in horror.

The door was wide open, and so were the windows. Everything had been turned out of the shed! There were boxes and cushions and sacks, all strewn on the ground in untidy heaps! Whatever had happened?

Janet put her tray down, afraid that she might drop it in her dismay. She looked at Peter in despair.

'Who's done this? Just as we were going to have a meeting too! It's too bad.'

Peter looked into the shed. It was quite empty, except for the shelves round the sides. He was puzzled.

'Janet – it couldn't be Susie, could it?' he said. 'I mean, this is an awful thing to do, throw everything out of our shed. I don't think even Susie would do that.'

'She might,' said Janet, almost in tears.. 'Oh, our lovely meeting-place!'

'Here come the others,' said Peter, as Pamela and Barbara appeared down the path together. They stared in amazement at the untidy mess on the ground.

'What's happened?' said Barbara. 'Are we too early?'

'No. We've only *just* seen all this ourselves,' said Peter. 'Hallo – here's Jack. Jack, look here.'

'My word!' said Jack. 'Who's done this? It can't be Susie. She's been with me all morning till I left just now.'

Colin and George came up just then, and the seven looked ruefully at the boxes and cushions thrown out so untidily. 'We'd better put them back,' said Janet. 'And we'll find out who's done all this to our secret meeting-place.'

They began to put everything back, and then they heard footsteps coming along down the path. Who was it? Peter looked to see.

It was the gardener, carrying a strong broom over his shoulder, a pail of water in his hand, and some cloths hanging on the side of the pail. He stared at the seven in annoyance.

'Hey, you! What are you doing? I've only just thrown all that rubbish out!'

'But why?' demanded Peter, indignantly. 'This shed is our meeting-place, and this isn't rubbish. We use it.'

'Oh, well, I don't know anything about that,' said

113

the gardener. 'All I know is that your father told me to clear out this place, burn all the rubbish, and do a spot of painting. He said it was going to rack and ruin, and he wanted it cleaned up.'

'I see,' said Peter, his heart sinking. If his father had planned this, there was nothing to be done. He turned to the others. 'Come on, let's find somewhere to talk,' he said. 'We can't meet in our shed for a while, that's certain. What a blow!'

'Never mind! We'll think of somewhere just as good,' said Colin. But nobody agreed with him. They thought the shed was the finest place in the world for Secret Seven meetings!

The Seven, followed by Scamper with his tail well down, went slowly up the garden path. Somehow it seemed dreadful not to have their usual meeting-place.

'We'll go to the summer-house,' said Peter. 'Oh, look, there's Mummy, Janet. We'll ask her about the shed.'

'Mummy!' called Janet. 'Why didn't you tell us the shed was going to be cleaned and painted – our own shed, I mean, where we meet? I do think *somebody* might have told us.'

'Oh dear, I quite forgot to tell you that Daddy wanted it cleaned and mended,' said Mummy. 'It was almost falling to bits here and there, you know. But you can have it for a meeting-place again when it's finished. It will look nice and bright and clean then.'

'But we like it old and dark and untidy,' said Peter mournfully. 'And I do think it's a pity to have it done in the holidays, Mummy, just when we want to use it.'

'Yes, I agree that that's a pity,' said Mummy, look-

114

ing very sorry. 'I would have stopped it if I'd known that it was to be done just now. Well – you'll have to find another meeting-place. What about the attic?'

'Oh no,' said Janet. 'It's no fun meeting in a *house*, Mummy, with other people in near-by rooms. We want a secret, lonely place, we do really.'

'Yes ... I suppose you do,' said Mummy. 'Well, I can't suggest one, I'm afraid. Go to the summer-house just for now.'

'We were going to,' said Peter, still very doleful. Soon they were all squashed into the little old summer-house. The girls didn't much like it, because it was rather earwiggy.

They began to eat the ginger biscuits. 'Rather soft, I'm afraid,' said Janet.

'Oh, I like them soft and squidgy,' said Pam. 'I hate them when you have to bite so hard they splinter in your mouth. I say, this is good lemonade! Did your mother make it, Janet?'

'No. I made it myself,' said Janet proudly. 'Peter, hadn't we better talk about where to have a new meeting-place?'

'Yes,' said Peter. 'And I vote that we all of us have a good hunt round to find somewhere, some absolutely secret place that even Jack's sister Susie won't find. It mustn't be too far away. I'll give you today to find one. Meet here this evening, in this summer-house again, at six o'clock.'

'Right,' said Colin. 'I think I know of one already.'

'Well, don't tell us now,' said Peter. 'We'll each give in our ideas this evening and put it to the vote to see

115

which is the best. We must do these things properly.'

'Yes,' said everyone, and took a drink of Janet's lemonade.

'What about the password?' said Jack. 'We were all so upset about the shed that we never even gave the password.'

'We've all got our badges on,' said Pamela. 'I had an awful hunt for mine. I put it in such a safe place that it was almost too safe for me to find!'

'Where was it?' asked George.

'I buried it in the pot of maidenhair fern my mother has in the drawing-room,' said Pam, with a giggle. 'And then forgot about it. It took me ages to remember it.'

'I thought it looked a bit grubby,' said Peter. 'I think that's a silly place.'

'Oh, I wrapped it in paper,' said Pam. 'But I forgot that Mummy watered it twice a week – so, of course, the paper soaked off and made my badge messy.'

'It's a good thing it didn't put out roots and grow!' said Peter. Everyone laughed.

'Peter, could we have a new password?' said Jack. 'Susie knows our last one. I'm most frightfully sorry, and I don't know how she knew it, unless she hung round our last meeting and heard it.'

'All right. We'll choose a new one,' said Peter. 'It's time we did, anyway. I must say that your sister Susie is getting worse and worse, Jack. I hope she's nowhere about just now.'

Jack got up and went out of the summer-house. 'Nobody's anywhere near,' he said. 'Quick – what's the **new password?**'

'Easter-egg,' said Peter. 'That's easy to remember, because it's the Easter holidays.'

'Easter-egg,' repeated everyone, in low voices. Pam took out a notebook and began to write it down.

'Don't *you* write it down, Jack!' said Janet, 'or Susie will find it. I wonder how she knew our last password?'

'Well, she called out, "Your password is Sugar-mouse" just as I was leaving,' said Jack. 'And I don't mind owning up now that I was jolly glad to hear it, because I'd forgotten it completely.'

'Sugar-mouse!' said Peter, in astonishment. 'It was nothing of the sort. Susie just made that up because she knew you'd forgotten it. She hoped you would rap on the door of the shed and yell out "Sugar-mouse" and make an ass of yourself.'

Jack went red. 'What was the password then?' he said. 'Janet, you tell me. Peter won't.'

Janet went red too. '*I've* forgotten it as well,' she said.

Pam blushed as red as Janet, so Peter knew she had forgotten too! He rapped on the summer-house table.

'The last password was a very simple one,' he said. 'It was "Thursday". Just that, "Thursday".'

'Golly, so it was,' said Barbara. 'I just couldn't remember if it was "Thursday" or "Friday".'

'*I* thought it was Sunday,' said Colin, with a laugh. 'It was a silly password to choose, Peter, too easy to muddle up with the other days of the week. "Easter-egg" is much better.'

Well, let's hope that Barbara and Colin don't mix it up with "Christmas present" or "Birthday gift"!' said Peter. 'Now – we've eaten everything, and Scamper's had his half-tart, and we've drunk all the lemonade – what about separating and hunting for a new meeting-place?'

'Right,' said everyone and got up. They all went off up the path to the front gate, and most of them were murmuring two words to themselves as they went.

'Easter-egg! Easter-egg! I must remember Easter-egg!'

Three

Plenty of ideas

At six o'clock that evening there was a continual noise of footsteps up the path to the little summer-house. Janet, Peter, and Scamper were inside, waiting.

'Easter-egg,' said Jack, walking inside. There was no door, for the summer-house was three-sided, with its fourth side open to the garden.

'Easter-egg,' said Barbara, walking in, too.

'Where's your badge?' asked Peter sharply.

'Oh – I've got it, it's all right,' said Barbara, feeling in her pocket. 'I don't know why I forgot to pin it on.' She pinned it on carefully and sat down.

The other three came along, each solemnly giving the password.

'For once nobody *yelled* it out,' said Peter. He took a notebook out of his pocket, and licked his pencil. 'Now then. I want your reports on any likely places to meet secretly. Colin, you begin.'

'Well, there's a fine big tree at the bottom of our garden,' began Colin hopefully. 'It's a great chestnut, and . . .'

'No good, I'm afraid,' said Peter, 'but I'll put it down. It would hardly be a secret meeting-place! Everyone would see us going down the garden to it, and people passing the wall nearby would hear us up there. Barbara, what's *your* idea!'

119

'Oh, it's a silly one,' said Barbara. 'There's an old hut in a field nearby our house, and . . .'

'I know it,' said Peter, scribbling in his note-book. 'Not a bad idea, Barbara. You, Pam?'

'I simply haven't any idea at all,' said Pam. 'I've thought and thought, but it's no use.'

'*Not* very helpful,' said Peter, putting a cross against Pam's name in his note-book. 'You, George?'

'Well, there's an empty caravan in a field not far from here,' said George. 'I know who owns it – it's a friend of my father's. I think I could get permission for us to use it.'

This sounded exciting. Everyone looked admiringly at George, who seemed quite pleased with himself.

'You, Jack?' said Peter. 'And don't suggest anywhere near *your* house, because of Susie.'

'I'm not going to,' said Jack. 'I'm not quite so silly as that. I've chosen somewhere a long way away, down by the river. It's an old boat-house that nobody ever uses.'

This sounded exciting too. Peter wrote it down solemnly. 'Now we've heard everyone's idea except mine and Janet's. We went out hunting together, and Scamper came too – and we've all got the same idea.'

'What?' asked everyone.

'Well, it's a cave in the quarry near the field where we grow potatoes,' said Peter. 'So it's on my father's farm, and not very far. It's absolutely lonely and secret, and goes back into the hill behind the quarry. Scamper found it, actually.'

'That sounds good – a secret cave,' said Pam.

'Well, we'll now put all our ideas to the vote,' said

Peter, and handed round slips of paper. 'Please write down on these papers what ideas you like best – but nobody must vote for their own idea, of course. I'll just go shortly over them again:

'Colin suggests a tree, but it's not a very *secret* place. Barbara suggested that old hut in the field near her house – but the roof's almost off and the rain would come in. Pam has no ideas. George suggests the caravan owned by his father's friend, a very good idea, but I don't honestly think we'd be allowed to use it because it's still furnished. I'd be afraid of breaking something.'

Peter paused for breath. 'Jack suggested the old boat-house by the river. Fine – but isn't it rather far away for a meeting-place? It's at least a mile away. And you know what Janet and I suggest – the cave. But that isn't a really comfortable place. There you are – please vote on your papers, fold them in half, and give them to me.'

Everyone solemnly wrote something on their papers, then handed them to Peter. He opened them and read them. When he looked up, his eyes were shining with pleasure.

'Er – well – it's very funny, but everyone except me and Janet have voted for the cave. We couldn't vote for our own idea, of course. So it's five votes for the cave – and the cave it will be. I'm glad – it's a smashing place really!'

'Is it? Let's go and see it straight away!' said Jack. 'It's not very far.'

'All right, come on then,' said Peter. 'We'll have a quick look, and then plan what to bring to it tomorrow. We'll settle into it at once.'

121

This was exciting. They all got up and went out into the bright sunshine. It was almost half past six, and as warm as could be.

'This way,' said Peter, and led the way down his garden and through a gate into a field. His father owned the farm-land at the back of the house, and it stretched away over the hills, the fields green with growing corn and root-crops.

Peter took them down a grassy path, past a pond with ducks on it, and then turned to the right towards the old quarry. Sand had been dug from it years ago, and it had then been abandoned. They all filed into the quarry and looked round.

Scamper ran in front. 'He'll show you,' said Peter. 'Just as he showed me and Janet this morning!' Scamper ran up to what looked like a rabbit path, over a little sandy hill, then down into a hollow behind. The others followed. Scamper stood waiting for them, his tail waving to and fro.

He ran through a gap in some thick bushes and disappeared. The others went through the gap too and looked for Scamper. He had gone!

'He's gone into the cave,' said Peter, grinning. 'You can see the entrance just there. It's all hung over with some plant that has sent long, trailing stems down, and has almost hidden the entrance to the cave. Come on – it's really quite exciting!'

Four

In the cave

THE Secret Seven crowded together to see the cave. There was no proper path to it, and they had to squeeze through close-growing bushes of bright-yellow broom to get to it. The bushes grew almost up to the cave entrance.

'No wonder Janet and I never spotted this cave before,' said Peter. 'We've been in this old sand quarry heaps of times, but never found the cave. It was only because old Scamper disappeared and we went to look for him that we found it. We were standing here, calling him, when he suddenly appeared under the trailing leaves that hide the cave! Didn't you, Scamper?'

'Woof!' said Scamper, and ran into the cave and back, as if to say, 'Do come on, it's a fine place!'

The trailing stems that hung down over the entrance certainly hid it very well. Peter pulled the greenery aside. 'It's like a curtain,' he said. 'Look – now you can see into the cave properly.'

Everyone bent their heads and looked in. It certainly was a fine cave!

'Nice and big, and with a lovely sandy floor!' said Jack. 'I don't see why you said it's not comfortable, Peter. Sand is lovely to sit on.'

'Oh well, I had to say *something* against it, as it was Janet's suggestion and mine,' said Peter.

By now they were all in the cave. Pam flung herself down on the sand. It was very soft indeed.

'Lovely!' she said. 'I'd like to sleep here in this sand. I could burrow my body down into it and make a lovely bed. It's a simply *wonderful* meeting-place, I think.'

'Nobody would EVER find it!' said George, looking

round. 'It's a bit dark, that's the only thing. It's that green curtain over the entrance that makes it so dark.'

Janet obligingly held the curtain back, and the sun streamed into the cave.

'Fine!' said Colin. 'We can have the curtain back when we're just playing about, and draw it when we're having a secret meeting. Couldn't be better. A cave with a ready-made curtain!'

'And look, the cave has a rock roof, all uneven, high here and low there,' said Barbara. 'And there are rocky shelves round the walls; we can use those to put our things on. We'll bring all kinds of things here! I expect we'll have to use this cave all the Easter hols, so we'll make it a kind of home as well as a meeting-place. Shall we?'

Everyone thought this was a very good idea. 'We'll bring the shed cushions here,' said Janet. 'And a box for a table.'

'And keep food here, and lemonade or orangeade,' said Jack. 'Won't it be fun?'

'Yes, and you'll have to be careful not to let Susie follow you here,' said Peter warningly. 'She'd just love to come here and mess things about, bring her silly, giggling friends with her too, I expect, and have a picnic or something in the middle of the cave.'

'I'll be very careful,' promised Jack. 'Well, I must say this is a jolly good place for the Secret Seven. Not too far away, perfectly secret, quite lonely, and our very own. Can any of us come here when we like, Peter? When there's not a meeting or anything planned? I'd love to come and read here by myself.'

'Yes. I don't see why this shouldn't be a kind of head-quarters as well as a meeting-place,' said Peter. 'Anyone can come whenever they like, but please leave it tidy, and don't go and eat all the food we leave here!'

'Of course not,' said everyone at once.

'If we come alone and want something to eat we'll bring it ourselves,' said Colin, and everyone agreed.

'Now, let's see. We'll come tomorrow at half past ten,' began Peter, but Jack interrupted before he could say any more.

'Oh, earlier than that, Peter! It's going to be fun; I'd like to come earlier. Can't we make it half past nine?'

'No, because Janet and I have jobs to do for our father and mother,' said Peter. 'We'll say ten, if you like. We can get our jobs done by then, I expect.'

'I've got jobs to do as well,' said Pam. 'I always help Mother with the housework in the hols. So does Barbara.'

'Well, say ten,' repeated Peter. 'And bring what you can to make the cave comfortable and homey. Bring books if you like – the cave's quite dry – and games.'

Everyone was sorry to leave the exciting cave. It really was a nice one, spacious, though the roof was not very high, and it was only in places that the Seven could stand upright – clean, with its floor of soft sand – and reaching back into a very nice, mysterious darkness, quite out of reach of the sunshine.

Peter held back the curtain of greenery till everyone had gone out. Then he let it drop into place and arranged it so that hardly a bit of the entrance showed.

Nobody at all would ever guess there was a big cave behind it, going right into the hill beyond!

Scamper came out last of all, his tail wagging madly. He liked the cave. It was exciting. There was no smell of rabbits in it, which was disappointing, but it was good fun to pretend there was, and to scrabble hard at the sand with his front paws, and send it showering into the air!

The Seven all walked back to the gate at the bottom of Peter's garden, and then up the garden to the front gate. They said good-bye, and went off to their different homes, thinking exciting thoughts.

Susie met Jack as he came in, and looked at his sandy shoes.

'Where have you been?' she demanded. 'I've been looking for you everywhere. Where did you get that sand on your shoes?'

'Ask no questions, and I'll tell you no fibs,' said Jack, pushing by her.

'You've been with the Secret Seven, I know you have,' said Susie, and she laughed. 'What's the password? Is it still Sugar-mouse? Ha, ha – I tricked you nicely over that, didn't I?'

Five

Settling in

NEXT day Peter and Janet felt very excited. They went down the garden to collect the old cushions they had had in the shed. The gardener had put them into another shed, together with the boxes, sacks, and other things.

He was very busy repairing the old shed. The two children peeped inside. It would certainly be nice and clean when it was all finished.

'I'd rather have the cave for the holidays though,' said Peter, and Janet nodded.

They were very laden indeed as they made their way down to the quarry. Scamper carried a bone in his mouth. He knew quite well they were going to the cave, and he wanted to take something too!

Peter and Janet were there before the others. They drew aside the curtain of greenery and went in. The curtain fell behind them.

'Don't draw it back yet, till the others come,' said Peter. 'They'll have to give the password outside the curtain before we pull it back. Otherwise we'd never know who was coming in! But the password will tell us it's the Secret Seven.'

Janet set down the cushions. Peter put down the box he had brought. It was heavy, because he had filled it with all kinds of things. He began to unpack.

'Hand me the things,' said Janet. 'I'll arrange them nicely on these rocky shelves. There's no hole we can use for a cupboard, but that won't matter. I say, isn't this going to be fun?'

Peter looked at his watch. 'It's almost ten,' he said. 'You go on arranging things, and I'll wait just at the entrance, behind the curtain, and ask for the passwords. The sand outside is so soft that we shan't hear anyone coming. I must watch for them.'

Almost immediately there came a soft shuffle outside. 'Password,' said Peter, in a low voice.

'Easter-egg!' said Colin's voice. Peter pulled aside the curtain of greenery, and Colin came staggering in, carrying a big cardboard box. He collapsed on the soft, sandy floor.

'Golly! I never knew books were so heavy! I've brought my whole set of "Famous Five" books to put on the shelves for anyone to borrow, and they've nearly dragged my arms out!'

'Oh, fine, there's one I want to read again,' said Peter, pleased. 'Find a nice even shelf of rock somewhere along the wall there, Colin, and put the books up neatly.'

A small cough came from outside the cave. Someone was waiting to be allowed in. 'Password!' said Peter, at once.

'Easter-egg!' said two voices together, and Peter lifted the green curtain. In came Pam and Barbara, both together, Pam giggling as usual. They both carried parcels.

'Janet will see to those,' said Peter, taking up his post

by the curtain again. Soon he heard the soft sound of feet coming quietly over the sand outside, and heard, too, the noise of people squeezing through the thick bushes of yellow broom.

'Password!' he said, and two voices answered together. 'Easter-egg!'

'Not so loud, idiots!' said Peter, and pulled aside the green curtain, grinning widely at Jack and George. He peered cautiously behind them.

'It's all right. I slipped off while Susie was at the bottom of our garden,' said Jack, staggering in. 'I've brought two bottles of drinks and two syphons of soda-water. Mother said I could, as her share towards the Secret Seven goings-on!'

'Goodo!' said Peter, pleased. He drew back the curtain and tied it with a bit of string, so that the sunshine flooded into the cave. He looked all round outside to make sure that no one was about.

'I think we're absolutely safe and secret here,' he said. 'This quarry has been deserted for years, and I don't expect anyone remembers there was ever a cave here.'

'Scamper would bark if anyone wandered near,' said Janet. 'Then we could quickly pull the curtain over the entrance and lie as quiet as anything!'

'Yes. Scamper would certainly warn us,' said Peter. 'Now, how are you all getting on?'

The cave was beginning to look quite cosy and furnished. The box-table was in the middle. Cushions were here and there on the sandy floor, ready for anyone to sit on. Arranged on the uneven ledges of the rocky wall were Colin's books and some of Jack's. Plastic cups had been neatly put in a row by Janet, and on a wider ledge she had put Jack's bottles and syphons.

A tin stood in one corner. It had in it some of the food that the Seven had brought, and on another ledge stood a tin of boiled sweets, a packet of oatmeal biscuits, and two bars of chocolate brought by Pam. A small jar of potted crab paste stood next to a jar of home-made strawberry jam.

'It all looks very good,' said Peter approvingly. 'Very good indeed.'

'Yes. We've found places for everything,' said Janet, pleased. 'That corner over there belongs to Scamper, by the way, that's where he's buried the big bone he brought with him. Please don't disturb it, anyone. You can stop sitting on it, Scamper. I've told everyone it's your own special corner.'

Scamper still sat there, however. To him a bone was a very precious possession indeed, and he had to make *quite* sure that everyone understood it was *his* bone.

'I'm hungry after all this,' announced Jack, 'I vote we choose something to eat. We've got a very well-filled larder!'

'I'll have a ginger bun,' said Colin. 'My mother made them yesterday. They're lovely. Let's begin with those.'

So there they sat, all the Secret Seven, happily munching ginger buns. The sun streamed in at the cave entrance, for the green curtain was still pulled back. What a lovely meeting-place – the best they had ever had!

Six

Jack is very puzzled

THE cave was a great success. On rainy days it was a wonderful place to lie in and read, or play games. Each of the seven burrowed into the sand and made his or her own bed or hole. Each had a cushion for their head. The shelves were always kept stacked with papers and magazines, and with food and drink.

'We couldn't have found a better place,' said Colin. 'Jack, does Susie ever bother about where you disappear to for hours on end?'

'Goodness, yes,' said Jack 'She keeps on and on about it. She knows our old shed is no longer a meeting-place, because she went to have a look at it. I have to be awfully careful not to let her follow me when I come here. Yesterday I turned round and there she was, keeping to the bushes beside the road, hoping I wouldn't see her.'

'What did you do?' asked Pam.

'I turned a corner and went off to the sweet shop instead of coming here,' said Jack. 'I do hope she won't find our cave.'

'Let's go into the quarry and play hide-and-seek,' said Janet, getting up. 'The sun's out again, and I'm longing to stretch my legs.'

So off they all went. Jack was chosen to shut his eyes and count a hundred before he began looking. The cave was to be Home.

Jack stood by a tree at the other side of the quarry, counting nice and slowly. When he had counted a hundred, he looked round. Could he see anyone behind a bush, or lying in the lush grass nearby?

No – not one of the others was to be seen. He moved cautiously round his tree, keeping his eyes open for a sudden movement somewhere.

He glanced towards the cave, which he could just see between a gap in the broom bushes that hid it so well. Then he stared. Someone was slipping into the cave! Who was it? He just couldn't see.

That's not fair, thought Jack. They haven't given me a chance to find them. Well, I'll soon find out which of the seven it is, and tell them what I think of them!

He saw a patch of blue nearby and recognized Pam's frock behind a bush. He rushed at her, but she escaped and ran squealing to the cave.

Then he found Barbara, Janet, and Scamper together, crouching behind a great hummock of sand. He ran to catch them and fell headlong over a tuft of grass. They rushed away, the girls squealing and Scamper barking.

He nearly caught Colin behind a tree, but Colin was too quick for him. Let's see – that only leaves one more, said Jack to himself. The first one I saw going into the cave – then the three girls – then Colin – myself – and so there's just one more. It's Peter or George.

He hunted here and there, and then suddenly fell over two giggling boys. It was Peter and George, half-buried in the soft sand. Jack grabbed at Peter and caught him, but George escaped to the cave.

'I'm caught all right!' said Peter, grinning. 'I'll be "He" next. Let's call out to everyone in the cave.'

'Wait a minute,' said Jack, looking puzzled. 'There's something I don't understand. Let's go up to the cave.'

Peter went with him to the cave, where the other five were waiting.

'What don't you understand?' asked Peter.

'Well, listen – first I saw someone slipping into the cave immediately after I'd finished counting,' said Jack, 'which wasn't really fair. Then I found Pam, then Janet and Barbara, then Colin, then you and George, Peter.'

'Well – what's puzzling you?' asked Peter.

'Just this – that makes *eight* of us, not counting Scamper,' said Jack. 'And what I want to know is, who was the eighth?'

They all counted. Yes, Jack was right. That made eight, not seven. Everyone said at once that they hadn't slipped into the cave before Jack discovered them.

'Well, who was that first person then, if it wasn't any of us?' said Jack, really puzzled. 'I tell you I saw somebody go into the cave before I discovered *any* of you. Who was it?'

Everyone began to look round uneasily. Peter pulled the green curtain back as far as he could, and the sunshine filled the cave, except for the dark places at the back.

'There's nobody here,' said Pam. 'Oh, Jack, do you suppose it could have been Susie?'

'I don't know. I only just saw *somebody*, but I haven't any idea who it was,' said Jack. 'And look here, surely that somebody must still be in here! I found

Pam almost immediately, and she rushed off to the cave. You didn't see anyone here, did you, Pam?'

'Of course not,' said Pam. 'If I'd seen Susie I would have smacked her!'

Peter took down a torch from the shelf of rock nearby and switched it on. He flashed it towards the dark corners at the end of the cave. 'Come forth!' he said, in a hollow voice. 'Come forth, O wicked intruder!'

But nobody came. The far corners of the cave, now lighted brilliantly by the torch, were quite empty.

'It's queer,' said Jack, frowning. 'Very queer. Give me the torch, Peter. I'll go and see if there's any corner or hole at the end of the cave that we haven't noticed.'

'Well, there isn't,' said Peter, giving him the torch. 'Janet and I had a good look when we first found the cave!'

All the same, Jack went to the far end and had a very good look round, flashing the torch everywhere. There seemed to be nowhere that anyone could hide.

He came back, still looking puzzled. 'Cheer up,' said Peter. 'You must have imagined someone, Jack. Anyway, *would* anyone come to that cave while we were all of us here, in plain view?'

'But that's just what we were not,' said Jack. 'We were playing hide-and-seek, and there wasn't a sound, and all of us, except me, were well hidden. Anybody coming here just then would not have heard or seen anything of us. They would have thought the place deserted.'

'Yes. I see what you mean,' said Peter. 'All the same, there's nobody here. So cheer up, Jack, and let's go on with the game. My turn to find you all. Go and hide!'

Seven

A real mystery

NOBODY said any more about Jack's idea that someone had slipped into the cave. Jack began to think he
really must have imagined it. Perhaps it was a shadow
from a cloud or something? They all played the game
of hide-and-seek again and again, and nobody saw
mysterious people slipping into the cave any more!

'It's time to tidy up and go home,' said Peter, at last.
'What a mess we seem to make when we've been in the
cave for even a short time!'

The girls shook up the cushions, and the boys gathered up the rubbish and put it into a bag to take home.
Then Janet put the rest of the food back on the shelves,
and tidied up Colin's set of 'Five' books.

'There!' she said. 'Everything tidy! If our mothers
came and looked in they would be most astonished.'

They all laughed. They went out of the cave, and
Peter pulled the green curtain carefully across. Then off
they went home.

'Same time tomorrow!' called Peter, when they all
said good-bye to him and Janet and Scamper at his
front gate.

'No! You've forgotten – we're all going to bike over
to Penton and see the circus come through,' said Colin.
'We're meeting at eleven at my house.'

'Oh, yes, how could I forget!' said Peter. 'We'll go to
the cave after dinner tomorrow afternoon.'

Next day they had a good morning, watching the long circus procession passing through the little town of Penton. Then they biked back for their dinners, and, at various times, set off to the cave.

Pam and Barbara arrived first, Pam very pleased because her granny had given her a tin of peppermints for the Secret Seven to enjoy.

'I'll put them beside the other tins,' she said. 'Hallo – look, Barbara, there's a tin on the floor of the cave. Who do you suppose knocked that down? We're the first here today!'

'Perhaps it overbalanced,' said Barbara.

'And I say, look – we left a whole bar of chocolate, a very big one, just *here*,' said Pam. 'I put it there myself. That's gone!'

'It's probably somewhere else,' said Barbara. Then she herself noticed something. 'Goodness, look – three of our cushions are missing! Has somebody been here?'

'It's Susie,' said Pam frowning. 'That's who it is. She didn't come with us to Penton today, so she must have come here instead! She has followed Jack sometime or other, and found out our meeting-place. Blow Susie!'

'Here are the others,' said Barbara. 'Let's tell them.'

They heard the password murmured outside the cave. 'Easter-egg' – then the curtain was pushed aside and in came Colin and George.

'Susie's been here!' said Pam angrily. 'Look, there are cushions missing, and our big bar of chocolate is gone, and a tin was on the ground.'

'And look, those currant buns we were saving for

today are nearly all gone!' said Barbara, opening a tin. 'Would you believe it!'

Soon Peter, Janet, and Jack arrived and were also told the news. 'But it needn't have been Susie,' said Peter, trying to be fair, though he felt perfectly certain it was. 'It could quite well have been a tramp.'

'He'd have taken lots more things,' said Pam. 'And what would he want with *cushions*! We might meet him down a lane carrying them, and we'd know he was the thief at once. No tramp would be as silly as that.'

'That's true,' said Peter. 'Well, Jack, you'll have to find out if it's Susie.'

'All right,' said Jack, looking troubled. 'I'll go now. But somehow I don't think it *is* Susie, you know. I can't help remembering that person, whoever it was, that I saw slipping into the cave yesterday.'

Jack went off to find Susie. The others each took a peppermint from the tin that Pam offered them, and settled down to read. Colin finished his book and went to get another. He gave an exclamation.

'One of my "Famous Five" books has gone! Has anyone borrowed it? It's *Five go down to the sea*.'

Nobody had. 'I know it's not Jack,' said Colin. 'He's just finished reading it. My word, if that's Susie again I'll have something to say to her!'

Jack came back in about an hour. 'Easter-egg' he said, outside the cave, and Peter called him in.

'Well,' he said, throwing himself down on the sandy floor, 'I've had an awful time. Susie says she's never been *near* our new meeting-place, she says she doesn't even know where it is! She flew into such a temper when I accused her of coming and taking things, that Mother heard her, and came to see what was the matter.'

'Oh, blow!' said Peter. 'You might have kept your mother out of this. What happened next?'

'Mother made me tell where our meeting-place is,' said poor Jack, looking really miserable. 'I couldn't help it, Peter, really I couldn't. She *made* me.'

There was a silence. Everyone knew that it was wrong, and also quite impossible, to refuse to tell mothers anything they wanted to know. But to give away their wonderful new meeting-place! How truly shocking.

'Was Susie there when you told?' asked Peter.

'Yes,' said Jack. 'She was, and she said she was jolly well coming to find the cave and make a real mess of it! I don't think she did come here this morning. She was with Jeff all the time in the garden. Mother said so.'

'Well then, who did?' said Peter, puzzled. 'It's a queer thief who comes and takes three *cushions*!'

There was a silence. Pam glanced round the cave fearfully. Who was it who came here? Jack had seen someone yesterday, and now the someone had come again today. WHO was it?

'Now that Susie knows about our cave, I think that someone must be here on guard whenever we're not here,' said Peter. 'I mean – we can't let Susie come and mess everything up. I can quite see that if it wasn't she who came and took the things this morning, she must be jolly wild with us for thinking it was.'

'I wouldn't be surprised if she brought Jeff with her

and turned the whole place upside down now,' said Jack gloomily. 'You don't know Susie like I do.'

'Well, let's make things jolly unpleasant for them if they *do* come,' said George. 'Let's balance a jug of water on that ledge over the green curtain. As soon as the curtain is moved, the jug will over-balance and pour water all over them.'

Pam giggled. 'Yes. Let's do that!'

'And let's do what my cousin once did to someone he didn't like,' said Colin. 'He got a reel of cotton and wound it all over and across the entrance to our summer-house – and he dipped it in honey first! Then when this awful boy walked into the summer-house, he walked right through the sticky threads and thought that an enormous spider's web had caught him!'

'How horrible!' said Pam, shuddering. 'To have sticky thread all over you like that!'

'Susie would hate it,' said Barbara. 'She loathes getting caught in spider thread. But who's got cotton or honey? Nobody here!'

'I can run indoors and get a reel of silk from my work-box,' said Janet, 'and there's some honey in a jar in our larder, I know. But aren't we being rather horrid to Susie?'

'No, Susie will only get caught in our tricks if she finds the cave and comes to turn it upside down,' said Pam. 'It will be her own fault if she gets caught. Nobody else's.'

'It's no good being soft-hearted with Susie,' said Jack gloomily. 'Actually, sometimes I think she's cleverer **than any of us!'**

Janet ran off to get the honey and the reel of silk. Barbara complained because her cushion was gone and she now had nothing to rest her head on.

'I suppose whoever took our cushions did it for some kind of silly joke,' she said. 'And probably threw them into the bushes somewhere.'

'I'll go and look,' said Colin, and got up. But the cushions were nowhere to be seen, and he soon came back. Janet came with him, having got the reel and the honey.

'We'll get the tricks ready when we go home to tea,' said Peter. 'I'll slip up after tea to make sure that no one's been into the cave, and I'll come last thing at night too.'

Just before they left they arranged the booby-traps. Janet ran the grey silk thread through the sticky honey, and the boys wound it back and forth across the entrance to the cave, twisting it round the plants that lined the edges of the cave entrance from top to bottom.

'There!' said Peter, at last. 'No one can get in without getting covered with thin, sticky threads! And what a shock they'll get too, when they draw back the curtain and get swamped with water from that jug! I've balanced it very carefully, so that at the slightest pulling back of the green curtain the water will pour out!'

Everyone giggled and wished they could be there to see the booby-traps catch any intruder. 'I hope Jeff comes with Susie, I can't bear him,' said Jack. 'And shan't I laugh if Susie comes back sticky and wet! Come on, let's go.'

After tea Peter went up to the cave to examine the

booby-traps. They were still there! The jug of water, half-hidden by leaves, was still in place, and he could see the grey, sticky threads gleaming behind the green curtain.

'Susie and Jeff haven't been yet,' he told Janet, when he got back. 'I'll slip up again just before it gets dark and have another look.'

So up he went once more to the cave, but again the booby-traps were still there, untouched. Susie won't come now, he thought. I'll be up here before nine o'clock tomorrow morning and watch out for her in case she comes then.

Eight

Scamper is a help

JACK came to see Peter just before nine next day. 'I came to tell you. that Susie's not been near the cave,' he told Peter. 'I kept an eye on her all yesterday evening and this morning. She's gone off to her music lesson now, so we're safe till twelve o'clock anyhow.'

'Right,' said Peter. 'Well, help me with the few jobs I have to do, and then we'll go up with Janet and Scamper. We'll try to get there just before the others come.'

So at five to ten, Peter, Janet, Scamper, and Jack made their way to the quarry and then up to the cave.

They looked up to where the jug was so carefully balanced on a ledge, and grinned.

'I'll get it,' said Jack, and climbed up to remove it.

'We'll have to break these threads ourselves,' said Janet. 'What a waste of booby-traps, wasn't it? Ooh, be careful, you'll get honey all over you!'

They broke the threads as carefully as possible, so as not to get themselves sticky, and went into the cave. And then they stood there in astonishment, gazing round as if they could not believe their eyes!

The tins were all opened – and emptied! Some were flung on the floor. Two more of the cushions had gone. A bottle of orangeade had disappeared, and so had a syphon of soda-water. The tin of peppermints had completely vanished, and also some more books. A torch that Colin had left on a shelf had gone too.

'But – but – how could anyone get *in*?' stammered Peter, utterly astonished. 'Our booby-traps were still there – those threads were quite unbroken. NOBODY could have come in, and yet look at this. I don't like it. There's something very queer going on in this cave – and I just don't – like – it!'

The three children felt scared. It was quite clear that *no one* had gone into the cave, because the sticky silk threads would certainly have been broken. But how could their belongings have been taken, and their tins emptied, if no one had been in the cave?

'You know,' said Jack, looking all round him fearfully, 'you know, Peter, I was quite certain I saw somebody slipping into the cave that time we played hide-and-seek. You kept saying I must have imagined it, but I didn't.'

'Well, certainly *somebody's* about, somebody who likes eating and drinking,' said Peter. 'And if he didn't get into our cave from the *outside*, he must know a way in from the *inside*!'

'But that's silly too,' said Janet. 'We know there's no way into the cave from the inside. We've had a jolly good look.'

'Scamper seems jolly interested in the cave this morning,' said Jack. 'Look at him sniffing and nosing round.'

Scamper certainly was interested. He ran here and there excitedly, giving little barks and whimpers, as if to say, 'I could tell you such a lot if only I could speak!'

He ran over to the place where he had buried his
bone, dug it up, and carefully took it to another corner
and buried it there. Peter laughed.

'He's afraid our visitor might find his bone – see how
deep he's burying it this time! Hey, Scamper, you're
sending sand all over us!'

Janet looked round at the untidy cave with its empty
tins and scattered books. Tears came into her eyes. 'I
made it all so nice,' she said. 'And we had such a lot of
good food here. Who is this horrible visitor who comes
when we're not here and steals like this? Where does he
come from? How does he get here if he doesn't come
in at the entrance?'

'Let's look all round the cave again, very, very carefully to see if there's another entrance somewhere,' said

Jack. 'There might be a small hole that someone could wriggle through, covered with sand.'

They looked thoroughly, Scamper sniffing too. But no, no matter how Scamper sniffed all round and about, or how the children dug here and there to find a hole under the rocky walls, nothing was found that would help to solve the mystery.

'And a very queer mystery it is too,' said Peter. 'I said I didn't like it, and I don't. I vote we clear up this cave and find another meeting-place. It's going to be no fun if we keep having our things stolen and messed about by some unknown visitor.'

'Yes. *I* don't feel as if I want to be here any more either,' said Janet. 'It's a shame. It's such a fine place. Well, the others will be along soon, so let's just clear up a bit, and we'll tell them when they come.'

It wasn't long before the others came, all four of them, chattering and laughing as they walked through the old quarry.

As soon as they arrived at the cave, Peter told them what had happened. They stared at his grave face and listened in astonishment to what he told them.

'It's jolly queer,' said George. 'I don't understand it. Taking food – and cushions – and books! It sounds like someone hiding somewhere and needing food, and something soft to lie on.'

'If one or two of us boys hid here in the cave tonight, we might see whoever it is that comes,' said Colin.

There was a silence. Nobody liked the idea at all. This mysterious visitor didn't sound a very nice person to lie in wait for.

'Well,' said Peter at last, 'I'm no coward, but considering that there really isn't any place in this cave that we could hide in without being seen almost at once, I don't see much point in your suggestion, Colin. I mean, the intruder, whoever he is, would probably see *us* before we spotted him. Anyway, I don't like the sound of him.'

'Nor do I,' said Jack. 'I vote we clear out of here and have another meeting-place. What's the sense of bringing stuff here and having it taken as soon as our back's turned?'

They began to clear up the cave. It was really very sad. Scamper watched them in surprise. Why were they looking so miserable? Why were they packing up everything? Well, he'd certainly better get his bone then! He couldn't leave that behind if everyone was leaving the cave!

He ran over to the corner where he had buried it. His sharp nose sniffed something else not far off on a low ledge of rock. Did it belong to the children? It didn't really smell like any of them. Scamper could always tell what shoe or glove belonged to any of the Seven just by sniffing it!

Scamper sniffed at this thing on the ledge, and then picked it up in his mouth. Perhaps it did belong to one of the children after all. He ran with it to Peter and dropped it at his feet with a little bark.

'Hallo, Scamper, what is it?' said Peter. He bent down and picked up a small, dirty note-book with a frayed elastic band round it. 'Anyone own this?' he asked, holding it up.

Nobody did. Jack came up, excited.

'Peter! It might have been dropped by our strange visitor! Look inside!'

Peter slipped off the elastic band and opened the little note-book. His eyes suddenly shone. 'Yes!' he said, in a low voice. 'It *does* belong to our visitor – and here's his name – look. My word, this *is* a find! He dropped it when he came raiding our cave last night!'

They all crowded round him in excitement. Peter's finger pointed to a name scribbled at the front of the note-book.

'Albert Tanner,' he said. 'He's our mysterious visitor. Albert Tanner! Who can he be? Well, we'll find out *somehow*!'

Nine

An exciting plan

'LET'S clear out of here quickly,' said Colin, in a low voice, looking nervously all round the cave. 'If Albert Tanner, whoever he is, is anywhere near, as he does seem to be, we don't want him to know we've found his note-book. We're all ready to go. Let's scoot off quickly, and examine the note-book in secret.'

'Good idea,' said Peter. 'Ready everyone? Come on then! Scamper, to heel!'

They left the cave and went out into the bright sunshine, each carrying a load. The tins, alas, were now empty, and very light to carry. Half Colin's 'Famous Five' books were gone, so he hadn't a great load, either. Most of the magazines had disappeared too. Evidently their mysterious visitor was quite a reader!

They went through the quarry and into Peter's garden. 'We'll go to the summer-house, I think,' said Peter. 'It's not very comfortable, but at least we can talk in secret there.'

Soon they were all sitting on the little bench that ran round the old summer-house, with Scamper panting on the floor in a patch of warm sunshine.

Peter took the worn note-book out of his pocket and opened it. The others crowded as near as possible to see what was in it. Peter turned over the pages.

'Albert Tanner has written his name in the front as you know,' he said. 'Which was kind of him, I must say – we at least know the *name* of our visitor now! There doesn't seem much else in the book, actually. Just a few notes of money and various dates, and a few words scribbled here and there. Let's see – yes – "potatoes, turnips, tomatoes, flour", just a shopping list, I suppose.'

He turned over a page or two. 'Another shopping list, and some figures jotted down. It doesn't seem as if this note-book is going to be of any use at all!'

Jack took it from him and looked through it too. At the back was a folded-in piece of leather to hold paper money. Peter hadn't noticed it. Jack slipped his fingers in to see if anything could be there.

Yes, a slip of paper, small and torn, with something scribbled on it in a different handwriting from Albert Tanner's.

'Look here!' said Jack. 'This was in the back of the note-book. See what it says? It's a note to Albert Tanner.'

'What does it say?' asked Janet, excited. 'Anything of use to us?'

'It's just scribble,' said Jack, screwing up his eyes. 'It says, "Daren't write it. Jim knows the place. He'll tell you. Meet him on post-office seat 8.30 p.m., 15th. Ted." '

'The 15th! That's today,' said Peter. 'Read it again, it's evidently an important message, but how mysterious! What's this "place" Jim is going to tell Albert? My word, if only we could know it! We could go to the "place" Jim says and have a good snoop round.'

154

A little feeling of excitement began to stir in everyone. Colin caught hold of Peter's sleeve.

'I'll go to the post-office seat tonight and sit there.
Perhaps I shall see this "Jim" and hear what he says to
Albert. I shall *see* Albert too!'

There was a silence, and the excitement suddenly
grew stronger. 'All of us four boys will go,' said Peter.
'Not the girls. Just us four.'

'You can't,' said Janet. 'You're going to see "West-ward Ho!" at the cinema. Mother's taking us both. And George is coming too, don't you remember?'

'Blow!' said Peter. 'Well, we can't get out of that without giving the whole thing away. Colin, you and Jack must go. And for goodness' sake listen with all your ears, and hear what's being said!'

'Right,' said Colin, thrilled. 'Can you come, Jack?'

'Rather!' said Jack. 'And what about us shadow-ing Albert and Jim, Peter? One of us could follow Albert, and the other one could follow Jim. It might be useful to know where Jim lives, and I must say I'd like to follow Albert if he goes back to the cave!'

'A jolly good idea,' said Peter. 'I only wish I could come too. But it's no good. I begged and begged to go to "Westward Ho!", and I can't get out of it now.'

They pored over the little note again, written in a bad handwriting, hurried and careless. Peter read it out aloud once more.

'Daren't write it. Jim knows the place. He'll tell you. Meet him on post-office seat 8.30 p.m., 15th. Ted.'

'Would there be something hidden in this "place" that is in the note, do you think?' said Janet.

'Yes. Probably,' said Peter, thinking hard. 'And if it's hidden, it's valuable. And if it's valuable it may be stolen goods.'

'Yes. Goods stolen by Ted, whoever he is, and hidden away!' said Colin. 'Or stolen by Ted *and* Albert – and Ted hid them – then got caught, perhaps, and went to prison. And now he wants Albert to find them.'

Everyone laughed. 'You've made quite a story of it!'

said Jack. 'I don't expect it's anything like that really. All the same, as soon as we know the place we'll certainly go there – if only we can get there before Albert does!'

'Yes, that's not going to be so easy!' said Peter. 'Maybe Albert will go there at once.'

'I hope he does!' said Colin. 'We'll be shadowing him, and he'll lead us right to this mysterious "place", wherever it is!'

'I wish I was going to be with you tonight,' said Peter longingly. 'It's an adventure, you know, and they don't come very often. I wish I was going to share it!'

Ten

What happened at half past eight

COLIN met Jack that evening at eight o'clock outside the post-office. It was dark, and there was no moon. They spoke together in low 'voices as they went over to the wooden seat nearby.

'What shall our plans be?' said Colin. 'The seat is just by that big chestnut-tree. Shall we hide behind the tree, or get under the seat, or what?'

'We mustn't both of us be in the same place,' said Jack. 'Otherwise if the men see us and send us off, we'll neither of us hear a word. I vote one of us gets *behind* the tree, and the other *up* the tree!'

'That's a jolly good idea,' said Colin. 'You'd better climb up the tree. I've got a stiff knee, and it's bandaged. I fell down our cellar steps today, and Mother made a tremendous fuss, and I was afraid she'd make me rest in bed or something! I nearly had a fit, thinking I might not be able to come this evening!'

'All right. I'll climb the tree,' said Jack. 'But I'd better do it now, before anyone comes. There's nobody about at all. I'll stand on the back of the seat, and you can give me a leg-up to that big branch that overhangs the seat.'

It wasn't long before Jack was perched in the thick branches of the chestnut-tree. Colin went behind the tree and leaned against the trunk, waiting. The church clock chimed a quarter past eight. Colin's heart began to beat faster – this *was* fun!

Ten minutes went by, and then someone came up. No, two people, arm-in-arm. Colin stiffened and held his breath. The two people passed talking together. Then someone else walked by smartly with a dog.

And then somebody came slouching along in rubber-soled shoes, a shadowy someone who kept out of the light of the street-lamps. He sat down on the seat, and Colin almost stopped breathing!

Jack peered down cautiously from the tree, but it was so dark that he could make out very little except that the man was smoking a cigarette.

Another shadowy figure appeared from across the road, walking silently. It joined the man on the seat. The two men sat a little apart, saying nothing, and the listening boys held their breath again.

'Cigarette?' said the first man, at last.

'Thanks,' said the second. The first man took a packet from his pocket and offered it to the other man. Then he struck a match and lighted the cigarette, which the second man had now put into his mouth. The flare of the match told him what he wanted to know.

'You're Albert,' he said quietly. 'That's right, isn't it?'

But, before Albert could even nod his head, something happened that made the two men almost jump out of their skins.

Colin sneezed! He always had a very loud sneeze indeed, but this one was tremendous! He didn't even know it was coming, and it gave him almost as much of a shock as it gave the two men!

'A . . .WHOOOOOSH – OOO!'

In a trice Albert had whipped behind the tree and got hold of the startled Colin. He held him in a grip of iron. 'What are you doing here? Hiding behind this tree?'

He shook poor Colin until the boy felt as if his head

160

would fly off. The other man came round the tree too.

'It's only a kid,' he said. 'Box his ears and let him go. We don't want any noise here.'

Colin got a blow on the head and went staggering away, almost falling. Albert ran at him again, and the boy fled for his life, terrified. Jack, up in the tree, felt very scared too. Should he go to Colin's rescue? No, by the time he'd got down the tree it would be too late. Ah, Colin had run away, so he was all right. Jack clung to the branch, trembling a little.

The men stood under the tree together. 'Better clear off,' said the first man, in a low voice to Albert.

'You've got something to tell me,' said Albert.

'Yes. The scarecrow!' said his companion, lowering his voice. 'That's where it is. Look by the scarecrow.'

'Thanks,' said Albert, and slouched off silently, and was soon lost in the shadows. Jack wished Colin could have shadowed him. *He* certainly couldn't shadow Albert, because it would take him a minute or two to get cautiously down the tree. Perhaps he could follow the first man, though.

By the time Jack was safely down the tree both men had completely disappeared. Jack made off as quickly as he could, feeling decidedly scared. Was Colin all right? He'd better go to his house and see if he could find out, without letting anyone else know why he had come!

When he arrived at Colin's house he saw a light in Colin's bedroom window. Good! He threw up a pebble and hit the window-pane first time. The window was opened cautiously, and Colin's head came out.

'Colin! It's me, Jack! Are you all right?' called Jack, in a low voice.

'Yes. Quite. That fellow gave me a jolly good box on the ear, but I got home all right, and no one saw me coming in. What about you? Did you hear anything?'

'Yes, but nothing *really* helpful,' said Jack. 'What a terrific sneeze that was of yours, Colin!'

'Yes, my goodness. I thought I . . .' began Colin, and then drew his head in quickly. Jack heard him speaking to someone in his bedroom, and ran out of the gate as quickly as he could.

The *scarecrow*! he thought. What does that mean? *I* don't know! Perhaps Peter will. Golly, I can hardly wait until tomorrow morning to tell him!

Eleven

Off they go again!

THE meeting in the summer-house the next morning was quite exciting. Peter and Janet and Scamper waited impatiently for Jack and Colin to come. Pam and Barbara came together as usual, then came George, and last of all Colin and Jack.

'Sorry we're a bit late,' said Jack. 'I went to call for Colin. His leg's still stiff so he couldn't walk very fast, though you ran fast enough last night didn't you, Colin?'

Colin grinned. He had a bruise on the left cheekbone near his ear, where he had been struck the night before. He felt rather proud of it.

'We've got news,' said Jack, feeling extremely important as he looked round at the expectant faces of the others.

'Well, buck up and tell us then,' said Peter impatiently. 'Did those two men meet? What did you hear?'

'Tell it all from the beginning,' begged Janet. 'I like to know every single thing so that I can see it in my mind's eye.'

'All right,' said Jack. 'Well, Colin and I met by the post-office at eight o'clock, and the men came at half past. Colin hid behind a tree, and I climbed up into it.'

'Jolly good,' said Peter approvingly.

'Just as the men were beginning to talk Colin did the

most TERRIFIC sneeze you ever heard,' said Jack. 'Honestly, I nearly fell out of the tree!'

'Goodness!' said Janet. 'Whatever happened then?'

'The men ran round the tree and found poor old Colin, and that bruise on his cheek is where he got hit,' said Jack. Everyone gazed in awe at Colin's bruise, and he felt very proud indeed.

'He had to run for his life, and there was I, stuck up the tree,' went on Jack, enjoying himself immensely. 'I can tell you, it was quite an adventure! Well, then the men spoke in low voices again, but I managed to hear the important thing.'

'What was it?' demanded Peter. 'You're so long-winded. Get to the point.'

'The first man – he must have been the Jim mentioned in the letter – he said "The scarecrow!"' said Jack, lowering his voice just as the men had done. '"The scarecrow! That's where it is!" he said. "The scarecrow!" Then the two men went off, and I hadn't time to shadow them because I was up the tree.'

'You did jolly well,' said Peter. 'Jolly well! It was a pity about Colin's sneeze. Still, you heard the main thing, Jack – and that was the word "scarecrow".'

'What does it mean, though?' asked Jack. 'Do *you* know? Does it mean a *real* scarecrow?'

'No. There's a tiny inn called "The Scarecrow" up on the common,' said Peter. 'I've often passed it when I've been in the car with my father. We'll go up there and snoop round. I bet that's where something is hidden, loot from some robbery, probably.'

'Oh, yes, *I* remember seeing that inn too, and thinking what a queer name it had,' said Janet. 'Peter, let's go *now*! Before Albert gets away with anything!'

'Yes. We'd certainly better go now, this very minute!' said Peter. 'We may find Albert there, digging away in some corner of the garden. It would be very interesting to see what he digs up!'

Everyone felt the delicious surge of excitement that always came over them when adventure was in the air. 'Get your bikes,' ordered Peter. 'Colin, is your knee too stiff to bike, do you think?'

'I can pedal all right with one leg,' said Colin, who wasn't going to be left out of this morning's excitement for anything. 'Come on, let's get our bikes, those of you who didn't come on them.'

'Meet at the cross-roads by the old barn,' said Peter. 'Wait for each other. Then we'll all set off together. My word, we're really on to something now!'

George was the only one who had come on a bike. The others set off to get theirs. Peter and Janet fetched their two from the shed, and set off with George to the cross-roads, Scamper running excitedly behind them. He knew when adventure was about, he always knew!

Soon everyone was at the cross-roads, even Colin, who could only pedal with one leg. Jack came last, looking hot and cross.

'What's up?' asked Janet, seeing how upset he looked. 'Did you get into trouble at home about anything?'

'No. It's Susie,' said Jack, with a groan. 'She says that she and Jeff went up to our cave this morning, you know I had to tell Mother about it in front of Susie, and when she saw we'd gone, she and Jeff decided to have it for their meeting-place! Isn't that maddening?'

'Well, let them if they want to!' said Peter. 'Much good may it do them! Albert will probably visit them as he did us and take their things! Serve them right!'

'I wonder how Albert gets into the cave if he doesn't

use our entrance!' said Janet. 'We know he used it once, because Jack saw him that time, when we were playing hide-and-seek. But he didn't use it when he robbed us of all those things. Those silk threads at the entrance weren't broken, you remember!'

'I imagine that our dear friend Albert may be some-where at the inn called "The Scarecrow"!' said Peter. 'He probably won't be using the cave much more if he finds what he's looking for!'

'Look, there it is – "The Scarecrow"!' said Pam, riding ahead. 'What a funny old inn, hundreds of years old, I should think. Come on, everybody – isn't this EXCITING!'

Twelve

The Scarecrow Inn

THE Secret Seven came near to the old inn. It was certainly a queer place, almost tumble-down. Outside a sign swung in the wind, creaking dismally. On it was painted a scarecrow in a field, and printed on it in big letters was the name.

'The Scarecrow,' said Peter, leaping off his bicycle. 'Here we are. Look out for Albert, everyone!'

They leaned their bicycles against a hedge and walked over to the inn. No one was about. The whole place looked completely deserted.

'But there must be somebody about!' said Colin. 'Look, there are a few hens pecking around.'

They went right up to the old inn. 'It seems to be shut,' said Peter, puzzled. 'Yes, look, there are bars across the windows and across the front door too, wooden bars, nailed on.'

'It must be closed down,' said Jack. 'Let's go round to the back. We can ask for a drink of water, or how to get to Penton, or something like that.'

So they all went round to the back door of the inn. A woman was in a little yard there, hanging out some washing, an old, grey-haired woman with a very disagreeable face.

'Er, could we have a drink of water, please?' asked Peter, in his politest voice.

'There's the well. Help yourself,' said the woman.

'Thank you. Is the inn closed now?' asked Peter.

'Yes. Been closed for months,' said the old woman, pegging up a sheet. 'I just caretake, and it's a lonely job up here on the common. You're the first people I've spoken to for about six weeks, except for the milkman and the grocer's boy.'

'Oh, then you don't know anyone called Albert, I suppose?' asked Peter, as innocently as he could.

'Now, don't you be saucy,' said the woman angrily. 'Who told you my old man was called Albert? You call him Mr Larkworthy, and mind your manners. See, there he is. I'll send him after you if you're cheeky!'

The Secret Seven saw an old bent man coming out of the inn with a stick in his hand, on which he leaned heavily. Goodness, they hadn't meant to be cheeky! How could they have guessed that the old woman's husband was called Albert?

'We didn't mean your husband,' said Peter hurriedly. 'We really didn't. We're just looking for someone called Albert that we thought we might see here this morning.'

'Well, I won't have any cheek from children,' said the old woman. 'You clear off, now, before I tell my husband to chase you.'

The Seven went away slowly, taking a good look at the little place as they went. They walked to their bicycles by the hedge.

'What do you think, Peter,' asked Jack. 'Do you suppose Albert came here at all?'

'No,' said Peter. 'We're on the wrong track. I think that cross old woman was speaking the truth. She prob-

ably hasn't seen anyone here for weeks! Goodness, I did feel awful when she said her husband's name was Albert! No wonder she thought we were cheeky!'

'I had a good look at that little garden,' said George. 'And it's quite plain that nobody has been digging in it to get anything buried there. Nothing but enormous weeds.'

'Yes. I had a look too,' said Peter. 'No, we're on the wrong track, as I said. The thing is, what do we do next? If only we knew where Albert was at this moment, it would be a great help!'

'It might not be,' said Jack, with a grin. 'He might be scaring Jeff and Susie in our cave!'

'I hope he is,' said Peter grimly. 'Just like those two to try to annoy us!'

'What are we going to do now?' asked Janet. 'Peter, do you suppose it's a *real* scarecrow we have to look for?'

Peter considered. 'Yes, it might be. I was so sure that the old inn was the place meant, that I didn't really think about proper scarecrows. But we can't go chasing over the countryside looking for all the scarecrows in the fields!'

'Yes, we can,' said Colin. 'Quite easily. All we've got to do is to separate, and bike all over the place, and whenever we see a scarecrow, get off and see if anyone has been disturbing the ground by it. I *bet* whatever is hidden is well dug-in beside a scarecrow.'

'Yes. It would be such a good place if the thief wanted to get the loot again,' said Peter. 'I mean, if stolen goods were hidden in a field in the ordinary way, they couldn't be marked in case anyone wondered what the mark

was for. A stick or a post or something would call
attention to the place and make the farmer examine it.
But a scarecrow is a *natural* mark and anything hidden
beneath it wouldn't be found until the field was reaped!'

'Yes. And the thief meant to get it before that, as
we know!' said George. 'Well, shall we go scarecrow-
hunting?'

'Yes,' said Peter, getting on his bicycle. 'But look out
for farmers. They mightn't be too pleased to see us walking all over their fields to get to a scarecrow!'

They all rode off together, Peter calling out orders as
they went.

'You take the west road, Colin and Jack. You the
east, Pam and Barbara. You take the north, George, and
Janet and I will turn at the cross-roads and take the
south. We shall cover most of the countryside then. Meet
at half past two this afternoon in the summer-house.'

Off they all went. 'Scarecrow-hunting!' said Jack
to Colin. 'What a game! I do wonder how many scarecrows we shall find!'

The Seven had a queer time, hunting for scarecrows! Pam and Barbara found a most fearsome one in
the middle of a field, his coat flapping like mad in the
wind.

They went to examine him, but as the soil was quite
hard all round him they knew that nothing had been
hidden and dug up beside *him*! So off they went to find
another.

Colin and Jack found two. One was in an allotment,
and although they were sure that it couldn't be the one
they were looking for, they went up to him all the same,

and examined the ground nearby.

A man came into the allotment with a spade over his shoulder. When he saw the two boys there he shouted at them angrily:

'You clear off, you two! These allotments are private. Are you the kids who've been taking broccoli from here?'

'No!' shouted the two boys. 'We were just having a look at the old scarecrow.'

'I'll scarecrow you if you come here again!' yelled the man, and Colin and Jack fled for their bicycles. The next scarecrow they found was in a field of young wheat, and no sooner had they walked over the field to the scarecrow than a farmer appeared with a dog. The boys just had time to make sure that the earth round the scarecrow was undisturbed before the dog flew at them.

'Ha! He'll bite you next time!' called the farmer, as the boys leapt on their bicycles.

'I don't think I like this scarecrow-hunting much,' said Colin, whose stiff leg was hurting him. 'That's twice we've had to run, and I just can't bend my knee properly.'

George, cycling quickly up and down country roads, thought he spied a scarecrow at the end of a field. He jumped off his bicycle and squeezed through the hedge – only to face a surprised and angry farm-labourer, hoeing vigorously.

'Oh – sorry – I thought you were a scarecrow,' said George very foolishly, backing away through the hedge. The farm-labourer, angry at being called a scarecrow, flung a clod of earth at George. It shattered into bits all over him. George spat some out of his mouth.

174

'Phoo! That was a good shot on his part!' said George, riding away. 'I don't know that I like this scarecrow business much!'

Peter and Janet had examined four scarecrows, for their particular roads ran between big farms, and great fields lay on either side. One scarecrow had thrilled Janet because a thrush had built a nest in the dented crown of the old scarecrow's hat. Peter could hardly get her away from it!

The other three they had found were not interesting, and quite plainly no one had been into the field to disturb the earth near any of the scarecrows.

Peter felt disheartened as he rode home beside Janet. 'All those scarecrows and not one of them any good to us,' he complained. 'I only hope the others have found the right one.'

They got home just in time for their dinner. Their mother looked in horror at their shoes, which were covered in mud from the soil in two very wet fields they had walked over.

'Where *have* you been?' she said. 'And what in the world were you doing to get your shoes so filthy? Take them off at once, and leave them outside.'

'We went to look at scarecrows, Mummy,' said Janet, 'and we found one with a thrush's nest in his hat! That's how we got our shoes so dirty. But we'll clean them ourselves.'

'You should go and see the scarecrow old James has put up in the oat-field,' said her father, who was already at the table. 'He tells me it's got a robin's nest in each pocket!'

'But how did he know?' said Janet in astonishment. 'He's almost blind, poor old man – he can't even see the clouds now, to tell him the weather.'

'Well, he's not too blind to see that somebody had been walking over his precious oat-field,' said her father. 'He followed the foot-steps, and they led him right to the scarecrow – and that's how he found the two robins' nests in the pockets!'

Peter pricked up his ears at once. 'Somebody walking over our oat-field to the scarecrow?' he said. 'Who, Dad – and why?'

'Goodness knows,' said his father. 'There are plenty of foolish townspeople who think they can walk all over growing fields! It was one of them, I expect.'

But Peter felt sure it was Albert! He looked at his mother. He really must go and see! 'Er – please could I just go quickly and look at those robins' nests?' he said desperately.

His mother looked at him in amazement. 'What – *now*? Just as dinner's ready? Don't be silly, dear. The nests won't fly away – they'll be there after dinner!'

Peter looked at Janet, who had read his thoughts. 'WHY didn't we think of our own scarecrow!' she blurted out. 'We see it from our bedroom windows each day. We –'

Peter gave her a sharp kick under the table, and she stopped at once. Goodness, she had nearly given the game away!

'Why all this sudden interest in scarecrows?' inquired her mother. 'I hope it soon wears off. I can't allow you to get your shoes like that again.'

The Scarecrow Inn

Peter and Janet longed for dinner to be over. As soon as they were allowed to go, they shot out into the garden, and slipped on their dirty shoes.

'It was *our* scarecrow we should have looked at!' said Peter. 'I could kick myself! Come on – let's go now and examine the soil round it. We'll take a fork, in case we may find something, though I'm afraid that Albert has got there first. Buck up!'

Thirteen

Everything seems dull now

PETER and Janet ran down the garden and out of the gate at the bottom. Round the potato-field and over a stile they went, and there was the oat-field, its green rows as bright as emerald!

In the middle of it stood the scarecrow put up by old James. He was a fine one, and wore one of James's old hats, cocked over on one side. He wore a ragged red jersey and an old tweed coat with sagging pockets. A robin flew out of one of them as the children went near.

The scarecrow's ragged trousers flapped in the wind against his two wooden legs. His head was a turnip in which old James had scraped eyes and mouth. He seemed to be grinning at them as they came up, and the wind shook him and made him jig to and fro.

But Peter and Janet didn't look at the scarecrow, or even at the robins' nests in the sagging pockets. They looked at the ground around his wooden legs.

And Peter gave a deep groan that really might have come from the old scarecrow! 'We *are* too late, Janet. Look, someone's been here. There are footprints all around and about, not only old James's hobnailed ones, but somebody with rubber-soled shoes – Albert's!'

'Yes,' said Janet, her eyes on the ground. 'And the soil has been well dug up. Something was hidden here, beside the old scarecrow. Oh, Peter, WHY didn't we look here first?'

'It wouldn't have been any good,' said Peter gloomily. 'I expect Albert came last night. He wouldn't come digging here in the day-time. He knew which scarecrow was meant, of course. We didn't! And all the time it was our own scarecrow!'

'Just dig round a bit and see if there's anything left,' said Janet.

'There won't be,' said Peter dolefully. 'I expect whatever it was was in a bag, a strong bag too, to resist the damp.' He dug about with his fork, but brought up nothing except a surprised worm. *'Blow!'* he said. 'I was so excited about this scarecrow business. Now we're too late, Albert has got the stuff, whatever it was, and will be off and away.'

'Yes, I suppose he will,' said Janet dismally. 'I wouldn't be surprised if he knew that it was hidden in this district and that was why he came and hid in our cave, so as to be on the spot to speak to that other man, what was his name? Jim? And to get the stuff easily.'

'I think you're absolutely right, Janet,' said Peter. 'And if you are, the stolen stuff, or whatever it was, must have *come* from this district too. I wonder if there have been any robberies lately.'

They had a look at the two cosy robins' nests, both of which had tiny feathered nestlings inside, and then walked back home. It was about half past two, and the other members of the Secret Seven were waiting in the summer-house.

They were very downcast at Peter's news. 'Well, we were none of us successful in our scarecrow-hunt this morning,' said Jack, 'and no wonder, if the loot had been buried by *your* scarecrow, Peter. What bad luck! If only we'd been able to dig by your scarecrow last night, perhaps we'd have got the hidden goods before Albert.'

'What shall we do now?' asked Pam. 'Everything seems dull suddenly, now that we've not got our cave any more, and the adventure has faded away.'

'I'm going up to the cave,' said Jack, standing up. 'I think I left my torch there, high up on a ledge. I hope Albert hasn't taken it! It's rather a nice one, and I'd like to get it if it's still there.'

'Right, we'll all come, just for the walk,' said Peter.

'We could take spades and dig in the old quarry, the sand is moist in parts, and you can model quite well with it. Let's do that.'

So they took four spades from the shed and three trowels, and off they went to the quarry. Jack went up to the cave and then stopped short in surprise.

Someone was there! He could hear excited voices. Then he frowned. He knew *one* voice – it was Susie's! Blow her, now she would mess about round them, and make silly remarks. Who was with her? It sounded like Jeff. What cheek to come to the cave! Just like Susie!

He went into the cave, still frowning. Susie and Jeff were right at the back, scrabbling about. Whatever were they doing?

'Susie!' he called sharply. 'What are you doing here?'

Susie turned round and then came quickly over to her brother. 'Jack! I *am* glad you've come. Something peculiar has happened!'

'What?' asked Jack impatiently. 'I think it's pretty peculiar that you and Jeff should come to *our* cave, even though we've left it.'

'Don't be cross, Jack. I really am glad you've come,' said Susie. 'Listen. Jeff and I came here, and we thought it was a lovely place. We made deep holes for ourselves. Mine's over there, look, and Jeff's is opposite, by the rocky wall. We thought perhaps you others might be coming, so we practically *covered* ourselves with sand, just left our noses out to breathe, and we waited for you so that we could give loud yells **and leap out at you** when you came in thinking nobody was here –'

Jack gave a snort. 'Is that all you've got to tell me? *Not* very interesting.'

'Oh, *do* listen, Jack,' said Susie. 'Well, we lay like mice, only our noses out, waiting for you to come in at the front entrance there, and then somebody came out from the *back* of the cave, and trod heavily on poor Jeff and went out of the entrance!'

'And yet we *know* the cave was empty when we came in,' said Jeff. 'We looked to make sure. But there's nowhere for anyone to hide or to come from, so who was this person, and how did he get here?'

Jack was now listening intently. This was news! He turned to the entrance of the cave and yelled loudly: 'PETER! JANET! EVERYBODY! COME HERE QUICKLY! QUICKLY, I SAY!'

Fourteen

What an excitement!

PETER, Janet, and all the others threw down their spades and trowels and raced to the cave at top speed. 'What is it?' cried Peter.

Then he saw Susie and Jeff and stopped. 'Clear out,' he cried. 'This is our cave, not yours.'

'Wait, Peter,' said Jack. 'Susie's just told me something queer.' He told the others what Susie had said, how she and Jeff had buried themselves all but their noses in the empty cave, and then someone had come from the back and walked out!

'So there *is* some way into this cave from the back,' he said. 'I know we've looked and looked, but there *must* be! Susie, did you hear anything at all before this fellow walked out of the cave?'

'Yes,' said Susie. 'I heard a kind of thud – so did Jeff.'

'As if someone had leapt down to the sandy floor,' said Jeff. 'Like this!' He jumped into the air and came down, making a soft thud.

'Then the way in from the back must be from somewhere up near the roof,' said Peter. 'Anyone got a torch?'

'Here's mine,' said Jack. 'I found it on the ledge where I'd left it.'

Peter took it. 'Come on,' he said. 'We're jolly well

going to solve this mystery. Wait though – Colin, keep guard at the front of the cave, in case that fellow comes back. Take a good look at him if he does.'

'Right,' said Colin, and limped to the front of the cave, though he would dearly have liked to be with the others.

There was quite a crowd at the back of the cave. Peter shone his torch on to the roof there. It was fairly high. He saw a rocky ledge jutting out and thought he would climb up to it. 'Give me a hand,' he said to Jack. 'Hold the torch for a minute, Janet.'

He was soon up on the ledge, and then shone the torch on to the roof again. He gave a sudden exclamation.

'What is it?' shouted everyone, almost dancing with excitement.

'There's a round hole here. You can't see it from where you are,' said Peter. 'And there's a rope-end hanging down. I can just reach it.'

The others craned their necks to see what Peter saw, but they couldn't. The hole was hidden by a jutting-out piece of rock, and it was only because Peter was high up on the ledge that he could see it at all. He shone his torch on the thick rope-end. It was well within his reach from the ledge on which he stood.

He stuffed the torch into his pocket. 'I can get hold of the rope,' he called down, 'and I think I can pull myself up by it. I'll try anyway.'

He caught the rope in both hands, and then by means of treading on first one narrow ledge of rock and then another, he managed to get right into the hole. He let go of the ledges with his feet and swung on the rope with his hands. He climbed up it as he did at gym, and came to a broad ledge, where he rested for a moment or two.

Then he stood on the ledge, putting his head up through the hole that still went upwards, and found that he was looking out of the hole into another cave above! He shone his torch around.

He gave a yell to the others down below, but to them his voice sounded curiously muffled and hollow. They were quite startled to hear it.

'I *say*! There's another cave here, a much smaller one! And some of our food's here, and all our cushions, and books and magazines! And there's a bag too, a small mail-bag that looks full of something!'

'What? What do you say?' yelled the others, almost overcome with excitement at all this shouting, and not being able to make out a word.

'PETER! What have you found?' cried Janet.

Peter came down the rope, found the ledge he needed to climb down from, and leapt to the ground. He pushed the others away as they crowded round him, and went to get some air at the front of the cave.

'Tell us! What did you find?' said Jack. 'We heard you yelling.'

'There's a cave up there with all our things in it. That fellow Albert used the cushions to lie on, because the floor is of hard rock, not soft sand,' said Peter. '*And* there's a bag, a mail-bag, I think. Probably full of registered envelopes! Goodness knows how long it was buried beneath our scarecrow.'

'My word, that's a find!' said Janet, her eyes shining. 'Now we know how our mysterious visitor got into the cave without passing through the front entrance, when he wanted to steal our things. How thrilled he must have been to find food and cushions and books!'

'Now listen,' said Peter. 'He may come back at any minute, but he won't dare to come into the cave while people are there. I'm going to tell Dad, and he'll phone the police. You stay here, all of you, till I come back, then Albert won't be able to remove the stolen mail-bag! I'll leave Scamper with you too.'

'Right,' said Jack, taking charge. 'We'll make a good bit of noise too, shall we, to scare him off if he comes! My word, fancy finding that cave above, Peter. You *are* clever!'

'Well, *I* really put you on to it,' said Susie. 'Goodness, I was glad to see you, Jack.'

'You were wrong to come to our cave, but for once in a way you were right to tell me what you'd seen,' said Jack sternly. 'Now, if you want to stay with us, behave yourself, Susie. Do you hear?'

'Yes, teacher,' said Susie demurely. 'I'll be a good, good girl. I'll –'

'Be quiet,' said Jack, 'or out you both go, you and Jeff!'

Susie looked at Jack's face and was suddenly quiet. They all were for a minute or two, thinking over the startling happenings of the last few minutes. Then they remembered that Peter wanted them to make a noise, so that Albert would not come to the cave to try to get that mail-bag! They began to talk and laugh.

Peter ran at top speed to find his father. 'Dad!' he called, seeing him by the barn. 'I say, DAD! Quick, I want you!'

Fifteen

A wonderful finish!

PETER's father could not make head or tail of the boy's breathless story at first. But at last he made out enough to call his wife.

'Will you telephone to the police and tell them to come at once, and go to the cave in the quarry?' he called. 'I'm off there with Peter. Tell you what's up when I get back!'

He went off with the excited Peter. Soon they were at the cave, where the others, talking loudly, were waiting anxiously. The green curtain was tied back now, and Peter's father gazed into the cave.

'I'd forgotten this old cave,' he said. 'I used to love it when I was a boy. Do you really mean to say there's a cave *above* it, Peter? I never knew that, and yet I played here heaps of times.'

'So did we,' said Janet. 'Come and see where the hole is that leads into the cave above, Daddy.'

'We had this cave for our Secret Seven meetings,' explained Peter, 'and we *couldn't* make out who took our things, or why. We didn't guess someone was in hiding in a cave above us! There's a mail-bag up there, Dad. Do you think the fellow stole it?'

'Probably. You'd better shin up and get it when the police come,' said Peter's father. 'I wonder how long it's been hidden there? Quite a long time, maybe.'

'No, only since last night,' said Peter. 'It was buried beside that scarecrow in the oat-field, Dad!'

'So *that's* why you were so interested in scarecrows all of a sudden,' said his father. 'I wonder if your mother has telephoned the police yet. Run back and see if they're coming, Peter.'

Peter set off through the quarry with Scamper at his heels, but half-way through Scamper left him and ran behind a hummock, barking madly. Peter followed him. He saw a curious mound in the sand, which, as Scamper leapt on it, put out hands and feet – and head!

'Call him off!' said a voice. 'Call him off!'

'Who are you?' demanded Peter, catching Scamper by the collar. 'I say, *I* know who you are, you're Albert, aren't you? Waiting till we're all gone so that you can fetch that stolen mail-bag and empty it! You meant to leave the bag up in that cave, stuff your pockets with the contents, and slip away free! You'll –'

'Now, now,' said a deep voice, 'what's all this, and who is this fellow lying in the sand? Ah, surely it's Albert Tanner! We've been looking for you, Albert, ever since that last mail robbery.'

It was the big Inspector of Police! Behind him was a stolid village constable, looking as if this kind of thing was very ordinary indeed.

The Inspector turned to Peter and beamed at him. 'Hallo, Peter! I knew as soon as your mother phoned that you were caught up into one of your adventures. Is Albert here anything to do with it?'

'Yes, sir,' said Peter. 'Look, my father's over there, by the cave. He's waiting for you.'

'Bring Albert along,' said the Inspector to his policeman, and Albert was duly brought along to the cave. As
soon as Peter's father saw him, he gave an exclamation.

'Why! It's Albert Tanner! I thought I told you never
to show your face in this district again, Albert!'

'You know him, sir, do you?' said the Inspector, getting out a big note-book.

'I should think I do!' said Peter's father. 'He was
brought up here on this land, in a cottage not far off,
and worked for me for a few years. But he was so dis-
honest I had to dismiss him.'

'That's how he knew this cave then!' said Peter. '*And* the one above. He must have explored like we did.'

Albert didn't say a word. He stood there, sullen and angry. The Inspector threw a glance at him. Then he turned to Peter's father.

'This man and another did a mail-bag robbery,' he said. 'The other man hid the bag somewhere, meaning to get it when the commotion about it died down. He worked on this farm once too, sir – his name's Ted Yorks.'

'Ted Yorks! Yes, he was here for years,' said Peter's father. 'He was a bad lot too, but a fine hedger and ditcher, which is why I kept him so long.'

'Well, as I said, these two planned this robbery,' said the Inspector, 'and the mail-bag was hidden, ready to be found and the contents shared between the two of them in due course. But Ted got caught and put into prison, where he is still.'

'But he managed to get a note out of prison to Albert, to tell him how to find out where he had hidden the bag!' cried Peter. 'I see it all now! Albert came to this cave to hide till he heard from Ted, because he knew the police here were still looking for him, and he didn't dare to show his face –'

'And when he got Ted's note, he went to meet that man Jim, the one on the seat by the post-office, and learnt that he had to look by the scarecrow!' said Jack. 'I heard Jim say "The scarecrow. That's where it is." And of course, Albert knew it was *our* scarecrow!'

'These kids know all about you, you see, Albert,' said the Inspector, looking at the surly man. 'Where did you put that mail-bag after you'd dug it up, Albert?'

'I'm not saying anything,' said Albert, 'except that I don't know anything about any mail-bag, and it's no use asking me.'

'I'll get the mail-bag, shall I, sir?' said Peter, much to the Inspector's surprise. He looked at Peter, quite astounded.

'The mail-bag? Don't tell me you know where *that* is?' he said. 'Right, get it.'

So off went Peter to the back of the cave, shinned up the wall, caught hold of the rope, and disappeared. Then a voice came down the hole.

'Stand by, everyone! Mail-bag on the way!' There was a heavy thud on the soft sand, and there was the mail-bag! Its fall had broken it open, and registered envelopes and packets came tumbling out.

'Whew!' said the Inspector, amazed. 'This is magic! Hey, Peter, any more mail-bags to come?'

Peter came down the hole, laughing. 'No, sir. That's the only one. Is it the stolen one?'

'Yes,' said the Inspector. 'Well, I'm afraid Albert won't be able to steal any more mail-bags for a long, long time. Take him away, Constable!'

Albert was marched away, still sullen and silent. 'Come in and have a word with my wife, Inspector,' said Peter's father. 'She must be longing to know what all this excitement's about. Peter, here's a couple of pound notes. Take all the Secret Seven out and give them a thumping good tea, ice-creams and all. You've done well, my boy!'

He went off with the Inspector, who waved a cheery hand to them. Peter turned to the others, beaming. He

192

waved the money at them.

'Look at that! We'll have a spread. Come on!'

Susie and Jeff went out of the cave with the others. Jack gave his sister a little push.

'You're not coming with *us*, Susie. We're the Secret Seven, and you don't belong. You go home.'

'Oh,' said Janet, seeing Susie's downcast face, 'couldn't she come just for once? I mean, she did tell you about Albert coming out of the back of the cave when she and Jeff were there, Jack, and it was because of that that we managed to find the other cave at last. *Couldn't* she come?'

'No. We're the Secret Seven,' said Jack, 'and Susie would only laugh and sneer at us all the time, like she always does. And Jeff too. No.'

'I won't! I think you're wonderful!' said Susie. 'Let me come. Just this once, Jack. I DO want to hear all about this exciting adventure.'

'You can come, Susie,' said Peter, taking command. '*And* Jeff too. Just this once. My word, it's a story worth telling, I promise you. It will take us at least four ice-creams each before the tale is told. It's a jolly good adventure, you'll have to admit that, Susie!'

It was, and Susie's going to say so, too, when she's heard it. Good old Secret Seven – they always get there in the end, don't they?

PUZZLE FOR THE SECRET SEVEN

CONTENTS

One

Off to the fair

'HALLO!' shouted a voice over the wall, and Scamper barked loudly at once. Peter and Janet looked up from their gardening.

'Oh, hallo, Jack!' said Peter, pleased. 'Stop barking, Scamper! Anyone would think you hadn't seen Jack for a month. Come on in, Jack. Any news?'

'Yes. Rather nice news,' said Jack, wheeling his bicycle in at the front gate. 'My mother won a pound at the whist drive last night – and she's given it to me to take all the Secret Seven over to the fair at Hilly-Down today. Can you and Janet come?'

'I say – how decent of your mother,' said Peter, and Janet beamed. She had so badly wanted to go to the fair, but she and Peter were saving up for their father's birthday.

'There's just one thing, though,' said Jack, seriously. 'Susie will have to come too – and she's got an awful friend staying with her, called Binkie. Mother says the money's for them too.'

'Oh well – we can put up with Susie for once in a way,' said Peter. 'After all, it's not as if we were going out to solve some mystery, or are in the middle of an adventure. You tell your mother we're very, very grateful. What time shall we meet?'

'Let's go after tea, when there are crowds of people at the fair,' said Jack. 'And stay till the lights are on. I love those great flaring lights they have. Let's meet at about five o'clock at the bus-stop in the High Street. And don't pay any attention to Susie and Binkie if they giggle all the time!'

'We certainly won't,' said Peter. 'Righto, then – meet you at five o'clock. Are all the others coming?'

'Yes. I've been round to them,' said Jack, getting on his bicycle. 'We'll have at least ten pence each to spend, and some of the others are bringing a bit more too. See you at five, then!'

He rode off, ringing his bell in farewell. Peter and Janet were pleased. 'We'd better ask Mother,' said Janet. 'Though I'm sure she'll say we can go – especially as we've promised to garden all day!'

Mother said of course they could go, and she would add twenty-five pence to the money Jack's mother had given. Scamper listened to it all, wagging his tail. He looked up at Peter and gave a little whine.

'He wants to know if he can go too,' said Peter, with a laugh. 'Yes, if you can keep up with our bikes, Scamper, old thing. You're getting a bit fat, you know!'

Scamper barked joyfully. There was nothing he liked better than an outing with the Secret Seven.

'You haven't had many meetings lately, down in your shed,' said Mother. 'Has the Secret Seven broken up?'

'Oh *no*, Mother!' said Peter and Janet together, quite shocked. Mother laughed.

'Well, a week of your Easter holidays has already gone, and you haven't asked me for cakes and lemonade for one of your mysterious meetings yet,' she said. 'And I bought quite a big tin of biscuits, thinking I'd have to supply you Seven with something to nibble at your meetings!'

'Nothing's happened yet for us to call a meeting about,' said Janet. 'But we've still got two weeks' holiday left.'

'Woof!' said Scamper, agreeing heartily, and wagging his tail.

'Your life is *all* holiday, Scamper!' said Peter. 'You don't do a single stroke of work – and it's no good your trying to tell me that you helped us with the digging this morning! All *you* were doing was digging up a bone you'd hidden!'

At five o'clock quite a crowd of children arrived on bicycles at the bus-stop in the High Street. First came Peter and Janet, punctual as usual, because Peter said that as leader he must always be on time. Just after came Colin, out of breath with racing along fast in case he was late. Then came Pam and Barbara together, with George shouting behind.

'Six of us,' said Janet. 'We just want Jack and Susie and Binkie. What a name! We once had a rabbit called Binkie, do you remember, Peter? It had a dear little twitchy nose, and teeth that stuck out.'

'Here they are,' said George, as three children came cycling quickly round the corner. 'Hallo, Jack!'

'Sorry we're last,' said Jack. 'But you know what Susie is – couldn't find her purse, didn't know where her bike was . . .'

'Oooh, you fibber,' said Susie. 'You know you kept us waiting while you pumped up your front tyre. Binkie, this is the rest of the wonderful Secret Seven that I told you Jack belonged to.'

Binkie beamed all round, and Janet nudged Peter in delight. 'She's like our rabbit!' she said, in a low voice. 'Exactly!'

Peter wanted to laugh, because Janet was right. Binkie had a funny little twitchy nose, and teeth just like a rabbit. She only needed nice long furry ears. She was a terrible chatterbox, even worse than Susie.

'Oh, I say!' she said, in a breathless voice. 'It's so nice to meet you all. Susie's told me all about you. And is this Scamper? Oh my, isn't he lovely? I've got a dog at home too, but he's a terrier, and you should see him catch a . . .'

'Shut up, Binkie,' said Jack, firmly. 'And please don't wobble on your bike when you ride with us. I never *saw* such a wobbler before!'

'Oh well, you see, it's because I always . . .' began Binkie, but nobody listened. They all rode off, chattering and laughing, Scamper running delightedly with them.

The fair was about a mile and a half away at Hilly-Down. It was in a big field, and as the children topped the last hill and looked down on the gay sight they were full of delight.

'All those tents and stalls, and flags flying and fluttering!' said Jack, as he cycled down the hill.

'And the roundabout! I can hear its music quite clearly,' said Janet. 'Oooh, Binkie, don't wobble so – you nearly had me off.'

They came to the entrance of the field, and went in. They stacked their bicycles carefully together in a corner, and Peter called to Scamper.

'On guard, Scamper!' he said, pointing to the nine bicycles. 'On guard, old boy!'

Scamper badly wanted to go with them, but he felt proud to be on guard. He wagged his tail and lay down by the bicycles. Peter patted him, and turned to the others.

'Now come on,' he said. 'Into the fair we go!'

Two

A good time – and a shock!

THE fair was very good indeed. The roundabout especially was voted 'smashing' by everyone.

'It's the *quickest* roundabout I ever knew,' said George, when they were all getting off after a very dizzy ride. 'I had to cling on to my giraffe for dear life. I was nearly swung off! Have we enough money to go again?'

'I don't want to go on again,' said Pam, trying to walk straight. 'I still feel as if I'm going round and round on my lion. Oooh, sorry, Colin – I didn't mean to bump into you. I just can't walk properly!'

Binkie was the same, and everyone laughed at the two girls, they were so dizzy. 'Let's go to the hoopla stall,' said Jack. 'But we won't let Pam or Binkie have throws, because they'll be too giddy to aim properly.'

That made both Pam and Binkie much more sensible, of course. In fact, Pam recovered so quickly that she threw best of the lot, and managed to get a hoop round a box of sweets, which she promptly shared with the others.

There was a coconut shy over in one corner, and here Peter shone, because he was an excellent thrower. He knocked down three coconuts, and the man in charge of the shy wasn't at all pleased! He handed Peter the coconuts with a very bad grace.

'However do you do it, Peter?' asked Jack, enviously. 'You *always* get a coconut when you go to a fair. And today you've got three!'

203

'Well, I pretend I'm bowling at a wicket,' said Peter, 'and the coconut I aim at is the row of stumps! It's easy if you think of it like that!'

Everyone immediately wanted to have another throw, but George shook his head. 'No. There's not enough money,' he said. 'Not even with Peter's twenty-five pence – unless you don't want to try anything else.'

But they all wanted to go on the swings, so, much to the coconut-shy man's relief, they moved off. 'Let's put these coconuts beside our bikes,' said Peter. 'I don't want to carry them about all the time. Scamper will guard them.'

Scamper was delighted to see them. He was lying by the pile of bicycles keeping an eye on everyone who passed. If anyone came a little nearer the bicycles than he thought they ought to, he stood up at once and growled. Two other dogs sat near by, admiring Scamper's fierceness. He was really feeling rather important.

Peter threw the coconuts down beside the bicycles. 'On guard, Scamper,' he said, and Scamper gave a short, sharp bark, as if to say, 'Yes, sir, certainly, sir!' He ran to the coconuts, sniffed them all over, then lay down again, keeping a sharp eye on the other two dogs.

The nine children spent every penny of their money, and then wished they had a little left to spend on some delicious-smelling hot gingerbread. This was being made in a little oven by a small, fat, gipsy-looking woman. It looked good and smelt even better.

'Want to buy some?' she asked Peter.

'Yes – but we haven't any money left,' said Peter. She laughed, and pushed a small batch of rather crumbly gingerbread squares over to them.

'Help yourselves. These are done a bit too much. I can't sell them.'

'Thanks! That's nice of you,' said Peter, and he and the

205

others helped themselves. He saw a pram near-by, with a baby laughing in it. It was rather a dirty baby, and the pram was old and broken-down and dirty too – but the baby was such a merry little creature that no one could help watching it as they munched the delicious gingerbread.

Janet went to play with the baby, and it held out its hands, and bounced up and down in delight. 'Does the baby travel about with the fair?' Janet asked the mother.

'Oh, no. We live up in a shack on the hillside,' said the little fat woman. 'My husband goes round with the fair when it wants extra help, and when it comes anywhere in the district I sell gingerbread.' She saw some people coming up, and began to shout. 'Hot gingerbread, real old-fashioned gingerbread, straight from the oven. Two pence a piece, only two pence a piece!'

'Come on,' said Peter, looking at his watch. 'We really ought to go now. We'll just wander once more round the fair now all the lights are up.'

'I like it better when it gets dark and they light those big flares,' said Janet. 'This is just the time I love. What a pity we've got to go!'

'I think I'll stay on a bit longer with Binkie,' said Susie. 'You like the fair when it's night-time, don't you, Binkie?'

'Oh, *yes*,' gushed Binkie, her nose twitching. 'It's so – so sort of romantic. It makes me want to write poetry. Oh, do let's stay, Susie. The others can go if they want to. I might be able to write a poem about it.'

'Binkie writes marvellous poetry,' announced Susie proudly. 'She won a prize at school for it. You ought to hear her recite it.'

This was the very last thing that anyone wanted. They stared at Binkie in horror, for it was plain that she was quite prepared to recite to them then and there.

'I said it was *time to go*,' said Peter, in a very deter-mined voice. 'And you and Binkie are to come too, Susie. We can't leave you here alone.'

'Oh yes you can. *I* don't belong to your silly Secret Seven,' said Susie at once. '*I'm* not under your orders.'

'Well, you're under *mine*,' said Jack firmly. 'And you know that Mother said you were to come back with *me*. And we are going RIGHT NOW !'

Susie said no more, but she scowled. 'She'll pay us out for this,' said Jack to Peter. 'Good thing we haven't a meeting coming on – she and Binkie would try to spoil it! Come *on*, Susie!'

They collected their bicycles from a delighted Scamper, and set off back home again. But on the way up the hill that led from the fair, George spied something that aston-ished him – a great light on the hillside, not far to the left.

'What's that?' he shouted, and stopped for the others to catch him up. 'Look – flames – and smoke! It's a house on fire!'

'My word, yes – we'd better see if we can help!' said Peter. 'Look, there's a telephone box just there, on the other side of the road, George. I'll telephone the fire-station, while you others cut across the field-path there, and see what's happening. Buck up!'

He rode to the telephone box and went inside, while the others opened the field-gate and then rode at top speed up the narrow path that led to the fire. *Was* it a house burn-ing fiercely – it didn't look as if much could be saved!

In the telephone box Peter asked for the fire-station, and spoke urgently into the telephone mouthpiece. 'Hallo! Fire-station? There's a fire up here on Hilly-Down Hill. It looks pretty fierce. Right—we'll stay here till you come!'

Three

The fire at Hilly-Down

PETER let the telephone-box door swing shut, jumped on his bicycle, and cycled along the same path as the others. He caught them up as he came to the fire, and stared in horror. Whatever had stood there on the hillside was almost burnt out!

'What was it? A house?' he asked, shielding his eyes from the fierceness of the roaring flames. 'I hope no one was in it!'

'A ginger cat was the only live thing we saw,' said George, looking very solemn. 'It shot by us as we came up. It must have been a small house, Peter. Did you get on to the fire-brigade?'

'Yes. They're coming. But it will be too late,' said Peter. 'Janet, don't cry. I don't expect there was anyone in the place.'

'My word – it must have been old and rotten to go up as quickly as that,' said Colin. 'What a crackling and roaring! Look out, Barbara – there are bits of burning stuff blowing about still.'

Peter took Jack with him, and the two boys anxiously walked all round the burning house, trying to see if there was anything they could do. But there was nothing to be seen but flames, now dying down a little, and tumbled, smoking pieces of wood. No wonder the poor old cat had been terrified!

Then came the sound of a clanging bell, and Colin called out in excitement. 'The fire-engine! Hasn't it been quick? Well, they can't help seeing at once where the fire is!'

'We left the field gate open, didn't we?' said George, and Peter nodded. 'Yes – and look, the fire-engine's coming through it now. Gosh, I wish *I* could drive it!'

The fire-engine came slowly up the narrow, rutted path, gleaming brightly in the light from the roaring fire. 'Anyone know if there's a well?' shouted a fireman, leaping down to unroll a long hose-pipe.

'There's a stream running down the hill just here!' called Jack, and the firemen went over to it. In less than a minute they were playing water on the flames, and a great sizzling noise arose.

'Like a million bacon rashers frying at once,' said Janet in wonder, and she was right!

'Did you see anyone about?' asked one of the firemen, as the flames died down under the water.

'No. Nobody,' said Peter. 'But the whole place was on fire when we came up – nobody could have been saved if anyone *had* been in there. But surely they would have run out, wouldn't they?'

'Might have been children asleep there,' said the man shortly. 'Whose is this shack?'

Nobody knew – but just then Peter saw someone hurrying up the field-path, wheeling something in front of her that bumped wildly over the ruts.

'It's the woman who was making gingerbread at the fair!' cried Janet. 'Oh – she said she lived in a shack on the hill-top. It must be *her* place! Poor, poor thing!'

It *was* the gingerbread woman. She came up quite breathless, her eyes staring in fright, the baby being almost bumped out of its pram.

'My Benny!' she shouted. 'Where is he? I left him here.'

'Well, Mam – we haven't *seen* anyone about,' said the chief fireman, and a little shiver of horror went through the children. No! No, surely no one could have been in that burning shack!

'Benny, Benny, Benny! Where are you, my little Benny?' screamed the woman. And then, to everyone's enormous relief, a child's high voice answered shakily from somewhere.

'Mammy! Mammy! Mammy!'

'He's safe,' said the little gingerbread woman, and tears ran down her cheeks. 'I'll go find him, mister. He won't come out while everyone's staring round. He's in the bushes somewhere, my little Benny.'

She took the baby out of its pram, and, carrying him in her arms, she hurried in the direction of a row of thick bushes a little way below the still-burning shack. 'Benny!' she called. 'Benny! Mammy's here. Everything's all right, love.'

And then, quite suddenly, it seemed as if there was a whole crowd of people staring at the dying fire – people who had left the fair, seen the flames, and come hurrying in at the open gate. Perhaps the woman's husband was there too? The children hoped so. Then he could comfort the poor little woman.

'What will they do for the night?' wondered Janet. 'Where will they sleep?'

'Oh, someone will lend them a barn, or take them in for the night,' said one of the firemen, busy rolling up the hose. 'It's a mercy no one was hurt. You kids go along home now. Thanks for letting us know.'

'I wish we'd some money left,' said Jack, thinking that

the pound his mother had given him would have been a godsend to the gingerbread woman just now.

Two policemen arrived, and one began taking notes. The other moved the crowd away. 'Move along, please,' he said. 'The fire's over. We can't do anything more. Will you move along, sir, please? And you too, madam?'

He came to the little crowd of children, still standing there with Scamper, feeling rather miserable.

'Are you the kids who warned the fire-station?' he said. 'Well, that was good work on your part. But get along home now, please. You can't do anything more.'

'What will happen to the poor woman and her children now?' asked Peter. 'I mean – she must have lost everything in the fire.'

'We'll look after her and the family,' said the policeman, stolidly. 'She'll be all right. That was only an old shack they lived in, not a house – they didn't have much of anything. You go home now, please, and let us do what we can for the woman.'

The fire-engine departed with a clanging of its bell, trying to make the crowd get out of its way. The children found their bicycles and wheeled them to the gate, Scamper following, wondering if they were going home. What an evening!

They all mounted their bicycles and rode along the road, very silent. Even Susie found nothing to say. Binkie began to talk first, the words suddenly pouring out.

'I've never seen a fire before, I've never seen a fire-engine so close. Ooh, wasn't it exciting? I've never . . .'

'Be quiet,' said Peter. 'You make it sound as if it was a sort of treat! Think of that poor woman!'

'Yes. *I'm* thinking about her too,' said George. 'I say, Peter – I think we ought to call a meeting of the Secret

Seven, and see if we can't plan something to help her. What about tomorrow morning at ten o'clock?'

'Fine idea!' said Peter, really pleased. 'I was just thinking the same thing myself. Secret Seven, those are your orders – be down in our shed, ten o'clock tomorrow morning.'

'Susie and me too?' said Binkie, thrilled.

'No,' said Peter. 'ONLY the Secret Seven. Susie – do you hear that? ONLY the Secret Seven!'

Four

Secret Seven meeting

NEXT morning, sharp at five to ten, Peter and Janet were down in their shed. On the door were the letters S.S., and everything was ready inside – boxes to sit on, some biscuits on a plate, and lemonade to drink.

'I hope everyone remembers the password, and their badges,' said Peter. 'It's rather a long time since we had the last meeting.'

'Wuff!' said Scamper, suddenly wagging his tail. Janet gave a squeal of laughter.

'*Scamper* knows it! He said it! Yes, Scamper, you've remembered the password – it was Wuff! Clever dog!'

Footsteps came up the path to the shed, and Scamper gave a little whine of welcome. He knew it was George. A knock came on the door, and a low voice said, 'Wuff!'

'Enter!' called Peter, and George came in, grinning, wearing his badge on his coat.

'I nearly forgot the password,' he said. 'But luckily I'd written it down in my diary! Here's someone else.'

It was Pam and Barbara. They knocked, and Peter called out immediately, 'Password, please.'

'Peter, we're not quite sure if it's Wuff or Woof,' said Pam's anxious voice.

'Wuff!' said Scamper at once.

'You're *not* to give the password away, Scamper,' said Janet, shocked. Barbara and Pam giggled outside the door. 'Thanks, Scamper. Wuff, Peter!'

'Come in,' said Peter. 'Just by the skin of your teeth, though! Who's that coming now?'

'Jack and Colin,' said Pam, as the door shut on her and Barbara. 'Oh, it's good to be here again, in our shed!'

Knock-knock!

'Password!' called Peter. 'And DON'T yell it.'

'We've forgotten it,' said Colin, in a very apologetic voice. 'I mean – it's so long since we had a meeting, and . . .'

'Can't let you in!' said Peter sternly.

'Oh, don't be such an ass, Peter,' said Jack angrily. 'You know I daren't write our password down in case Susie finds it – and it's awfully difficult to remember it when we have had so many. I know it's something to do with a dog. Is it Whiskers?'

'Wuff, wuff, wuff,' said Scamper, and Pam gave a squeal of delight. Then a voice came from somewhere in the bushes outside.

'The password is Wuff, Jack, Wuff!' and then came a burst of very loud laughter from two people.

'SUSIE! BINKIE! I TOLD you not to follow me!' cried Jack angrily. 'How do *you* know the password?'

'Oh, come in, come in,' said Peter, opening the door. Jack and Colin went in, looking angry, and Peter went over to the bushes. He spoke sternly to the two giggling girls behind them.

'Spoil-sports! Go and giggle somewhere else. If you are here in two minutes' time I shall take the hose-pipe and water this bush thoroughly. And I *mean* that!'

There was a scuffling noise, and the two girls ran off, still giggling. Susie knew that Peter meant what he said, and she didn't want to be hosed! Peter went into the shed and slammed the door.

To everyone's great relief, he said nothing at all about passwords. 'Now,' he said, taking his place on his box. 'About this business of the fire. I've . . .'

But before he could go on, Scamper began to bark madly. He ran to the door and scraped at it, still barking.

'Scamper! What's all this row about?' demanded Peter. 'If it's those two girls again you're to go and chase them away. Do you hear?'

Scamper was delighted to see Peter opening the door. He dashed out at once, and the Secret Seven looked after him to see if he was chasing Susie and Binkie.

But he wasn't. He was dancing round two legs in corduroy trousers, his tail wagging in delight.

'Oh, it's Dad's shepherd,' said Peter, in surprise, and called to the fine-looking old fellow on the near-by path. 'Hallo, Matt! Did you want my father? He's gone to market, I'm afraid.'

'Oh. I was afeard he'd be gone,' said old Matt, taking his cap off and scratching his thatch of grey hair. 'Well – maybe you'd give him a message for me, Master Peter?'

'Yes, of course,' said Peter. 'What is it?'

'Well, likely you know there was a fire last night over on Hilly-Down yonder,' said Matt, 'and Luke Bolan and his wife had their shack burnt out, and they've nowhere to go . . .'

'Yes – we all saw it,' said Peter soberly. 'And I telephoned for the fire-brigade, Matt.'

'You did? That was smart of you, Master Peter,' said Matt. 'Well, now, I've got an idea to put up to the master – but you say he's at the market?'

'Yes. He won't be home till after dinner,' said Peter. 'What's your idea, Matt?'

'There's an old caravan up by my sheep-hut,' said Matt. 'I lived in it afore the master built me my hut, and I only use it now to store my goods in. Proper broken-down old thing it is – but it would house Luke Bolan and his wife and kids for a bit, Master Peter, if so be as the master would let him use it. They haven't anywhere to go, see?'

'Oh, I'm *sure* my father would let them have it,' said Peter, and Janet nodded at once. 'Anyway, let's go and ask Mother. She'll know if Dad would give permission.'

So the whole of the Secret Seven, with old Matt and Scamper too, went up the garden-path and round the house to where Peter's mother was weeding her lettuce bed. She was most surprised to see them with the shepherd.

'Why, Matt!' she said. 'Is anything the matter?'

Matt told her what he had said to Peter, and she listened carefully. 'Of course the Bolans can have the caravan until they can find somewhere else,' she said. 'I know the master would say that. That poor woman – all her things burnt up like that! We'll certainly have to do something to help her. You go back to the Bolans, Matt, and tell them they can move into the old caravan at once. You can take your things out and store them in your own hut for a time, can't you?'

'Oh yes, Ma'm,' said Matt. 'And I can give them a rug, and lend them my little old table.'

'We'll see what we can do too,' said Peter's mother, and she turned to the Secret Seven. 'Will you let me come to your meeting for once?' she said. 'Because I think we can all help in this – and if I'm there I can help you to make sensible plans. It's a thing we must do together.'

'Of course, Mother!' said Peter, delighted. 'Come along now, this very minute! We'd LOVE to have you!'

Five

All kinds of plans!

THE Secret Seven filed into the shed after Peter and Janet's mother. Peter shut the door.

'I'm glad you didn't ask me for the password, Peter,' said his mother, smiling. 'Dear me, I do feel important, coming to one of your meetings. It's very nice of you to let me.'

'We're very pleased, Mother,' said Janet, and all the others nodded in agreement. Everyone liked Peter and Janet's kind, generous mother.

They began to talk about the fire, and the homeless Bolans.

'There's Luke Bolan, Mother, who goes round with the fair,' said Peter, 'and there's Mrs Bolan, who visits any fair that comes into the district, and makes hot ginger-bread to sell. We hadn't any money left to buy it, but she gave us all some!'

'That was really very kind of her,' said his mother, surprised.

'And there's a dear, smiley little baby,' said Pam. 'Rather dirty, but a little darling.'

'And there's a boy called Benny,' said Janet. 'We haven't actually seen him, Mother. He was in the shack last night when it was burnt down, but he ran out and hid in the bushes. Poor Mrs Bolan was so afraid he would be inside the burning shack.'

'Yes. You told me last night,' said her mother. 'Well, now, let's think. I suggest that each of you should go home and tell your mothers about what has happened – and tell them that we are going to lend the old caravan to the Bolans, but that as all their things were burnt, we want to try and give them as many really necessary things as we can . . .'

'Do you mean kettles and things?' asked Pam.

'Yes – and perhaps an old mattress to sleep on,' said Peter's mother. 'There won't be room for a bed, of course. A folding chair would be a good idea – and a small mattress perhaps for the little boy and the baby. They will want food too.'

'Well, I'm really glad that the Secret Seven have something to do,' said Peter, pleased. 'It makes us much more of a real club then. What can *you* give, Mother?'

'There's an old mattress in the loft,' said his mother, thinking hard. 'And I can send up at least one saucepan – and I've an old blanket, and . . .'

'Well, if all our mothers can find something or other we'll be able to make that caravan really cosy,' said Janet, looking forward to the job. 'I vote that everyone goes home after this meeting, and finds out what he or she can bring – and then comes back here to another meeting as soon after dinner as possible . . .'

'And we'll draw up a list of things, and choose what we think Mrs Bolan will need!' said Peter. 'Mother can help in that, can't you, Mother?'

'Oh yes!' said his mother, smiling. 'And when we've decided what to take we'll get the farm-van, and pile everything into it. We'd better take a scrubbing-brush or two, because I expect that old caravan will need cleaning!'

'This *is* going to be fun,' said Barbara. 'I'm good at scrubbing! I only hope Mrs Bolan won't be there, because it would be wonderful to see her face when she comes to the van, and sees it all clean and furnished ready for her!'

'Oooh yes – I'd like to get it all quite perfect,' said Pam. 'Shall we go off home now?'

'Yes,' said Peter. 'The sooner the better! Now mind you tell your mothers what *my* mother has said – and I bet they'll all rush round and see what they can find.'

The Seven stood up, excited, and Scamper wagged his tail eagerly, jumping up at Peter. 'Do you want to help too, old fellow?' said Peter. 'Well, we'll take you with us! Now remember, Secret Seven – back here after dinner – say as near half-past two as possible. And REMEMBER THE PASSWORD!'

'Wuff!' said the rest of the Seven at once, and made Scamper bark in delight.

'Thank you, Mother, for coming to our meeting,' said Janet, hugging her mother. 'We'll bring you our lists this afternoon and let you say which things would be best to take up to the old caravan. Won't Matt be surprised to see us?'

'He certainly will,' said her mother. 'He's a kind old fellow!'

Everyone cycled home, eager to tell their mothers about the morning's meeting. Peter and Janet went to find the mattress in the loft. Yes, there it was, rolled up in thick brown paper, and tied with string. They dragged it to the trap-door of the loft, and let it slide down the ladder – BUMP! It landed at the bottom very suddenly, and Scamper tore down the stairs in a great fright.

Mother went to her linen cupboard, and her blanket store, and found two old sheets and a blanket, warm and cosy. She chose a saucepan from the kitchen, and a teapot and jug from the dresser there. She rummaged out an old oil-stove too, to air the caravan.

Peter and Janet carried everything to the hall, and stored it there ready for when the farm-van called that afternoon, as Mother had arranged.

Just before half-past two the other Secret Seven members arrived, each with a list or some notes scribbled in a notebook.

Nobody forgot the password this time, and Scamper was really very funny when they all arrived at the shed. He said 'Wuff' before they did!

Peter collected the lists, and read them over. 'Golly – your mothers have been jolly generous!' he said, pleased. 'Everyone's offered a blanket – and our mother did too. Let's take the lists to her, and let her decide which things will be best for the caravan. At this rate we'd have enough to furnish a dozen caravans!'

They took the lists to Peter's mother, and she checked them quickly with a pencil, crossing off duplicated articles.

'This is fine!' she said. 'Did you arrange to have the things ready, all of you?'

'Oh yes,' said everyone.

'Very well – I think I can hear the farm-van outside now,' said Peter's mother. 'We'll pack our own things into it – and then collect what we want from the other houses. Come along!'

It was fun going round in the van and collecting so many things. Everyone's mother was very kind, and said that they were pleased to think that the Secret Seven was doing such a fine job.

'And now we'll drive up to the old caravan,' said Peter's mother. 'And really set to work! We're going to have some fun!'

Six

An afternoon of hard work!

'DID Susie and Binkie try to interfere, Jack, when you asked your mother for a list of things she could spare?' said Janet.

'Oh yes – and they were very cross when I said it was Secret Seven business,' said Jack. 'I told Susie there was nothing to stop her saving up a bit of money and buying something on her own. But she always wants to butt in on the Secret Seven!'

'I think perhaps you might have let them, just for once,' said Peter's mother.

'But, Mother – you don't understand,' said Peter at once. 'If we let Susie in just ONCE we'd never get rid of her. And, anyhow, we don't want eight people. We're the Secret *Seven.*'

The farm-van stopped at a field-gate, and Peter jumped down to open it. A grassy road led round the hill to where old Matt the shepherd had his hut and kept his sheep.

The van jolted slowly over the rough road, and the kettle and saucepans rattled and clanked inside. Everyone was sitting on the two old mattresses and blankets – it was quite comfortable! At last the van jolted to a stop, and the driver called out, 'We're as near the caravan as I can get, Ma'm. And here comes old Matt.'

The shepherd opened the door of the van and smiled all over his face as he looked inside and saw so many people.

223

'Why, you've come too, Ma'm,' he said. 'That's fair kind of you! And what a lot of goods! That old caravan won't know itself. I've been cleaning it up a bit, but it's still pretty dirty.'

'We'll soon make it nice and clean!' said Janet, jumping out. 'Come on, Mother!'

How hard they all worked that afternoon! They washed and scrubbed and swept. Peter mended two shelves to hold pots and pans. George stacked the mattresses neatly rolled up, inside the caravan. 'It will be quite easy for Mrs Bolan to untie them tonight!' he said.

Matt came back again about two hours after. He had been rounding up some of the sheep, and his old dog was with him. Scamper ran to him to play, but the sheepdog lay down, put his nose down between his paws, and shut his eyes.

'He can't be bothered with you, Scamper!' said Peter, grinning at the surprised spaniel. 'No – leave him alone. He's run for miles, getting the sheep in, and he's tired. Matt – have you been able to tell the Bolans about this caravan yet?'

'Yes, young sir,' said Matt. 'They were that pleased. Mrs Bolan wouldn't believe it at first. I didn't tell her you were going to furnish it, though. I thought that would be a nice surprise. She'll be along any time now.'

'Well – we've just about finished,' said Peter. 'Come and look, Matt.'

Matt could hardly believe his eyes when he saw the spick-and-span caravan, looking so cosy inside. He stared in wonder.

'There now – who'd have thought it?' he said. 'And the master talked of chopping it up for firewood next winter!'

'There's Mrs Bolan, look – with the old pram!' said Janet. 'And the little boy. She's got something piled on the pram – two loaves of bread and a few parcels. Oh, poor things, of course, all their food was burnt too! We never thought of bringing any for them!'

'Yes, we did,' said George. 'My mother sent a few tins. I've put them on the shelves that Peter mended. I expect Mrs Bolan will be sure to have brought milk for the baby.'

'We could get the shepherd to bring up milk each morning,' said Peter. 'Couldn't we, Mother?'

Mrs Bolan wheeled the pram towards them, looking surprised and a little scared to see so many people outside the old caravan. She smiled nervously. Matt went up to her in his slow, kindly way, speaking to her as if she were one of his nice old sheep.

'Come along now, Mrs Bolan, don't you be afeard, we'm all friends here. This here's the caravan you can have, so mistress says, and right cosy they've made it. Take a look inside.'

Peter's mother came forward. 'We were so sorry to hear of the fire last night,' she said. 'Oh, what a dear little baby! And what's the little boy's name?'

But as soon as Benny felt her hand on his head he turned and fled away, hands outstretched in front of him, stumbling as he went. Janet started after him.

'Leave him be,' called Mrs Bolan. 'He's so scared now, poor lamb, what with the fire and all!'

Janet stopped. The boy, about eight years old, was small for his age, and looked a little strange. He had enormous dark eyes that stared rather blankly at them, and a shock of very black, curly hair round his small brown face. He made his way into a bush and crouched there, peering out like a small animal, listening to everything that was said.

Mrs Bolan was now admiring the caravan. 'Why, there's everything we want!' she said, looking round in pleasure. 'Even tins on the shelf! And clean as a new pin too! It's right kind of you, Ma'am, to do all this for me. I cried my eyes out last night when that old shack of ours went up – a nasty place it was, cold and draughty, but it was our home.'

'When's your husband coming?' asked Peter, hoping to see Luke's pleasure too.

'Oh Luke – Luke's real upset,' said Mrs Bolan, looking worried. 'We lost a few precious things in that fire, you see. I lost my sewing-machine, and Luke lost his banjo and . . .'

'Oh – does he play the banjo?' said Colin. 'So does my uncle. What a pity it was burnt.'

The baby began to cry, and Mrs Bolan bent over her. 'I must give her some milk,' she said, 'and then I'll settle into the van. My, we're lucky. I'll send Luke down to thank you properly, Ma'm as soon as I can.'

'Shall we go now?' said Peter, and his mother nodded. She turned to Matt.

'You can bring up some milk for the baby each day, can't you, Matt?' she said to the kindly old shepherd, and he nodded.

'Well, good-bye then, Mrs Bolan,' said Peter, and everyone called out some little message too. 'Good luck! We hope the caravan will be comfortable! Tell us if there's anything else we can do!'

Peter went over to where Benny was hiding. 'Good-bye, Benny,' he said, but the strange little boy didn't answer. His great dark eyes wandered up to Peter's face, and yet Peter felt as if he was not really looking at him. What a curious child!

Seven

Susie and Binkie are a nuisance

As the Secret Seven went down the hill in the farm-van, glad to have done a really good job, they saw a man in the distance, walking slowly up. 'I bet that's Luke Bolan,' said Janet. 'I hope he'll be pleased when he sees what we've done for him.'

'I expect he will,' said her mother. 'But you must remember that even though he has a roof over his head now, he and Mrs Bolan have lost every one of their possessions – except that old pram! And it's a terrible thing to lose things you have had for years and years – like Luke's banjo.'

'Are they expensive?' asked Jack.

'Good gracious yes!' said Colin. 'My uncle paid a mint of money for his!' And he began to pretend that he was playing a banjo, strumming with his fingers and making a banjo-like noise that made everyone laugh.

'Do we have another meeting soon?' asked Barbara. 'I wish we could. It was nice to have the two we've just had.'

'Well, let's,' said Peter. 'Even though there isn't anything to have a meeting about, we could talk and have a bit of fun. Mother, can we get out of the van now and walk over the fields? It's such a nice afternoon.'

'Yes – and if you'd all like to come back afterwards to a late high tea, I'll have it ready for you,' said his mother. 'You really have worked very hard, and you must be getting hungry already! I'll telephone to tell the other mothers.'

228

'Oh Mother! You really are a pet!' said Janet, and everyone agreed. 'Of course we'd like high tea – what shall we have? Eggs? Ham?'

'Wait and see,' said her mother, laughing. 'Well, out you all get, and I'll drive on alone. Good-bye for an hour or two!'

The Seven leapt out of the van, Scamper too, and set off across the fields. It was a wonderful spring day, with

the birds singing madly and primroses everywhere. Cow-slips nodded on the hillsides too, and celandines shone out from the ditches.

'They're so shining-bright that they look as if they've been polished,' said Barbara.

A voice suddenly hailed them, and the Seven stopped. 'Ahoy there! Wait for us!'

'Blow! It's Susie and Binkie,' said Jack in disgust. Sure enough it was – and they came leaping down the hill at top speed.

'Hallo! What happened about the caravan?' yelled Susie.

229

They told her, and she and Binkie listened with interest. 'You might have let us help!' said Susie reproachfully. 'Even though we don't belong to the Secret Seven.'

'Well, we said you could buy the Bolans anything you wanted to,' said Janet. 'Why don't you? You could take it up to the caravan yourselves.'

'Well, we jolly well will,' said Susie. 'Can we come with you now, or are you the high-and-mighty Secret Seven again, all on your own?'

'Don't be an ass,' said Peter. 'You can see we're not holding a meeting just at this moment, so of course you can come with us.'

'Binkie's made up a poem,' said Susie, with a sudden little giggle. 'All about the Secret Seven.'

'Well, we don't want to hear it,' said George, feeling quite certain that it wouldn't be a very polite one.

'It's got a chorus,' said Susie. 'Hasn't it, Binkie? Let Binkie say the poem, Peter, and we can all join in the chorus.'

'Don't you let her, Peter,' said Jack, at once. 'You've no idea how rude Susie and Binkie can get when they put their heads together.'

But Susie was not going to be stopped, nor Binkie either. Binkie began to chant lines in a loud, sing-song manner, dancing about in front of them.

'Oh see the Secret Seven
So very smug and pi,
Eyes turned up to Heaven,
When they come walking by!
They think they're very clever,
Alas, we don't agree,
We think the Secret Seven
Are silly as can be!

230

'*Chorus, please* . . .' And here Susie joined in at the top of her voice –

'Silly as can be, Silly as – '

But that was too much for the Secret Seven. With one accord they ran at the irritating Binkie and the aggravating Susie, yelling loudly.

'How dare you make up that song! Shut up! You horrible girl! Be quiet! We'll . . .'

But Susie and Binkie were racing away at top speed, laughing at the anger of the Secret Seven. 'Serves you right for not letting us help this afternoon!' yelled Susie, stopping for a moment. 'You just look out for us! We'll pay you out for that!'

Then off they raced again. 'I thought this would happen,' said Jack gloomily. 'I'm very sorry about it – but I can't help having Susie for my sister. As for Binkie – think what you'd all feel like if you had to have a girl like her staying a whole week with you!'

'It's a very rude and untruthful song,' said Barbara, who always hated being made fun of.

'It's just a *little* bit funny too,' said George, but nobody would agree with him. They were now walking beside a field where a scarecrow stood, and stopped to have a look at him. A rook stood on his old black hat, and he looked very comical.

The wind waved his torn old tweed coat about and made him seem alive. 'He's got Daddy's old trousers on,' said Janet, with a laugh. 'The ones Mummy didn't like because they were too light and showed the dirt so much. And someone's tied a dirty scarf round his neck. It looks like the one our cowman used to wear – red with white spots!'

The rook bent over the scarecrow's face and pecked it.

231

'Shoo!' shouted Peter indignantly. 'You're supposed to be scared of him. Shoo, rook, shoo!'

The rook gave two loud caws that sounded exactly as if it was laughing, spread its big black wings, and flew off slowly, cawing as it went.

'I bet it's saying something rude – like Binkie,' said George. 'I say, I'm awfully hungry now. What about that tea your mother promised us, Peter?'

That made them all hurry off at once. Eggs, ham, cold sausages, cheese, a fruit cake – they could eat the whole lot. So could Scamper. WUFF-WUFF!

Eight

Matt has surprising news

THE tea was ready by the time the Seven poured into the farm-house. They washed and made themselves tidy and then settled down happily at the table. What a spread!

'Cream cheese!' said Jack, in delight.

'Ham and eggs!' said Pam hungrily. 'My favourite!'

'Now just help yourselves,' said Peter's mother, smiling round. 'You deserve a treat after all your good work this afternoon. I saw your sister Susie and that friend of hers as I came home, Jack, and nearly asked them in too.'

'Mother! What an *awful* idea!' said Peter, helping himself to two cold sausages, a hard-boiled egg, and a slice of ham. 'That girl Binkie made up a very rude song about us. If you'd asked her in she might quite well have had the nerve to sing it at the tea-table.'

'I'd throw the cream cheese at her if she did,' said Jack, quite fiercely.

'Oh no you wouldn't,' said Peter's mother at once. 'I don't make cream cheese for that kind of thing. Colin, you haven't taken nearly enough ham.'

'He's dreaming!' said Pam, giving him a nudge. 'Wake up, Colin – whatever are you thinking of?'

'Well, actually, I suddenly thought of a sort of poem about Binkie,' said Colin, blinking his eyes suddenly, as if he were coming out of a dream.

'A poem! Surely *you* don't write poems, Colin!' said Janet, amazed. 'How does it begin?'

'Well, it begins like this,' said Colin, and then changed his mind. 'No, I'd better not tell you.'

233

That made everyone press him all the more, of course, and at last he grinned and recited a few lines, a little afraid that Peter's mother, who was listening, might not approve.

'Oh Binkie has the habit
Of a funny little rabbit,
Twitching up and down her little nose . . .'

The next line was lost in gales of laughter. 'Oh Colin – that's *exactly* Binkie!' cried Jack in delight. 'I shall recite it to her whenever she and Susie start that awful Secret Seven song.'

'How does it go on, Colin?' asked Janet, looking at him in admiration.

'Well, I've only got as far as two more lines,' said Colin. 'And in her mouth beneath
Are little rabbit teeth . . .
I can't think of the last line yet!'

'It doesn't sound awfully kind,' said Peter's mother, and that made Colin go red and say no more.

'Well, but Susie and Binkie aren't kind either,' argued Janet. 'Let's think of a last line:

'And in her mouth beneath,
Are little rabbit teeth . . .'

'No, don't,' said Colin, anxious not to displease Janet's mother. He frowned hard at Janet, and tried to kick her under the table, but only succeeded in kicking poor Scamper, who gave a loud and indignant yelp.

'Oh sorry, Scamper, sorry!' said Colin, and slid under the table to comfort Scamper – and to change the subject too!

'Well, that was a simply smashing high tea, Mother,' said Peter when the meal at last came to an end. 'I wish I could begin all over again, but I can't.'

'It's funny – but when I tasted that cream cheese at the beginning of the meal I thought it was just about the nicest thing in the world,' said Pam. 'But now I can't even bear to look at it!'

'We'll help wash up,' said Barbara.

'Oh thanks,' said Janet. 'Shall we *all* wash up, Mother? We'll be very, very careful.'

'Yes. That would be nice of you,' said her mother, and took up her mending while the Seven went in and out, taking the dirty dishes to the kitchen.

'We'll have a meeting tomorrow, if everyone approves,' said Peter, wiping the dishes carefully. 'Can you all come at ten?'

'No. I've got to go errands,' said Pam. 'I could come at eleven though.'

It turned out that eleven o'clock was all right for everyone, so it was duly arranged. 'We'll have to have a different password,' said Peter, 'because Susie and Binkie know the last one.'

'Wuff,' said Scamper, looking up.

'Yes, that's right. You really are too clever for words, Scamper!' said Peter, grinning. 'Well – you can choose the next one. Go on – tell us what you'd like.'

'Thump, thump, thump,' went Scamper's tail on the floor, as he looked up happily at Peter. He did so love being talked to.

'Thank you, Scamper. "Thump" is our next password,' said Peter gravely, and everyone laughed. 'I don't somehow think anyone will forget that!'

Nobody did, of course, and next morning when the knocks came on the closed shed door, where Peter and Janet awaited the others, the password was said at once. '**Thump!**'

235

And each time it was said Scamper thumped his tail joyfully on the floor of the shed. He had never chosen the password himself before, and he felt very, very proud!

Soon all the Seven were sitting down in the shed, talking. They wondered how the Bolans were getting on in their caravan. They wondered if Matt had remembered to take up a bottle of milk when he called for his own that morning. Then George asked Jack if Susie and Binkie knew he had come to the meeting.

'No. I slipped off when they were climbing trees in the garden,' said Jack. 'They keep *on* singing that silly song about us. I tried to remember the one that Colin made up about Binkie, but I couldn't. How does it go, Colin?'

But before Colin could tell him, someone came up to their door and rapped on it.

'Who's there?' called Peter. 'You can't come in unless you know the password. We're holding a meeting.'

'It's me, Matt the shepherd,' said a voice, and Peter opened the door at once. Matt stood there, looking rather cross.

'Have any of you been taking the clothes off that old scarecrow I dressed out in the field for the master?' he said. 'The crows are down there in their hundreds! They don't take fright at a turnip head and sticks – it's only when a scarecrow's dressed and looks like a man that they keep away.'

'No. No, of course we haven't taken the clothes!' said Peter, astonished. 'We wouldn't dream of it!'

'Well – you see if you can find out who did!' said Matt. 'I'll have to tell your father about it this evening. You just find out for me, will you?' And away he tramped, leaving the Seven too astonished for words. Now, WHO would do a silly thing like that?

Nine

Crash!

THE Secret Seven looked at each other in astonishment. 'Why, we saw the old scarecrow yesterday,' said Peter. 'There was a rook on his head – so the birds can't be as scared of him as old Matt said!'

'But who could have taken the clothes?' said Jack. 'I mean – they were pretty old and torn, weren't they?'

'Well, the scarecrow has worn them for a long time,' said Janet. 'I wouldn't have thought they were much good for *any*one!'

'They wouldn't be worth a single penny,' said Peter. 'I must say I'm surprised at Matt thinking *we*'d had anything to do with it!'

'Well, we did once do something silly with a scarecrow,' said Janet. 'Don't you remember? We planted some seeds in our own little gardens, and when the birds came and pecked them up we fetched an old scarecrow out of the wheat-field and stood him in the middle of our own seeds! Daddy was very cross – but Mother said we hadn't meant any harm, we were too little then to understand.'

The others laughed at the picture of Janet and Peter dragging a scarecrow all the way to their own small gardens. 'All the same – I expect that's why Matt thought it was you,' said Colin.

'I suppose – I suppose it couldn't be Susie and Binkie, could it?' asked George.

Everyone thought it was very likely! 'It's just the silly sort of thing they *would* do,' said Jack. 'They would think it very, very funny – and they'd know we'd be questioned and feel jolly puzzled.'

'Well – you'd better ask Susie about it,' said Peter to Jack. 'And if she starts giggling and won't say anything, just say you'll report to *us* and we'll take the matter in hand, as we have been asked to find the clothes.'

'Yes. That sounds very official,' said Jack approvingly. 'I must say it would be a good idea if Colin finished his poem about Binkie, and even made one up about Susie. Those two want taking down a peg.'

'Well, to change the subject,' said Peter. 'Does anyone want to go to the cinema tonight? Janet and I are going, and we'd love to have some of the Secret Seven with us.'

'I can't come,' said Jack. 'If I ask about it, Mother will say that Susie and Binkie are to go too. And I'm *not* going to sit beside two giggly girls all the evening.'

'And I can't come,' said Pam. 'Barbara and I are going out to tea with a friend.'

'I could come,' said Colin, and George nodded his head too. 'That would be four of us. We'll meet you at the cinema, five minutes before the film starts. What about the scarecrow clothes now? Do we bother to look about for them, or not?'

'Not till Jack has asked Susie and Binkie if they know anything,' said Peter, getting up. 'Well, that's the end of this meeting. I'll let you all know when there's another. I wish something exciting would happen – *not* like that. horrid fire, though!'

That evening Janet and Peter met the other two at the cinema, paid for their tickets, and went in. It was a good film, and they all enjoyed it. They sat it out to the end and then left the cinema. It was a very dark night, with not a star to be seen.

Peter and Janet were on bicycles, but the other two were walking. 'Good-bye!' said the two cyclists and went off in the darkness, their lamps sending a wavering light in front of them.

Colin and George walked off slowly, talking as they went. All the shops were shut, but some were still lighted, so that, although shut, their goods might still be displayed to any passer-by. The boys looked into them as they passed.

The bicycle shop was lighted up, and they stopped to admire the new racing bicycle in the middle of the window. The next lighted shop was an antique shop, which sold all kinds of interesting things – old pictures, ornaments, tea-sets, musical instruments, chairs, and other furniture.

The boys stopped to look at a picture of a long-ago battle, and then walked on again. At the corner Colin suddenly exclaimed, in panic, 'I say – I believe I've lost my watch. Blow! I *shall* get into a row. Do you mind if we walk back and look for it, George? I might have dropped it in the cinema, of course.'

The boys turned and went back very slowly, George's torch lighting up the pavement, as they hunted for the watch. And then the torch flickered faintly – and went out, leaving them in black darkness.

'Look at that now – the battery's gone just when we needed the torch!' groaned Colin. 'Why didn't I bring mine as well? We can't look for the watch in this darkness, that's certain.'

Someone passed them, walking softly in the road, not seeing the two boys standing still on the dark pavement, messing about with the useless torch. He passed so silently that the boys jumped.

'He walked as quietly as a policeman!' said George. 'I say – what about going after him, and if he *is* a policeman, we'll report the loss of your watch – then if anyone takes it to the police-station it will be returned to you at once – before you get into a row about it!'

'Good idea!' said Colin, and they went after the silent passer-by. They could just make him out in the distance as he passed a lighted shop.

They were almost up to him as he came near to the lighted antique shop, and were just about to call out to him, when he stopped and looked all round him in a curiously cautious manner.

'He's not a policeman after all,' said Colin. 'I say – what's he doing?'

Things then happened very quickly indeed! The man took something from beneath his coat and threw it at the lighted window of the old antique shop!

CRASH!

The glass splintered at once, and fragments flew all about, glittering in the light from the shop window. The horrified boys saw the man snatch at something in the window and then race off with it at top speed.

He passed by them, and Colin put out a foot to stop him. But the man swerved and raced on, passing under a nearby lamp-post, and then disappearing into the night.

'After him!' shouted George, and they tore round the corner where the man had gone. But he was nowhere to be seen in the darkness – and certainly could not be heard, for his tread had been absolutely silent.

What an excitement there was then! The crash of breaking glass brought people flocking into the street, shouting and calling. A policeman appeared as if by magic – and someone ran out of the antique shop, joining

in the clamour. Good gracious! Colin and George had
certainly got something to tell the Secret Seven!

Ten

Very surprising

COLIN and George ran up to the antique shop. The little man who owned it was wringing his hands as he saw his smashed windows, and everything inside covered with broken glass.

'What's all this?' said the big policeman, looming up silently, and taking out a notebook. 'Who did this?'

'A man,' said someone. 'I just caught sight of him across the road. I couldn't tell you what he was like, though. He raced off at once.'

'What's been taken, sir?' said the policeman to the shopkeeper.

'Oh, that I can't say till I've had a good look,' said the man. 'My word – that picture's done for – that battle picture. The flying glass has cut it to bits – and the brick has smashed that lovely old vase. I don't rightly know what was in the window, sir, till I ask my assistant. He did the window for me yesterday, when I was away. Oh my word, what a mess!'

There was quite a crowd now, round the shop, and soon another policeman came. Colin and George wondered if they ought to say that they, too, had seen the man smash the window, and were just screwing up their courage to do so, when one of the policemen saw that there were a few children in the crowd.

'You get off home,' he said sternly. 'Go on now. You can't help us, you only hinder us. Clear off!'

Colin and George slipped away at once. They had seen

242

all they wanted to, and they were pretty sure that they couldn't give much help. Also, they didn't much like the thought of being stared at by so many people if they went up to the policemen and spoke to them. Why, some of them might think that they had smashed the window, and were owning up!

'We MUST get Peter to call a meeting tomorrow and tell the Secret Seven about this,' panted George as they ran home. 'I don't expect we can *do* anything. But I think we *ought* to tell the others.'

Colin agreed. Anyway, it would be most exciting to relate the story to them! How he wished he and George had managed to trip the man up, and perhaps catch him. What a thrill *that* would have been!

Colin telephoned to Peter the next morning. 'Peter – is that you? Listen, George and I saw a thief smash a window coming home from the cinema last night and steal something out of the antique shop. We actually *saw* the man. Do you think we could have a meeting about it? It's really very exciting.'

'My word – did you actually *see* him?' said Peter. 'Dad heard about it from his cowman, and told us at breakfast – and Janet and I groaned because we thought we'd been just too early to see it happen.'

'Well, we had to go back to see if we could find my watch,' said Colin. 'If we hadn't done that we'd have missed all the excitement. What time shall we come to the meeting, Peter? George and I can go round and tell the others now, if you like.'

'Right. Well, bring them along as soon as possible,' said Peter. 'Janet and I will be waiting down in the shed.'

It was quite an excited group of children who met in the shed some time later. All of them had heard of the smashing of the window, but nobody except Pam knew what had been stolen.

She listened quietly to the story told by Colin and George, as did the others. Peter and Janet wished that Colin had discovered that his watch was missing before he had said good-bye to them – then they, too, would have seen the excitement.

'Actually,' said Colin, 'I *hadn't* lost my watch, after all! I found it on my dressing-table when I got home!'

'*Did* you?' said George. 'Gosh – and to think how we searched every inch of the pavement! By the way, does anyone know if the man has been caught yet?'

'Not so far,' said Peter. 'My father had to see the police this morning about a dog that's worrying our sheep – and the policeman told him they hadn't the foggiest idea who the thief was – or why the man wanted to steal anything from the antique shop. Dad didn't hear what was stolen, however. Does anyone know?'

'Yes, *I* know,' said Pam at once. 'It was a very, very old violin, worth hundreds of pounds! It was in the very front of the window, with a card telling its history. The man took that, and the bow too!'

'Ah – he must be a violinist, then,' said Peter, saying what everyone was thinking. 'They'll be checking on all the local violinists, I expect.'

'I hope they won't question Miss Hilbrun, the violin teacher at our school!' said Pam. 'She's a wonderful player – but I'm sure she would go into a dead faint if a policeman wanted to ask her questions. She even had to go and sit down for half an hour once, in the middle of teaching, because someone let the piano-lid drop with a bang!'

'I bet you were the one that did that,' said Jack.

'I was not. It was your sister Susie,' said Pam. 'You might have guessed that! Oh dear – it really makes me smile to think of our mouse-like Miss Hilbrun throwing a brick into a window to steal a violin!'

'Listen, George and Colin,' said Peter. 'According to the policeman Dad spoke to this morning when he was reporting that dog, nobody seemed to know exactly how the man was dressed or what he looked like. Did *you* happen to notice? You ought to have done, because that's one of the rules of the Secret Seven – always to be observant, and keep our eyes open.'

'Well – yes – I think I can tell you more or less what he looked like,' said George, though Colin looked rather blank. 'I can't say that I actually noted it all – but I did get a jolly good view of him in the bright light from the window, just as he smashed it – a sort of quick photograph of him in my mind, if you know what I mean.'

'Tell us, then,' said Peter, taking out his notebook. 'It might be jolly useful. We could look out for him if we know, for instance, what he's wearing.'

'Well – he was medium size,' said George, half-shutting his eyes to picture the man in his mind. 'And he had a very torn old coat of brown tweed – *very* torn. And trousers that were a kind of light grey and very dirty. And a black hat with a hole in it. And, oh yes – a scarf round his neck with red-and-white spots.'

Peter gave a loud exclamation. 'George! Do you know what you've just described EXACTLY? The clothes that were stolen from the *scarecrow*!'

Eleven

A very interesting meeting

THE Secret Seven stared at Peter in the utmost amazement. What! The violin thief had been dressed in the clothes stolen from the scarecrow? But WHY?

'You don't suppose it was the *scarecrow* who stole out in the night and took the violin, do you?' said Pam, with one of her sudden giggles.

'Don't be silly. You know the scarecrow hasn't any clothes now – unless Matt has found some more for him,' said Janet.

'This is very, very interesting,' said Peter slowly. 'It certainly rules out jokers like Susie or Binkie.'

'Well, I *did* ask them,' said Jack, 'and honestly I couldn't make out whether they knew anything about the scarecrow's clothes or not, they giggled so. I half thought they *did*, as a matter of fact.'

'Well, they couldn't have. They were just pulling your leg,' said Peter. 'Now let's think carefully about this, and if anyone has a sensible remark, please make it. We know two things – one, that a man stole a very valuable old violin last night – and two, that for some reason he wore old clothes belonging to a scarecrow. Now what do we make of that?'

'Well, if the violin was old and valuable, and was obviously the one thing he had made up his mind to steal, it's clear that he must have been a violinist himself, or know about the value of old ones,' said Colin at once. 'The odds are that he is a musician, if not a violinist.'

'And he wore those awful old clothes as a disguise so that if he were seen he couldn't possibly be recognized,' said Barbara.

'And he didn't want to buy them at an old clothes shop or borrow them from any tramp, in case of questions being asked,' said Jack.

'So he spotted our scarecrow and took the clothes from *him*!' said Peter. 'And presumably he will throw them away now or hide them somewhere.'

'He might put them on the scarecrow again,' suggested George.

'No. He'd be afraid that it might be watched,' said Peter. 'Anyway, it's sure to be dressed up again now. No – he'll either burn or bury those clothes.'

'We could look for them – only we'd probably never find them!' said Janet. 'I mean – there's the whole countryside to hide them in!'

'Yes, that's true,' said Peter. 'Well – has anyone any other suggestion?'

Nobody had. It seemed impossible to hunt for a violinist they didn't know who had been dressed in clothes he had probably already hidden away!

'Do we know any first-class violinists who would love a valuable old violin?' asked Pam hopefully.

'Well, yes we do,' said Peter, 'but none of them would dress up in scarecrow clothes and smash a shop-window. I mean, there's old Mr Scraper at school, who teaches the violin – but I can't possibly imagine him doing things like that. Or Mr Luton, our churchwarden – he plays the violin too, so does his wife. But they wouldn't go about smashing windows. No – it must be someone a bit mad, I think, who has an urge to steal and use a really precious old violin.'

'But yet sensible enough to use the scarecrow's clothes as a disguise!' said Jack.

'Yes. Well, it's a puzzle. I don't really see that there's anything we can do to solve it at the moment,' said Peter.

'Except look out for old clothes stuffed in a ditch or a bush, or buried somewhere.'

Scamper suddenly began to bark loudly, and everyone looked up. 'I bet that's Susie,' said Jack, in disgust. 'We've got to go and see my granny this morning, and Susie said she'd call for me here. I *told* her not to! Interrupting our meeting!'

The rude Secret Seven song came on the air at that moment, sung lustily by two voices – Susie's and Binkie's.

> 'Oh see the Secret Seven,
> So very smug and pi,
> Eyes turned up to Heaven,
> When they come walking by!
> They think . . .'

Colin flew to the door and opened it. He sang at the top of *his* voice – and he had a really loud one –

> 'Oh Binkie has the habit
> Of a silly little rabbit,
> Twitching up and down her little nose!
> And in her mouth beneath
> Are lots of rabbit teeth
> And that's the way a little Binkie grows!'

The Secret Seven listened in delight. That would serve Binkie right for making up such a horrid poem about *them*! They hadn't heard the end of the poem before, because Colin had only thought of it that very minute!

Susie marched right up to Colin, red in the face with anger.

'You've made Binkie cry with that song!' she said. 'How dare you? I'll pay you out, you Secret Seven, for making up such an unkind song about my best friend.'

'Well, Binkie started it, with her rude Secret Seven

song,' said Colin stoutly. But all the same he felt rather
ashamed of making Binkie cry. Perhaps it *was* rather an
unkind song.

'Jack, you're to come now,' ordered Susie. 'Granny will
be waiting for us.'

'All right, all right. Don't order me about,' said Jack.
He turned to the others. 'What about this afternoon?' he
said. 'Are we going anywhere?'

'We might go up and have a look to see how the gingerbread woman, Mrs Bolan, is getting on in her caravan,'
said Peter. 'Mother has given us some baby clothes to take
up, and I thought I'd take my old toy bus for Benny.'

'Right. I'll be along about half-past two. Is that all
right?' asked Jack.

'Make it three,' said Peter, and the others nodded.
'We'll keep an eye open for scarecrow clothes on the way,'
he added, lowering his voice.

'*I* heard you,' said Susie, at once. 'And what's more, I
know you and the others think that Binkie and I were the
idiots who took the scarecrow clothes, but we didn't. Jack
asked us about them. It's just about time you Secret Seven
made a mistake about something! You think you're too
clever for words. So look out – else you'll be sorry!' And
away she went with Binkie.

'Now what exactly does she mean by *that*?' said
Peter.

249

Twelve

Scamper makes a find

AT about three o'clock that afternoon the Secret Seven set off through the fields to go to visit the Bolans' caravan. Scamper raced along with them as usual.

'We shall pass the scarecrow on the way,' said Colin. 'I wonder what he's wearing now?'

He was fully dressed again, in a curious collection of clothes. He wore a woman's hat with a feather in – a raincoat full of holes, and old macintosh trousers, very torn. He stood there looking rather forlorn and ashamed of himself.

Janet gave a squeal of laughter when she saw his hat.

'That's the hat that the cowman's wife used to wear in church!' she said. 'I've often and often watched that feather waggling in it when she fell asleep on a hot Sunday!'

'And those trousers belong to the cowman,' said Peter. 'He must have got a new pair. I think the macintosh is the shepherd's. My word – the old scarecrow looks peculiar now, doesn't he? Hi, Scarecrow! Where are your other clothes?'

The scarecrow flapped his sleeves dismally and didn't answer! They left him standing sadly in the field, and went on towards the Bolans' caravan, up by Matt the shepherd's hut.

On the way they had to pass over a small bridge across a gurgling stream. Scamper, hearing the water, ran joyfully ahead. Now he could get a drink!

But he stopped before he came to the little stream and

began to sniff about in a ditch in the greatest excitement.

'What's up, Scamper?' called Peter. 'What are you scrabbling at?'

Scamper was certainly excited. He barked, and scraped vigorously with his front paws. The Secret Seven came up to him and looked down in amusement. Then Janet gave a little cry.

'Peter! Look – what's that sticking out of the hole he's made? It looks like a bit of cloth. Oh, PETER! It couldn't be the scarecrow clothes, could it?'

'Well – this does look a bit like old grey flannel – and we know that the scarecrow's trousers *were* flannels!' said Peter, feeling a little surge of excitement welling up inside him. 'Go on, Scamper. Find it, then, find it!'

Scamper scraped at top speed, flinging out earth behind him, and covering the Seven with it. Soon he had got firm hold of whatever was there, and tugged it right out in triumph.

'Wuff!' he said. 'Wuff, wuff, wuff!'

Peter picked up the piece of grey flannel. It didn't look like trousers. It looked more like a torn piece of skirt. He looked down at Scamper, who was busy burrowing again in the hole he had made, giving little whines of excitement.

'He's got something else there,' said Jack. 'Maybe the old hat.'

Yes – in half a minute Scamper brought up an old hat – but what a hat! It was a very old straw one, with a ribbon round it – a ribbon that Pam recognized only too well!

'Peter! That's one of our old school hats and the school ribbon we wear at our school! This hat has never been on any scarecrow! Whatever does it all mean?'

'Wuff!' said Scamper again, in delight, and put his nose right into the hole he had made. He brought out a large and extremely smelly bone, which he proudly laid at Peter's feet.

'Good gracious!' said Peter, amazed. 'So that's why you dug down there – you smelt the bone! But why in the world did anyone bury the . . .'

And just then there came the sound of someone exploding into laughter. What an explosion that was! The Seven turned at once – and there were Susie and Binkie, rolling about on a bank of grass, behind which they had been spying on the excited Seven!

'Oh, I'll die of laughing! Oh, I can't bear it! Oh Scamper, you're a perfect wonder! Oh, I've got such a stitch in my side!'

That was Susie, of course. She went off into a cascade of laughs again, and Binkie joined her, shouting out just like Susie.

'Oh did you see their faces when they found your old school hat, Susie? Oh, I'm dying of laughing! I can't laugh any more, I'm crying with laughter! Oh, that smelly old bone! Good old Scamper!'

Scamper couldn't make out why Susie and Binkie were rolling about and squealing. He thought they must be hurt, and he put his tail down and ran over to them, whining.

'Come back, Scamper,' said Peter, and Scamper ran back, surprised at Peter's stern voice.

'I suppose you think this is funny,' began Peter, calling to the two girls. 'Well . . .'

'Oh yes, we do think it's funny!' laughed Susie, wiping her eyes. 'The funniest thing that ever happened. You were all so solemn!'

'Oh come on – let's leave them to their silly giggling,' said Jack furiously, and the Seven walked with great dignity to the little stream and crossed the bridge. But after a little while Pam gave a sudden giggle. She looked round apologetically.

'Sorry,' she said. 'But honestly it *was* rather funny.' And she gave another little giggle.

Barbara couldn't help joining in. 'We must have looked funny, poring over a bit of Susie's old school skirt and her old school hat,' she said, and began to laugh.

And then, of course, everyone saw the funny side, and they roared with laughter, just as Susie and Binkie had. Oh dear – how easily they had been taken in!

'It was really rather clever of them to think of burying the bone at the *bottom* of the hole, and putting the other things on top,' said Janet. 'I mean – they must have planned it very well, really. They knew we were coming up here . . .'

'And that old Scamper would smell the bone, and scrape a hole,' said Jack. 'And that we'd get all excited to see the piece of cloth there. Oh dear — we were properly taken in. Well, they've paid us back all right.'

'Here we are, almost at the caravan,' said Peter. 'And there's Mrs Bolan, look, doing some washing outside. Hallo, Mrs Bolan!'

Thirteen

An odd little boy

MRS BOLAN looked up as the children came towards her.

'Well, it's nice to see you,' she said, smiling her nice smile. 'Oh – what's that you've brought me, miss? What a lovely little coat – and a little dress too. The baby won't know herself!'

'And I brought this for Benny,' said Peter, producing the bus. 'Where is he?'

'Somewhere about,' said his mother, and called: 'Benny! Where are you, love? Benny, there's a present for you.'

But no Benny appeared. 'He's hiding,' said his mother. 'He's scared of visitors.'

'Doesn't he go to school?' asked Pam, looking all round for the little boy. 'Or is he too young?'

'He's eight,' said Mrs Bolan. 'He's never been to school. He wouldn't like it, and it wouldn't be any good. Poor Benny – he hasn't had much luck in his life. Oh land's sake, look at that baby now, hanging half out of her pram! What I'll do with her when she can walk, I *don't* know. But there, maybe Benny will look after her – he loves his little sister.'

The girls wandered off to look inside the caravan. It looked cosy and comfortable, but not very tidy or very clean.

'Did we give you everything you needed?' asked Janet. 'We tried to think of everything.'

'Yes, love – all except needles and cottons!' said Mrs

Bolan, laughing. 'You wouldn't believe how much I've wanted those – to run up little curtains for the windows, and to mend up my clothes – these I stand in are the only ones I've got – all the others were burnt.'

'Oh – we never even thought of needles and cottons – or scissors either,' said Janet. 'I expect you wanted scissors too didn't you, Mrs Bolan?'

'Oh yes – but Luke left me his penknife,' said Mrs Bolan, squeezing out her washing. 'And Matt the shepherd is good to me – he brings me other little things, you know.'

'We'll come up again as soon as we can, Mrs Bolan,' promised Janet, 'and bring you a small work-basket. I never use my old one; you can have that. Is there anything else?'

'Well, I suppose you haven't an old bucket to spare, have you?' asked Mrs Bolan. 'You did bring one, but Benny's gone off with it, bless his heart. He plays little tunes on it with a stick – he's clever at that, and it keeps him happy, poor lamb.'

'Yes, we'll bring you a bucket too,' said Peter. 'As soon as we can. Listen – what's that noise?'

'Oh, that's Benny with his bucket!' said Mrs Bolan. 'Sounds quite like music, doesn't it! Dinga-dinga-dong-dong, dinga-dinga-dong-dong! Benny, you bring me my bucket!'

There was silence after that, and Mrs Bolan shook her head. 'No good going after him,' she said. 'He'll hide himself somewhere, and keep as still as a rabbit in its burrow.'

'Is your husband still down at the fair?' asked Peter.

'The fair's moved on,' she answered. 'Didn't you know? Luke's gone with it. It moved off this morning, and Luke

255

won't be back with me for a few days. I shall miss him, up here alone on the hills. But old Matt there, he keeps coming to see if I'm all right!'

Janet thought she was a brave, cheerful, and generous little woman. She remembered how she had given them a batch of her hot gingerbread at the fair, when they had no money to pay for it.

'There's Benny!' said Jack suddenly, and beckoned to the small boy, who took no notice at all. He had appeared beside some gorse bushes, and stood staring across at them, scarcely blinking his great dark eyes.

'There now – you see he's hidden that bucket of mine somewhere, just as I said!' said Mrs Bolan. 'Benny, you come over here. There's a lovely present for you, a beauty. It's a bus! You come and get it.'

Benny stood quite silent, still staring. The children thought him a very odd little boy indeed, but he was a striking and lovely child, and Janet longed to give him a hug. He began to walk over to them, slowly and carefully, as if afraid of falling. He stopped fairly near and stared towards them again.

Peter went over to him with the bus. He held it out, but the child made no attempt to take it. So Peter put it gently into his hands, and at once the boy clutched it, and ran his fingers all over it in delight.

When he found the little hooter that said 'Toot-toot!' his whole face lighted up and he smiled sweetly.

'Toot-toot-toot!' he sang, in a tuneful little voice. 'It's a bus, Mammy, a bus. Is it for me, Mammy?'

'Yes, for you,' said his mother. 'Say thank you nicely to the young gentleman.'

'Thank you,' said Benny, looking at George, instead of at Peter. Janet thought he had the strangest eyes she had ever seen, dark, beautiful, and deep, but without any expression at all.

Scamper ran up and pushed his head against Benny's leg. Benny backed away, half scared, and Peter called Scamper to him. Benny went off back to the bushes, carrying his precious bus.

'Goo!' said the baby, bouncing up and down in her pram. 'Goo-goo!' She wanted attention too, and Janet went over to her at once. She was as lively as Benny was quiet. She put her fat little hand against Janet's cheek.

'She likes you,' said Mrs Bolan, smiling. 'Now stop bouncing, you little monkey, or you'll have the springs out of that old pram!'

'It's time to go,' said Peter, looking at his watch. 'Mrs Bolan, we'll bring you a bucket, and needles and cotton and any other little thing we can think of as soon as we can! I'm so glad you like the caravan.'

'Oh, it's fine,' said Mrs Bolan cheerfully. She was now pegging up clothes on a line that stretched from one tree to another. 'Thank you for coming.'

The Seven went off together, with Scamper trotting in front, sniffing at everything. When he came to the hole where the bone had been he remembered that he had left his precious, magnificent bone up at the caravan site, and bounded back to fetch it.

'Well, I'm glad we went up there,' said Janet. 'But Benny puzzles me. What a queer little boy – and I really do think he ought to go to school. He's eight! I'll tell Mother about him, and perhaps she can arrange something.'

'Here comes Scamper again,' said Peter. 'Pooh, take that bone away from me, Scamper – it's the smelliest, nastiest one I've ever known!'

Fourteen

Something very queer

Two days went by, and the Seven were very busy with all kinds of things. Peter and Janet lime-washed the hen-houses for their father, with Scamper watching in great interest.

'You look a bit peculiar, Scamper – splashed with white from the lime-wash drips,' said Janet. 'Why *must* you sit exactly under where we're working – you get all the splashes!'

George was busy too, with Colin, rigging a fine ship they had made together. Jack was helping at home. The two girls, Pam and Barbara, were earning a little money by weeding onion beds.

'Horrible job!' Pam told Peter, when she saw him. 'The weeds *will* grow all tangled up with the onion stems, and we keep pulling up tiny onions with the weeds, and have to replant them! Still – we earn five pence an hour!'

They often spoke about the stolen violin, especially Colin and George, who spent a good deal of time together on the ship. It was they who had seen the window being smashed, of course, and it was interesting to talk about such an exciting happening.

'It rather looks as if this business about the stolen violin is fading out,' Colin said to George. 'My father asked the police if they'd heard anything about it, or had an idea of who the thief was, but they hadn't.'

'Well, they won't now,' said George. 'The man's gone off with it. I expect he's a hundred miles away!'

Peter and Janet finished their job in the hen-houses, and

258

decided to take a day off.

'We think we'll go for a walk, Mother,' said Peter. 'May we have sandwiches?'

'Yes, dear. I'll make you some,' said his mother. 'If you're going near old Matt the shepherd, take him this letter, will you? It didn't come till after he'd fetched his milk this morning.'

'Right,' said Peter. 'We'll go to the woods, I think, and see how far the bluebells are up, and have our picnic there – and then we'll go home over the hill where Matt has his sheep.'

'And we'll look in on the Bolans,' said Janet. 'I love that little baby. Oh Mother, can you give me an old pair of scissors, please? I promised Mrs Bolan I'd take her a pair, and some needles too. You did send a bucket up by Matt, didn't you?'

'No. Matt said she could borrow his,' said Mother. 'Anyhow till that monkey of a boy brings back the pail we sent before.'

'He's not a monkey at all,' said Janet, remembering the big-eyed, solemn little boy. 'He's a queer little fellow. He only took the bucket to play tunes on!'

The children set off with their sandwiches, Scamper running joyfully ahead. It was a wonderful day again, and the sun was as hot as June. Primroses nestled every-where, and little wild anemones danced gaily in shady corners. Janet skipped along happily.

'It's lovely to have a day all to ourselves after sticking to that lime-washing job for hour after hour,' she said. 'I wonder if any bluebells will be out. It's terribly early, but you never know.'

The woods were full of springing bluebell leaves, their long green spikes standing guard over the flowers pushing

up between them. Janet found one flower right out, its
bells a lovely blue.

'Here's one! And another! Oh, I wish we could find a
white one. That's so very, very lucky!'

'Better not pick any,' said Peter. 'They would only be dead by the time we get home!'

They had their lunch in the bluebell wood, with the blackbirds and thrushes singing loudly overhead, and a little robin hopping round their feet, waiting for a crumb. Then they went on again, climbing the hills to where Matt the shepherd kept his sheep.

He wasn't in his hut, so they left his letter there, and then went across to where the Bolans had their caravan, a little way off. But that was shut too, and no one was about, not even Benny.

'The sheep are on the opposite hill today,' said Peter, sitting down on the grass. 'What a lot Dad's got now, hasn't he? And how the lambs have grown!'

'It must be rather nice to be a shepherd up on the hills, living by himself with the sheep and the lambs he loves,' said Janet, sitting down beside him. 'Oh look – isn't that old Matt coming up the path over there? And his dog too!'

It was. He smiled when he saw them, and his eyes shone as blue as the sky. Janet wondered why so many people who lived in the open air had such very blue eyes. She ran to meet the old shepherd and slipped her hand into his hard, horny one.

'Well, missie, 'tis nice to see you and your dog,' said Matt, leaning on his big crook. ' 'Tisn't often old Matt has visitors. Me and my dog here, we don't see much company.'

'What about the Bolans? You see them, don't you?' asked Peter.

'Oh yes – and Mrs Bolan is a right kind woman,' said Matt. 'I haven't seen her husband. He comes home at odd times, mostly late at night. He works in the fairs, you know. But that boy Benny – he's a queer little fellow, now.

Sits and stares at nothing for hours! It's my belief he's not right in the head.'

'Oh dear!' said Janet. 'Perhaps that's why he doesn't go to school, then. Poor little boy.'

'I'd like to set him on my knee and tell him a tale,' said Matt. 'But as soon as he hears anyone coming he's off like a frightened rabbit. I'm wondering if he was scared last night, if he heard what I heard!'

'Why? What did you hear?' asked Peter, in surprise.

'I don't rightly know, young sir,' said Matt, screwing up his wrinkled forehead. 'I were in my hut, half asleep, when I heard it. It was about half-past nine, and a dark night too! What a wailing it was! What a sad, sad noise! It rose up and down, up and down, till I couldn't bear it and went out on the hillside to see if some animal was in pain – and yet it sounded like no living thing. But there was nothing there. As soon as I called out, the wailing stopped.'

Peter and Janet listened in astonishment. What a queer tale! Wailing? Who would be wailing? And why?

'The noise went high and it went low,' said Matt. 'I never did hear such wailing before. It fair went through me, and gripped my heart. I were right down glad when it stopped!'

'Do you think it will come tonight?' asked Peter. Matt shook his head.

'How do I know? Mebbe – and mebbe not. I asked Mrs Bolan about it this morning, and she said she hadn't heard anything. But it were wailing all right!'

'Janet, I'm going to get Jack to come up here and listen with me tonight!' said Peter, as Matt got up to fetch his pipe. 'Wailing! That's something very queer. We'll find out what it is!'

Fifteen

Up on the hills at night

PETER and Janet longed to tell the others this new, queer piece of news. They raced down the hill, with Scamper at their heels.

They passed Jack's house on the way and called in to see him. He was having a jigsaw competition with Susie and Binkie, who at once began to chant the Secret Seven song under their breath. Most annoying!

'Jack, can you spare a moment?' asked Peter. 'We've some rather queer news.'

'What is it?' asked Susie at once, her quick, bird-like eyes staring brightly at Peter.

'I'm afraid it's Secret Seven news,' said Peter coldly. 'Can you come, Jack? You can finish your jigsaw afterwards.'

'Yes, of course,' said Jack, and got up. 'Back in a few minutes,' he said to Susie and Binkie and marched out with Peter and Janet.

'I'm glad you came,' he said, taking them into another room. 'Mother has made me play with those two girls all day. Oooh – girls! What a bore they are.'

'Thank you very much, Jack,' said Janet indignantly. 'Perhaps I'd better go, and leave you with Peter.'

'No. No, of course not!' said Jack, in alarm. 'I didn't mean *you*. You're fine. It's just those two that get on my nerves.'

Peter snorted. 'Fat-heads,' he said. 'They must lead you an awful life, Jack. But listen, I want you to do something with me tonight. It's not exactly to do with anything the

Secret Seven have been working on, but it's rather queer.'

He told Jack what Matt had said. Jack was amazed. 'He must have been dreaming, don't you think?' he said. 'I mean – what would go wailing out on those hills? If it was an animal, caught in a trap or something, poor thing, old Matt would recognize its wail or howl. If it's something he couldn't place he *must* have been dreaming!'

'I didn't think of that,' said Peter. 'Of course, it might have been a dream – but he said he got up and went out of his hut and still heard it. It stopped when he called out, though.'

'When he woke up, I expect!' said Jack, with a grin.

'Well – perhaps it's not worth bothering about,' said Peter, rather downcast.

'I think it is – and if you don't go, I shall get Pam and Barbara, and we'll go,' said Janet unexpectedly.

The two boys looked at her in surprise.

'No,' said Jack at once. 'It's not right for girls to go by themselves up on the hills at night. 'I'll go with Peter, of course I will. Shall we ask Colin and George, Peter?'

'Yes. We'll make a sort of adventure of it,' said Peter, pleased. Then, as Janet opened her mouth to argue, he frowned. 'And don't you start asking if you and the other two girls can come, Janet, because you CAN'T!'

'All right, all right,' said Janet, looking rather sulky. How tiresome to be a girl and kept out of so many exciting things!

The boys quickly arranged everything. Jack said he would go round and tell Colin and George, and they would all be outside Peter's front gate as soon as it was dark.

'Bring torches, for goodness' sake,' said Peter. 'There's

no moon, and if it's a cloudy night it will be as dark as pitch.'

'Come on – we'd better get back home,' said Janet, looking at her watch. 'We're late for tea already.'

They went quickly out of the room – and heard a stifled giggle. They stopped indignantly.

'Have those two girls been listening?' demanded Peter. 'We shut the door. Surely they aren't mean enough to listen through the keyhole?'

'Susie and Binkie would do *any*thing,' said Jack desperately, and raced after the giggles that could still be heard in the distance.

Peter was very cross, and so was Janet. Why ever hadn't they gone into a corner of the garden, where nobody could possibly hear a word? Well, the only blessing was that they had spoken in fairly low voices, so perhaps Susie and Binkie hadn't heard anything much.

Jack went round to tell Colin and George, and to see if they would like to join in the little adventure. They both laughed at the 'wailing' old Matt had heard, but said they would certainly come.

'We *were* going to the cinema tonight, but we'll come with you and Peter instead,' said Colin.

'Half-past seven outside Peter's front gate,' said Jack. 'No bikes. We'll have to walk up those hills – and let's hope the scarecrow doesn't chase us when we pass his field!'

'It was a funny business about his clothes, wasn't it?' said Colin. 'We never found out anything about those – they just vanished. Right, Jack – you can count on us.'

So, when it was nice and dark, the four boys met outside Peter's gate. Janet was there too, to see them off. 'I *wish* I could come,' she said, still hopeful that she might.

265

But it was no good! The boys said good-bye and strode off up the dark lane, leaving poor Scamper behind too.

It took them some time to get up to where old Matt had his hut.

'We won't let him know we're here, in case he's cross about it,' said Peter, in a low voice. 'I vote we sit down behind this bush. I wonder if Matt is in his hut.'

'Yes. I can see a crack of light,' said George. 'He's there all right. Now, we'd better sit absolutely still and quiet, so that the wailer won't guess we're listening or watching.'

So the four boys sat there in utter silence, jumping once when an owl gave a sudden hoot, and straining their ears when some small creature ran over the grass.

And then suddenly the wailing began! Good gracious! What a horrible noise! Woooooo-ooh! Waaaaa-ah! Eeeeeeeeee! The boys clutched one another, their hearts thumping violently.

'It sounds right behind our bush!' whispered Peter. 'Let's creep round and shine our torches!'

'Woooooo-oooh! Waaaaa-ah! Eeeeeeeee!'

'Now – quick!' said Peter, and round the bush they went.

Sixteen

The strange wailing

THE four boys switched on their torches as they stumbled round the great gorse bush – and almost before they got there, they heard another noise – *not* a wail – which filled them with surprise and anger.

They shone their torches on two figures crouching there, both holding their sides with laughter.

'Susie! Binkie! You beasts!' cried Jack, in horror and anger. 'You listened to what Peter said this morning. You've spoilt EVERYTHING!'

'Was our wailing good?' asked Susie, half-choking with laughter. 'Did old Matt hear us too? And the Bolans? We call ourselves the Weird and Wonderful Wailers – did you know?'

A tall figure suddenly loomed up in the light of the four torches. It was Matt the shepherd.

'What's this?' he said sternly. 'What are you children doing here at this time of night? What was all that yelling?'

'It wasn't yelling – it was Binkie and I wailing,' said Susie. 'Didn't you hear it last night, Matt?'

'What I heard last night wasn't made by any silly child,' said Matt solemnly. 'You be off before the *real* wailing starts. Yes, all of you. And you, Miss Susie, I'll tell your father of you, so I will. Coming up here in the dark of night!'

'Oh no – please don't tell Dad,' said Susie, really alarmed, and got up in a hurry.

'Come on, Susie,' said Binkie, feeling scared by the stern shepherd. 'Quick!'

And she ran off down the hillside, shining her torch in front of her, Susie following close behind. Jack went after them. 'Wait for me, you idiots. You'll get lost. SUSIE! Wait for me! I'll take you home.'

'You be off too, lads,' said Matt, to the other three. 'If so be as you should hear what *I* heard, you'll be tearing down the hill as if a hundred dogs were after you. Now go. Good night to you.'

And with great dignity the old man walked back to his shack. The boys heard the door shut. They switched off their torches, feeling angry and uncomfortable.

'That Susie!' said George. 'Horrible girl! And Binkie too. Coming up here like that! I must say you were an ass, Peter, to let Susie overhear what you told Jack.'

'Yes. But honestly you don't expect people to listen at keyholes,' said Peter. 'Though Susie will do anything, of course, to make fun of the Secret Seven. That's all she does it for.'

'Well, shall we push off home too?' asked Colin. 'I must say this is all very disappointing.'

'We'll wait just a bit – in case the real wailing, that Matt told us about, does happen to come again,' said Peter. 'He said he thought it came about half-past eight – and it's gone that now.'

'Well – five more minutes, then,' said Colin. 'But I'm pretty certain old Matt dreamt it all.'

They sat silently for five minutes, in the pitch-black darkness. Not a star was to be seen in the overclouded sky. An owl hooted again, and the wind made tiny noises in the gorse-bush behind them. Then a bird in a nearby bush unexpectedly gave a little chirrup and was silent again.

'Better go now,' whispered Peter, and rose to his feet. The others stood up too, and Peter took a few steps forward.

Then he stopped very suddenly indeed, and so did the others. Their hearts began to beat fast again, and Colin clutched hold of George.

A strange, sad wailing came on the air – oh how strange and how sad! It rose up through the night, high and full of beauty, and then fell again to a lower note, mournful but still pure and lovely.

Not a sound was to be heard except that strange, unearthly noise. Even the wind seemed to be listening, holding its breath, as were all three boys. They stood transfixed, clutching one another, not making any other movement.

They heard Matt's door open. The old shepherd must have heard the wailing too. It wasn't a dream of his. It was real!

There it was again, filling the night with mournfulness, and yet with beauty too – what a strange, strange sound to hear up on the lonely hillside.

'What is it?' whispered Colin at last.

'Don't you know?' said Peter. 'It's someone playing a violin! That's all it is. But oh, what wonderful playing! No tune. Just playing like the wind plays, or the trees, going on and on and on!'

'A violin!' said George. 'Of course! But I've never heard one played quite like that before. Who's playing it? And why, out on this hill in the dark night?'

Then they heard Matt's voice, stern and clear in the darkness.

'Who are you? Come forth and show yourself!'

The sounds stopped at once, and not another note was

heard. Matt stood at his door for a few minutes and then went inside his hut. The boys heard the door shut.

'Sit down here,' said Peter, in a low, excited voice. 'I want to say something.' They all sat down, and in the darkness Peter spoke urgently.

'That violin! It must be the one that was stolen! I've never heard a violin played like that before – the notes were so pure and so lovely. And to think that Matt called it wailing!'

'Well – it *was* a kind of wailing – violin music often does wail,' said Colin. 'But it was beautiful. Yes – I bet it was the stolen violin. But who was playing it?'

'Luke Bolan!' said Peter promptly.

'How do you know?' asked George.

'Well – we know he plays the banjo, so he may be able to play the violin too,' said Peter. 'And his banjo was burnt in the fire – so maybe he stole that violin to make up for it.'

There was a silence after this. Then Peter spoke again. 'The next thing for us to do is to find the violin – he probably hides it in his caravan,' he said. 'Let's go quietly over to it now, and see if there's a light inside. Better be very careful, because if Luke was playing it on the hillside, he may still be out there. No torches on, please!'

The three boys crept over towards the caravan. Would they see Luke inside, with the violin? The *stolen* violin?

Seventeen

Where is the violin?

At first the three boys could not see the caravan at all, the night was so dark. They stumbled forward as quietly as they could, holding out their hands in front of them.

'Sh!' said Peter suddenly and stopped. The others bumped into him. 'Look!' whispered Peter. 'You can just see the outline of the caravan against the dark sky. Isn't that it?'

'Yes,' whispered back Colin. 'But there's no one there – it's quite dark.'

'Strange!' said Peter. 'Well – let's go as close as we can. Stop if you hear the slightest noise.'

They crept right up to the silent caravan. Not a chink of light was to be seen. Peter crept up the steps and listened. Ah – there *was* a sound inside! But what was it?

'It's someone crying!' said Colin. Yes – there was some-one sobbing quietly, like a child!

'It must be little Benny, left all alone in the van,' said Peter. 'Is the pram anywhere about?' He switched on his torch to see. But it was not in its usual place beside the caravan, and was nowhere to be seen. The sobbing still went on inside the van.

Then a voice made them jump almost out of their skins. It was old Matt again! He must have seen their torches and come over from his shack.

'Didn't I tell you lads to clear off home?' he said. 'Master Peter, does your father know you're out? And what are you doing on the steps of that caravan?'

'Matt – that wailing – it was someone playing a violin!' said Peter.

Matt stood silent a moment. Then he spoke in a voice of wonder. 'Young sir, you're right! But never did I hear a fiddle played like that afore. A-wailing and a-woe-ing! Who played it? There's no one in the Bolans' caravan, except young Benny tonight, that I do know, for the Bolans asked me to keep an eye on it, while they went down to see someone about a cottage.'

'Oh – then it's poor little Benny crying in there because he's frightened of the wailing too!' said Peter. 'Shall we go in and comfort him?'

'No. He's afeard of people,' said the shepherd. 'But he's not afeard of old Matt! You let me see to him, Master Peter. I'll rock him to sleep like a weakly lamb! It's only that violin that's scared him. And that's a strange thing to be sure – someone up here making such mournful music at night!'

Matt walked into the dark caravan, making soft, comforting noises in his deep, kind voice. Peter flashed his torch swiftly inside, and saw Benny's dark head on a pillow in a corner. Old Matt bent over him.

The boys left the caravan in silence, and began to walk home. They were filled with curiosity and were extremely puzzled.

Peter spoke first. 'I don't understand all this. It *must* have been Luke playing that violin somewhere on the hillside. But why? Matt seems quite certain that he and Mrs Bolan went off to the town, and left Benny in the van. They took the baby with them, of course, as the pram is gone. Well, then – why did Luke Bolan apparently come back, all on his own, and play a violin?'

'I don't know,' said Colin. 'But I'm perfectly certain in

my own mind that it was Luke who stole that violin, and uses it to comfort himself with because his banjo has been burnt. He may have felt his wife down in the town for an hour or two, and come up here to play it.'

'Well – where do you suppose he hides it?' asked George. 'He must hide it jolly carefully somewhere – because if it were found he'd go to prison for theft!'

'He probably hides it in his caravan, under the mattress – or in the bread-bin, or some such place,' said Peter. 'I think we ought to come up tomorrow and see if we can find it. Luke will be off to some fair or other, earning his living, and we know Mrs Bolan takes the baby and Benny to go shopping. Janet and I met her in the town the other morning.'

'All right. We'll come up here tomorrow,' said George. 'I feel as if I MUST get to the bottom of this. It's all so strange – the fire – the missing scarecrow clothes – the stolen violin – the wailing in the night – and yet no one about to play the violin!'

'Look out!' hissed Colin suddenly, and the three stopped walking very suddenly. A figure stood not far off, still and silent in the big field. Peter chuckled.

'Ass! It's our old friend the scarecrow! I'm glad to see he's still wearing his new clothes. Come on – we shall all get into awful rows if we're much later!'

'What time shall we meet tomorrow?' asked George. 'Shall we all go – the whole Secret Seven? We'll take something up to the Bolans as an excuse for calling.'

'Right. As near ten o'clock as you can manage,' said Peter. 'Then we can get back in good time for lunch.'

They parted at Peter's front gate and went to their homes, thinking over the night's adventure – for it really had been an adventure! All except that silly business when Susie and Binkie tried to upset everything!

'I hope to goodness they don't get to hear that we're going up to the caravan tomorrow,' thought George as he went home. 'Jack really ought to be more careful. He deserves to be chucked out of the Secret Seven if he can't keep Susie and her giggling friend in order!'

Jack somehow managed to keep Susie in complete ignorance of what was happening, and arrived at Peter's in good time the next morning. Everyone was there. A very brief meeting was held, at which Peter explained to the girls and to Jack exactly what had happened the night before. They listened in astonishment and envy, especially poor old Jack, who had had to escort Susie and Binkie home!

'Gosh – to think it was someone playing a *violin*!' said Jack. 'I wish I'd heard it. Blow Susie! I bet it was Luke Bolan playing it! My word – what a bad lot he is – smashing a window to steal a really valuable old violin!'

'Come on,' said Peter, standing up. 'Yes, you too, Scamper. Mother's given us some butter and biscuits to take up to Mrs Bolan, so they will make a nice excuse for seeing her, if she happens to be there. If she isn't we shall have a chance to look inside the van to see if the violin is tucked away somewhere.'

Off they all went, Scamper running beside them, his tongue hanging out. Where were the Secret Seven off to now? Scamper didn't care if they were going to the moon, so long as he could go with them!

Eighteen

An unexpected find

THE Seven arrived at Matt's hut and looked inside it. The shepherd was not there – in fact, they could see him a long way off, rounding up sheep on the opposite hill. He waved to them and they waved back. His dog was with him, working hard.

'Now to see if the Bolans' van is empty,' said Peter, and they went across to it, carrying the biscuits and the butter. Scamper trotted on in front, his long tail waving happily to and fro.

'Mrs Bolan! Are you there?' called Peter. There was no answer at all.

'The pram's not here,' said Janet, sorry that she wouldn't see the dear little baby.

'Is the door locked?' asked Peter anxiously. 'I hope to goodness it isn't.' He ran up the steps and knocked. 'Mrs Bolan! Are you in?'

There was no answer. He pushed gently at the door, and it yielded, opening a little.

'I'll just put the butter and biscuits on the shelf!' he called to the others, and went right inside. The caravan smelt musty and rather unpleasant, and was not very tidy. The big mattress still lay on the floor, as if Mrs Bolan had left in a hurry and hadn't troubled to tidy anything. Even the dirty breakfast cups and plates were still left on the shelf.

'Can we come in too?' called Janet.

'No. I'll just have a quick hunt round myself, and then one of you can come in, and check round to see that I haven't missed any hiding-place,' said Peter. 'We'd get in

275

each other's way if we all came in, it's so small. It shouldn't be difficult to find a violin hidden here.'

The others stood outside, some on the caravan steps, some on the grass, peering in to see what Peter was doing. He searched very thoroughly indeed.

'Nothing under or in the mattress!' he called. 'Nothing in the cupboard. Wait, there's a shelf almost in the roof of the caravan – there's a long box there – that might be it!'

He took down the box and opened it – but it was quite empty except for a few mildewed papers that might even have belonged to Matt, when *he* had the caravan!

Peter searched everywhere. Then he came to the door, rather disappointed. 'No go!' he said. 'The violin is definitely not here. I suppose it might be hidden under a bush somewhere – but I don't think so, because that would ruin it – even if it had a case, which it hasn't. The case was left behind in the shop. Janet – you come up and search.'

Janet leapt up the steps, and the others watched her searching too. Peter told Colin and Jack to look *under* the caravan as well, for there were a few things there. But no – the violin was certainly not among them. It was very, very disappointing.

Then suddenly Janet gave a loud squeal, and made everyone jump. 'What is it?' they cried.

'Look what I've found hanging behind the caravan door!' she cried. 'It was opened flat against the wall, and I didn't think of looking behind it till this moment. Look!'

And she displayed something very, very surprising to the rest of the Seven. Not the stolen violin – but the stolen scarecrow clothes!

Yes, there they were – the old tweed coat, the dirty hat, and grey flannel trousers!

Everyone stared in amazement, recognizing the clothes at once.

'But – but – how did they come to be in the caravan?' said Janet.

'Easy! Luke stole them from the scarecrow, wore them as a disguise to steal the violin, then came back to the van and hung them behind the door!' said Jack. 'Who would bother about old clothes in a van? No one would know they once belonged to a scarecrow!'

'Oh dear!' said Pam. 'I can't help feeling awfully sorry for poor Mrs Bolan. I'm sure she didn't know Luke stole the scarecrow clothes – or the violin. Where *can* that violin be? It simply *must* be hidden somewhere!'

'Well, it's certainly not here,' said Peter. 'And as I'm sure it's not hidden in the bushes, there's only one place I can think of!'

'Where's that?' asked the others, eagerly.

'In the baby's pram,' said Peter. 'No one would ever think anything was hidden in such a place, certainly not a valuable violin. I bet that's where it's kept.'

'But Peter – it would ruin a violin to be bounced about on all day – and the baby is a very bouncy one!' said Pam.

'It could easily be wrapped round and round in some thick material,' said Peter. 'Easily! I bet I'm right!'

'Well – what do we do *now*, then?' asked Colin. 'We *think* Luke stole the scarecrow clothes to disguise himself – we *think* he stole that violin because his banjo was burnt – we *think* he plays it out on the hills at night – and now we *think* it's hidden in the baby's pram. But we can't prove a single thing!'

'If we could only look inside the pram, we should know,' said Jack.

'But how can we do that?' asked Peter.

'Sh!' said Jack suddenly. 'Look who's coming!'

They turned in a hurry – and saw Mrs Bolan hurrying along with the baby in the pram. It was howling loudly. Benny ran by his mother's side, holding on to the pram.

At first Mrs Bolan didn't see the children beside the caravan. Peter shut the door hurriedly, and then they all went towards her, hardly knowing what to say.

'There, there, little love,'. she was saying to the baby. 'You're starving, aren't you, poor lamb!' She picked it up and turned to take it to the caravan, suddenly startled to see the seven children. She tried to smile her usual smile – but her face was worried and anxious, quite without its usual cheerful expression.

'Why, good morning, my dears,' she said. 'I'm just going to feed the baby. I've been down the town all the morning, and she's starving, poor mite. I meant to be back before this!'

She hurried into the caravan, and Benny went too.

'What about looking into the pram now?' said Pam, in a low voice. 'It's our only chance. Oh – I DO hope the violin isn't there!'

She bent over the pram and pulled away a dirty covering. Peter burrowed deep down into the well of the pram, surprised to find his fingers trembling. He felt something long and hard, wrapped in thick cloth! He pulled it out.

He unwrapped a little of the cloth – and part of a violin handle showed at once! 'Yes – it *is* the violin!' said Peter, shocked. 'Now what do we do?'

279

Nineteen

Little Benny

A LOUD voice made all the Secret Seven jump. They looked up, to see a man walking up to them – a tall, stooping fellow, with thick black hair and eyes exactly like Benny's – Luke Bolan. He looked very angry.

'You give me that! Poking and prying! I'll box your ears, the lot of you!'

'Are you Luke Bolan?' said Peter. 'Well, isn't this the violin that was stolen from the antique shop?'

There was a scream from behind them, and Mrs Bolan came flying out of the caravan, Benny behind her.

'Luke! Luke! Leave those children be! Don't you dare harm them. Oh, look at that now – they've found the violin!' And to the children's utter dismay, she covered her face with her hands and began to sob. Benny began to sob, too, in fright, pulling at her dress.

Luke took the violin roughly from Peter, and held it up in the air as if he were going to dash it to the ground and break it. But Mrs Bolan held his arm at once.

'No, Luke, no. That would only make things worse. What do you children know about this? How did you find out?'

'It's too long a tale to tell,' said Peter. 'But Colin here actually saw your husband smash the window and take the violin – and he saw that he was wearing our old scarecrow's clothes: and I'm afraid we've just seen them hanging in your caravan. And now, of course, we've found the violin!'

'Oh Luke, Luke, what have you done to us?' wept Mrs Bolan. 'You'll go to prison, sure as the sun is in the sky – and then what's to happen to me and the children? All our things burnt – and me left with the baby and poor little Benny!'

Luke put his arms round her, looking very sad indeed. Mrs Bolan flashed round on the children.

'I was going to put back that violin in the shop this very morning! Yes, that I was – and Luke here, he'll tell you the same. We didn't know it was so valuable! Luke thought it was so old-looking that it wasn't worth much!'

'I see,' said Peter, suddenly understanding. 'Of course – it does look very, very old. But didn't Luke see the notice beside it?'

'Yes,' said Luke. 'But that didn't mean nothing to me.'

'Luke can't read,' said Mrs Bolan, wiping her eyes. 'He never went to school – he lived in a caravan all the time he was a child, and wasn't anywhere long enough to get schooling. If he'd have seen the notice and read how old and precious the violin was, he'd never have taken it – would you now, Luke?'

'No, that I wouldn't,' said Luke. 'I never thought it was worth more than a few pence – and I'd not got even those, after our shack got on fire. I meant to have gone in and paid later. But I needed that violin right bad.'

'Why? Just because your banjo was burnt?' asked Colin, rather scornfully.

'Banjo? No, I didn't care so much about *that*!' said Luke, surprised. 'I can always borrow a banjo. No, young sir, it was for my Benny here I wanted the violin.'

'Benny! But – but surely he can't play a violin!' cried

281

Janet, amazed.

'Benny, love – do you want to give us a tune?' said Mrs Bolan, bending over the scared-looking little boy. He couldn't understand what was going on, and he was very frightened. Why was his mother crying?

Luke took the violin from the pram, where he had laid it when he went to comfort his wife. He put it into the eager little hands that went out for it – Benny's small brown hands, that seemed to come alive when they felt the smoothness of the old violin.

He walked a little way away, and stood with his back to them. He put the violin under his chin, and raised the bow – and on the air came once again that strange 'wailing, unearthly and beautiful, that the boys had heard the night before. No tune – just a series of beautiful sounds as if Benny was singing his own strange thoughts.

'He's playing to himself – just as the blackbird sings to himself, listening all the time,' thought Janet.

'No, no, Benny – play "The Dancing May-Tree!"' called his mother. 'Not your own tunes!'

And straightaway the boy swept into the merriest, gayest dance that the children had ever heard – joyous, breath-taking, astonishing. They gasped in wonder.

Mrs Bolan smiled round at them. 'There! That's an old gipsy tune. Benny plays them all! My little Benny! You've never heard him play, have you? He . . .'

'Well – we did hear him last night, when it was dark,' said Peter. 'And old Matt heard him the night before. But he only played that kind of *wailing* music of his own, and Matt was puzzled and told us about it.'

'So we came up last night to see if we could hear it too – and we did,' said Colin. 'But we knew at once that it was someone playing a violin most beautifully. And we

guessed the violin was a very good one – the stolen one, in fact!'

'Oh Benny, Benny – and I left you asleep in bed!' said Mrs Bolan. 'And so I did the night before. You got out of bed, found the violin and took it out to play on the hillside – is that what you did?'

Benny didn't answer. He didn't even turn to face his mother. He was rubbing the bow gently on the strings, making a curious sound like the wind in the trees. Janet suddenly realized that that was exactly what he *was* playing – the actual little song that the wind was whispering in the nearby birch-tree!

'But he's a genius!' she thought. 'I hardly know which is the violin and which is the wind.' Then she spoke out loud.

'Mrs Bolan! Benny's wonderful! He's a little genius! Oh, why don't you send him to school? Why don't you let him be taught music properly?'

'Benny wouldn't be any good at school, Miss,' said Mrs Bolan, and she drew the child to her. 'Why, surely you know what's the matter with him? My Benny is blind.'

Blind! Now the children knew why those great dark eyes had no expression in them, and why Benny was so careful when he walked! Poor, poor little Benny.

'Music is the only thing that keeps him happy,' said Mrs Bolan. 'And when he lost his own violin in the fire it seemed as if his heart was broken. That's why Luke took that old violin, Miss – just to make our little Benny happy again!'

Twenty

Meeting of the Secret Nine!

THE Seven looked at Mrs Bolan, and then at the silent, mysterious little Benny. Janet felt tears coming to her eyes. What could they do to help this gifted little boy? SOMEthing must be done! But the Secret Seven couldn't do it. No, the grown-ups must come into this – they always knew what to do!

And so it was that the Seven went to Peter's father and mother that morning, and poured out the whole story to them.

'We don't know what to do now, Mother,' said Peter, when the tale was ended. 'The violin must go back to the shop – but Daddy, poor Luke mustn't be put into prison! Benny must go to school, and he *must* be taught music – and he must have a violin of his own. The Secret Seven are quite prepared to buy one for him, even if they have to save for a year.'

'You're a good set of kids,' said his father, pleased. 'This is a most remarkable story, I must say! I don't know how you Seven get mixed up in things of this sort! Now first, about the violin. We can quite well give it back without any harm coming to Luke. Matt tells me he's a good enough fellow – and I don't expect he would have stolen that violin if he hadn't been so upset at Benny's being burnt.'

'He simply loves Benny!' said Pam. 'But how can the violin be given back without Luke coming into it?'

'There's a reward offered for its return – and if returned in good condition, no questions will be asked,' said

Peter's father. 'I propose to take it back myself, and say that I can't explain how it came into my possession – but that the man who took it is very sorry – and naturally I could not take any reward. That should settle that.'

'Oh good!' said all the Secret Seven, and the Scamper thumped his tail on the floor.

'And what about Benny?' asked Janet.

'I think I can help there,' said her mother. 'He can go to one of the wonderful schools run for blind children, and his gift for music will be developed to the utmost. He won't mind so much leaving his mother if he can have his precious music, and he will have all his holidays with her, of course!'

'Oh, thank goodness!' said Barbara and Pam, together. It had been a terrible shock to the Seven to learn that little Benny, with his beautiful dark eyes, was blind. But now it wouldn't matter so much – he would always be happy with his music!

'Well – it isn't often the Secret Seven have a Secret *Nine* meeting!' said Peter's father, smiling. 'I must say that Mummy and I feel highly honoured, Peter. Grown-ups are quite a help sometimes, aren't they?'

'Oh Daddy – we couldn't do without you!' cried Janet, and gave him a sudden hug. 'Do you *mind* taking the violin back to the shop? You're sure you won't be arrested?'

'Quite sure,' said her father. 'And what's more, if the Secret Seven really do mean to get money together to buy little Benny a violin, I'd like to help too – and so would Mummy, of course. I could have a look at the violins in the music shop, and see if there's one that would suit a small boy – so that Benny won't fret for his own burnt one any more.'

286

'Oh YES!' cried all the Seven together, and Scamper thumped his tail once more. He had no idea what was going on, but he was certainly enjoying it all. What other dog in the world would be allowed in at an important secret meeting like this?

Peter's father lost no time in dealing with the violin. He never told the Seven exactly what had passed between him and the antique-shop dealer – he merely said that all was well, and that Luke's name had not been mentioned.

'But I shall have a word or two with Luke myself,' he said. 'Just to make sure that he knows he was *almost* in very serious trouble.'

'Have you got another violin for Benny?' asked Janet anxiously.

'You can go up to Mrs Bolan and tell her to take Benny down to the music shop tomorrow, and they will let him try their smaller ones,' said Daddy. 'And then bring her here for Mummy to talk to her about school for Benny. Dear me, we do seem to be meddling in other people's affairs!'

'Not meddling – just giving a helping hand!' said his wife. 'As for the Secret Seven, Peter, you'll have to keep them all up to the mark, you know – and help to pay for Benny's violin!'

The Seven kept their word, of course. They had never in their lives been so busy earning money in holiday time! They found themselves jobs of all kinds, and even Susie joined in!

'Binkie's gone home, thank goodness,' said Jack. 'So Susie is just a bit more sensible. Mother says we're to allow her to get a job and give us the money if she wants to. She says it will do Susie good.'

'Oh well – if it's possible to do Susie good by all means let her work hard!' said Peter. 'But all the same, she is NOT going to come to our next Secret Seven meeting.'

When the day of the meeting came, two days before they went back to school, what a pile of money they had to count – plenty to buy the violin that Benny was already very, very happy with! He was to take it to the blind school with him, and that pleased him very much.

'Well – you've all worked jolly hard,' said Peter, looking round at the Seven. 'It's been rather exciting, hasn't it? Thanks for all your money, Secret Seven. Oh, and here's a bit more.' He emptied several coins on to the up-turned box in front of him.

'Who's that from? Susie?' asked George.

'No. It's from Scamper!' answered Peter, with a laugh. 'He gave up two large bones and one little one in order to help Benny – and here's his money! Thanks most awfully, Scamper! You're a brick!'

'Wuff!' said Scamper happily. 'Wuff-wuff-wuff-wuff-wuff!'

'He says it's a pleasure to help us!' said Peter solemnly. 'And he really *does* like the Secret Seven!'

So do we, Peter. So do we!

SECRET SEVEN FIREWORKS

CONTENTS

One

What's happened to the Secret Seven?

PETER, Jack and Janet were walking home from school one fine October day, when someone came skipping up behind them. It was Susie, Jack's sister.

'Hallo, you three!' she said. 'What's happened to the Secret Seven? You never seem to have meetings now.'

'Nothing's happened to the Secret Seven,' said Peter. 'Don't be silly.'

Susie began to chant a little song just behind them.

> 'The Secret Seven's falling to bits.
> It doesn't meet any more.
> The only thing that is left of it
> Is the silly S.S. on the door!'

'*Susie!* You little horror!' said Jack, angrily. 'Singing like that in the street about the Secret Seven! Falling to bits! You don't know what you're talking about.'

'Oh, I *do*,' said Susie, skipping in front of them now. 'I know you haven't met for ages – I know. Jack's lost his badge – I know you can't use Peter's shed for meeting-places – I know . . .'

Peter, Janet and Jack glared at the smiling, irritating Susie.

'What do you mean – you know we can't use our shed?' demanded Peter. 'You've been snooping.'

'No, I haven't. My ball went over your wall, Peter, and I ran to get it – and I saw your shed full of onions! *Onions!*' Susie laughed loudly. 'So I knew you couldn't be meeting there – and I've a very particular reason for asking if the Secret Seven is still going on or not.'

Peter stopped at once, and the others stopped too. *Now* what was Susie up to? Why was she so anxious to know about the Secret Seven?

'What's this silly, particular reason?' asked Peter, sharply, 'Go on – tell us.'

'Well, you see – if your Secret Seven has stopped, I thought *I'd* like to form a Secret Seven Club of my own,' said Susie, solemnly, with a wicked glint in her bright eyes. 'I thought I'd ask Leonard, and Harry and . . .'

'What! Copy *us*!' said Janet, in scorn. 'Well – *I* wouldn't want to be a copy-cat like that!'

'And anyway, forget about it,' said Peter. 'The Secret Seven is meeting this very Saturday morning. Isn't it, Jack?'

This was the first that Jack had heard of any meeting but he nodded his head vigorously. 'Yes. Let me see – ten o'clock, wasn't it, Peter?'

'That's right,' said Peter, giving Janet a little nudge in case she should say *she* hadn't heard of any meeting.

'It'll be a pretty smelly meeting, sitting on top of all those onions,' said Susie. 'Shall I help you to clear them out of the shed?'

'*No!*' roared Peter and Jack together.

Janet gave Susie a push. 'Go away!' she said, fiercely. 'You're just *trying* to be annoying. Fancy thinking *you* could run a club!'

'I could, easily,' said Susie. 'You just wait and see!'

She skipped off, leaving the other three feeling really furious. 'Can't you possibly keep that sister of yours in order, Jack?' said Peter. 'Like I do Janet?'

'You do *not* keep me in order,' said Janet, at once, and

stalked off ahead of the two boys. They looked at one another.

'*Girls!*' said Jack, in a disgusted voice, low enough for Janet not to hear. 'They're all the same.'

'Except that Susie is a bit worse,' said Peter. 'Now look, Jack, we'd better have this Secret Seven meeting, as we've said we're going to. It's an awful bore, really, because we'll have to turn all those onions out and put them somewhere else. I hope my father won't mind!'

'Well, look, let's all come at a quarter to ten, not ten, and help you,' said Jack. 'We can easily tell the others in good time.'

'All right,' said Peter. 'Quarter to ten, then – and tell Susie if she dares to so much as put her nose round the door of our shed, I'll . . . I'll – well, I really can't think of anything bad enough to do to her.'

'What shall we have a meeting about?' said Jack. 'Nothing much has happened – no mystery or anything to work on. But we must have something to *talk* about.'

'Well, we will,' said Peter, an idea suddenly coming into his head. 'What about planning for Bonfire Night? It will be here in a couple of weeks or so, and we ought to start saving up for fireworks, and decide about a guy – and where to burn him.'

'Golly, yes!' said Jack, thrilled. 'Of course – that's what we'll have the meeting about. If we don't start saving up soon we shan't have any fireworks on Guy Fawkes Night. Jolly good idea of yours, Peter.'

'And for goodness sake find your badge,' said Peter. 'Susie said you'd lost it.'

'What a tell-tale!' said Jack. 'I *had* lost it. It went to the cleaner's on the lapel of my blazer – Mother didn't notice it. And I was awfully upset when the blazer came back without it, and grumbled like anything. That's how Susie knew it was gone.'

'Well, you'd better get your mother to make you a new one,' said Peter. 'Can't have anyone turning up without a badge, you know.'

'All right, all right. Why don't you lose *yours* for once?' said Jack. 'Then you'd know what it feels like. How was *I* to know that my mother was going to send my blazer to the cleaner's all of a sudden?'

Peter gave him a friendly punch. 'Don't be so touchy! Tell George about the meeting on Saturday, will you? And I'll tell Colin. Janet will tell Pam and Barbara.'

'Right,' said Jack, as Peter swung in at the gate. 'There's one good thing to be said for Susie – she's made us call a meeting! I shall look forward to it. So long, Peter!'

'So long!' said Peter, and ran down the path that led to the shed where the Secret Seven met. He opened the door – and a dozen onions rolled out at once. He kicked them back.

'You wait till Saturday!' he said. 'You'll have to get out of here, and make room for the Secret Seven! Janet – Janet! Where are you? I say – won't it be fun to have one of our meetings again!'

Two

Password, please!

ON Saturday morning Janet and Peter were down by their shed, together with two or three barrows of all sizes, ready to wheel away the onions stored there. The gardener hadn't been at all pleased when he heard that his precious onions were to be taken out of the nice dry shed.

'But, Gardener, we asked Dad, and he *said* we could put them into the old summer-house,' said Peter.

'Rain blows in there,' said the gardener.

'Dad said we could take the old tarpaulin sheet and cover them over with that,' said Janet. 'You see, Gardener, this really *is* our shed. We meet here. You know we do.'

'Not for weeks you haven't,' said the gardener. 'Well, I'm busy – you'll have to move the lot yourselves. Take you a good time, too!'

'Oh, there'll be seven of us,' said Peter. 'Many hands make light work, you know.'

'You be careful that too many cooks don't spoil the broth,' said the man, and walked off, his rake over his shoulder.

'That was quite bright of the gardener,' said Janet, astonished. 'We'll have to tell the others that. Now let's see – three barrows; and look, wouldn't it be easier to *shovel* up the onions, instead of picking them up in twos and threes as we said?'

'Now *you're* quite bright!' said Peter. 'I'll go to the tool shed and see what I can find. Hope the gardener's not there. He's a bit gloomy this morning. If the others come, ask them the password and see they've got their badges on.'

Janet began to put the onions into one of the barrows. She had put in about twenty when Colin and George came along.

'Hallo!' said Janet. 'Password, please.'

'It's so long since we had a meeting that we've forgotten it,' said Colin. 'Anyway, we'll hear it when the others come. It's only when we enter the shed that we have to say it. Do *you* know it, Janet?'

'Yes,' said Janet. 'But I had to look it up in my diary. I'd better not tell you it, in case Peter is cross. Come on – help me with the onions. Oh, wait a minute. Have you got your badges on? Good! Peter told me to look and see.'

'This sounds quite like old times,' said Colin. 'We oughtn't to have gone so long without a meeting.' He began to scoop up onions in his hands.

'Here are Pam and Barbara,' said Janet, hearing foot-steps. 'Hallo, you two! Password, please!'

Colin and George pricked up their ears at once. Aha – now they would know it!

'Wee Willie Winkie,' said the two girls together, and Janet nodded. 'That's right,' she said. 'Er – password, boys?'

Colin and George repeated it solemnly, and Pam gig-gled. 'You'd forgotten it,' she said. 'I say – what a lot of onions.'

Peter came back at that moment with Scamper at his heels. He carried one big spade and two small ones.

'Password!' said George, pointing at him. 'And it's *not* Jack the Giant-Killer!'

'Quite right. It's Wee Willie Winkie!' said Peter, with a grin. 'Isn't it, Scamper?'

'Wuff,' said Scamper, pleased to see so many people.

'Let's see – Jack's not come yet,' said Peter. 'Ah – here he is. Has he got his badge on? He said it had gone to the cleaner's on his blazer, and hadn't come back. I told him he'd have to ask his mother to make him another.'

'Hallo, hallo!' said Jack, coming up at a run. 'Am I last? Sorry – but I quite forgot that I'd lost my badge. I went to ask Mother to make one and . . .'

'But that looks like your *old* one on your coat,' said Janet. 'A bit scruffy!'

'It *is* my old one,' said Jack. 'And what's more Susie found it for me! She said that when cleaners find brooches or badges or anything like that on clothes sent to be cleaned, they pop them into an envelope and put them in a pocket. And Susie looked in the breast pocket of my blazer, and there was my badge, inside a little envelope. I'd have been awfully late if she hadn't found it.'

'Well! Fancy *Susie* doing you a good turn!' said George, astonished. 'Good for *her*! We're all here now – let's buck up and move all these onions and get on with the meeting.'

It didn't take long for the seven of them to shovel up the onions into three barrows and wheel them away to the summer-house. Soon they were all neatly piled there and Peter and Jack pulled the old tarpaulin over them to keep them dry.

'Now we'll go back to the shed and hold our meeting,' said Peter. 'We'll get a few boxes to sit on, and after the meeting we'll clear up the shed and make it neat and tidy again.'

Back they all went to the shed. Peter was surprised to

see that the door was now shut, and even more surprised to find Scamper there, growling at it! What *was* the matter with him?

Peter tried to open the door. It was locked from inside! A familiar voice came from the shed, with an aggravating little giggle at the end of it.

'Password, please!'

'*Susie!*' yelled everyone, and Peter shook the door angrily.

'Susie, how dare you? This is *our* meeting-place. Open the door at once.'

'In a minute. I just wanted to sit here and think what a horrible shed this is,' said Susie. 'Pooh! It smells! Now, when I have *my* club, I shan't meet in an onion shed, I shall meet in a . . .'

'Susie! *Will* you open the door?' yelled Peter, banging on it furiously.

'On one condition,' said Susie. 'And that is that you let me walk out without speaking to me or touching me. Otherwise I shall sit here all morning and hold a Secret Seven meeting by myself.'

Peter knew when he was beaten. 'All right, you fathead. Come on out. We want to hold our meeting before the morning's gone. But we'll pay you out for this!'

The door opened and Susie sauntered out, grinning all over her cheeky face. Nobody said a word, though everyone longed to shout at her. She disappeared up the garden path, Scamper giving a few small, rather astonished barks.

'Good riddance to bad rubbish!' said Pam. 'Come on – do let's begin our meeting. My word – I'm glad Susie's not in the Secret Seven. *What* a nuisance she'd be!'

Three

Plenty of plans

THE Seven trooped into the shed and looked round. 'Better get a few boxes, as you said, Peter,' said Janet. 'Pam, you come with me – I know where there are some. You boys sweep out the shed a bit. It's messy with onion skins.'

Before long all the Seven, with Scamper thumping his tail happily on the ground, were seated on boxes round the shed. They felt quite tired after all their shovelling and wheeling of barrows!

'Now, we've met to discuss plans for Bonfire Night,' said Peter, in a business-like way. 'It's still some time ahead, but it takes a good while to save up money for fireworks. Also we'll have to discuss a guy.'

'I vote we make a guy *exactly* like Susie,' said Pam. 'Awful girl!'

'No. Susie would simply *love* that,' said Jack, at once. 'She'd go round boasting about it. I vote we make a nice *big* guy –one that would look fine on top of a bonfire.'

'Oh yes – and let's have a *smashing* bonfire!' said Barbara. 'The biggest we've ever made. We made a pretty big one last year, but I'd like a most enormous one. I love to see the flames blaze high!'

'Right. We'll have a great big bonfire – and a guy to match,' said Peter. 'That means we'll have to begin collecting stuff for it at once. It takes ages to build a big pile of burnable stuff.'

'Where shall we have it?' asked Colin.

304

'In my garden,' said Barbara. 'Then the next door kids could see it.'

'No. It's too far for us all to bring wood there,' said Peter. 'Actually I think it would be a good idea to have it in the big field just at the bottom of our garden here – for one thing there's a lot of dead wood in the hedges and in the little wood nearby, and it wouldn't be very far to carry it.'

'Yes. That's a good idea,' said Jack. 'We could have a simply enormous one out there in the field. We could meet in the wood, and collect dead twigs and branches together – that would be more fun that getting it on our own and dragging it here.'

'Right. That's settled then,' said Peter 'We're getting on. Now about saving up for fireworks.'

'We'll all bring what we can, as we usually do,' said Barbara. 'I've got a bit of money in my savings box already that I can bring. Who shall be treasurer?'

'Better vote for one,' said Peter. He took out his notebook and tore a page from it. He then tore the page into seven neat strips, and handed a strip to each person. 'Everyone got a pencil?' he said. 'You haven't, Pam – well take mine for a minute. Now – write down the person you think would be a good treasurer – someone to hold the money for us, and keep it safe, and count it each time we bring any. They'll have to keep the figures in a book, so that we know what we've got, and who brought it. Ready? Write the name down then of the one you want. If must be someone good at figures, of course. We don't want a muddle made of our money.'

They all sucked or chewed their pencils and frowned. A good treasurer? One who could manage figures well? One who wouldn't make a muddle?

They each scribbled a name on their piece of paper, folded it and handed it in to Peter. He unfolded each one – and then grinned.

'Hm – well!' he said. 'You all seem to think *I'm* the one – six votes for me! Thanks awfully.'

'But there are seven of us!' said Pam, surprised. 'Who didn't vote for you?'

'*I* didn't vote for myself, silly!' said Peter. 'Actually I voted for Jack. Well, that's settled. We'll meet here in the shed each Saturday at ten o'clock – unless we make different plans. Bring any firework money you have then. And when it's all written down in our fireworks book, we'll go off into the field and the wood and collect stuff for the bonfire.'

'Good,' said George, pleased. 'It's fun to be doing something again. We oughtn't to let so much time go by without a meeting.'

'What about a guy?' asked Colin. 'Who's going to see about him?'

'I think the three girls had better make a big, stuffed body,' said Peter. 'They are more likely to get stuff for the guy than we are. And they can sew better than we can.'

'Gracious – you can't sew at *all*!' said Janet. 'I've just thought of something. Mother said that old eiderdown off your bed was no good now – it's got the moth in. We could use that for the body – all nicely squashed up.'

'Oh *yes*,' said Barbara. 'That's a very good idea. And I believe we've got a dirty old rug somewhere in the loft at home too – that would help to make a good fat body!'

'Well, you girls have got some good ideas,' said Peter. 'We'll decide about clothes at another meeting. We'd better see the size of the guy's body before we try to fit him out with clothes.'

'Don't make him *too* enormous,' said Jack. 'Else we shan't be able to get old clothes to fit him!'

'Well – I think it's time we brought this very interesting meeting to an end,' said Peter. 'What about sweeping out this shed, and getting that old table we had, and putting up a shelf again?'

'Yes. We'll do that,' said Colin, getting up. 'Oh sorry, Scamper – did I tread on your tail? Hallo – who's this coming? If it's Susie, let's all chase her up the path!'

But it wasn't Susie. It was Peter's mother, carrying a tray of lemonade and biscuits.

'I don't know the password!' she said. 'But please let me in. If I say "Lemonade and biscuits!" will that do?'

'Oh Mother – you *are* a brick!' said Peter, in delight. He opened the door. 'Come in – we're all here – and we've had a *marvellous* meeting, and made all kinds of plans!'

'Well, it's nice to see the Secret Seven together again,' said his mother, setting down the tray on a box. 'There now – there are a few dog biscuits for Scamper, because I know he doesn't like being left out.'

'Wuff-wuff!' said Scamper, gratefully, and licked her hand.

Everyone settled down to eat and drink. They felt very happy. They had made plans – good ones too – and they could all work together once more, and meet each week – perhaps oftener.

'Well – here's to Bonfire Night!' said Peter, lifting up his glass. 'And a Jolly Big Guy!'

Four

Saturday morning

THE next Saturday morning all the Seven met again. 'Wee Willie Winkie!' said everyone, and passed quickly into the shed. Peter shot a sharp look at each of them – yes, they all had on their badges – good!

The shed looked very neat and tidy now, swept out, and with sand sprinkled all over the floor by Peter, except where an old rug lay, given by Pam's mother. Two shelves were up, and on them stood some plastic cups and a plate or two. There was also a tin of toffees, and a second tin in which were home-made biscuits made by Peter's mother.

Scamper went to sit under the biscuit shelf, looking up longingly, giving little whines every now and again.

'No, Scamper – it's not biscuit-time yet,' said Peter. 'Don't take any notice of him, anyone. He's had a good breakfast already. Scamper, be quiet.'

'I've got a report to make on the guy,' said Pam, importantly. 'He's coming along nicely.'

'Fine,' said Peter. 'Tell us about him.'

'Well, we took Barbara's old rug,' said Pam, 'and Janet's old eiderdown – goodness, it *was* moth-eaten! It's a good thing it's going to be burnt.'

'And we did a bit of rolling up and shaping,' said Janet, 'and really, it's not a bad body at all. Would you like to see it? It's just behind the shed, covered over with an old rubber sheet.'

'You shouldn't leave it there,' said Jack. 'Susie might get it.'

Janet went to fetch the guy's body. It certainly was

quite fat, and the girls had really managed to shape it very well. It had a round head, a plump body, with a rope tied round it for a waist, and plump arms and legs.

'We haven't made the feet and hands yet!' said Janet. 'It's not bad, is it?'

Scamper was amazed to see such a curious-looking creature. He barked frantically, and seemed quite scared of it. The children laughed at him.

'Wait till it's all dressed up, Scamper,' said Janet. 'You'll bark all right then!'

'If any of us have old clothes that will fit this big fellow, please bring them to our next meeting,' said Peter. 'Or give them to Janet before that, if you can.'

'The guy had better be kept in here, hadn't it?' said Jack. 'If Susie comes snooping round, she *might* find it outside – and she's still thinking of making a club of her own, you know. If she does, they're sure to make a raid on the shed!'

'All right, we'll leave it here – right at the back, in its rubber sheet,' said Janet. 'I'm glad you all approve of it. Please don't forget to look out some nice big clothes – and a big hat or cap. We shall put a mask on him, and he'll look really fine.'

'Now about money,' said Peter. 'Anyone brought any?'

To everyone's delight, the money poured in! Five pence from Pam, ten pence from Barbara, eight pence from Colin, nine pence from George, three pence from Jack, and twenty pence between Peter and Janet.

'Fifty-five pence already,' said Peter, writing down names and money quickly, and adding it up. 'Pretty good.'

'Sorry about my three pence,' said Jack. 'But my Gran

had a birthday this week, and I spent most of my money on a present. I'll bring more next week. Dad has promised me fifteen pence if I'll clean up the garage for him. I'll bring that.'

'That's all right,' said Peter. 'We've made a jolly good start. Now, what about a biscuit or two, and then we'll set off to look for dead wood for our bonfire.'

'Wuff!' said Scamper, at once, thumping his tail on the ground.

Everyone laughed.

'I don't know whether you deserve a biscuit, Scamper,' said Peter. 'You haven't brought in any money – you didn't help with the guy, and . . .'

'Wuff-wuff-wuff!' said Scamper, running over to Peter and putting a paw on his knee.

'He says, can he have a biscuit if he goes and picks up dead wood with us,' said Peter, solemnly. 'Shall we let him?'

'Yes!' shouted everyone, and Scamper received the very first biscuit out of the tin. Everyone took one, and then, locking the shed behind them, they set off, munching their own biscuits, to the field behind Peter's garden.

'Let's choose a place for the bonfire,' said Peter. 'Not too near the hedge, in case it gets burnt.'

'Just here then,' said Jack, walking to a nice flat patch. 'It's well away from the hedge, and we can all dance round it with plenty of room to spare, and let off fireworks.'

Everyone agreed, and Peter nodded. 'Another thing settled,' he said. 'Hallo, look – there's Dad's hedger-and-ditcher man. He might let us have all the trimmings to burn!'

An old fellow was standing a little way up the hedge, slashing at it with a sharp-edged tool. He was cutting away the untidy new growth made that year, and was shaping the hedge skilfully. The children went to him and watched him, admiring the way he cut and trimmed.

'Good morning, Burton,' said Peter. 'You're making a jolly good job of that. Do you like hedging and ditching? You've cleared out the ditch well.'

'I likes any job that takes me outdoors,' said the old fellow. 'Sun and wind and rain, that's what I likes.'

'Could we have the hedge trimmings, do you think?' asked Peter. 'For a bonfire on Guy Fawkes Night?'

'You be welcome to them,' said Burton. 'I'll leave this little lot here for you. Take them any time.'

'Oh good,' said Peter. 'We'll do that. Come along, all of you. We'll be off to the wood now, and hope we'll find stacks of dead wood. We're going to have a jolly busy morning!'

And across the field they ran to the wood, Scamper barking joyfully. What were the Secret Seven up to now? Scamper would help them, whatever it was!

Five

A nasty-looking lot

THE Seven shuffled through the dead leaves in the wood. Except for the evergreen trees, the wood seemed very bare, and full of light. Peter kicked at a fallen branch.

'Here's a nice bit of wood for our fire! Let's make it the beginning of our collection, and bring whatever we find to this spot here under this big tree. Jack and I have brought plenty of rope. We can tie the whole lot up here when we've collected it, and drag it home.'

'Good idea,' said Colin. 'Let's separate then and hunt in different directions.'

The wood was full of dead twigs and fallen branches. There had been a great gale three weeks before, and a good deal of dead or rotten wood had been blown down. The children were delighted to see so much. Soon they each had quite big bundles.

'I'm going to put my lot down where we planned we would,' said Pam. 'I keep dropping bits now. I've got so much.'

'I'll do the same,' said Janet. 'My word, look at Jack over there. He's dragging along half a tree! That's a jolly good find!'

It was fun in the wood, shuffling through the dead leaves, hunting for firewood. One by one the Seven dragged their finds through the trees to the place they had arranged, under the big tree. Soon quite a good pile was there – big twigs, little twigs, small branches, big ones –

and good gracious, here came Peter, Jack and Colin dragging a most enormous branch!

'We'll have to chop this one up smaller,' panted Peter.
'I say – we *are* getting on, aren't we?'

'Let's go to the hedger's old hut and sit down for a bit,'
said Jack. 'I'm really quite puffed. I've got two packets of
sweets to share out. Let's go and sit down and eat
them.'

'Good idea,' said Peter, and the Seven set off to
Burton's little hut, where he often had his dinner on a
rainy day. It was just inside the wood, overgrown with
brambles and ivy, and in the summer-time it was so green
with the leaves that it could hardly be seen.

'I haven't been here before,' said Pam, as they came
near to the hut. 'It must be nice to have a little hut all your
own like this. I suppose Burton won't mind us sitting in it,
will he?'

'Oh no. Janet and I have often been inside,' said
Peter.

Scamper suddenly began to bark as they came near the
hut. Peter looked at him in surprise. 'What's the matter,
old thing? There's nobody about – not even a rabbit!'

The spaniel stood quite still, his silky nose pointing
towards the shed. 'Wuff-wuff-WUFF!' he barked.

'Can't be anyone here,' said Peter. 'Go and look,
Scamper. You're just making a fuss.'

Scamper went slowly and stiffly over towards the shed,
growling. Everyone watched, puzzled. He went right to
the shed door, and then let off a loud volley of barks. An
angry voice came from the shed.

'Clear off!' Then a stone came flying out, narrowly
missing the surprised Scamper.

Peter raced up to the shed at once, and stood angrily at

315

the door, glaring at three men inside. 'What do you mean by throwing stones at my dog? You nearly hit him. You might have lamed him.'

There came the sound of scornful laughter and then a stone came spinning out of the shed door and caught Peter on the ankle.

Scamper gave a fierce growl and darted forward. Peter just caught him in time before he went into the shed.

'You'd better get out of this shed,' cried the boy, angrily. 'It doesn't belong to you. It's Burton's hut. I'll fetch him over here to you if you don't clear out.'

He stood glaring at the three laughing men, and one of them sent another stone skimming through the door. It just missed Scamper. 'I'll go and get Burton,' shouted Peter, and turned to go. He ran back to the others, who were all standing together, amazed.

'I'm going to get Burton,' panted Peter. 'Watch and see if the men go.'

He shot off to find Burton, but before he had time to come back, the three men came out of the shed, stood at the doorway a few seconds, and stared at the watching children. One of them shook his fist. The boys pushed the three girls behind them, as the men walked towards them. But they turned off between the trees, and disappeared, talking in low voices.

'What a nasty-looking lot,' said Janet, relieved to see them go. 'I wonder what they were up to in that shed?'

'Planning some kind of mischief, I should think,' said Colin. 'It would be a jolly good meeting-place for three rogues.'

'I've got a notebook,' said Jack. 'I'm going to jot down what the men are like – just in *case* it might be useful.'

'But how could it be?' said Pam.

'You never know,' said Jack. 'Hallo, here's Peter. Didn't you get Burton?'

'No – he's gone off somewhere,' panted Peter. 'Those men gone?'

'Yes,' said Colin. 'And Jack's just going to jot down some notes about them. We think they're probably plotting some kind of mischief. Let's see – one man was short and dark, and had a crooked nose . . .'

'Yes,' said Jack, writing. 'And one was big and fat, and had a moustache. No hat. Gingery hair.'

'And the third one was thin, and limped,' said Pam. 'His ears stuck out too. I noticed them.'

Jack finished scribbling and put his notebook away.

'Now let's take all our stuff back,' he said. 'Where are the ropes, Peter? Let's have the sweets in our own shed – I don't fancy Burton's shed after those scruffy-looking men have been there!'

Six

The bonfire is begun

PETER had three lengths of rope tied round his waist, and he now untied them and gave one each to Jack and George.

'Make a big bundle of wood and tie it with the rope,' he said. 'Come on, girls – you help me with my bundle!'

They were soon busy tying up the collected wood into enormous bundles. Then they put the ropes over their shoulders, and set off through the trees, pulling the bundles across the field to the place planned for their bonfire.

'This is fun,' said Janet, as she and Peter dragged one great bundle over the field. 'Oh Pam – look, some of our bits have dropped out. You walk behind and pick them up for us.'

In about half an hour's time all the twigs and rotten branches were piled up well. The Seven stood back and looked at the heap proudly, Scamper wagging his tail as though he too had helped with the bundles! But all he had done was to carry one long twig back in his mouth, banging it against Peter's legs!

'There!' said Peter. 'That's a jolly good beginning, I must say. I tell you what, if anyone has half an hour to spare, I think they should pop along and collect a few more bits and pieces, Janet and I might be able to in our dinner-hour next week.'

'And I could race along from afternoon school perhaps, on my bike, at four o'clock sometime,' said George. 'It would still be light enough to hunt about.'

'Good,' said Peter. 'Every little helps, as my Dad says when he wants us to go weeding, and hopes we'll do half the garden!'

'Let's go and sit down and have Jack's sweets,' said Pam. 'I feel quite tired out.'

They left the pile of wood and went to sit in their own shed. Peter unlocked the door and they went in.

'I'm keeping the door locked because I've got our firework money in that box on the shelf,' he said. 'And also because of the guy. Susie just *might* come along and do something silly to it.'

'She wouldn't touch the money, though, you know that jolly well,' said Jack at once.

Peter nodded. 'Yes. I know that, of course. Come on – hand out the sweets, Jack. It's nearly dinner-time, but I bet they won't spoil our appetites. Not mine anyway, because we're having steak and kidney pudding, and *nothing* would put me off that.'

'*Why* did you have to mention steak and kidney?' groaned George. 'You've made me feel so hungry that I could eat all Jack's sweets at one go.'

Jack hastily stuffed the sweets back into his pocket. His hand touched his notebook, and he remembered that he had written the three men's descriptions in it. He drew it out, and read them out loud.

'It will be funny if we meet them again,' he said. 'We shall know where they're going – probably to Burton's hut in the woods.'

'We shan't meet them again – not in Burton's hut or anywhere else,' said Colin. 'They were just tramps, wandering over the country. They sat down for a rest in the hut, I expect.'

'Oh well – you never know,' said Jack, rather damped,

319

and put his notebook back into his pocket. 'When's our next meeting, Peter?'

'Can you manage Thursday afternoon, after school?' said Peter. 'Not for finding wood, but just for seeing what guy clothes we get and if anyone has some more money. Then we shan't have to spend so much time on those things next Saturday morning; we can get straight on with collecting wood for the bonfire.'

'Right,' said Colin, and George and Jack nodded too.

'Pam and I may not be able to come,' said Barbara. 'We may have an extra dancing lesson then. We're in a concert soon, you know.'

'Well, come if you can,' said Peter. 'Same password – and badges, of course. There's our dinner-bell. We must go. See you on Monday, chaps!'

They all departed, and Peter and Janet and Scamper went up the path to their house.

'Wash your hands!' called their mother. 'My goodness me, you *are* dirty!'

'We've been collecting wood for our bonfire,' called back Janet. 'We won't be a minute.'

They told their mother all about their morning as they ate their steak and kidney pudding very hungrily indeed. When they came to the piece about the three men in the hut, their mother looked up sharply.

'Now listen – you are not to go into the wood unless there are at least three or four of you – certainly not alone. I don't like the sound of those men. There are some very bad men about in these days.'

'But Mother, they were only tramps,' said Peter. 'And anyway, Scamper was with us.'

'Well, if you go into the wood you are to take Scamper

with you,' said Mother. 'And you are not to let any of the girls wander about without you boys. Now that's an *order*. Do you understand, or shall I get Daddy to say so?'

'No – of course not. We'll do exactly what you say,' said Peter, surprised. 'Mother, you should just *see* our bonfire pile of wood – it's awfully big already.'

'I shall have to come and watch it when you set it alight,' said his mother. 'And see the fireworks too. By the way, Janet, if you want to earn firework money, you can do a little job for me.'

'Oh good. What, Mother?' asked Janet.

'You can turn out the linen cupboard and put back everything tidily for me,' said his mother. 'That will be a five pence job if you do it well.'

'Right, I'd love to,' said Janet. 'I like arranging things. I'll do it this very evening. Our next meeting is on Thursday, you know.'

But their next meeting came before Thursday after all. Something very exciting happened – and it was Colin who called the meeting, not Peter!

Seven

Colin has some news

On Monday evening, when Peter and Janet were sitting quietly doing their homework, the telephone rang. Mother went to answer it.

She called to Peter. 'It's for you, Peter. Colin wants to speak to you. He sounds very excited.'

Peter shot to the telephone at once, and Janet went too. What had happened? Colin had walked part of the way home from school with Peter that afternoon, and hadn't seemed in the least excited about anything.

'Hallo? Peter here,' said Peter, and at once heard Colin's excited voice. 'Peter, can I come and see you *at once*? Something's happened. I want to call a meeting of the Secret Seven as soon as possible – tomorrow after school perhaps. Can I come right along now? I'll only be a minute or two on my bike.'

'Goodness – what's the matter?' said Peter, astonished. 'A meeting? Whatever about?'

'Can't tell you now. People might hear,' said Colin. This sounded very mysterious indeed.

'Well, come along at once,' said Peter. 'Better come to the shed. We'll be alone there. See you soon.'

He put down the receiver, and stared at Janet, who was just beside him.

'What is it?' she said, excited.

'Don't know,' said Peter. 'He's coming in a few minutes – to the shed. He wants to call a meeting of the Secret Seven tomorrow. Whatever *can* be the matter?'

'I'm coming down to the shed too,' said Janet.

'No, you're not,' said Peter. 'All right, all right – don't look so fierce. I'll let you come, but remember, not a word to anyone unless I say so.'

'As if I *would* say anything!' said Janet, scornfully. 'Mother! Mother, where are you? Peter and I are going to slip down to our shed for a minute. Colin wants to see us about something important.'

'Aha! Secret Seven business, I suppose,' said her mother. 'All right, but put coats on, please. It will be cold down there tonight.'

They put on their coats and slipped down to the shed, with Scamper trotting happily at their heels. Peter unlocked the door, and lighted a little oil-lamp his mother had given him for the shed. He set it carefully on a box.

The two waited patiently for Colin, trying in vain to think what could have excited him so. It must be something very important if he wanted to call a meeting! Any member had the right to do this, though as a rule it was only Peter who did so.

Jingle-jingle! That was a bicycle bell. *Click* – that was the front gate. Then came the sound of footsteps as Colin hurried down the path to the shed, wheeling his bicycle.

He rapped at the door. 'Wee Willie Winkie,' he said, in a low voice, and Peter opened the door at once.

'What's all the excitement about?' Peter asked. 'Sit down and tell us.'

'I'll begin at the beginning,' said Colin, whose face was red with cycling fast and with excitement. 'You know where my granny lives, don't you? Not far from my house, but round the corner?'

'Yes,' said Peter and Janet together.

'Well, she's away,' said Colin, 'but she's coming back

tomorrow, so my mother asked me if I'd take some new-laid eggs to Granny's house – we keep hens, you know – and give them to Greta, her Austrian maid, so that Granny could have some poached eggs when she gets back. It's her favourite meal.'

He stopped and rubbed his hot face with his hanky.

'Go on,' said Peter. 'Do come to the point.'

'I *am*,' said Colin. 'Well, I took the eggs and ran up the road and round the corner. There was a light in the hall as usual – but I didn't knock at the front door, because I always go in the back way. It saves Greta coming to the door. Well, I slipped round the back way, and got to the kitchen door. It was shut, but not locked.'

'Wuff!' said Scamper, suddenly, and made them all jump.

'It's all right – he only saw a mouse run over the floor,' said Janet. 'Do go on.'

'I went inside,' said Colin. 'Greta wasn't in the kitchen, so I went through to the sitting-room. There was a light there, and I wondered if Granny had got back a day early, I pushed open the door – and my word *what* a mess I saw! Phew!'

'What kind of a mess?' asked Peter, thrilled.

'Everything upside down – drawers pulled out and emptied on the floor. The cupboard broken open. And then I saw Granny's safe – that was broken open too! She had it behind a big mirror – I didn't know that before. Someone had taken down the mirror, found the safe and smashed it open. It was empty!'

'*Colin!* How *awful!*' said Janet.

'Where was Greta?' said Peter. 'Surely *she* hadn't done all that!'

'Of *course* not,' said Colin. 'I suddenly heard a wailing

noise, and rushed out into the hall. I traced the noise to the kitchen – and then to the larder, which was locked on the outside. I unlocked the door – and there was poor Greta inside, locked in!'

'What did you do next?' asked Peter, really excited.

'I telephoned the police,' said Colin. 'I felt frightfully important, ringing up the police-station. Two men came round at once – and by that time my mother and father were there too, because I phoned them as well.'

'But why do you want to call a meeting of the Secret Seven about this?' asked Peter. '*We* can't do anything.'

'Well, listen,' said Colin. 'I heard Greta giving details of the robbers to the police – three men – and she described two of them *exactly* as Jack described those men in his notebook – the men we saw. Greta didn't see the third – but I'm *sure* they must have been the men we saw in Burton's hut – and for all we know they were planning the robbery then!'

'Whew!' said Peter. 'Think of that! Yes – we'll certainly call a meeting tomorrow. After afternoon school sharp at quarter past four. My word – what a thrill!'

Eight
Another meeting

TUESDAY seemed a very long day indeed to the Secret Seven. They longed for afternoon school to be over so that they could race off to the meeting-shed, and hear all that Colin had to say. He had actually been called out of school that morning by the police, who wanted to ask him questions!

'I bet he feels jolly important,' said Jack to Peter, as Colin walked out of the schoolroom. 'I'm longing for our meeting, aren't you?'

The meeting time came at last. Everyone was at the shed very punctually indeed, except Jack, who arrived last of all, panting for breath.

'Wee Willie Winkie,' he gasped. 'Sorry to be last, but it was Susie's fault. She wanted to know what was up, and when I wouldn't tell her, she went and hid my bike – and her own too – so I had to run all the way here on my feet.'

'Sit down,' said Peter. 'Colin, begin your story, please.'

Colin told it all over again. He was sorry that it was his granny's house that had been robbed, but he couldn't help feeling very thrilled that he had been the one to discover the robbery, and telephone the police.

'So Greta saw two of the men, but not the third,' said Peter, when Colin had finished. 'Have you brought your notebook, Jack? I rather think we shall find the description of the third robber there!'

Jack fumbled for his notebook, his face alight with excitement. 'To think I wrote down all their descriptions –

just by chance, really, because I happened to have my notebook!' he said. 'Wait a minute – yes, here are my notes. Colin, how did Greta describe the two men *she* saw?'

'She said one was very short and dark,' said Colin, 'and she specially noticed that his nose was crooked, and she said he had bad teeth.'

'Well, that answers exactly to my first description,' said Jack, excited. 'I've got "One man was short and dark, and had a crooked nose". I didn't notice his bad teeth.'

'The crooked nose is enough, really,' said Colin. 'Well, that was one man. Greta said the second man was thin, and had ears that stuck out from his head. She said she thought he was lame, but she wasn't sure about that.'

'Ha – she's right!' said Jack, looking at his notes again. 'Listen. I've got one man down as thin, and noted that he limped – well, that's Greta's second robber, no doubt about that! You say she didn't see the other one?'

'No – she said that the men burst in at the kitchen door, and she saw the first two quite clearly. The third man was behind them, so she couldn't describe him. The first two leapt at her, and she fell to the floor, poor Greta. They turned her on her face, and the third man bound her hands, and then they bundled her into the larder and locked the door. She wasn't really hurt – only scared stiff.'

'She must have been thrilled to see you when you opened the larder!' said Janet.

'She was! I undid her hands, and she put her arms round my neck and hugged me, and said hundreds of things in German, which I couldn't understand at all,' said Colin. 'Then she sat down, plump, on a chair – and *most* unluckily it was where I'd put the bag of eggs.'

Everyone roared with laughter, and then stopped, look-ing rather guilty.

'We oughtn't to have laughed,' said Janet. 'It's all very serious – but honestly – when I thought of poor Greta sitting down on Colin's eggs, I just couldn't help myself!'

'Well, Greta laughed too, when she found out,' said Colin. 'Actually she laughed and cried at the same time. Gosh, I did have a time – seeing to Greta, and telephoning the police and Mother and Dad – and waiting for the police to arrive – well, honestly, I half thought it must all be a dream!'

'I bet you did,' said Peter. 'Did you tell the police that you thought we'd seen the three men?'

'Yes, I did,' said Colin. 'But I didn't say anything about Jack writing down the descriptions of them, because I thought perhaps he'd like to tell them that himself. I mean – it might be an important clue.'

'Jolly decent of you,' said Jack. 'Shall we go to the police together, straight away now, Colin, with my note-book?'

'Yes, you'd better,' said Peter. 'They'll be interested to know we've got descriptions of the third man. Or rather, that you have, Jack. Good thing you wrote them down – you just *never* know when a thing like that is going to be useful.'

'I think we'll go now,' said Jack, getting up, looking rather important. 'Come on, Colin.'

'Thanks for calling the meeting, Peter,' said Colin. 'Can we have another soon – to tell you what happens at the police-station when Jack and I give them the third man's description?'

'Rather – tomorrow, same time,' said Peter. 'And I'll see if my mother will let us have tea down here in the shed. See you tomorrow then, Jack and Colin.'

They were just getting up when Scamper began to bark loudly and excitedly. Then there came a loud knock at the door, which made them all jump.

'Open in the name of the law,' said a queer, deep voice.

'Gracious – it's the police again,' said Colin, and opened the door.

There was no one there! The Seven stared out into the half-darkness, feeling just a bit scared. Scamper raced out, barking, and stopped by a bush. Peter ran up to it, and shone his torch there. A delighted giggle greeted him.

'*Susie!*' yelled everyone, in a fury.

'Please, Peter, I've brought poor Jack's bicycle for him to ride home on,' said the maddening Susie. 'I thought he'd be pleased.'

'You horrid little snooper!' shouted Jack. But Susie had gone, slipping away in the darkness. How much had she heard? *What* a little wretch she was!

Nine

Susie really is annoying

COLIN and Jack cycled off to the police-station at once, Jack with his precious notebook in his pocket. When they got to the station, they found the sergeant there, a man they liked very much. He had already seen Colin twice – once when the police had gone to his granny's house, in answer to his telephone call, and once when they had called him out of school that morning, to ask him questions.

'Hallo, Colin – you again!' said the sergeant, and smiled. 'Well – got any more burglars to report?'

'No, sir,' said Colin. 'But Jack here has the description of the third man – the one Greta didn't see.'

'Well, I'm blessed!' said the sergeant, and pulled a note-pad in front of him. 'We've got pretty good descriptions of two of the men, but not the third. Greta didn't see him, as you just now said. How do *you* know what he was like? You said you didn't see anyone yourself, at the house.'

'No, sir,' said Colin. 'You see, it's like this. We were out in the woods last Saturday, and we came to a hut, and inside were three men. They were pretty awful to us and we thought they might be up to some mischief. So Jack here wrote down their descriptions. Jack, give your notes to the sergeant.'

Jack handed them over. The sergeant read them quickly. He whistled when he came to 'One was big and

fat, and had a moustache. No hat. Gingery hair.' He put
the notebook down and looked at Jack.

'Good work, son,' he said. 'Really, kids are pretty smart
nowadays! Your description of two of them is excellent –
we're pretty certain we know who they are, though we
don't know *where* they are. I can't place the third one –
the big, fat fellow, with a moustache and gingery hair.
What was he dressed in? Did you notice?'

'Well no,' said Jack, trying to remember. 'They were all
pretty dirty and scruffy. Nothing outstanding in their
clothes, as far as I can remember. Did you notice anything
in the way they were dressed, Colin?'

'No. I just think they were in overcoats of some sort,'
said Colin, frowning. 'Two of them wore hats or, caps –
and I know one hadn't a hat – that was the red-haired
fellow, of course. We all noticed his hair, because he had
no hat.'

'Well, this is a great help,' said the sergeant, giving Jack
back his notebook. 'I expect those thieves are miles away
by now, but keep your eyes open, will you – you and the
others?'

'We certainly will, sir,' said both boys together. They
said goodnight, and left the police-station, both feeling
very thrilled at having been able to help.

'We'll tell the others all this at the meeting tomorrow
night,' said Jack. 'Golly, I'll have to race home! I've loads
of homework to do. Wait till I see that sister of mine –
pretending she was the police tonight, and making us
open our shed-door to her! Perhaps she won't interfere so
much in future though – she's having two friends to stay
with her – both girls, whose mother's in hospital. Susie will
be so busy looking after them that she won't have time to
interfere with the Secret Seven.'

'Good thing!' said Colin, who heartily disliked the aggravating Susie. 'We don't want her poking her nose into this!'

They parted and went their separate ways. Jack went to find Susie as soon as he got home, to tick her off for breaking in on their meeting that night.

'Susie!' he yelled, as soon as he got in. 'Where are you? What do you mean by pretending to . . . oh, sorry, I thought you were Susie!'

'No. I'm Doris, who's come to stay,' said the girl he had thought was Susie. 'And this is Hilda, my sister. It's nice of your mother to have us. I hope we shan't be in the way.'

Jack looked at Doris and Hilda, and he didn't much like what he saw. They grinned at him impudently, he thought, and he didn't look forward to having *three* giggling girls talking about him, and nudging each other, and playing jokes on him. One was bad enough!

'Open in the name of the law!' said a voice – Susie's, of course. 'Oh, Jack – did you really think I . . .'

'You behaved abominably,' said Jack. 'Breaking in on our meeting like that. I was ashamed of you.'

'We're going to make a little club ourselves – Hilda, Doris and I,' said Susie. 'It's called the Tiresome Three.'

'I should think it's a very good name,' said Jack. 'So long as you don't make yourselves tiresome to *us*, and keep away when we're meeting.'

'Oh, the grand Secret Seven!' said Susie. She turned to the giggling Hilda and Doris. 'You've no idea how solemn their silly old meetings are,' she said. 'Passwords, badges, nobody else allowed in, oh, they think they're too grand for words. You look out, Jack – the Tiresome Three might come and join you one night!'

'Shall we raid their shed?' said Doris. 'That's what my

brother and his club did to another club – they got a lot of things, they got . . .'

'If you *dare* to interfere with us, *any* of you, I'll – I'll pull your hair off!' cried Jack, exasperated, and marched out of the room, boiling over.

'What a bad-tempered brother you've got, Susie,' he heard Hilda say, and he very nearly turned back to pull her hair. He went to his room and sat down, frowning. Never mind! *Let* them laugh and giggle! The Secret Seven were helping the police, and he couldn't see the Tiresome Three helping *any*one!

'I'll have to warn the Seven that Susie and the others mean to make trouble,' he thought, as he took his home-work from his school bag. 'Thank goodness we've got old Scamper – he always barks when anyone comes near the shed. How *dare* Susie do the things she does!'

Ten

A wonderful guy

PETER asked his mother if he could have the Secret Seven to tea the next day, Wednesday.

'You see, Mother, what with one thing and another, there seems to be a lot to talk about and plan – Bonfire Night, of course, and now this business of Colin's Granny being robbed, and us having seen the three men . . .'

'We'll see to the tea ourselves, Mother, you don't need to do a thing,' said Janet. 'And we won't scamp our home-work, we promise you.'

'All right, dears – of course you can have a Secret Seven tea,' said their mother. 'I'll cut the bread and butter, and I'll bake you some biscuits, and you can buy some buns or something at the baker's. I shan't have time to make cakes too. Do you want lemonade or tea?'

'Oh, lemonade – no, orangeade for a change!' said Peter. *'We'll* carry everything down, Mother, and we'll wash up, too. You're always so *decent* about the Secret Seven.'

'Well, if you want to know something – I'm very glad I've got a decent son, who runs a decent club, helped by a very decent sister!' said Mother, laughing.

Everyone was very punctual at the meeting, and their eyes shone when they saw the spread provided for them.

'I'm glad I didn't eat too much dinner today,' said Colin, eyeing the currant bread and butter, and the jam sandwich that Janet had bought, and the big plate of home-made biscuits.

They talked as they munched away at their tea, Scamper gnawing happily at a great big bone. Jack told them about Susie and the Tiresome Three. Peter groaned.

'*Don't* say they're going to play silly tricks on us – really, I'm getting awfully tired of Susie,' he said.

'Well, it doesn't much matter if they raid us while we're *here*,' said Janet. 'The door's locked. And if they come when we're not here, the door will still be locked! Even Susie wouldn't break the window, surely, to get in!'

'How are you getting on with the guy?' asked Jack.

'We'll show you, when we begin the meeting,' said Janet. 'We've got some fine clothes for him! Pam's father was a brick. When he heard about the guy, he rummaged through his old clothes, and sent some.'

'You see, Dad's big and rather fat,' said Pam. 'So his clothes should fit the guy beautifully.'

'And George's father gave George a wonderful cap for the guy,' said Janet. 'Your father must have an awfully big head, George – the cap's enormous.'

'He *has* got a big head,' said George, proudly, 'It needs to be big, he's terribly brainy, you know.'

'And our dad gave us some old gum boots – his field boots, simply colossal,' said Peter. 'They might be too big even for the fat legs of the guy!'

'We'll dress him up after the meeting,' said Janet. 'He's there, waiting at the back – he'll be glad to be dressed. He needs a mask, too.'

'I'll slip up to the shops and get one as soon as I've finished tea,' said Colin. 'I don't like guys without faces – they look horrid. I bet old Scamper won't like the mask, though!'

'I hope you've all remembered to bring a little firework money,' said Peter.

'Yes,' said everyone, and Peter grinned, very pleased. He couldn't help thinking that his club must be about the best in the kingdom! Even their dog always behaved well!

The boys carried back the tea-things when tea was over. Then they settled down to the meeting, and Peter took the firework money from each member. He added up the total. 'Whew! One pound and five pence – pretty good, you know – and there's still some time to go. We mustn't forget we've still got to build our bonfire higher.'

'We can collect more wood on Saturday morning,' said George. 'Now, what about dressing the guy?'

They pulled the fat, shapeless body out from its rubber sheet, and sat it on a box. Scamper growled at it at once. He didn't like it at all.

They began to dress it, laughing. It wasn't at all easy.

'It seems as if the old guy just *won't* help us!' panted Jack, trying to pull a pair of enormous trousers over the guy's plump legs. 'Don't be so *awkward*, guy!'

'It's a good thing Pam's father is such a big man,' said Barbara. 'The guy is larger than we thought! What about some braces?'

'Oh, we don't need those. We can safety-pin the trousers to his body,' said Janet. 'There, the trousers are on at last – they make him more real, somehow.'

'Now the coat,' said Jack, taking up a rather stained old tweed coat, that didn't match the trousers.

'That's the coat my dad used when he was plastering and painting our kitchen,' said Pam. 'My mother said she was glad to see the back of it! Aren't the buttons nice? Half-yellow and half-brown. Too good for the guy, really!'

'Well, it fits him beautifully,' said Peter, laughing as he did up the buttons. 'Feeling warmer now, Mr Guy? Colin, what about you going to buy a mask before the shops shut?'

'Right,' said Colin, and slipped out of the shed door. 'Shan't be long.'

The others began to pull the boots on to the guy's plump legs. It really was a hard job.

'He's an obstinate fellow, this guy,' said Jack. 'Wants to go bare-foot, I suppose! There – that boot's on, thank goodness. Stop growling, Scamper. Anyone would think you didn't like our beautiful guy!'

Scamper's growls suddenly became louder and he ran to the door. 'Susie! The Tiresome Three!' said everyone. But they were wrong.

It was Colin, carrying a mask, and in a great state of excitement. He waved an evening paper at them.

'I say! There's news about the thieves who got into my granny's house. They've caught two of them. It's all printed here. Stop messing about with the guy, and listen.'

'Shut the door,' said Peter, sharply, afraid that Susie might be lurking outside, and Colin banged it at once. He sat down on a box, and opened the paper. 'It's here – in the stop press news – this bit in the corner,' he said. 'I'll read it to you.'

Eleven

One up to the Tiresome Three

'Go on – do read it,' said Janet, impatiently.

'It is reported this afternoon that two of the thieves who robbed Mrs Strangeway's house on Monday night, have been caught by the police. They had not left the district. The third man ran away and escaped. The police have a full description of him. He is stout, tall and has a moustache and red hair. Unfortunately the stolen articles have not yet been recovered. Anyone having seen a man of the above description is asked to contact the police.'

'Gosh!' said Peter, as Colin finished reading. 'So they've got two of the men already. What a pity the other fellow escaped.'

'Yes – and took the stuff with him, I suppose,' said Colin gloomily. 'My poor old granny is in an awful state, as you can imagine. She had to go to bed with shock as soon as she got back, and my mother sent for the doctor. If only she could get back the things she prized most – my grandfather's silver cups – the ones he won for all kinds of sport – and the jewellery that's been in her family for years. I wish the police had got the stolen stuff instead of the robbers!'

'Probably the two thieves who were caught will soon confess where they hid it,' said Pam.

'Well, I should think the third man, who wasn't caught, will certainly go and take the things from whatever hiding-place they are in now, and hide them somewhere else!' said Peter. 'Just in case his pals gave away the hiding-place! He could then wait a bit till all the hue and cry had died down, and take them for himself!'

'Yes, I suppose he could,' said Colin, laying down the paper. 'Fancy the men still being in the district. You'd have thought they would have got away as soon as possible.'

'I bet the man who's free will have put a hundred miles between himself and the police by now,' said Jack.

'If he hasn't, he'll find it difficult to move about in the daytime,' said Colin. 'You can shave off a moustache, but you can't hide your fatness – or your ginger hair.'

'You *can* hide your hair – dye it, say – or wear a hat, silly,' said Barbara.

'Let's get on with the guy,' said Janet. 'What do you think of him, Colin?'

She and Pam pulled the guy in front of Colin. He looked very queer in his big trousers, carefully safety-pinned in place, his enormous dirty old tweed coat, and large rubber boots. Scamper began to bark angrily again.

'He simply can't bear our guy,' said Pam. 'Did you get a mask, Colin? Oh yes, there it is. Put it on the guy, then we can put the cap on his head.'

Colin carefully fitted the big mask over the front of the guy's head. Everyone roared with laughter. The guy seemed very real now he had a face!

'Isn't it odd – you've chosen a mask with a red moustache!' said Janet. 'Like the robber who got away! Mr Guy Fawkes, are you sure you're not the third robber?'

The guy stared solemnly at her, and Scamper growled again. He really did not like the guy at all.

340

'Take the mask off and squeeze the head a bit to make the mask fit better,' said George. 'It sticks out over his chest too much.'

They took off the mask, and pummelled the stuffed head till it was a better shape. Then on went the mask again, and Scamper gave another volley of angry barks.

'Now the cap,' said George, and solemnly placed it on the guy's head, screwing it round a bit to give it a jaunty, rakish look. The Seven laughed uproariously. The guy looked really comical with his cap on.

'How do you do, Mr Fawkes?' said George, and shook him by the hand. 'I hope you are feeling well, and looking forward to warming yourself on our bonfire next week.'

'He looks awfully uncomfortable sitting on that box,' said Janet. 'And he's heavy to hold up straight. Can't we get him an old chair, or something, to sit in? He'll last a lot longer on top of the bonfire if he's sitting up.'

'I think there's an old chair, with arms, in the stables,' said Peter. 'Nobody uses it now. Let's go and get it, shall we?'

They all trooped out of the shed, Scamper too, leaving the guy sprawled over his box.

'Back in a minute, Mr Fawkes,' said Colin, politely, and made the others laugh.

They made their way to the stables, and there sure enough, in a corner with other jumble, was the old chair. Its cane seat was almost gone, and part of the back. But it still had its two arms.

'Just the thing,' said Peter, pleased. 'We can easily put a bit of wood over the rotten cane seat, for him to sit on. Give me a hand, Colin.'

They took the old chair back to the shed, Peter shining his torch as they went. When they came in sight of the shed, glowing by the light of its little oil-lamp, they stopped in a hurry!

Peter's torch had picked up something standing against the shed, near the open door. Whatever – whoever – was it?

'It's – it's our *guy*!' cried Janet in fright. 'Look – he's walked out of the shed – he's standing there! Peter! Look at him!'

Yes, there was the guy, sure enough, leaning against the shed, quite still, his mask looking exactly like a face. And then – and then came the sound of suppressed giggles from somewhere nearby!

'*Susie!*' yelled Jack, in fury. 'You've taken our guy and stood him outside. Wait till I get you three – how *dare* you!'

There came the sound of more giggles, and then scampering feet. The Tiresome Three, having made their first raid, were gone!

'They've hung him on a nail, look,' said Peter, angrily seeing that the guy's neck was neatly impaled on an old nail at just about the right height. 'Golly – didn't he look real, leaning there against the shed? What on earth possessed us to go off and leave the door open? We must have been mad!'

'Wait till I get home,' said Jack, grimly. 'I'll tick those girls off properly. Here – let's take the guy into the shed again. Come along, Mr Fawkes. Sorry you've had such a silly trick played on you, poor old fellow!'

Twelve

Jack can be tiresome too!

THE Secret Seven were really very angry to think that the Tiresome Three had actually dared to go into their meeting-shed, and take out the guy.

'What idiots we were to leave the shed open, even for those few minutes!' groaned Peter. 'But Scamper didn't bark or growl as he usually does when there's anyone hiding near.'

'I expect they arrived at the very minute we went off to get the chair,' said Colin. 'Just a bit of sheer luck for them, that's all. For goodness sake lock the door each time you leave the shed, Peter. They'll steal the whole guy next, and burn him on their own bonfire. Are they going to have a bonfire, Jack?'

'Don't ask *me*,' said Jack. 'As if they'd tell me anything! Those two girls, Doris and Hilda, are even worse than Susie, it seems to me! Giggle, giggle, giggle, all the time. I expect they *will* have fireworks and a bonfire – I don't know about a guy.'

They sat the guy down in the chair, having first put a sheet of wood under him to stop him sinking down through the broken cane seat. He sat there, his arms on the arms of the chair, looking as if he wanted to smoke a pipe or read a newspaper!

'He's not a bad guy at all,' said Barbara. 'I've never seen such a nice *plump* one before. We could perhaps get him an old pipe – we could stick it into his mouth for him.'

'I say – it's getting pretty late,' said George, looking at his watch. 'I've got homework to do. I must go. That was a jolly good meeting, even if it had an annoying ending. Don't forget to thank your mother for us, Peter. Jolly fine tea!'

The meeting broke up, for not only George had homework to do. Soon the shed was in darkness, the door securely locked, and the key in Peter's pocket. The guy sat there in his chair alone.

Jack cycled back home, fuming with rage. Susie really was behaving badly. What a sister to have! He went to put his bicycle away, and suddenly spotted a faint light in the summer-house down the garden.

'Hallo – who's there?' he thought, and crept down to see. He heard low voices, and recognized them at once.

'Susie – and the others! A meeting of the Tiresome Three, I suppose!' thought Jack, grimly. 'All right – *I'll* do a little snooping this time!'

He stood close to the windows of the summer-house, thinking that it was a remarkably cold spot to choose for a meeting-place. He grinned to himself. What a fine revenge for Susie's surprise that night!

He heard Susie's voice. 'We can't let the Seven crow over us with a guy like that – and firework money for tons of fireworks – and the biggest bonfire in the district!' she said. 'I wouldn't mind if they'd let us *share* in the fireworks and *see* the bonfire, and help to burn the guy – but they're jolly mean, all of them, and they just won't share a thing.'

'Well, we'll raid them again,' said a voice – it sounded like Hilda's. 'What about their bonfire? Where is it? Can't we raid that?'

'I don't know where it is,' said Susie. 'I can find out,

though. I'll ask Jack quite nicely – and I bet he'll tell me!'

There were a few giggles, and something that Jack couldn't catch. He began to boil with fury. Raid the Secret Seven's *bonfire*! What a nerve!

'It's a pity we've so little money for fireworks,' said Doris. 'They're so frightfully expensive – and it's no fun unless you have a lot. And we haven't a guy, either.'

'It's not much good having a guy unless you've got a bonfire to burn him on,' said Susie. 'Didn't their guy have marvellous clothes? I wish we could get hold of some like that!'

Then came more talk that Jack couldn't hear. The Tiresome Three must have put their heads close together, and were making plans. *What* plans? Jack had great forebodings. What were these awful girls going to do next? He *certainly* wouldn't tell them where the bonfire was! Well, he might *hint* – but it would be a hint that would send them quite in the wrong direction!

Jack began to smile. Yes – he could send the Tiresome Three on a long, long walk – with no bonfire at the end of it! It would serve them right.

Then he thought he would give the girls a fright to pay them out for their night's mischief. He opened his mouth and gave a weird and wonderful groan that startled even himself.

'Oooo-ah-oooo-ee-AHHHH!'

There was a sudden silence in the summer-house. Then he heard Susie's scared voice. 'Gracious! Whatever was that?'

Jack groaned again, ending with a most blood-curdling yowl. With three terrified shrieks the Tiresome Three stumbled out of the summer-house and fled up the garden at top speed. Jack went into the summer-house and collapsed on the seat, holding his sides with laughter.

'Oh my! I really didn't know I could groan like that!' he said. 'Well – I'll saunter into the house now, and pretend I've just come from the Secret Seven meeting.'

So in he strolled, hands in his pockets, humming a tune. The girls turned to him at once, still looking scared.

'Jack! Did you hear a perfectly frightful noise as you came in through the garden?' asked Susie.

'What do you mean? The cat mewing?' said Jack. 'Don't say you're scared of *him*! Or do you mean the old brown owl? You girls! If you heard a mouse squeak you'd skitter off in fright! And by the way, I suppose you think that was funny, taking our guy out of the shed like that? Well, it wasn't. It was just plain mean.'

'Well, aren't *you* mean?' demanded Susie at once. 'You won't share your guy and we haven't one. You won't share your fireworks – and we've none! And I bet you won't even tell us where your bonfire will be – you won't even let us *see* that!'

'Where *is* the bonfire?' said Hilda, looking very innocent. 'Fancy not even telling us that!'

'Oh, I'll tell you where you'll find a bonfire we've built,' said Jack. 'You know Haylings Field, that runs up that very steep hill? Well, you'll find a bonfire there, all ready to light. Now don't you be mean and light it! I don't trust you three giggling fatheads an inch!'

He strolled out of the room, and the Tiresome Three grinned at one another.

'Easy, wasn't it?' said Susie. 'We'll go there tomorrow! *And* we'll pull their bonfire to bits!'

Thirteen
Face at the window

Jack cycled round to Peter's early the next morning to tell him the joke he meant to play on the Tiresome Three. Peter grinned.

'Jolly good idea! I'll cycle up Haylings Hill with you now, and we'll take a few miserable twigs – and a note to put under them! When will the girls go up, do you think?'

'After afternoon school, I imagine,' said Jack. 'Only Susie has a bike, so they'll have to climb all the way up on foot – and you know how steep it is.'

'I'll write a note now,' said Peter, getting out his note-book and pencil. He scribbled something and signed it, then passed it across to Jack.

'YOU CAN HAVE THE WHOLE OF THIS BONFIRE IF YOU LIKE. HOPE YOU EN-JOYED YOUR CLIMB. A GOOD LAUGH FROM — THE SECRET SEVEN.'

Jack chuckled. 'Jolly good. That will make them wild – they'll have all that long climb for nothing! All the same, we'll have to keep an eye on our *real* bonfire, Peter. I wouldn't be in the least surprised if they didn't come and look for it and kick it about, when they find they've been tricked into going up to the top of Haylings Hill.'

'Yes. We'll certainly keep an eye on it. One or other of us had better keep guard there, I suppose,' said Peter. 'What's to-day – Thursday. We'll all meet this afternoon, I think, and we'll take what money anyone brings, and arrange for two of us to go and buy fireworks on Saturday. Better not leave it too late or the best ones will be gone.

Let's see, Bonfire Night is on Sunday – that means we'll have to hold it on Monday.'

'Why not Saturday?' asked Jack.

'Colin said he might not be able to come,' said Peter. 'He asked me *not* to make it Saturday. I'd better get my bike and ride up Haylings Hill with you straight away, or we'll be late for school. Gather a few sticks and twigs while I get it.'

Soon the two boys were cycling off at top speed. In their bicycle baskets was a collection of small twigs. They grinned when they looked at them.

Haylings Hill was very steep indeed. They had to get off their bicycles near the top and push them. At last they were at the summit, and hurriedly arranged a criss-cross of twigs as if for a small fire. Peter stuffed the note under the twigs, so that a corner of it showed.

'There! I hope the Tiresome Three will enjoy their climb!' he said. 'Come on – it's getting late. Thank goodness it's all downhill now!'

The Secret Seven met again in their shed that day at a quarter past five, when everyone had had tea. Scamper was delighted to see them, and leapt round in delight. He couldn't imagine why the Seven were meeting again so soon, but he was certainly glad to welcome them. The little oil lamp was lighted, and the shed looked warm and cosy.

The guy sat sedately in his chair while Peter collected a little more money. 'One pound fifty pence,' he announced. 'Jolly good. Now, who'd like to come and choose the fireworks with me tomorrow at dinner-time instead of waiting till Saturday? I thought three of us could go – and the rest can say now if there are any particular fireworks they'd like us to get.'

It was decided that George and Pam should go with
Peter. Then Jack, grinning all over his face, told the
Seven how he had done a bit of snooping on the Tiresome
Three, and heard their threats of raiding the bonfire – and
how he had told them they would find a bonfire laid on
the top of Haylings Hill.

'And we went up there this morning, Peter and I, and
put a silly little twig fire ready, with a note from the Secret
Seven!' he said. 'I bet the Tiresome Three have taken a
long walk up there after afternoon school today!'

'They'll be furious,' said Janet. 'I hope they won't come
and raid *our* bonfire.'

'I don't think they know where it is at present,' said
Jack. 'As soon as I hear that they do know – or are looking
for it – I'll tell you. Then we can be on our guard.'

'Grrrrrr!' said Scamper, suddenly, and made them all
jump.

'Can it be the Tiresome Three back from the hill
already?' said Jack, startled. 'What's up, Scamper?'

'Grrrrrr!' said Scamper again, and all the hairs on his
neck rose up. He ran to the door and listened intently.

Pam suddenly gave a loud shriek, and made everyone
jump violently. Janet turned on her angrily. 'What did
you scream like that for? That's just what the Tiresome
Three want – to scare us and make us yell out!'

Pam pointed to the little shed window with a shaking
finger. 'A face looked in there,' she said. 'I saw it.'

'Then it *is* Susie and her friends!' said Jack, fiercely.
'Why didn't we draw the curtain across?'

They all ran to the door and pulled it open, and Scamper ran out, barking. He sniffed all round, and then stood
still, growling again.

'They've gone,' said Peter, shining his torch all round.

'Perhaps they came to raid the guy – take him away or something in revenge. Shut up, Scamper. There's nobody here now.'

They all went back and Peter drew the curtain across the window. 'Better break up the meeting now,' he said. 'Meet here on Saturday morning, please, and we'll finish building the bonfire. Jack, tell Susie we saw her – or one of the others – peering in. And tell her we hope they enjoyed their long walk!'

'I will,' said Jack, and cycled off. To his great astonishment he met Susie, Hilda and Doris at his front gate, walking wearily into the drive. Doris was almost in tears.

'You beast!' said Susie, angrily. 'Sending us all the way up there, to the top of Haylings Hill! That silly little bonfire – and the horrid note. Doris has hurt her ankle, falling on the hill – she could hardly get home. You're *mean*!'

'But – but wasn't it you, then, peering in at our shed window?' said Jack, amazed.

'I don't know what you're talking about,' said Susie. 'So don't try and be funny. I tell you, we've only just got back – and I'll have to see to poor Doris's ankle *at once*.'

They went round to the garden door, leaving Jack feeling puzzled – and rather sorry for his trick. He really hadn't meant anyone to fall down the hill.

But *who* had looked through the window? He had better telephone Peter immediately!

Fourteen

A dreadful shock

JACK telephoned Peter as soon as he had a chance. 'Peter? I say – it *wasn't* Susie or her friends who came and peeped in at our window tonight. They'd only just got back from Haylings Hill when I arrived home. Doris had hurt her ankle and was limping.'

Peter whistled. 'Who was it, then? Wait a minute, here's Dad. Dad – I say, Dad – you didn't peep in at our shed window tonight, did you?'

'No,' said his father. 'But the gardener was working late today – I expect he saw your light there, and peeped in.'

'Oh – so that was it,' said Peter, and told Jack. 'Anyway, the shed's locked,' he said. 'No one can get in. See you tomorrow, Jack.'

Susie was very, very angry about Jack's trick. 'I've a good mind to tell Mother,' she scolded. 'You should just *see* poor Doris's ankle. Well, you just look out for yourselves, you mean, horrible Seven. We're going to find your bonfire and pull it to bits! And if only we can get hold of your guy, we'll take him and burn him ourselves!'

'Don't be silly,' said Jack. 'The shed's locked, you know that. Yes, I know you found it unlocked the other night, but that was only for a few minutes while we went to get a chair for the guy. I tell you, I'm sorry about Doris's ankle. Now leave me in peace.'

But Susie wouldn't, and poor Jack had to retire to his bedroom. He wished once again that he and Peter hadn't played that trick on Susie and the others. Once Susie made up her mind to pay him out for anything, she usually did! Suppose she found their big bonfire? That would be the end of it!

Next day Peter, George and Pam went off to buy the fireworks. They managed to get all they wanted, except for some called Moon Rockets.

'They'll be in tomorrow morning,' said the shop-woman. 'You call for them then. And I'll have some in called "Catch-me-if-you-can" – little ones that rush about in the air, and hop all over the ground.'

'Oh, well will you keep some for us?' asked Peter. 'We've saved one pound fifty pence altogether – and we've spent just over a pound already. I'll keep the rest of the money and bring it in tomorrow for the other fireworks. I'd certainly like some of the Moon Rockets!'

He put down one pound and five pence in silver, and picked up the parcel of fireworks. George and Pam had helped to choose them and were very pleased. Peter put the rest of the money into his pocket.

'Forty-five pence,' he said. 'I'll make a note of what we've spent when I get back home, and put the change into the box on the shelf. If anyone has any more firework money they can add to it when we meet to make the bonfire bigger tomorrow morning. There's no meeting to-night.'

He popped into the shed when he got back, and put the money away safely. He took a look at the guy, and decided to ask his father for an old pipe. 'We didn't do anything about that,' he thought. 'And he *does* look as if a pipe would suit him!'

He asked his father later on in the evening. 'A pipe? Well, my old pipes are my favourite ones really,' said

his father. 'Still, wait a minute. I've got one with a broken
stem. Your guy won't mind that, I'm sure.'

He found it and gave it to Peter. Scamper ran to the
door and barked.

'Take him for a turn round the garden with you,' said
Peter's mother.

'Right!' said Peter. 'Come on, Scamper – walkies!
We'll take the pipe to the guy. Coming, Janet?'

'Got the key of the shed?' asked Janet. Peter fumbled in
his pocket. Then he felt in his other pocket.

'Blow!' he said. 'Where is it? Gosh – surely I locked up
the shed when I popped in with the money. Oh, *don't* say
I left the key in the lock!'

'Quick – come and see,' said Janet, thinking at once of
the Tiresome Three. They pulled on coats and tore down
the garden to the shed, Scamper leaping about madly.
They came to the door, and Peter shone his torch on the
lock.

'Look – I *did* leave the key in it,' he said. 'What an
absolute fathead I am! I really don't *deserve* to be the
leader of the Secret Seven. Thank goodness Susie hasn't
been along and taken it!'

He unlocked the door and they went into the shed,
Peter holding the pipe for the guy. Janet gave a sudden
yell and clutched his arm.

'Peter! *Peter!* Look at the guy! His clothes are gone!
Susie *has* been here. Oh, why ever did you leave the key in
the lock?'

Sure enough, the guy sat in his chair, wearing his mask
and nothing else. He looked very foolish and fat as he
sprawled there.

'The only thing the Tiresome Three have left him are
the safety pins that pinned his trousers,' said Janet, tear-

355

fully. 'Oh Peter! Our lovely guy – the best one we've ever had! Whatever will the others say?'

Peter was simply horrified. To think that this was all his fault! He looked round the shed, hoping vainly to find the clothes thrown into a corner. But no – there wasn't even the cap to be seen.

'Come back to the house,' he said, dolefully, and locked the door carefully, putting the key into his pocket. 'This is simply awful. I'll get on to Jack straight away and tell him what the Tiresome Three have done.'

Jack was just as horrified as Peter and Janet, when he heard the news. He could hardly believe his ears.

'So *that's* where Susie and the others went this evening, is it?' he said. 'I thought they were having one of their silly meetings down in the summer-house, but they must have gone to our shed. My word – I'll go for Susie over this!'

He slammed down the receiver and went to find Susie. She and Hilda and Doris were sitting by the fire, reading. Jack exploded angrily, and pulled Susie's hair hard.

'What have you done with our guy's clothes? So *that's* where you disappeared to this evening – you went stealing!'

'Don't be funny,' said Susie, looking most astonished. 'We were up in the attic all evening, looking out jumble for Mother's sale.'

'You were *not*!' shouted Jack. 'Don't tell untruths. WHERE ARE THOSE CLOTHES?'

Fifteen
Oh, that Tiresome Three

Susie and Doris and Hilda looked quite alarmed when Jack shouted so loudly.

'I tell you,' began Susie, raising her voice too, 'I tell you *we* haven't got the clothes – but I'm jolly glad to hear your silly old guy has lost them. Ha ha!'

'Where did you hide the clothes?' shouted Jack again – and at that moment his mother put her head into the room.

'Jack! Stop shouting. What's the matter?'

'Susie and Doris and Hilda have taken the clothes off our guy,' blurted out Jack, forgetting that it was a mean trick to tell tales. But he did feel so very, very angry! 'And they are telling fibs about it. Oh yes you are, Susie, I know you!'

'That's enough,' said his mother. 'Go up to your room, Jack, and cool off. I'll speak to Susie.'

Jack stamped out of the room, boiling with rage. He looked into Susie's room, hoping to see the guy's clothes stuffed under the bed or in the wardrobe, but there was nothing there. He went into his own room and waited.

Soon his mother came in.

'You are not to say another word to Susie and her friends about that guy's clothes,' she said. 'You've upset the girls very much – and Susie told me how you and Peter tricked them into climbing all the way up Haylings Hill. I'm ashamed of you.'

'But, *Mother*,' said Jack, 'please listen. Mother, *please* ask Susie where she hid the guy's clothes.'

'I'm not going to discuss the subject at all,' said his mother, and shut the door. Jack sat and fumed. He didn't even dare to go down and telephone to Peter. He felt sure that the Tiresome Three would be giggling over his shoulder if he did.

The Seven had to meet at the shed the next morning – and it was a sad and sorry company! They gazed at their wonderful guy, now so bare and ugly, wearing only his mask, and Pam burst into tears.

'All the clothes I brought!' she sobbed. 'It's too bad! I think your mother ought to go to Susie's mother, Peter, and complain. It's *stealing*.'

'Well – not exactly,' said Jack, uncomfortably. 'I mean – I'm sure Susie will give them back after Bonfire Night, it's just one of her silly *tricks*. I was so angry last night I could have shaken her to bits!'

'It's all my fault, I'm afraid,' said Peter, humbly. 'If I hadn't left the key in the lock, it would never have happened. I take the whole blame. Susie just took her chance – it was a real bit of luck for her – just like when we left the door open to get the guy that chair. That was a bit of luck for her too.'

'Well – we'll have to try and get some more clothes,' said Colin. 'There's an old raincoat hanging in our garage. I'm sure nobody wants it. I'll get that. And somebody can surely get hold of another cap. The guy will just have to make do with those!'

'We bought the fireworks,' said Pam, changing the subject, very sorry for poor unhappy Peter. 'Fine ones! And we kept back forty-five pence to buy some of those new Moon Rockets. Shall I pop up to the shop and see if they're in, Peter?'

'Yes, do,' said Peter, taking the money-box from the

358

shelf. 'The money's here.' He shook the box, suddenly looking alarmed. He put it down quickly on the little table and took off the lid. Then he looked up, dismayed.

'The money's gone,' he said. 'Not a penny of it left. Forty-five pence all gone!'

There was a dead silence. Even Scamper did not move an ear. Then Jack spoke, his words falling over one another.

'If Susie took it, it was only a joke, Peter. Really, it was. She – she's not a thief.'

'Well, didn't she steal the guy's clothes?' demanded Barabara. 'I wouldn't put anything past the Tiresome Three!'

'No, no, wait,' said Peter. 'I feel like Jack – I don't believe Susie would ever *steal*. After all, she's Jack's sister. I think she and the others may have taken the clothes and the money to pay us out – meaning to keep them till after Bonfire Night and then give them back . . .'

'Yes – yes, that's what they'll do,' said Janet. I'm sure of it. Jack, just tell Susie you know they've got our money, but you jolly well want it back after Bonfire Night. We'll have to get the Moon Rockets then. We shouldn't have had such a feud on between us. It's getting too silly for words.'

'All right,' said Jack. 'And now for goodness sake let's go and collect wood for the bonfire. I can't sit here a moment longer. I feel too angry for words.'

They all got up and went out, Peter locking the door very carefully indeed. They walked rather silently to the field and looked at their bonfire.

'Someone's been digging round and about it,' said George. 'I wonder what for.' He stamped down the rough clods, and looked at the bonfire. 'It wants a good bit more on!' he said. 'Cheer up, Jack, cheer up, Peter. You look as if you've done a whole page of sums wrong!'

Even that joke didn't bring a smile to anyone's face. What a blow to lose their guy's clothes *and* the rest of the firework money! What a blow that Peter hadn't locked the door last night!

They followed the same plan as before, collecting wood and piling it at the edge of the wood, then roping it and dragging it to the bonfire. It soon grew very big, and the Seven began to feel more cheerful when they thought what a blaze it would make. Scamper ran round with twigs in his mouth, looking very busy indeed. He even began to take them off the bonfire too, but that was soon stopped!

'Look – look, there's Susie and the others!' said George, suddenly. 'They must have been hunting about for our bonfire.'

'*Where are our guy's clothes?*' yelled Pam, suddenly remembering how much trouble she had gone to in getting them.

'*We* haven't got them!' shouted back Susie.

'You have!' cried Pam. 'Don't you go near our bonfire. We know you'd take that away too, if you could.'

'Be quiet, Pam,' said Janet.

'We don't want a silly bonfire like this,' shouted Susie. 'Why, it'll fall to pieces if it's kicked. Look!'

And to the Seven's horror she and Hilda and Doris ran round it, kicking away some of the twigs. *Well!* Whatever next!

Sixteen

Keep guard on the bonfire!

As soon as the Seven ran across the field towards the bonfire, Susie and the others disappeared.

'You wait!' called Susie. 'We'll come back, and you won't find much of your bonfire left!'

'We'll just have to put someone on guard,' said Peter, dolefully. 'I'm beginning to think it was a great mistake to quarrel with Susie. She's too clever.'

They finished the bonfire, keeping a good look-out for the Tiresome Three, but not another sign of them did they see.

'Better take it in turns to watch the bonfire this afternoon,' said George.

'No. I know a better idea than that,' said Jack. '*I'll* watch Susie and the other girls. I won't let them out of my sight. And tonight I'll take them to the cinema, so that I know they'll not be up to mischief. Mother said she would give me the money for it. Mind you, I shan't *like* doing it, but it's the only sensible thing I can think of.'

'It's a very, very good idea,' said Janet. 'And it does mean we won't have to stand about in this cold field all day, watching the bonfire! Do you want Peter to keep you company tonight at the cinema? It would be rather awful for you to have those three girls all to yourself.'

'All right,' said Jack, gratefully. 'It would make things a bit easier.'

So that night Peter and Jack solemnly took the three giggling girls to the cinema. His mother was very pleased.

362

'I'm glad you've made up that silly quarrel,' she said to Jack. 'I knew the girls hadn't taken those clothes – it wouldn't be a bit like them to do a thing like that.'

Jack said nothing, but thought privately that it would be *exactly* like them. He had kept an eye on the three girls all the afternoon, and knew that they had not gone near the bonfire. And they would be safe under his wing at the cinema and until bedtime. That was something!

Next morning, which was Sunday, the three girls went to church, Jack with them. But in the afternoon Susie grew restive.

'Let's go for a walk,' she said to Hilda and Doris. Jack pricked up his ears at once. Ah – where to? The bonfire field?

'I'll go with you,' he said.

'No thanks,' said Susie. 'I don't particularly want to be under your eye any more. What do you think we are going to do? Kick your bonfire to pieces? I bet that's what you're thinking.'

As that was exactly what Jack *was* thinking, he couldn't help going red. And then, just at that moment, his father called him.

'Jack, old son, come and give me a hand with cleaning the car, will you?' he said.

'Er – well – I thought of going for a walk with the girls,' said poor Jack.

'*We* can spare him, Dad,' said Susie, with a wicked grin. 'So long, Jack. Be good!'

And away went the three girls, leaving Jack to go out to the garage and begin hosing the car. Blow! Now he couldn't possibly keep an eye on them. Wait – hadn't he better telephone Peter and tell him to guard the bonfire? It would be so awful to have such a beauty spoilt now!

'Can I go and telephone Peter, Dad?' he asked his father. 'I've – er – just remembered something important.'

'Well, wait till you've finished the hosing,' said his father. 'It can't be so terribly important that you have to go at once!'

So, for three-quarters of an hour Jack worked on the car, fuming. Suppose Susie and the others were ruining the bonfire now? How maddening it would be! He was very glad to rush off to the telephone as soon as his father gave him permission.

'Peter? Is that you? Listen, Susie and the others have gone out for a walk – but it's just *possible* they may go to the bonfire field. Keep an eye there this afternoon, will you?'

'Right,' said Peter. 'Thanks for phoning.' He called to Janet. 'Hey, Janet – that was Jack. He says Susie and her friends have gone out for a walk – will we keep an eye on the bonfire.'

'Oh my goodness – we'd better go out into the field straight away!' said Janet, and flew to get her coat. Peter fetched his and they went into the garden, and down to the bottom. In a few minutes they were out in the bonfire field.

No one was there. The field was empty. Probably Susie had taken her friends quite a different way! Peter glanced at the bonfire.

What a shock he got! He clutched Janet's hand and pointed to the bonfire, unable to say a word. There was very little of the huge pile to be seen. It had been scattered over a wide area. Big twigs, little twigs, branches – there they lay on the grass.

'They've destroyed it,' said Janet, and tears came to her

eyes. 'Oh, how *could* they? It was such a beauty too – so high and wide. Oh Peter – why didn't Jack telephone sooner? We could so easily have driven Susie away.'

Peter was very red in the face. He stared at the ruined bonfire, his mouth set and angry. 'Susie must have gone mad,' he said at last, and marched over to what was left of the great heap.

'What's this hole?' said Janet, in surprise, as they came up to where the bonfire had been built. 'It looks as if Susie and the others had a spade and scattered the wood everywhere and then dug a hole. Honestly, they must be mad! What are they up to, Peter?'

'I don't know,' said Peter, staring. 'Let's go and phone Jack. Wait a minute, though – surely that's Susie and her friends coming up the field? It *is*! let's go and tackle them – let's see what they've got to say! Come on!'

Seventeen

A spade – and a button!

PETER and Janet met the Tiresome Three as they drew near the bonfire. Suzie gazed at the ruined pile of wood in amazement.

'What's happened!' she said. 'Have you been kicking your bonfire about?'

'No – *you're* the ones who have done that,' said Peter, his voice trembling with anger.

'We've only just come!' said Doris, indignantly. 'You saw us!'

'So you say – but it's quite clear you've been here before,' said Peter. 'You're good at mean tricks, aren't you?'

Susie looked at him and then at the bonfire. 'Well, I won't say that we wouldn't have spoilt it a *bit,*' she said. 'But we wouldn't have destroyed it like this – and who dug that hole in the middle?'

'Don't pretend,' said Peter, in disgust. Janet suddenly tugged at his arm.

'Peter – Peter, they're *not* pretending! They're just as surprised as we are! Peter, it *wasn't* them!'

'Peter won't believe you,' said Susie, scornfully. 'Jack won't, either. Well, it just happens to be the truth, see – we've *only – just – come*! So what about looking round and finding out who really *did* do all this?'

Peter and Janet stared at her. She spoke very earnestly indeed.

'You think we took your guy clothes, and your money – and now you think we've ruined your bonfire. Well, we didn't. And that's the *truth*!'

And with that, Susie, Hilda and Doris marched off, heads in air, leaving Peter and Janet still staring, unable to say a word.

Janet found her tongue at last. She turned to Peter. 'Peter, they truly are not pretending. They certainly didn't ruin our bonfire – and I don't believe they did the other things either. Anyway, I never *could* believe that Susie took our money. It's someone else, Peter, *someone else* who is playing tricks!'

'But who?' said Peter, bewildered. 'And why steal the clothes off the guy? It seems such a mad thing to do.'

'Let's look round a bit,' said Janet. 'We might find footprints or something. And I wish I knew who had been digging about like this. It seems so *mad* somehow. Look at this big clod of earth thrown up. Do you suppose Burton knows anything about it? He knew we were making a bonfire, because we asked him for the hedge trimmings to burn.'

'Well, yes – Burton *might* have seen someone about!' said Peter. 'I wonder if he's around anywhere? He usually helps to milk the cows on Sunday, so that the cowman can get a bit of time off.'

'I think that's him over there,' said Janet looking in the direction of the wood. 'Perhaps he's going to his little hut. Let's go after him and ask him if he's seen anyone messing about in this field.'

They ran after the figure in the distance, but the man disappeared between the trees.

'Yes – I think it *is* Burton,' said Peter. 'Come on – I bet he's gone to his hut!'

They made their way into the wood till they came to the little overgrown hut. They called loudly. 'Burton! Burton! Are you there?'

There was no answer.

'I'm going inside,' said Peter, and disappeared through the half-open doorway. Janet followed him.

'No – he's not here,' said Peter, looking round. It was rather dark in the shed, but as his eyes grew used to the dimness, something caught his eye – something that glinted a little. He picked it up.

'A spade!' he said. 'And look, Janet – it's Burton's! It's got his name burnt across the handle. He always burns his name on his tools, in case they get stolen.'

Janet looked distressed. 'Peter! You don't think it could be *Burton* doing all these things, do you?' she said, anxiously. 'I like Burton. But – but – *someone's* been messing about round our bonfire with a spade – and this one's got Burton's name on it!'

'You mean it might have been Burton peering in at our window, and walking in when the door was unlocked and taking the guy clothes for himself?' said Peter. 'He certainly needs a few decent clothes! And taking our money too! But we've had Burton for *ages*, and Daddy thinks he's a wonder. It *can't* be old Burton – unless he's gone mad!'

'Well, this is certainly his spade,' said Janet. 'Oh, I can't *bear* it to be Burton! If we tell Daddy he'll lose his job.'

Peter looked round the hut again, puzzled and worried. It was bad enough to have thought that the Tiresome Three might have played mean tricks – but it was worse still to think of old Burton doing such peculiar things!

He saw something small and round lying on the floor, and picked it up.

'A button,' he said. 'Look, Janet – it seems familiar, somehow. Do you recognize it?'

Yes, Janet did! 'Of *course*, don't you remember? The guy's old tweed coat had buttons like this – half-yellow and half-brown! The thief has been here – sat down here – and a button fell off the coat. I expect he was wearing it. Peter, who in the world is it? That coat's too big for Burton, surely.'

'He *could* have had it altered,' said Peter. 'Come on – let's go home. There's something queer about all this.'

Eighteen
Jack has a sudden idea

PETER and Janet went home feeling rather upset and extremely puzzled.

'Better tell all the others tomorrow at school what has happened,' said Peter. 'If they could each bring something to eat, and Mother would let us have lemonade again, we could have a quick tea, and then go out and rebuild the bonfire. We've got the guy all right, and we've got fireworks – not as many as we hoped, but still, enough to have a bit of fun.'

'Yes, it's disappointing that our grand plan for a wonderful guy and lashings of fireworks has been spoilt – but we'll just have to make do with second best,' said Janet.

So, after afternoon school on Monday, the Seven met once again in the shed, with Scamper to welcome them as usual. The girls had been told by Janet at school what had happened the day before, and the boys had been told by Peter. They sat down, opened their bags of cakes and biscuits, and accepted lemonade from Peter.

'Well,' began Peter, 'you know more or less what happened to our bonfire yesterday – *ab*solutely ruined – and you know that Janet and I think it wasn't Susie and her friends after all.'

'You said it was probably Burton, the old hedger-and-ditcher,' said Colin.

'Well, it wasn't,' said Peter, and this was news to everyone but Janet. 'My father happened to mention him this morning, and said he had been ill for some days and in bed. So it certainly *wasn't* him.'

'Probably some tramp then, who peered into our shed, saw the nice warm clothes the guy was wearing, and stole them – and the money too,' said Jack. 'But what *I* can't understand is, who ruined our bonfire – and what's the sense of making holes round it?'

There was a silence – and then, quite suddenly Jack smacked his hand down so hard on his knee that everyone jumped almost out of their skin.

'We're blind!' said Jack. 'We're idiots! We're complete fatheads!'

The others stared at him in alarm. Whatever did he mean!

'Hold on, Jack, old thing,' said Peter. 'What's up? You look as if you've seen a ghost or something!'

'Well, I haven't. But I think I've spotted the person who's been stealing our things and spoiling our plans!' said Jack. 'Of course, of course, of *course*!'

'Who is it?' demanded Peter.

'Well, who could it be but the third thief who escaped when the other two were caught – the ones who robbed Colin's Granny!' said Jack. 'Don't you *see*?'

'The third thief – but . . .' began Peter.

'Yes! He knew the police had a full description of him, it said so in the papers! So he had to get other clothes – *and he got them from our guy*!' said Jack.

'Of course! Don't you remember, he was tall and fat!' said Janet. 'He'd need big clothes – and he must have spotted them on our guy . . .'

'Yes – that time he peeped in at our window!' half shouted George. 'It wasn't the gardener or Burton, it must have been that thief!'

'He needed money – and took ours!' said Barbara.

'And do you know what I think? I bet the other two

thieves buried the stolen valuables in our field!' cried Peter. 'And that's what all the digging's for – those holes – those thrown-up clods! He stole Burton's spade for that!'

'And since Burton's been ill, the thief must have been sleeping in his old hut!' put in Pam. 'And that's how that button came there – he was wearing the guy's coat and it came off.'

Scamper felt the excitement round him and began to bark, wagging his tail hard. Peter patted him.

'Quiet, Scamper, quiet. You shall join in the excitement in a minute. Listen, all of you. That thief is still somewhere in the woods – maybe in Burton's hut this very minute. I don't believe he has found those hidden valuables – and he won't leave till he does. Well then . . .'

'Well, then, we'd better tell the *police* what we think!' cried Jack. 'Or he may find the hidden goods and disappear. Aren't we idiots not to have thought of it before? All that fuss and excitement over that robbery – and here we've had the third robber hanging about our shed for ages!'

'And we thought it was poor Susie,' said Janet. 'Honestly, I feel awful about that.'

'Look – don't forget it's Bonfire Night,' said Barbara. 'Telephone the police straight away, or we'll never have time to rebuild our bonfire, take the guy out and let off the fireworks. *Please* don't let's spoil Bonfire Night.'

'All right, all right,' said Peter. 'I'll go and tell the police what we think – though they may not believe it, of course. Jack, you and George take out the guy. Pam, you're responsible for the fireworks. Janet, remember the matches for the bonfire. Colin and Barbara, start rebuilding it as quickly as you can!'

'Right, Captain!' said Jack. 'Scamper – lead the way!'

'And for goodness sake look out for the thief!' shouted Peter, as he ran out of the shed door to go in and telephone. 'I bet he's still about somewhere!'

Nineteen

Quite a lot happens

EVERYONE obeyed orders, and very soon the guy, in his old raincoat and cap, was being carried out of the shed in his chair, and down the garden into the field. Pam followed, hugging the big parcel of fireworks. Janet raced up to the house for a box of matches.

Soon they were all in the field. It was getting dark now, and they would have to use their torches before long.

'Blow!' said Jack, feeling a few spots of rain on his face. 'I believe it's going to rain!'

Colin and Barbara set to work to build up the scattered bonfire heap. It wasn't very easy in the half-darkness. Jack and George helped too, once they had set down the guy.

Colin suddenly pulled Janet's coat. 'I say,' he said, in a whisper. 'Look – is that someone over there – on the other side of the field?'

Janet looked – and what she saw made her nudge Jack and George. 'Be very quiet!' she said, in a low voice. 'Look over there!'

They all looked across the misty, rainy field, and saw what Colin had seen . . . a man, digging, digging, digging! He hadn't seen them away in the distance, for he had his back to them.

'The third robber!' whispered Janet. 'What do we do now?'

'Take no notice at all,' said Colin. 'Just keep him under our eye till the police come. That's about all we can do.'

'Can you see if he's dressed in our guy's old clothes?' whispered Pam.

'No – it's too misty now, and he's just too far away,' said Colin. 'But it *must* be the thief – else why is he digging? Come on. Build up the bonfire. Stick the guy on top. Pretend we're going about our own business and haven't even noticed him.'

So they all rebuilt the bonfire at top speed, and then, with a great heave, set the guy and his chair firmly on top.

'He's sitting there beautifully,' said Jack. 'Firm as anything. Blow this rain – I don't believe our bonfire will light up at all. Everything's getting soaked.'

'I think it's terribly disappointing,' said Pam. 'Every single thing's gone wrong with our wonderful bonfire plans! Everything!'

'Shut up – the fellow's coming across the field,' said Colin, in a low voice. 'Don't be afraid – we've got Scamper. Get on with the bonfire, and talk, and don't take any notice.'

The man was now almost up to them. Pam glanced round and gave a little cry, which she choked in her throat – he was wearing the trousers, the tweed coat, the rubber boots and the cap in which their guy had first been dressed! Scamper had now begun to bark and growl. The man spoke roughly.

'Clear out of this field. It belongs to the farmer. You're not allowed to have bonfires here.'

'My father is the farmer it belongs to,' said Janet. 'He knows we are building it here. Please be careful of our dog. He bites.'

The man lifted his spade as Scamper jumped round him, barking, and the children all yelled at once.

'Don't you hit him!'

'Stop that!'

'Put that spade down, don't hit the dog!'

'Scamper, come here!'

What would have happened next nobody knew – for quite suddenly two cars drew up on the road side of the field, and six dark figures leapt out.

'The police!' shouted Jack, excited. 'Look – they've come already!'

In a trice the man was off in the rainy mist, with Scamper at his heels and the six children after him. He kicked out at the dog and struck him on the leg. Scamper yelped and came limping back to Janet.

'Here's the man, somewhere over here!' shouted Jack, waving his torch. The dark figures fanned out and came across the field. Then suddenly someone ran panting up to them from behind – and it was Peter, who, after telephoning the police, had stopped to tell everything to his mother, and had then raced down to the field to join the others.

'My word – the police have been quick!' he said. 'They believed my story – every word of it! Did I hear you say the man was here in the field?'

'Yes – Scamper went after him and so did we,' said Jack. 'But he kicked him and hurt him. Watch out for the man – but let's keep together. The fellow ran off over in that direction. He's sure to be caught, the police are all round the field.'

Scamper limped off, barking. *He* had caught sight of the man. It was maddening for the Seven to stand in the half-darkness, and hear shouts, and the sounds of running footsteps, and not be able to see a thing in the rain that was now pouring down.

Scamper gave a yelp as if he was in pain, and the Seven ran to him. Peter felt his leg anxiously. 'I don't *think* it's broken!' he said.

A policeman came up. 'Did you see that fellow on this side of the field?' he said. 'I'm afraid we've lost him in this rain. Good gracious – whatever's that thing right over there?'

'It's our bonfire,' said Peter. 'And the poor old guy's sitting on top, waiting to be burnt – but he'll be so wet through we'll have to give up all idea of it, I'm afraid.'

'Gave me quite a turn, seeing the guy up there on that heap,' said the policeman. 'Well – I'm afraid we'll have to give up the chase. The man may have slipped into the wood – we'll never get him there.'

The Seven heard the policemen gathering together, and then by the light of their torches making for the two police cars.

'Blow!' said Peter. 'Now that fellow won't be caught. He may be a mile away by now.'

'He's not, said Janet, suddenly, right in his ear, in a voice shaking with excitement. 'He's not! Peter – he's sitting up there on our bonfire! He's got the guy's raincoat on – but I saw his rubber boots in the light of my torch. *That's* where he's hiding, Peter! He knew we wouldn't light the bonfire in this rain!'

Peter let out a long breath of amazement, and walked over to the bonfire. Yes – Janet was right! What a hiding-place! There sat the thief, in the guy's chair, the raincoat over his clothes, the mask on his face – on the top of the bonfire! Thrown down behind was the real guy, robbed of his coat and mask.

'Stay here and fiddle about round the bonfire,' Peter said in a low voice to the others. 'I'll take Scamper in case he smells the man up there and barks – and I'll try and catch the police before they drive off. Stay here now, while I rush across the field.'

379

Twenty

Bang! Crash! Whoosh!

PETER tore right across the field. He shouted as he came near the cars, and waved his torch. One car was just driving off, but stopped.

'We've got the man!' he shouted. 'He's sitting on top of our bonfire, dressed in the guy's raincoat and mask, but we saw his boots. Come quickly.'

Everything then happened very, very suddenly. The police raced across the field, the man leapt off the bonfire, Scamper limped on three legs to stop him – and over went the thief! Before he could get up, he was caught! He began to shout and struggle.

'You go back home, you kids,' said the sergeant. 'You'll get soaked. Sorry your bonfire night's been spoilt – you'd better have it tomorrow! We'll be digging up this field in the morning, and maybe we'll get the buried goods before you light your bonfire! We'll come and dance round it if we do!'

The Seven watched the policemen disappear through the rain, the prisoner held tightly. Janet gave an enormous sigh.

'I suddenly feel dreadfully tired,' she said. 'Let's go in. I'm soaked.'

'Well, it was very exciting, but not much of a bonfire night – especially after all our wonderful plans,' said Jack.

'And poor Scamper's hurt,' said Peter. 'I don't feel like having a bonfire night at all, now. Let's give up the idea –

and not bother about it tomorrow. After all, we've not got an enormous lot of fireworks – and our bonfire's soaked – and so is our guy. Come on in.'

But next morning they all felt very differently! The sergeant telephoned to say that they could have the third robber's guy clothes if they wanted them – they had found the man's own clothes. 'And I have another little surprise for you,' he said.

'What?' asked Peter.

'Well – I'm very pleased with your help,' said the sergeant. 'And I am sending along a bumper box of fireworks, with my best thanks. Enough for about twenty of you! Have a good time tonight!'

'Oh – thanks a lot!' said Peter, thrilled.

All the others were delighted too, when they heard, and great plans were made after morning school.

'My mother says you are all to come at five and she'll give us a smashing tea – and Dad will come out and set the bonfire going with us,' said Peter.

'And Burton's coming back today and says he'll build the bonfire sky-high,' said Janet. 'The other wood is soaked through. He'll bring some dry branches from the wood-shed.'

'There's just one thing more,' said Peter. 'Jack I feel *awful* about Susie. Simply awful. I mean – we accused her and the others of – of –'

'Go on – say it – of stealing!' said Jack. 'Well – *they* didn't have any fireworks last night either – I expect you'd like them to come to our show tonight, wouldn't you?'

'Yes. Yes, we'd *all* like them to,' said Peter. 'But do you think Susie will *want* to come? After all, we were pretty beastly in the things we said.'

'Let's write her a note from everyone of us,' said Janet. So between them they wrote a note, and Jack gave it to Susie. She looked most astonished and opened it at once.

'*Dear Susie,*' she read,

First of all we're very sorry for all the awful things we said. We really are. We would be awfully glad if you and Hilda and Doris would come to our firework party to-night. We've been sent the biggest box of fireworks you ever saw. Please do come and help us to set them off. Come to tea in the shed first. The password is Wee Willie Winkie.

With many apologies to you from

The Secret Seven.'

'Gracious goodness!' said Susie, her eyes shining. 'Wait till Hilda and Doris see this! Come to your *party*? I should jolly well think we will! And I *say* – does it really mean that we can meet in the shed with you – and say the password?'

'Yes – but only just this *once*,' said Jack. 'And please do behave yourself, Susie, and tell Hilda and Doris to as well.'

'Oh, I *will*,' said Susie. 'My word – *what* a surprise!'

And so, for the first time, Susie actually said the password and was admitted to the Secret Seven shed with Hilda and Doris. Not to a *meeting*, though – just to a tea-party. She was really very nice, for she waved away every-one's apologies, and smiled round in delight.

'Don't apologize! I've said just as awful things as you did, and done them too! We did our best to spoil your bonfire night – though that thief did far more than we did! And thanks *most* awfully for letting us come here and say the password. I never, *never* thought you'd do that.'

Everyone warmed to the generous-natured Susie, and Janet began to wonder however they could have thought such dreadful things of her and the others. 'But oh dear – I wouldn't be surprised if Susie's nice behaviour doesn't last very long,' she thought. 'Or ours either, come to that! So we must make the best of tonight!'

They certainly did. Come out to the field and listen.

BANG! CRASH! WHIZZZZZZZZ! Whoooosh-ee-whoooosh-eewhooosh! *That* was the first Moon Rocket!

Sizzle-sizzle-sizzle – the bonfire is burning high – what a sight the flames are! And there's the old guy, plump and wobbly, dressed in coat, trousers, boots and cap, sitting high on top. Bang! A rocket flew by his ear, and made him jerk his head.

'He's laughing! The old guy's laughing!' shouted Janet, dancing round the bonfire. 'He says he's as warm as toast at last!'

BANG! Good-bye, Secret Seven, see you again soon! WHOOOOOOSH! Look out, Peter, that rocket went very near your nose! CRASH! What in the wide world was *that*?

Only one figure is missing from the Grand Firework Party. Guess who it is? Yes, it's dear old Scamper. He's terrified of bangs and crashes, so he is lying comfortably in his basket by the fire, pretending that he can't go because his leg is bandaged!

Good-bye, Scamper! Give the Secret Seven a lick from us when next you see them!

GOOD OLD
SECRET SEVEN

CONTENTS

One

A meeting is called

ONE morning after school, Peter went to find his sister Janet.

'Hey, Janet!' he said. 'I'm calling a Secret Seven meeting for tomorrow morning. Jack's uncle has given him a lovely present, and he wants all the Seven to share it.'

'What is it?' asked Janet. 'A game of some sort?'

'No. You'll have to wait and see,' said Peter. 'It's Jack's surprise, not mine. Will you write out a few notes and tell the others to come – 10 o'clock sharp. Thank goodness it's Saturday tomorrow.'

'Wuff,' said Scamper the spaniel. He loved Saturdays too. He knew he would have Peter and Janet all day long then.

'Yes, *you* shall come to the meeting as well,' said

Janet, patting his soft golden coat. 'But do you know the password, Scamper?'

'Wuff-wuff!' said Scamper at once, and the children laughed.

'Quite right – the password *is* "wuff-wuff",' said Peter. 'What a good memory you have, Scamper!'

Scamper wagged his tail, and said 'wuff-wuff' again. 'Better not say it too often, Scamper,' said Janet. 'Or that awful Susie might hear you.'

Susie was Jack's sister, and *not* one of the Secret Seven, though she badly wanted to belong. She loved to find out whatever password the Secret Seven were using, and it really was quite difficult to stop her.

Janet scribbled four cards – one to Colin, one to George, one to Pam and one to Barbara. 'There!' she said, 'I'll take them round on my bike. I don't need to write to Jack, as he's asked for the meeting himself. Is he going to bring this present of his tomorrow, whatever it is?'

'Yes,' said Peter. 'I'd better tidy up the shed where we meet – and I'll ask Mother what she can spare for us to eat. I *think* Cookie is baking today, so I'll go and tell *her* about the meeting, too!'

Next morning Janet and Peter went down to their shed at a quarter to ten, carrying a good many things. 'I've tidied it up,' said Peter. 'Gardener had been in and taken two of the big flower-pots we used as seats, but I found two boxes instead.'

The shed-door had on it the two big letters S.S., standing for Secret Seven. Janet and Peter looked at them proudly.

'Secret Seven!' said Janet. 'Best club in the world! I *shall* enjoy a meeting again – it's weeks since we had one – we've been so busy with school things.'

In they went, and shut the door. Now no one would be allowed in unless they gave the password. Peter set down the things he was carrying, and looked round proudly. 'Didn't I clean the shed well?' he said. 'I even cleaned the windows. It's nice and warm too, isn't it?'

The shed backed on to the hot greenhouse, and so gained some of the heat from there. It was pleasantly warm on this cold November day. Janet began to set out some coloured mugs, taking them down from the shelf.

'Mother thought we'd better have hot cocoa this cold day,' she said. 'I'll fetch it as soon as everyone is here. I bet Jack will be first with his wonderful present, whatever it is! Where's Scamper?'

'I don't know. He didn't come down with us. I expect he'll turn up,' said Peter. 'He's probably chasing his old enemy – the stable cat. He *still* thinks he can catch her, though he never will.'

'Look what Cookie's given us,' said Janet, showing Peter a tin full of buns. 'Currant buns warm from the oven – and a home-made macaroon for each of us!'

'Good old Cookie!' said Peter, sniffing at the warm buns. 'One of these days I'll buy her a medal. Buck up, Janet – the others will be here in half a minute. I hope they'll all remember the password! Listen – here comes the first one. I bet it's Jack.'

Two

That awful Susie!

A FIST banged on the door, and Peter called out at once. 'Password, please.'

'Wuff-wuff!' said a voice, rather loudly.

'Enter,' said Peter, 'and DO remember not to say the password so that everyone can hear it for a mile around!'

'Sorry!' said George, coming in at the door, a grin on his face. 'Did I sound like Scamper? I tried to.'

'Well, you didn't,' said Janet. 'You sounded exactly like yourself. Sit down, George. We thought you were Jack. He said he'd be here early, because he has something to show us.'

Knock-knock – somebody else had come. 'Password!' yelled Peter, and the answer came at once. 'Wuff-wuff! Wuff-wuff!'

In came Pam and Barbara, beaming all over their faces. 'Hallo! We're not the last. Good!'

Bang-bang! 'That must be Jack,' said Janet, as Peter called out 'Password, please!' But it wasn't. It was Colin. He marched in and shut the door smartly. 'Hallo, everyone! I say, it's nice and warm in here! What's the meeting called for? Anything special?'

'Yes,' said Peter. 'Jack asked me to call it. He has something jolly interesting to show us. I can't think why he's not here. It's past ten, and he said he'd be early.'

'I bet it's that awful sister of his who's stopping him coming,' said Pam.

'But how could she know about our meeting?' said Peter. 'Jack wouldn't tell her, I'm sure.'

'Here's Jack,' said Barbara, as more footsteps came down the path to the shed. Someone gave the door such a bang that they all jumped. Before Peter could call out 'Password' a voice shouted it loudly. 'WUFF-WUFF'.

'Enter!' cried Peter, sure it was Jack's voice. The door flew open – and there stood Susie, Jack's sister! She grinned round at them.

'Thanks for inviting me to your meeting,' she said, and shut the door behind her. She sat down on a box before anyone could stop her.

'Susie! How dare you!' shouted Peter and Janet together. Peter threw the door open. 'Go away!' he said. 'You know you've no right here. You don't belong to the Secret Seven.'

'Well, you'd better *let* me belong then,' said Susie. 'Because my mother says that the present Jack had from our Uncle Bob is to be shared between us! And as he's bringing it here to show you today, *I've* come to share it too.'

Someone else came down the path, carrying something over his shoulder – something long and straight. There was a loud knock on the door, and the password was said very clearly.

'Wuff-wuff,' said Jack's voice. It was exactly like Susie's, so no wonder everyone had thought she was Jack!

'Enter!' called Peter. Jack came in, carrying his load carefully. He glared angrily at Susie.

'How did she know our password, Jack?' asked Peter, sternly. 'Did you tell her?'

'No, he didn't. I just hid in a bush outside and listened,' said Susie. 'You needn't glare at me like that, Jack. Mother said I could share that present, you know she did.'

'Can't we turn her out?' said Pam, who didn't like Susie at all. 'She always tries to spoil everything!'

'You just *try* to turn me out!' said Susie, fiercely. '*I* don't want to come to your silly old meetings – but I tell you, I'm going to share Jack's present as much as any of *you* are.'

Peter looked at her in despair. What could you do with a girl like Susie? If they tried to turn her out she would probably shout and yell, and bring his mother down to see what was the matter – and Mother might even *agree* that Susie should stay and hear what Jack said about his present.

'Tomorrow Binkie, my friend, is coming to stay with me,' said Susie. 'And I've said *she* can share the present too – my half of it, I mean.'

'*Binkie* – that awful little rabbit-face?' said George, in horror. 'That silly giggler – that . . .'

Everyone groaned. Susie alone was bad enough, but when she and Binkie were together the two girls were impossible.

'Well – what are you going to do?' asked Susie. 'All rush on me together and throw me out? Or let me stay here at the meeting?'

Peter made up his mind quickly. On NO account could Susie attend one of the Secret Seven meetings. On the other hand they couldn't throw her out. She would make such a fuss! Very well then – he must declare the meeting ended, and say that there would be *no* proper meeting, but just a talk about Jack's present, whatever it was.

'I declare this Secret Seven meeting ended,' he said, in a loud voice. 'We will all go indoors and see Jack's present in our playroom. I will NOT have strangers present at our secret meetings.' He got up, and all the others stood too – except Susie.

'All right, all right – you win,' she said. 'Your mother would be cross with me, I know, if I go indoors with you. She'll think I've interfered. But just you listen for a minute, and hear *my* side of the question!'

Three

Jack's present

BUT before Susie could go on, footsteps pattered up to the shed-door, and someone scraped at the bottom. 'Password!' shouted Peter, and a doggy voice answered at once, 'WUFF-WUFF-WUFF!'

'Enter, Scamper,' said Peter. 'But you said too many wuffs! Clever dog, to remember the password!'

That made them all laugh, even Susie. Scamper trotted in and licked everyone in delight. Then he lay down at Peter's feet, panting. 'You're late, Scamper,' said Peter. 'But it doesn't matter because I've declared the meeting ended. Susie, if you've anything to say, say it, and go.'

'All right,' said Susie. 'That thing Jack has brought is a present from our Uncle Bob, who was once a sailor. It's a telescope – and a jolly fine one, too!'

'A *telescope*!' said everyone, excited. Yes – now they could see that it was. Jack began to take off the wrappings sulkily, as Susie went on talking.

'Well, Jack's idea was to bring it down here and give it to the Secret Seven,' said Susie. 'But Mother said Uncle Bob meant *me* to share it – and I didn't see why you Secret Seven should have it all. I knew I'd never see it once it was installed in this shed. So I argued with Jack...'

'Shouted the place down, you mean!' said poor Jack.

'And Mother heard, and she came, and she said Jack *was* to share the telescope with me, though she was pleased that the Secret Seven could look through it too. And Jack said he didn't care what Mother said, he wasn't going to let me share any of it – so I shot off by myself and came to the meeting to tell you all this.'

'And left me behind with Mother in a real rage,' said Jack. 'I'm so sorry, everyone. I meant to leave the telescope here in the shed, so that we could all use it, and look at all sorts of things in the distance – the different cars going along the hillside road – the castle on the hill – the herons on the old pond – it would have been such fun.'

'Yes – fun for *you* – but not for me!' said Susie. 'And what about Binkie? *You* want to share the telescope with Peter and Janet and the rest, don't you – well, *I* want to share it with Binkie!'

'I shouldn't think Binkie knows what a telescope *is*!' said Jack. 'Her head's full of wool, not brains! *She* won't want to use a telescope.'

'Now listen,' said Peter; making up his mind quickly. 'You'll *have* to share with Susie, Jack, if your mother says so. But why shouldn't we keep it down here in the shed, so that *any* of us can use it at any time? Not at a special meeting or anything like that.'

'We'd have to keep the shed locked, then,' said Jack. 'This telescope is quite valuable, Uncle said. But that means that Susie will have to know where the key is!'

'Well – as long as she doesn't try to come to any of our meetings again and spoil them as she has spoilt today's, I don't see why she shouldn't know where the

key is,' said Peter. 'We've got to be fair about this, Jack. I bet *my* mother would say I'd got to share with Janet if someone gave me something fine like this telescope. Let's be fair.'

'All right,' said Jack gloomily. '*Be* fair. But don't blame *me* if Susie and Binkie spy on us and find out all our secrets and passwords and everything.'

'Let's have something to eat and drink,' said Janet. 'We'll all feel better then. You'd better have some too, Susie. Being cross always makes people hungry.'

'Well, I'm *not* hungry,' said Susie, getting up. 'But thank you all the same, Janet. I know when I'm not wanted. I only came to say I'm *going* to share the telescope.'

'Wait a bit,' said Colin, seeing that Susie was near tears, for all her boldness. 'Before you go we'd better arrange where the key is to be hidden. Then you'll know where to look for it.'

'Tell Jack, and *he* can tell me,' said Susie, stalking out of the door. 'Goodbye, stuck-ups! Wait till I tell Binkie about this!'

She slammed the door so hard that Scamper jumped and began to bark. Jack looked round at the others, feeling ashamed of his sister.

'Susie's got such a temper,' he said. 'I'm so sorry about this.'

'Let's not talk about Susie,' said Janet. 'She didn't go off because she didn't want to share our food – she went because she was afraid she was going to cry. And I can just imagine how awful she'd feel if she did – in front of all of us!'

So nobody said another word about Susie, but tucked into currant buns and macaroons and hot cocoa. Scamper had his share, and thoroughly enjoyed himself. He went to sniff all round the big, strange-looking parcel that Jack had brought into the shed.

'No one seems interested in my telescope except Scamper,' said Jack, in a forlorn voice. 'And I was so very excited about it.'

Peter clapped him on the shoulder. 'So are we! Come on – let's see this wonderful present!'

Four

The wonderful telescope

THE wrappings were soon off – and the Seven crowded round as Jack put the big telescope together, and showed them how the long tube could be stretched out even longer.

'You've no idea how far the telescope's eye can see,' he said. 'When I looked through it this morning before I came, I could see the scarecrow in the field half a mile from our house – and what is more I could see a sparrow or some bird sitting on his hat!'

'Do let's look through it,' said Janet, excited. 'Let's take it out into the garden, and train it on something far away.'

So they carried it out into the garden, and set it on its little stand on the broad top of the low garden wall. Jack was very clever at adjusting the lens so that it focused properly, and made everything as clear as could be.

'Now that's exactly right,' said Jack, looking through the telescope. 'I've trained it on that little cottage over on the slope there. Before you look through the telescope tell me what you can see with your bare eyes.'

'Well – the cottage, of course,' said Pam. 'And something in the garden, I can't see what.'

'And somebody on the path. That's about all,' said Barbara.

'Right. Well, look through the telescope and you'll see a whole lot more!' said Jack. 'You first, Peter – you're our leader.'

So Peter looked through the long telescope, and immediately gave a loud cry. 'Jack! It's marvellous! I can see Mrs Haddon as if she was just over our wall – and I can even see the jug she is carrying. And that's a pram in the garden – and I can see the baby's teddy bear sitting up at the end of it! And . . .'

'Let *me* have a turn,' said Janet, itching to have a look. 'Good gracious! *I* can see something sticking out of the chimney! It must be a sweep's brush. Yes, it is! And there's a cat sitting just inside the window! Oh

Jack – it's as if I've magic eyes that can see for miles! Oh, aren't you lucky to have a telescope like this? What fun we'll have!'

Jack was very pleased at the excitement his telescope caused, as one after another the Secret Seven peered through it. 'We can have great fun with it,' he said, proudly. 'We can watch the birds and see everything they do. We can examine every aeroplane that comes overhead. We can . . .'

'Children! Whatever *are* you doing standing still out in the cold for so long?' suddenly cried a voice. 'You'll get colds, all of you! What's that you've got?'

'It's a telescope, Mother,' called Janet. 'It belongs to Jack. He's sharing it with us.'

'How lovely! But do you know how late it's getting?' called her mother.

'Well, we'll put the telescope away now,' said Jack. 'I'm supposed to get home to an early lunch. Come on – help me with it, Colin.'

Soon the telescope was safely in the shed, wrapped up very carefully.

'It's jolly good of you to share it with us,' said Peter, 'and to say we can all use it when we like. But I think we'd better say that I or Janet must be told when anyone comes to borrow it – we'll be *responsible* for it, see? Is that understood, everyone?'

'Oh yes! We'll come and tell you when we want to look through it,' said George, and the others agreed. 'But suppose you're out? We'd better know where the key of the shed is to be kept, Peter.'

'Oh – of course,' said Peter. 'Let's think now – somewhere fairly easy to get – but yet well hidden. What about under this flat stone here, just by the shed? Scamper, you're the only one not allowed to touch the stone or the key. Understand?'

'Wuff,' said Scamper solemnly and wagged his tail. He watched while Peter carefully slid the key under the stone.

'I'll have to tell Susie where it is,' said Jack, in rather a small voice.

'I know. We promised that,' said Peter. 'She will *have* to go into our shed, but we'll be careful not to leave any Secret Seven secrets about! Tell her where the key is – and say she MUST put it back under the stone if she ever uses it.'

'Right,' said Jack. 'Er – what about a new password, Peter? Susie knows our last one.'

'Good gracious, yes. I'd forgotten that,' said Peter. 'Well, I think it's quite obvious what we'll have! The next password, members, is – TELESCOPE!'

Then off they all went, and Peter and Janet carried everything carefully back to the house. Scamper followed them, wagging his tail. 'Wuff-wuff!' he said, and Peter laughed. 'No – that's our *old* password, Scamper. You'll have to remember the *new* one!'

Five

Through the telescope

THE telescope was a great success. The Secret Seven found it a most fascinating pastime to peer through it at all kinds of things, and there was much coming and going at the meeting-shed.

'I'm writing an essay on gulls in wintertime,' said George, arriving one dinner hour, complete with sandwiches to eat. 'I thought I'd set up the telescope and watch the gulls on your father's fields, Peter – there are always so many there, at this time of year.'

So there sat George, solemnly chewing ham sandwiches, and peering through the telescope at the excited gulls foraging in a newly ploughed field. No wonder he had ten out of ten for his essay!

Colin wanted to see the big jet-liners that flew steadily on their way overhead. 'I could almost see what the people in it were having for dinner,' he told an astonished Janet. But she wasn't interested in planes – she loved to swing the telescope round on its stand, and watch the people walking or riding on the distant road.

'It's almost as if they were in the garden,' she said. 'Peter, I saw old Mrs King riding on her tricycle, and I counted the onions in her net-bag – twelve she had. And I saw that horrid little Harry Jones ride by the greengrocer's cart and quickly take an orange off it as he went.'

'You'll turn into a peeping Tom if you don't look out,' said Peter. 'I bet young Harry would be horrified if he knew you were watching him across dozens of fields!'

The telescope was used at night too, and the Seven marvelled at the way in which it brought the moon so close to them. They had to take the telescope indoors for that, because Peter's mother said it was too cold to stay outside with it.

Susie came to use it too, of course, with her friend Binkie, who was just as giggly as ever. They found the key and went into the shed. They took the telescope into the garden and rested it on the wall. Peter saw them there, and went out to them.

'Oooh, run, Susie – here's Peter!' giggled Binkie, pretending to be scared. 'Oh, don't eat us, will you, Peter! Oooh, I'm frightened of you.'

'I only came to see that you knew how to use the telescope,' said Peter, coldly. 'I thought Susie might want help.'

Susie was busy looking through the telescope. She had it trained on a house some way off – then she swung it to another house. 'There's Mr Roneo painting his greenhouse,' she said. 'The ladder's awfully wobbly. And now I can see Miss Fellows cleaning her window from inside. Now I'm looking at the roof of that big old house – I can see it sticking up above the trees. There's a skylight set in the roof – it's being opened – someone's climbing out! Oh! oh! oh!'

Her sudden loud screaming made Peter jump in fright. 'What's the matter? What's happening?' he demanded. 'Let me see.' But Susie fended Peter off and kept her eye glued to the telescope. 'Someone else has climbed out on the roof now!' she cried. 'And he's chasing the first man. Oh, he's fallen off the roof! Peter, what shall we do? We'd better tell your mother, and get help.'

'Mother's out,' said Peter, worried. 'I'll rush off myself and see what I can do. There's a doctor who lives opposite that old house. I could get him if he's there. My word, what a bit of luck you happened to look through the telescope just then!'

He tore off down the garden – but when he came to the gate, he heard a noise that made him pause. It was the sound of delighted giggling!

He stopped at once – and then strode back angrily. 'What are you laughing at, Binkie? Susie, *did* you really see a man fall off the roof – or not?'

'Well – he might *not* have fallen off,' said Susie. 'I'll look again.' She put her eye to the telescope and peered through it once more. 'I can still see him! He's got his foot caught in the roof gutter now – oh, POOR man, he's hanging upside-down by one foot. Now here comes the other man, he . . .'

'Idiot!' said Peter, angrily. 'All made up, of course! I might easily have gone off to that house and taken the doctor too, and hunted for an imaginary man down in the garden. I suppose you think that's funny?'

'Oh we do, we do!' said Susie, with tears of laughter in her eyes. 'It's *awfully* funny, Peter – you should just have seen your face of horror. This is a most wonderful telescope. I wonder what I'll see next. *You* have a turn,

Binkie, and see if you can spot anything interesting too.'

'You can both clear off,' said Peter, and took firm hold of the telescope. 'If *this* is the kind of thing you're going to use a telescope for, I shall lock it up. GO HOME, BOTH OF YOU!'

And dear me, he looked so fierce, and Scamper began to bark so loudly that Susie and Binkie actually obeyed him, and fled for their lives!

Six

A face at the window!

IT wasn't until Janet thought she would turn the telescope on to the big hill where the ruined old castle of Torling stood, that anything really exciting turned up. The castle wasn't much more than a few standing walls, and one great ruined tower in which jackdaws nested.

Janet liked the jackdaws. They sometimes flew down to the farm, and pecked about with the hens, talking all the time in their chattery voices.

'Chack-chack-chack!' they called to one another. Jack and Pam were with Janet the last time she had gone to watch the jackdaws in the fields, and Jack had made them laugh by saying that he kept wanting to say 'Yes, sir!' every time a jackdaw called 'Chack!'

'It sounds exactly as if they're yelling at me,' said Jack, 'just like our games master does at football!'

'Chack! Chack!' called a big jackdaw at once, cocking his head on one side and looking up at Jack. 'Chack! Chack!'

'There! He heard what I said,' said Jack, and they all laughed.

The jackdaws nested in the ruins of the old tower, but now that it was November their young ones were grown, and were flying with them. The little colony must have numbered at least a hundred. Janet could see them from her bedroom window, and had often wished the old tower was nearer the farm, so that she could watch the antics of the birds more closely.

'And now I *can*!' she thought. 'We've got that lovely telescope that brings everything so near! Why didn't I think of watching the jackdaws before!'

She went to fetch it, first telling Peter in case he wanted it himself. 'It's really too cold to sit out in the open air with it today,' he said, as he took the key out from under the stone. 'Better take the telescope indoors, Janet. I'll carry it in for you. We could put it up in the boxroom at the top of the house – you'd be out of the way then – and the big window there looks right up the hill to the castle.'

Soon Janet was sitting in the boxroom, surrounded by all kinds of junk, her eye glued to the bottom end of the telescope tube. She had trained it carefully on to the top of the faraway hill, where the jackdaws circled round the tower, a hundred small black dots in the far distance.

But now, seen through the telescope they became birds, not dots – birds with outspread wings, circling and rising and falling in the misty November day. They played tricks on one another, chased each other, pretended to tumble and then swept away crying 'chack-chack-chack' as if they were laughing. Janet laughed too.

And then she suddenly stiffened on her chair. She was looking at one of the old windows at the top of the tower, through which some of the jackdaws had been flying – but now there were no jackdaws there; they had flown away as if suddenly scared, when something appeared in the window-opening, peeping cautiously over the stone window-ledge.

'What is it?' thought Janet. 'It's not a bird. Surely it can't be a cat? No – it isn't – my goodness me, it's a *head* – a man's head with a hat on – no, a cap. What in the world is he doing?'

The head remained at the window for a few minutes, and then disappeared. Janet knew that there were dangerous, broken steps at one side of the tower,

leading almost to the top and she guessed that whoever
it was who was there would now be climbing down.
She trained the telescope downwards – and caught
sight of something moving past one of the lower
windows. The man was half-way down!

'Look at that!' she said out loud, astonished. 'Someone's hiding in that old tower! Whatever for? It's
ruined and tumble-down and deserted – and dangerous too, because it's gradually subsiding! I must tell
Peter!'

She yelled for him and he came up to the boxroom.
Janet told him what she had seen, and he too looked
through the telescope at the old castle. But he could see
nothing moving there, except the jackdaws, who were
now once more settling here and there on the castle
walls.

'Whoever it was has gone into hiding down below,'
said Janet, beginning to feel excited. 'So the jackdaws
aren't frightened any longer. Who can it be, Peter?'

'Can't imagine!' said her brother, puzzled. 'Nobody
ever goes there in the winter – and anyway, it's supposed to be dangerous now. Some stones fell down this
spring, you know – right off the top of the tower! Are
you quite *sure* you saw a face at the window? Which
window was it?'

Janet told him, and Peter gazed at it through the
telescope, moving it downwards to other openings. He
gave a sudden exclamation.

'Yes! There *is* someone there! I saw something
moving down below – on the ground floor. I'm sure
someone passed quickly across the doorway, just

inside! No wonder the jackdaws keep flying up in fright!'

'We must tell the Secret Seven,' said Janet, excited. 'You never know, Peter – this might be something mysterious, something that . . .'

Peter laughed. 'It's probably just some tramp looking for shelter! Still, we'll tell the others and see what *they* think!'

Seven

Susie is very annoying

NEXT day, when Peter walked home with Jack and George after school, he told them what he and Janet had seen through the telescope. 'Janet saw a face – the head of a man wearing a cap,' he said. 'And I distinctly saw someone moving behind the great doorway of the castle. I think there's a man hiding up there.'

'Well, if he were hiding, surely he wouldn't give himself away by peering through windows and walking across open doorways!' objected Jack. 'I expect it was just a chance visitor.'

'Look, Jack – anyone hiding up there would never, never imagine that anybody could *possibly* spot him in the castle, far away from everywhere, at the top of that hill!' said Peter. 'It was only because we were using your powerful telescope that that man was seen! He could never be spotted with the naked eye.'

'Yes – you're right there,' said George. 'I didn't think of that. The castle is so lonely and deserted on the top of that steep hill that anyone might judge it safe to hide there in the wintertime. But it must be jolly cold! Where does he sleep, do you think?'

'Down in the old dungeons?' suggested Peter, with a shiver. 'Have you ever seen them? You go down about a hundred steps into a cold, dark, echoing place – rather like a most *enormous* cellar! Hundreds of years ago prisoners were kept down there.'

417

'How horrible people must have been in those days!' said George. 'I couldn't even keep a dog or cat down in a cellar!'

'What about us going up to the old castle and having a snoop round?' said Jack. 'I've never been there.'

'Well, it's rather dangerous now, my dad says,' said George. 'But the dangerous places have warning notices up, so I dare say we'd be all right. After all, we're pretty sensible, or Peter wouldn't allow us to belong to the Secret Seven!'

That made the others laugh. 'Quite right,' said Peter. 'No fatheads allowed in the S.S. Club! Well, what about it – *shall* we go up to the castle? We could bike or walk, whichever you like.'

'Bike,' said Jack. 'It's true we'll have to walk up most of the castle hill, it's so steep – but it will be fun to coast down.'

'Right. Saturday morning, then,' said Peter. 'We'll ask Colin if he'd like to come, but not the girls – the hill would be a bit steep for them.'

But the three girls had quite other ideas about that. 'Too steep indeed!' snorted Janet, when Peter told her what he and the other boys had planned. 'I bet I could ride right up that hill and get to the top before you did! We're *all* coming, see? Pam and Barbara, too. This is a Secret Seven thing, and we'll all be in it. Anyway, *I* discovered there was someone hiding in the castle, not you!'

'All right, all right, all *right*,' said Peter, backing away. 'Don't bite my nose off. I'll ring up Jack and tell him it's to be a Secret Seven outing. We'll all wear our badges.'

So he rang up Jack, and told him that Janet insisted on the three girls coming.

'What a nuisance!' said Jack. 'It's quite a way to the castle – and we'll have to bike slowly or the girls won't keep up with us.'

'What's this you're phoning about?' said Susie, suddenly appearing at the door of the room in which Jack was phoning. 'Are you going on a spree or something? I'd like to come too. It would be a treat for Binkie.'

'Well, you're *not* coming!' said Jack. 'It's a Secret Seven outing. And do shut up a minute. Can't you see

I'm phoning?' He turned back to the telephone. 'Sorry, Peter. Susie came barging in just then. She said *she* wanted to come too, with Binkie!'

'What a truly horrible idea!' said Peter into the phone. 'They can't, of course. I won't have them.'

'Have you spotted that fellow again, hiding in the castle?' asked Jack, thinking that Susie had gone out of the room.

'Don't talk about that on the phone,' said Peter, quite cross. 'Anyone might hear! It's *our* secret!'

'Sorry,' said Jack, humbly. 'All right, then – we all of us meet at a quarter to ten, Saturday morning, outside your front gate. Is Scamper coming?'

'No. Too long a run for him,' said Peter. 'Goodbye for now!'

Susie pounced on Jack as soon as he had finished. She had been hiding behind an arm-chair, listening! Jack glared at her in rage.

'You've been *listening*! Well, a fat lot of good it will do you!' And he stalked out of the room.

'Who's hiding in the old castle? And why are they there, do you think?' asked Susie, following Jack out of the room. 'Go on – tell me. How do you *know* anyone's there? It's too far to see people in the castle. I don't believe it!'

'You forget that we have a telescope, Miss Clever!' said Jack, coldly, and ran up the stairs. Susie made a rude face behind his back.

'Well, *we're* coming too, Binkie and I,' she said. 'We'll be the Secret Nine, instead of the Secret Seven! So there!'

Eight

Up at the castle

JACK knew perfectly well that Susie would keep her word, and that she and Binkie would follow the Seven on their journey to the old castle. He kicked himself for not having made certain that his annoying sister was out of the room before he finished phoning. He would remember to search thoroughly in future.

With a sigh he went to see Peter, not daring to telephone him again, in case Susie was about. He told him of Susie's threat.

'Well – fancy letting out what our plans were, with *Susie* in the room!' said Peter, in disgust. 'You really *are* a mutt! Never mind. We'll simply start half an hour later – but for goodness' *sake* don't let her guess that!'

So, at quarter past ten on Saturday morning, the Secret Seven assembled outside Peter's front gate. All of them had their bicycles with them, and in the baskets were bottles of lemonade, and biscuits. This was Janet's idea, and everyone thought it a very good one.

Jack was the last to arrive, and he pedalled up in a hurry. 'Sorry I'm late,' he said. 'I had to make sure that Susie and Binkie weren't lying in wait somewhere, meaning to come with me!'

'Where are they?' demanded Peter.

'I don't know. But their bikes are still in the shed, so we're safe,' said Jack, thankfully. 'I asked Mother where they were, and she said she heard them talking about going shopping – so *that's* all right!'

'All the same – we'll keep a look-out till we're safely on the way,' said Peter. 'I will *not* have those two messing up our plans.'

They saw no sign whatever of Susie or Binkie and soon forgot about them. After all, if their bikes were in the shed, they couldn't go far!

When they came to the steep road that wound up round the castle hill, they panted and puffed – and one by one leapt off to walk. It really was *too* steep to ride up. The road did not go to the castle, but passed by it some way off. A footpath over a stile led to the old ruin, and when they came to this the Seven piled their bicycles on top of one another in the hedge, and were soon over the stile. They carried their lemonade and biscuits with them, planning to eat and drink in the shelter of the castle.

It was still some way off up the hill. They all kept a sharp look-out for signs of anyone looking out of the windows, but could see nothing at all.

The jackdaws circled overhead all the time, calling loudly, disturbed at seeing so many children. 'Chack, chack!' they called. 'Chack, chack!'

And Jack answered at once. 'Glad you know me! How are you all?'

'Ass!' said Peter, laughing. 'My word – what an enormous number there are! Now, what shall we do first? Look round the old place – go down into the dungeons and snoop around? Eat our biscuits?'

'Let's go inside and eat there,' said Barbara. 'The

wind's jolly strong out here, and I'm cold. I'm hungry, too. We can snoop round afterwards.'

So they all trooped up the broken steps, and in at the great entrance to the castle, where once enormous gates had hung. They stopped in the vast hall inside, and stared in surprise. It was piled high at one side with twigs of all kinds and sizes!

'Who put those here?' said Jack, puzzled. 'Oh, of course – the jackdaws! They nest in the tower chimney, and these twigs must have fallen down from their nests for years and years!'

They looked up the tower. They could see the sky through a square hole at the top where smoke once rose from the enormous stone fire-place far below, in the hall. This was almost completely hidden by the fallen twigs, which had spread out on to the hall floor as well. They cracked loudly as the children trod on them.

A big wooden notice, with DANGER painted on it, was placed further down the hall, in a carved stone door-way. The children peered through it, and saw a big room, with one wall crumbling dangerously. It looked as if it might fall at any time.

'We can't go in *there*,' said Peter, at once. 'I shouldn't think anyone would hide in *that* room – I imagine it would be a pretty dangerous hiding-place!'

'Sh!' said Janet, in a low voice. 'Don't talk about hiding-places – if anyone *is* hiding here, they'll hear you.'

'You're right,' said Peter. 'Let's go further down the hall – we'll find plenty more old rooms, I expect, all crumbling away! Come on – and look out for any signs of people hiding!' he added, in a whisper. 'Follow me!'

Nine

An exciting time!

IT wasn't until they came to what seemed to be a dark kitchen-like place, with a huge stone sink in one corner, that they found anything at all exciting. Jack suddenly stopped and pointed.

The others looked, and saw what appeared to have been a fire, made of sticks, half-burnt through. Pam gave a little cry as she bent over them.

'Why – the sticks are still warm! It's not long since this fire was lighted!'

'Sh!' said everyone, looking over their shoulders, feeling that whoever had lighted that fire, might still be about.

Peter felt the twigs. Yes, they were certainly still warm – and what was more, it looked as if someone had stamped out the little fire in a hurry, for it was curiously flattened!

'Talk in loud voices about ordinary things,' commanded Peter, in a whisper. 'And keep your eyes open.'

They followed Peter up some steps to a stone bench in a crumbling recess in the wall. A newspaper had been left there, and they pounced on it.

'What date is it? It might tell us whether anyone has been here recently,' said Colin. He shook it open.

'No – no use,' he said. 'Look – it's dated 16th September – ages ago!'

'Left by some visitor, probably – maybe trippers

were still visiting the castle then,' said Peter. 'Come on – let's have another look round.'

To their great disappointment they could find nothing of any use at all. A few cigarette ends – one or two dead matches – a paper bag that had once held sweets. 'No – I can't say that these are any help,' said Peter.

'I vote we sit down and have our biscuits,' said George, at last, tired of hunting in every corner. 'I'm filthy dirty – just look at my hands!'

'I say – do you suppose these steps go down to the dungeons?' called Barbara. Everyone turned to see where she was. She stood below a big hand-printed notice. It said 'THE DUNGEONS. UNSAFE. DESCENT FORBIDDEN.'

'Yes. Look at the notice, ass,' said Peter. 'Well – we don't go down those steps, that's certain! I don't particularly want an old wall to fall on top of me!'

'Let's have our biscuits sitting on the old stone bench here,' said Jack. 'It will just about take us all. What a castle! The things that must have happened here!'

They all sat down, crowding on to the uneven old seat. It felt very cold and hard! Soon they were munching their biscuits, and drinking their lemonade out of the little bottles.

'Do you really think anyone's here besides us – hiding somewhere?' said Pam, in a whisper.

'Quite likely,' answered Peter, also in a whisper. 'Probably down in the dungeons! Nobody in their sense would go down there, with that danger notice up!'

'I don't like to think of someone hiding down in that

horrible dark dungeon,' said Barbara, a picture of a dreadful damp, smelly, black place coming into her mind. 'I do hope to goodness we don't hear any noises coming from there.'

'Don't be a fathead,' said George. 'Nobody's down there – why should . . .'

He stopped very suddenly, as a curious noise suddenly came to his ears. Everyone heard it, and stiffened in fright.

It sounded a little like a very unhappy owl, 'Ooooo!' it wailed. 'Ooo-oo-OOOOOOO!'

Pam clutched Barbara and made her jump. 'What is it? Did you hear?'

'Shut up,' said Peter, sharply. 'Listen, everyone. Someone's down in those dungeons.'

'Oooh-ah-oooh-eeeee!' wailed the voice.

Pam gave such a shriek that everyone leapt to their feet. She tumbled down from the seat and ran howling down the stone passage to the hall.

Jack went after her, and the others were just collecting their bags and bottles when another noise made them jump. It, too, came from the dungeons.

'Bang! Bang-bang! Bang!'

'Quick – run!' shouted Peter, clutching Janet, and pushing her in front of him. 'Back to our bikes!'

'Is that someone shooting?' asked Barbara, fearfully, as they ran, hearing a few more 'bangs' coming from the dungeons.

'Goodness knows!' said Peter. 'Gosh, look how scared the jackdaws are now – and what a row they are making! Whatever can be going on in that castle?'

Ten

Another meeting

WHEN they had reached their bicycles safely, they paused to put their bags and bottles into the baskets. Peter was beginning to feel a bit ashamed of their hurried flight.

'Do you think we boys ought to go back and find out what those bangs were?' he said. 'I mean – I don't *think* they were gun-shots, you know – they weren't loud enough.'

'You go if you want to. *I'm* not rushing into danger,' said Colin. 'Something's certainly going on there. Tell the police if you like – and leave *them* to deal with it. What with that half-warm, stamped-out fire of twigs – and those howls and bangs – it's enough to scare grown-ups, let alone *us*!'

'Let's have a meeting about it!' said George. 'We ought to decide what we're going to do. We *know* there's somebody there – so why is he hiding? And what's he doing down in the dungeons, popping away like that? Is he trying to scare us off? Has he something to hide?'

'Let's have a meeting as soon as we get back,' said Janet.

'I can't. I've a music lesson at quarter past twelve,' said Pam. 'Please, *please* don't have a meeting without me.'

'Well, three o'clock this afternoon, then,' said Peter.

'And mind you remember the password – telescope – and wear your badges.'

'*I* can't come then,' said Jack, 'and neither can George. We've got football practice. Make it tomorrow evening.'

'All right. Tomorrow evening then – six o'clock – and be punctual,' said Peter. 'And if I've got time I'll take a look at that castle through the telescope this afternoon. There really *is* something going on there!'

They rode home rather gloomily, all the boys now wishing they had gone into the dungeons – or at least peeped down – to see what was going on. 'Still, we hadn't any torches,' said Peter. 'We couldn't have seen a thing. It sounded awfully like owls, didn't it – but it couldn't have been. Owls hoot but they don't make bang-bang noises!'

Jack rode home, hoping that Susie and Binkie were out still and wouldn't ask him questions about his morning. He peeped into the shed and saw that the girls' bikes were still there. Good! They must still be out doing their Saturday shopping!

As soon as Peter was home, he fetched the telescope from the shed, while a delighted Scamper danced round him. The spaniel had not been at all pleased at being left behind that morning, and had lain by the fire, sulking – but now he was so glad to see Peter and Janet again that he could hardly keep still!

Peter took the telescope to the boxroom and set it up. Scamper sniffed at the bottom end with much interest.

'You look up it with your eye, not your *nose*,' said

Peter. He set his right eye to the telescope, and trained it on the castle – good gracious, was that someone standing in the great doorway!

But before he could see properly, Scamper jumped up to lick him – and over went the telescope! 'Idiot!' said Peter, crossly, and hurriedly picked it up. It seemed quite all right. He set it up again and peered through it excitedly.

But now the doorway was empty. No one stood there. Peter felt really vexed. 'Couldn't you have waited a bit to lick me?' he said to Scamper. 'Oh goodness – now there's *Mother* calling me – and by the time I get back to the boxroom, it'll be too late to spot whoever it was!'

His mother kept him busy for the rest of the morning, and in the afternoon he had to do his homework. He longed to go up and look through the telescope. So did Janet.

There was nothing interesting to be seen when at last they managed to peer through it. In disappointment they took it down to the shed again, and locked it there as usual.

'Cheer up, Peter,' said Janet. 'We're having a meeting tomorrow night, and I've a box of toffees! It will be fun to talk about our morning at the castle.'

On Sunday evening everyone arrived quite punctually, and the password was rattled out five times. 'Telescope!' As George said, it would be easier to remember *that* password than forget it!

They settled down in the warm shed, all seven of them. Peter glanced round to see if they were wearing their badges. Yes – everyone had the S.S. on their coats. Janet handed round the toffees, and they began to talk about the previous morning.

'Someone's hiding at the castle, for *some* reason, that's certain,' began Peter. 'And that someone doesn't want anyone else to know he's there – and scared us away. I feel silly now – I'm sure the man who's hiding there knew we were kids and would run for our lives if he made scary noises!'

'Yes. I've been thinking that too,' said Jack.

'Oh, but they sounded so *awful*,' said Pam, and she gave a little shudder. 'I wouldn't go there again if you gave me a thousand pounds.'

'Well, we're not offering you anything like that,' said Peter. 'So stop shuddering, and talk sense. I think now that we were rather cowardly.'

'But those *bangs*!' said Barbara. 'They sounded so loud and frightening. And those moans and howls!'

'Now let's be sensible,' said Peter. 'I don't suppose . . .'

And then he stopped very suddenly indeed, for from outside the shed came two or three mournful yowls exactly like those the Seven had heard yesterday morning! 'Ooo-oo-OOOO!'

Everyone jumped violently, and Scamper barked and ran to the door, scratching it angrily. There was a dead silence in the shed, except for Scamper. The moaning suddenly stopped.

Then the bangs began! Pop! Pop-pop! POP!

'I'm scared,' whispered Pam, and clutched at Barbara, making her jump.

'Ooo-ooo! Pop-bang-pop!'

Then came a most familiar sound – a giggle, hastily stopped midway. Jack and Peter gave cries of fury and rushed to the door.

'SUSIE! BINKIE! YOU BEASTS!'

The door was flung open so suddenly that the two giggling girls outside were taken by surprise. Jack leapt out and caught Susie. Binkie ran, but came back to help Susie and was caught too. They were both dragged into the shed and set down with a bump on two boxes.

'And now will you just tell us the *meaning* of all this!' said Peter, so angry that he could hardly get the words out of his mouth.

Eleven

Susie's tale

'I SHAN'T say a word if you shout at me,' said Susie. 'And Binkie and I will yell the place down if you're unkind to us.'

'Unkind! UNKIND! Well, what about you and Binkie!' cried Janet. 'Interfering in all our plans! It was *you* down in that dungeon, wasn't it – yowling and – and – well, what *were* you doing to make those bangs?'

'They weren't bangs – they were loud pops,' said Susie, with a sudden giggle. 'The same as we made down in that dungeon. Look – I'll show you!' The two girls looked highly pleased with themselves.

And to the great disgust of the Secret Seven she took a small bundle of coloured rubber out of her pocket and blew hard into it. It swelled up into a truly colossal balloon! Susie held it away from her and Binkie promptly jabbed it with a large pin. POP!

'*That's* what scared you away – balloons popping – and yowls!' said Binkie, giving them a wicked grin, and putting the big pin back under her coat lapel. 'Did our hoots and yowls sound awful coming up those old stone steps?'

'You'd no right to go down into those dungeons,' said Peter, severely. 'Didn't you see the notice? Don't tell me *you* put that notice there!'

'No, we didn't. But it wasn't there when I went up to

see the castle with some friends in the summer,' said Binkie, 'so I guessed it couldn't be *very* dangerous to go down! It was only printed by hand too – not properly, like the other notices.'

'So it was,' said Jack, remembering. 'I say – do you suppose that whoever is hiding there wrote out that notice himself, to stop people prying in the dungeons?'

'And stop them finding something he had hidden there!' exclaimed George. 'It's just like Susie to disobey warnings.'

'*Did* you see anything hidden there?' said Peter. 'Tell us at once.'

'Yes, we did,' said Susie. 'But unless you ask me politely, I shan't tell you anything.'

Peter glared at her. Exasperating, irritating girl! She grinned cheekily at him. 'Say "please, Susie",' she said.

And poor Peter had to do as he was told! He just *had* to know what was down in the dungeons.

'Please, Susie,' he said, quite fiercely.

'Not like that. Really *politely*,' said Susie.

'Susie! I'll shake you to bits if you go on like this!' said Jack suddenly. 'I'm ashamed of you – talking to Peter like that. I'll – I'll . . .'

'All right, all right. I'll tell you what we saw,' said Susie, hastily, knowing quite well that her brother would certainly give her a really good shaking if she was cheeky much longer. 'Listen, all of you.'

Everyone listened intently as Susie told what had happened to her and Binkie yesterday morning. Binkie sat beside her, nodding her head every now and then as Susie related her story.

'Well,' began Susie, 'we knew you were all going up there, of course, and we knew you thought there was someone hiding in the castle, because we heard what Jack said on the phone. So we thought we'd go too, and get there *before* you, so that we could play a few tricks.'

'Yes – but how did you get there? Your bikes were in the shed. I saw them,' said Jack.

'Have you forgotten that there are such things as buses?' said Susie. 'We just caught the bus that goes up the hill and stops at the top. We hopped off and made our way over the fields to the castle – to the *back* of it, not the front, in case you came early.'

'*Buses!* Why didn't we think of that!' groaned Jack. 'So you were there a long time before us?'

'Oh yes – and when we came up to the back of the castle, very quietly, just in *case* anyone was there, we saw someone sitting on an old stone, painting the castle.'

'Painting a *picture* of it, she means,' put in Binkie, seeing that some of the Seven looked rather astonished. 'Goodness – she jumped like anything when we came up behind her, because she hadn't heard us coming over the grass.'

'Did you talk to her?' asked Peter. '*We* thought it was a man there, not a woman. The person I saw through the telescope seemed to have a man's cap on.'

'Oh, this woman had no cap – but she wears her hair

sort of piled up on top of her head. I suppose it looked like a cap, in the distance,' said Susie, who was now enjoying herself thoroughly. 'Well . . .'

Scamper suddenly growled and ran to the door. 'Someone's coming!' said Peter. 'Who is it?'

There was a knock at the door, and then came Cookie's cheerful voice. 'I won't come in, I know you're talking secrets – but I'm leaving a plate of jam-tarts out here. Seven – is that right?'

'No, nine – ten, counting Scamper!' called Susie, cheekily, before anyone else could say a word. 'It's a Secret *Nine* Meeting tonight!'

'Well, one of you must come and fetch two more then,' said Cookie's voice, and off she went, back to the house.

'Secret *Nine* indeed!' said Janet, very cross. She frowned angrily at Susie. 'You certainly *won't* get any tarts!'

'Right. We'll say good-bye and go home then,' said Susie. 'Come on, Binkie!' And the two of them got up and went to the door!

Twelve
Susie has plenty to say!

PETER groaned. He knew when he was beaten! 'All right – you win!' he said. 'Come back and sit down. Colin, go and get three more jam-tarts – old Scamper can have one then.'

Colin departed, with Scamper at his heels. The rest of the Seven sat and looked at Susie in disgust. What a girl! She smiled cheekily all round. This certainly was Her Evening! Aha! She was teaching those stuck-up Seven a lesson!

Colin came back at once with the tarts, and they all began to eat them, Scamper too.

'Well, about this artist woman,' said Susie, with her mouth full. 'She said we'd better not go into the castle because it was dangerous, so we thanked her for her warning – but, of course, we meant to go without her seeing us!'

'You *would*!' said Jack.

'We stopped and talked a bit, just to see if she had anything interesting to say,' said Susie. 'But she hadn't, really. She just said she loved the old castle, and was painting it, hoping to sell the picture. She said she kept her paints and things inside, because nobody ever came in the winter, so they were quite safe.'

'This looks as if all our suspicions were silly,' said Peter, feeling rather small.

'She was awfully interested in us, too,' went on Susie. 'Wasn't she, Binkie?'

'Oh yes – she asked us a lot of questions – and she laughed like anything when Susie said Jack and the others were coming up to hunt a man hiding in the castle.'

'You told her *that*!' cried Peter, angrily. 'How dare you? You'd no right to give our plans away.'

'Well, they were silly plans, so it didn't really matter,' said Susie. 'She asked me how in the world you could see anyone in the castle from this farm – we told her you lived here, Peter – and she was *very* interested to hear about the telescope we keep down in this shed, and how easily we could see the castle with it.'

'SUSIE! You surely didn't give that away too – how *could* you? Now she'll know we're watching what's happening,' groaned Peter. 'Honestly, you must be a nitwit to jabber like that to a stranger.'

'And *you* must be a nitwit to think anything peculiar is going on up at the castle,' said Susie. 'Just a woman artist painting a picture! *No* one's hiding there. She said that she goes down to sleep in the village on the other side of the castle each night – and except for us, not a soul has been to the castle since she came. Ha ha – what about your mystery now?'

The Secret Seven felt very small indeed – and very angry. It had all been so exciting – and now Susie had interfered, and there was nothing left!

'Did you see anything at all in the dungeons?' asked Peter, after a pause.

'Only things that I suppose belonged to the artist,' said Susie. 'Let's see – what was there, Binkie?'

'Pictures,' said Binkie. 'Pictures without frames.

Rather dark and ugly, *I* thought. I suppose the artist had painted them. They were all covered up, of course. We just peeped at them. There was a pile of rugs too, and some tins.'

'The artist said she'd take another day or two to finish the picture, and when it rained she went into the castle for shelter,' said Susie. 'That's how it was you saw her peeping out of that window, I expect. She has all her meals there too, except breakfast and supper. She just opens a tin.'

'Funny sort of life,' said George. 'Well – that's that! If only we'd gone behind the castle *we'd* have seen her too. We just went straight in at the front. You were watching out for us, I suppose, and shot down into the cellar to blow up your stupid balloons.'

'We nearly died of laughing when we heard you yelling with fright, and listened to you racing out of the castle,' said Binkie, and went off into one of her giggling fits.

'Oh do shut up,' said Jack, tired of both Binkie and Susie. 'Go home. Get out of our sight.'

'We thought we'd like to use the telescope, if you don't mind,' said Susie, putting on a most polite voice. 'The moon's rather good tonight.'

'No. This meeting is ending,' said Peter, firmly. 'Scoot, you two girls. I think your behaviour was *disgraceful*.'

'You sound like Miss Cummings, our form mistress,' said Susie, in delight. 'Do say all that again!'

'Oh clear out!' said Peter, at the end of his patience. 'And don't *attempt* to do anything funny with our telescope tonight. I forbid you to!'

'But it doesn't belong to *you*,' said Susie, flaring up at once. 'It's half mine. I only *let* you use my half-share in it, I . . .'

'Susie! Be quiet, and come home with me,' said Jack, and he took his sister's arm very firmly indeed.

'I'm ashamed of you!'

He dragged her out of the shed, and Binkie followed. Peter heaved a sigh of relief.

'Thank goodness, we've got rid of them! *What* a pair! Well, let's hope that's the last we'll hear of them for some time!'

Thirteen

The telescope again

Susie and Binkie were angry with Jack for hauling them away. 'We wanted to look through the telescope again,' complained Susie.

'No, you didn't – you were just being annoying,' said Jack, fiercely.

'Let go my arm,' said Susie. 'I want to walk by myself.'

'Well, just behave yourself then,' said Jack, quite relieved to let such a wriggler go. The two girls darted off at once, and Jack saw them racing up the road towards home. He heaved a sigh of relief. What COULD anyone do with a sister like Susie?

But Susie and Binkie didn't go home. No – Susie was quite determined to have her way and take out the telescope that night. She didn't *really* want to – it was just obstinacy. She had asked for it – had been refused – and that had made her determined to get her own way. Just like Susie!

So, instead of going round the corner and home, the two girls slipped into a gateway, waited till Jack had gone plodding past, and then raced back to Peter's again. They were puffing and panting so much that they hadn't enough breath left to giggle. But they were very thrilled to think they had outwitted poor Jack, who would be almost home by now. Ha! Ha!

In a trice they were down at the shed. It was in

darkness now, and well and truly locked. The girls found the key under the stone, and unlocked the wooden door.

They each had a torch, and it was not difficult to set up the telescope on the low garden wall as usual.

'We'll just have a quick look at the moon, so that we can say we saw it through the telescope,' said Susie. 'And then we'll put it away. Won't the Secret Seven be wild to think we got our way after all!'

They were soon looking through the long tube of the big telescope. The moon was not at all obliging, and stayed behind clouds, so that the night was dark, instead of light.

'Swing the telescope round a bit and look at the old castle,' suggested Binkie. 'Then we can say we saw that too.'

So Susie trained the telescope on to the castle, far away on its steep hill. It was just a great dark shadow in the night, only visible because of the light from the half-hidden moon.

'There,' said Susie, 'now we can ... oooh – I say – Binkie, there's a *light* in the castle!'

'In the *castle*! What do you mean? Let *me* see!' said Binkie, and glued her eye to the bottom of the telescope. 'Yes! There *is* a light. It's somewhere on the ground floor – is it shining out of the entrance?'

'I don't know. Might be one of the downstairs windows,' said Susie, pushing Binkie aside. 'Yes, there it is – quite clear! What does that mean, do you suppose? That woman said she never slept in the castle – she went down to her lodgings for tea and stayed there!

It's a signal to someone, I should think. Yes – that must
be it. Perhaps there *is* something going on, after all!'

'Good gracious! Let's go and tell Peter then,' said
Binkie, excited. 'Or shall we keep it to ourselves?'

'No – we'll tell Peter,' said Susie. 'He'll be *furious* to
think we've discovered something else! Come on!' So
off they went to find Peter and Janet. They were up in
their playroom, doing jigsaws, and were really amazed
to see Binkie and Susie again!

'Look here!' began Peter angrily, but Susie stopped
him.

'We've got news!' she said. 'There's someone up at

the castle, signalling with a light! We saw it! We looked through the telescope. Come and see.'

But Peter only laughed, and sat down to his jigsaw again. '*Another* of your silly jokes,' he said. 'I wonder you're not tired of them. If you think we're going to be taken in again, you're mistaken. Now, if you don't clear out and *keep* out, I'll call Mother. We've had enough of you both for tonight.'

'But Peter – we looked through the . . .' began Binkie, and was promptly pushed out of the room by Peter and Janet, and Susie was hustled off too. The playroom door banged, and the two girls heard the key being turned in the lock.

'All right! You'll be sorry!' shouted Susie. 'You'll be VERY sorry tomorrow that you didn't listen to us!'

And down the stairs they went, almost crying with rage. There *was* someone signalling in that castle, there *was*!

Fourteen

A horrid shock

NEXT morning Janet and Peter went down to their shed after breakfast to clear up the things left there the evening before.

'We've twenty minutes before we need to start for school,' said Peter, looking for the key under the stone. 'Hallo – the key's not here! What's happened to it? I know I put it there last night.'

'Susie must have taken it!' said Janet, frowning. 'Just to spite us. The little nuisance!'

They went to the shed-door to see if Susie had torn off the green letters S.S. that were always there. Good – they were still there – but as they turned away from the shed, Janet gave a cry of surprise.

'Peter! The key's in the *lock*! Susie forgot to hide it – the idiot! Anyone might break into the shed and take things if it isn't locked.'

They went in, feeling cross. Everything seemed all right – and then Janet frowned. Something was missing, surely? What was it?

'The *telescope*!' she cried suddenly. 'Peter – where's the telescope? It's gone!'

'Susie's taken it!' said Peter, so angry that he stammered over the words. 'Just because I said she wasn't to use it, and because we wouldn't believe her silly story last night about someone signalling in the castle! I'm going to telephone Jack.'

Jack was horrified when he heard Peter's news. He fetched Susie at once.

'You just go to the phone and tell Peter where you've hidden the telescope!' he said. 'It's not in the shed.'

'But we put it back safely,' said Susie, sounding so amazed that Jack felt she must be speaking the truth. 'We did, really.'

'Did you lock the door?' said Jack. Susie looked at Binkie – and then she went very red.

'Oh Jack – no, I don't think I did. I was so cross because Peter wouldn't believe me, that I just shoved the telescope into the shed, slammed the door – and ran off with Binkie. I can't remember locking it, or hiding the key.'

'We forgot,' said Binkie, in a very small voice. 'Yes, we forgot. Oh that lovely telescope, Jack! Has it been stolen?'

'I expect so,' said Jack, going back to the telephone. 'Of all the idiots! One of these days, Susie, you'll get into serious trouble. It's a jolly good thing it's *our* telescope, not anyone else's.'

He told Peter that Susie and Binkie *had* put back the telescope, but had forgotten to lock the door. Peter was very angry. 'So any prying thief snooping round the shed at night could get in,' he said. 'And of course he'd take the telescope – it would be the most valuable thing there! I'll have to tell my dad, Jack.'

'Oh not just yet!' begged Jack. 'Susie would get into such trouble. I know she's an awful girl, but she *is* my sister, and – well – you know how I feel.'

'Right, Jack. We'll wait till tonight, and see if any-thing turns up,' said Peter. 'Better have a meeting – half-past five, sharp. But DON'T tell Susie.'

'I won't. But she's so worried and upset that I really don't think she'd even *think* of trying any tricks!' said poor Jack. 'I'm awfully worried too. I know it looks as if Susie and Binkie took the telescope themselves, out of spite – but Susie doesn't tell lies, you know, however annoying she is in other ways.'

'I know she doesn't,' said Peter. 'All right. Five-thirty tonight. I'll tell the others.'

So at half-past five that night a rather subdued Seven met once more down in the old shed. Scamper couldn't *think* what was the matter with them, and ran about wagging his tail and trying to cheer them up.

It was a very serious meeting. Everyone already knew about the telescope, because Janet had told the girls in break at school, and Jack and Peter had told George and Colin. Now – what was to be done?

Fifteen
Exciting plans

'JACK – you'd better say a few words to everyone about Susie,' said Peter.

So Jack explained how Susie had forgotten to lock the door, and was very, very sorry, and asked the Seven to forgive her and Binkie. 'She says they'll do ANYTHING to help us get it back,' finished Jack. 'I'm most awfully sorry myself – and jolly thankful that it belonged to me and Susie. I'd have felt dreadful if it had belonged to anyone else.' He felt pretty dreadful now, but *that* would have been just *awful*.

'We're sorry too, Jack,' said Peter. 'And we do believe you when you say that Susie *didn't* take the telescope.'

'I think we ought also to believe her tale of the light that she said she and Binkie saw in the castle last night, when they looked through the telescope,' said Jack, earnestly. 'I know Susie is really most annoying, but *honestly*, Secret Seven, I have never, never once known Susie to tell a lie. She plays jokes, I know, and makes us believe silly things – but she never tells a thumping fib – and if she says she saw a light in the castle last night, then she *did*.'

'I see,' said Peter. 'Well, what do the others say? Do we believe it or not?'

'*I* believe it,' said Pam. 'Susie's a fathead and a nuisance, but I've never known her to tell even a small fib

452

at school to get herself out of trouble. She's too proud to do that. She'd rather take her punishment.'

'She's more like a boy, really,' said Barbara, which made all the boys look scornfully at her. 'Well, you know what I mean,' she went on. 'She's brave – and bold, and don't-care-ish – and she doesn't cry if she hurts herself, and she'll stick by her friends through thick and thin. If she were a boy I'd like her awfully – but as she's a girl, she's just a nuisance.'

This rather remarkable speech by the quiet Barbara surprised everyone.

'I know what you mean, Barbie,' said Janet. 'Let's forgive Susie – and let her help if she wants to.'

But the boys drew the line at that. No – they didn't want Susie's help. Secretly they felt that she might be a bit too clever for them!

'Well – to come back to the point,' said Peter, 'we'll say that we believe what Susie said about seeing a light in the castle – and that means that the woman artist she saw wasn't telling the truth when she said she didn't stay there at night – and it does seem to mean, too, that the light must have been a signal! All right – to whom was she signalling – and why?'

'I think we boys ought to go up to the castle tonight and have another snoop round,' said Colin. 'I feel ashamed now that we ran away as we did! I'd feel better about it if we went up again, and tried to find out what really is going on.'

The other boys nodded. They felt the same. 'But no girls,' said Peter, firmly, seeing that Janet was about to speak. 'NO GIRLS.'

'There's *one* thing we haven't tried to solve,' said George. 'And that is – who on earth stole the telescope! The ordinary thief wouldn't want a thing like that – difficult to sell, and no real use to him! I should have thought he'd have taken the rug off the floor, or our lamp – something like that.'

'Yes, you're right,' said Peter. Then they all jumped as Jack slapped his knee and gave a cry. 'Listen! I bet I know who stole our telescope! *Whoever is hiding in the castle took it!* Susie told that woman artist about the telescope, and how we could see the castle with it, and even saw someone at the window – and if there is any funny business going on up there, that woman would know that our telescope would show it to any of us down here – if we happened to look through it at an awkward moment for them!'

'So someone popped down here last night, found the shed-door unlocked, went in and stole the telescope so that we couldn't spy on them!' finished Peter. 'Too easy for words! Blow Susie! If only she'd locked the shed, I bet they wouldn't have got in.'

'The thing is – what sort of funny business could be going on, up in the old castle?' wondered Janet. They all frowned and thought hard.

'It would make an awfully good hiding-place for anything stolen,' suggested Pam. 'Those dungeons would be fine for that.'

'But Susie said there was nothing there but pictures without frames,' said Colin. 'I suppose that woman had painted them, and was storing them there till she could get them framed.'

'Don't be an ass,' said Jack. 'If there were a lot there, it would have taken anyone *weeks* to paint them. But I tell you what they *might* be! *Old* pictures – valuable ones!'

'Well, they would be framed, if so,' said Barbara.

'Not if they were stolen,' said Jack. 'Nothing easier than to take pictures out of their frames, roll them up, and spirit them away!'

'I think that's rather far-fetched,' objected Janet. 'Honestly I do.'

'All right,' said Jack. 'There's only one thing to do, as far as I can see – and that's to go up there tonight, and watch. Susie said that woman must have been signalling with a light last night. Right – she was presumably signalling to *someone* – probably telling them that the goods were there – they could come and fetch them – or something like that. In which case . . .'

'*Somebody* might go for them tonight!' said George and Jack together.

There was a silence, and everyone thought hard. Then Peter spoke firmly.

'This is what I think our plan should be. We four boys will bike up there again after supper tonight. We will snoop round and see what we can find out. I bet our telescope's hidden up there! If we think we need help, or that Dad ought to know and get busy too, we'll signal with one of our bike lamps. Wave it up and down!'

'Oooh – this is exciting!' said Pam. 'How many times will you wave?'

'Twice if everything's O.K., and we can't find anything wrong. Four times if we'd like Dad to come up. More than four times if it's really *urgent*. Got that?'

'Yes,' said everyone, fervently, their eyes shining with excitement.

'Pam and Barbara, you come round after supper and watch with me,' said Janet. 'But wait a minute, Peter – how can we see your signals? We haven't the telescope now, remember, and we can't see any signals without that. The castle is too far away.'

'I've thought of that,' said Peter. 'You must borrow Dad's field-glasses – and I think, when we've been gone about half an hour, you'd better tell him the whole story, so that he's ready to come if we need him.'

'This is too exciting for words!' said Pam. 'Field-glasses! How clever you are, Peter. Of course, field-glasses can see nearly as far as a telescope – they will pick up any signal easily.'

'The meeting is ended,' said Peter, and Scamper got up with a sigh of relief and stretched himself. What a dull meeting – no buns, no biscuits, just talk, talk, talk – and hardly a laugh, and not one single pat! No – Scamper didn't at all approve of meetings like that! He stalked up the path with his tail down.

'Ooooh – twice if it's O.K. – four times if they want Peter's father to come – and six times if it's urgent!' said Barbara to Pam, as they went home. 'Pam – don't you think that the Secret Seven have a *thrilling* time?'

Sixteen

After supper

AFTER supper that night, Peter disappeared to get his
bicycle, and to meet the others. 'Now remember,
Janet,' he said, as he went out, 'borrow the field-glasses
and use them – but you needn't ask Dad for them for a
while – give us time to get well away, or Dad might
come after us, and if there's nothing going on up there,
it would be a shame to drag him out when he's tired;
but be sure and WATCH FOR ANY SIGNAL.'

'Oh I will, Peter, I will,' said Janet, wishing she was
coming too. 'Oh, *why* am I a girl? I do so want to
come. Are you taking Scamper?'

'No. It's too far for him,' said Peter. 'Sorry, Scamper, old thing. Stay home!'

Scamper turned away sadly, tail down again, very
miserable. Didn't Peter love him any more? This was
the second time that he had gone out without him.
Scamper walked down the garden some way behind
Peter, wondering where he was going. He watched him
take out his bicycle. He saw the other boys come up one
by one, and his tail went down even further.

He could bear it no longer when he saw the boys ride
off. He would follow them! They would go faster than
he could run, but somehow he would smell their trail
and follow, 'Wuff,' said Scamper to himself. 'Peter
won't know. But I feel as if I MUST be with him tonight!'

457

And so a lonely figure padded up the road after the bicycles, holding its nose in the air, sniffing, sniffing, trotting away after the four boys. Good old Scamper!

Meantime Janet was watching the clock. She was glad when the two other girls came. Time was going very slowly indeed. She waited until the boys had been gone about half an hour, and then she decided to ask for the field-glasses, and tell her parents what was happening! Would they be cross? Well, it couldn't be helped, she must just bear it.

She found the field-glasses and went to the sitting-room where her father and mother sat, her mother knitting and her father doing his accounts.

'Dad,' she said. 'May I borrow your field-glasses, please?'

'What in the world for?' said her father, astonished. 'At this time of night too!'

And then out everything came – the whole story, higgledy-piggledy at first, so that her parents couldn't make head or tail of what she was telling them. But gradually they understood what had been happening – and why Janet wanted the field-glasses!

'Bless us all!' said her father, quite astounded. 'What on earth will you children be up to next? This is a silly business – cycling up to the castle in the dark! As if anything serious could be happening there! Peter's idea of stolen pictures is *nonsense*!'

'Wait a minute, dear,' said his wife. 'I read something in the paper about valuable old paintings being stolen from Lord Lunwood's house – they were cut from their frames – and must have been rolled up and taken away quite easily – in a suit-case, I think the paper said . . .'

Janet gave an excited little scream. 'Oh *Mother* – the pictures Susie and Binkie saw were just rolled up, too – *not* framed – oh MOTHER !'

And now her parents really did sit up and take notice. They questioned Janet quickly, and were most astonished at all she told them.

'So the four boys have gone up to the castle, all on their own !' said her father. 'This is really a most extraordinary story, Janet, I feel rather worried.'

'You needn't be,' said Janet. 'The boys can look after themselves, Dad – they always have! We can watch for their signal, and see if they need help.'

'I'm not waiting for any signal!' said her father, firmly. 'I'm going up now – and I'm taking Matt the shepherd with me, and Gardener as well!'

'Oh dear!' said Janet. 'We were supposed to wait for a signal. Peter *will* be cross!'

'Well, I shan't mind *that*!' said her father, and went out to get Matt and to tell him to fetch the gardener. They were all to go up in the car.

Janet held the glasses carefully. Then she suddenly remembered that she hadn't seen Scamper for some time. 'Wherever is he?' she thought. 'Poor old Scamper! I expect he's sulking in a corner somewhere, because the boys went off without him. I must find him and comfort him!'

She went back to where Pam and Barbara were patiently waiting in the playroom for her, and told them quickly what her father was going to do. They whole-heartedly approved.

'Grown-ups always seem to know *at once* what's the best thing to do,' said Pam, thankfully. 'That's one of the differences between them and us! Where are you off to now, Janet?'

'To look for old Scamper,' said Janet. 'Come with me.'

But, of course, they couldn't find Scamper. He was nowhere about, and Janet suddenly felt sure he had gone trailing after the boys. She was very glad.

'Scamper's always a help, anyway,' she said to the

others. 'Come on – we'd better go up to the boxroom now and watch for signals through the field-glasses. Oh dear – I feel all worked up!'

But though they looked and looked through the glasses, each taking a turn, no signal came!

'This is awful,' said Janet, when an hour had gone by. 'No "All's Well" signal – and no "Something's Wrong" signal – and no "Urgent" signal – nothing at all! Whatever CAN be happening?'

Seventeen
Up in the castle

QUITE a lot had been happening! The boys had set off
on their bicycles, all feeling excited. They didn't know
that Scamper was padding a long way behind them,
sniffing most exciting night-smells as he went. He smelt
a hedgehog somewhere in the ditch nearby, but paid
no attention. Then he smelt rabbits in the field, and he
longed to scatter them. But on he trotted! He was determined to find Peter and see what he was up to. It
wasn't fair of Peter to leave him behind!

Peter was now almost at the castle, with the others
cycling behind him up the steep hill. How they
panted – but as long as *Peter* was still valiantly pedalling, they meant to as well! They were very thankful to
see him jump off when he came to the place in the
hedge where they had all flung their bicycles before! It
had been a hard climb.

'Switch off your lamps,' said Peter. 'I think it will be
safe to leave the bikes here. Only the bus comes by
usually at night – very few cars.'

They were soon walking cautiously up the grassy hill
towards the castle, which loomed above them like a
gigantic black shadow. Each of them had a torch, but
nobody used one, for fear of warning anybody in the
castle. Peter suddenly stopped, not far from the old
ruin.

'Go cautiously now,' he commanded. 'In single file –

and remember, if trouble comes, one of us must signal with his torch. It doesn't matter which of us – so watch out in case it's necessary.'

They came quietly to the castle. Not a sound was to be heard. It was in complete darkness. When they stepped cautiously inside, their rubber shoes making no sound, a rustling noise began above their heads, and they stopped in fright.

'It's only the roosting jackdaws!' whispered Peter. 'They must have heard our quiet tread! Wait till they settle again.'

Soon there was complete quiet once more. The boys went on down the great hall – and then Peter caught sight of something that made his heart beat quickly.

'Look – there's a light of some sort in that old kitchen-room,' he whispered to the others. 'Stay here. I'm going to see what it is.'

He tiptoed off to the entrance of the huge old room – and stopped in surprise at what he saw. Someone was there – a woman. She had lighted a fire of sticks to keep her warm, and it was burning brightly. She was lying on her side, facing the little fire, her eyes closed.

'So it was *she* who had stamped out that half-burnt fire we found the other day, the twigs still warm!' thought Peter. 'She must have seen us coming, and hurriedly put it out. I hope she's really *sound* asleep!'

She seemed to be. She was lying on a mattress, wrapped all round in rugs (the ones Susie saw down in the dungeons, thought Peter) and didn't move at all. Beside her Peter caught the gleam of a clock's

luminous hands, and then his ears picked up its
quick ticking.

He tiptoed away and whispered what he had seen to
the others. 'She's fast asleep by a fire of twigs. I expect
she's here to watch out for anyone coming in the day-
time who might discover the secrets of the dungeon. It
was really quite a good idea to pretend to be an artist
and paint the castle – she could sit all day and keep
guard, then!'

'Well, she didn't spot *us* the other day!' said Jack. 'I
say – if she's asleep, I don't think much can be happening tonight, do you? I mean – wouldn't she be
awake if somebody was coming in answer to her signal
last night?'

'Yes. I suppose she would,' said Peter. 'Oh well – we

can at least go down to the dungeons and see if those pictures are there! If they are, we could pick them up and go home with them – then the thieves would have a real shock when they came – they'd find them gone!'

'Good idea!' said George, pleased. 'Let's go down now – but for pity's sake don't let's wake that sleeping woman! Go carefully.'

So, very warily indeed, the four boys went down the old stone dungeon steps. These were much broken and worn, and the boys were glad of their torches to see where they were treading.

'Here we are!' said Peter, when they came at last to the bottom of the steps. 'Whew – what an *awful* place!'

It certainly was! It had great stone walls, black with the dirt of centuries, and the floor was of uneven stone too. Peter shone his torch round and saw great iron staples in the wall.

'I bet plenty of poor wretched prisoners were once roped to those for months – perhaps years,' he said, and everyone shivered at the thought.

'It's not *damp* here, though,' said Jack. 'I thought all dungeons were damp and smelly.'

'Well, this is on a hill, so any water would drain away,' said Peter. 'And, of course, that's why this is a good hiding-place for valuable pictures – it's perfectly dry! Damp would have ruined them at once.'

'Well – where *are* the rolled-up canvases that Susie told us about?' said Jack, flashing his torch all round. 'There's straw here – where maybe tramps rest at times – and some old newspapers – but I can't see much else!'

Jack was right. There were no rolled-up pictures to be found, though they searched everywhere in the great old dungeons.

'Well – I suppose the men have been here already and taken them,' said George, in disappointment.

'Or else Susie made it up!' said Colin. 'Another of her little tricks!'

'No,' said Jack. 'I am certain she didn't make that up. Binkie saw the canvases too, you know. And yet – if the thieves *have* been to fetch them, why is that woman still here? It must surely mean that she has hidden them somewhere else – maybe because she was afraid that the girls had seen the pictures, and might tell someone.'

'Yes. That's more like it,' said Peter. 'But where can they be hidden? They must be somewhere easy to get at, if the men are coming here for them. They wouldn't want to spend ages getting them out of some difficult hiding-place!'

'Well – there's nothing for it but to do a bit of hunting ourselves!' said Colin. 'Come on! And let's hope we find our telescope somewhere too!'

Eighteen

An exciting discovery

So, treading very quietly indeed, not daring even to cough, the boys began to look for a likely hiding-place. They hunted in every corner, except in the room where the woman lay asleep, and at last came to the conclusion that the pictures must be somewhere there. It seemed to be the only place left!

'She's probably hidden them under her mattress,' said Peter, with a small groan. 'But let's have one last think. Where would *we* hide them if we had to? And remember, they *could* be straightened out flat.'

Silence. Everyone thought hard. Then Colin whispered loudly: 'I know where *I'd* hide them – under all the mess of twigs the jackdaws have dropped for years, at the base of the big tower!'

'Jolly good idea!' whispered back Peter. 'Fine hiding-place! We'll go and look. Quietly now!' he admonished, as a scramble started.

They tiptoed to where the mass of twigs lay heaped everywhere on the floor, and shone their torches all around. 'It looks as if that pile over there has been messed about a bit,' whispered George, shining his torch on a heaped stack. 'Hold my torch. I'll scrabble about and see.'

He stepped over the masses of twigs, and they cracked loudly beneath his feet. He stopped in a hurry, and waited a moment, afraid that the noise would wake the sleeping woman. Then he leaned forward and began carefully to scrape away the twigs that seemed to have been freshly heaped-up.

His hand felt something underneath, and he gave a small cry. 'I believe I've found something!' he whispered, and pulled out what looked rather like a roll of thick paper.

'Yes! It's one of the pictures Susie must have seen down in the dungeons!' said Peter, thrilled. 'See if there are any more.'

Yes – there were plenty more, all neatly rolled up, some of them inside one another. George handed them all out to Peter and Jack. It was a very thrilling moment indeed!

And then they heard something that startled them very much, and made them jump almost out of their skins! A bell! A loud bell that rang and rang and rang, breaking the dark silence so suddenly that the boys felt rooted to the spot. Then the noise stopped, and there was silence again.

'What was it? A telephone bell ringing?' whispered Colin.

'Sounded more like an alarm clock going off,' whispered George, surprised to find himself trembling.

'Of course! It was the clock we heard ticking near that sleeping woman!' said Peter. 'She had set it for a certain time! Maybe the thieves are coming soon, to get the hidden pictures, and she wanted to be sure to be awake. We'd better hide!'

They tiptoed to a small recess in the great wall, and crouched there, their hearts beating fast. Peter and

Jack had the rolled-up pictures. They waited there, quite silent.

They heard movements after a minute or two, and then the light of a lamp came from the kitchen-like room where the woman had been sleeping. The light came nearer, and the crouching boys saw the woman pass their recess, holding the light before her to see the way. They huddled in the dark shadows, hardly daring to breathe!

She passed right by, went to the great entrance, and stood there. 'She's signalling!' whispered Peter. 'I bet that's to say "All's Clear – come and get the goods"!'

'Oh goodness! The girls at home will see the signal and think it's *ours!*' groaned Jack. 'I wonder how many times that woman's waving.'

'Let's get out of here,' said Colin. 'I don't want to be found by whoever's coming up to the castle. Let's go now, whilst we've time.'

'Well, we should have plenty of time, if the thieves have to come from any distance,' said Peter. 'But maybe they're hiding somewhere near, so we'll have to look out! Come on – we'll rush by that woman – she *will* have a fright! Let's hope we can signal with our torches when we get out on the hillside!'

They all left the dark little recess and raced to the entrance, where the woman stood, the lamp still in her hand. She gave a scream when they pushed past her, and tried to catch hold of Colin.

'Stop! Who are you? Stop, I say!'

But the boys did not stop. They tore out into the darkness. Then Peter had a shock – he tripped over something and fell headlong – and down went all the others too! Before they could get up, firm hands had hold of them, and each boy was pulled roughly to his feet. A bright torch was shone into their faces.

'Kids!' said a man's voice. 'Four boys! What on earth are you doing here, I'd like to know!'

Three men stood there, dark shadows in the night, lighted only by the torch they held towards the four boys. They had neatly tripped each of them as they came racing out into the darkness.

'Let me go!' yelled Peter, and kicked out hard. The man holding him tightened his grip.

'Quite a little spitfire,' he said, mockingly, and shook him hard. The woman came up, then, amazed.

'I've not seen them before,' she said. 'They must have been hiding in the castle.'

'Are the things safe?' said the tallest man, sharply.

'I'll see,' she said, and went off. The boys waited, their hearts thumping. They knew that the pictures were certainly *not* safe in their hiding-place. No – they were well down the hillside now, where they had rolled after Peter and Jack had kicked them, as soon as the men caught hold of their arms. How they hoped that nobody had seen the rolls of pictures bumping down the hillside in the darkness!

The woman came hurrying back. 'They're gone!' she said. 'Not a single one there. These boys must have taken them and hidden them somewhere! Whatever made them come here! They *couldn't* have known anything about them!'

'We'll soon find out,' said the tall man. 'Shove the boys into the dungeons and keep them there till they tell us what they are doing here at this time of night – and where they've put the pictures!'

And then, very roughly indeed, the four boys were pushed into the castle, and down into the dungeons! What a horrible thing to happen, just as they had been about to go home in triumph!

Nineteen

A friend in need!

'I SAY! This is a sickening thing to happen!' said Peter, rubbing himself where he had fallen against the hard stone floor. 'What bad luck to run headlong into those men!'

'Peter! What happened to the pictures?' said George, in a whisper.

'We managed to drop them and give them a good kick down the hill,' answered Peter. 'I hope they're still rolling!'

'What are we going to do?' asked Colin, who felt decidedly scared.

'I don't see that we can do *anything* at the moment,' said Peter. 'What a pity we weren't able to signal to the girls, after all! Then we'd know help was coming.'

'What do you suppose those men are doing?' asked George. 'Looking for the pictures?'

'I should think so,' said Peter. 'They'll be down here soon enough, when they can't find them anywhere!'

Nobody liked hearing that! Their hearts sank. Peter began to wonder if he could possibly get out of the castle and signal home. No. He couldn't. One of the men would be sure to be watching at the top of the dungeon steps.

And then something most astonishing happened! There was no *man* at the top of the steps – only the woman, who had been told to shout if the boys tried to escape. Quite suddenly the boys heard her give a scream, and then she shouted, 'Oh, what is it, what is it?'

Then something bounded down the steps at top speed, and flung itself on top of Peter, whining in delight!

'*Scamper!*' cried Peter, in the utmost astonishment. 'Whatever are *you* doing here? How did you find us? Oh good dog, clever dog! Oh, how glad I am to see you!'

Scamper whined and barked and licked every one of the boys. What a long, long trek he had had, following their trail – but now, here he was, *just* at the right moment! He leapt up at Peter, and went almost mad with joy.

The boys felt braver at once. Scamper would be a real help! The woman's screams had brought the men up at once, and they shouted to her.

'What's happening? What is it?'

'Oh, something pushed by me in the dark and shot down into the dungeon!' she said. 'It *seemed* to be a dog!'

Scamper immediately produced an extremely fierce growl down at the bottom of his throat – it startled even Peter, who was used to Scamper's barks and growls.

'Urrrr. URRRRRR, URRRRRRR!'

'You be careful of our dog!' yelled Peter. 'He'll attack you if you don't let us go.'

'You tell us where you've put those pictures and we'll let you go all right,' came back the angry answer.

473

'Otherwise we'll keep you here for a week!'

'Stuff!' shouted back Peter. 'Our people will soon come after us. *We* don't mind staying here. Makes a nice change!'

All the same, the boys didn't at all like being down in the dungeons. They were dark and full of shadows – and they were very cold indeed! One of the men decided to give the boys a scare and came rushing down the steps, hallooing at the top of his voice. He certainly startled the boys – but as he also had the effect of making Scamper go wild with rage, it didn't do him much good! The spaniel flew at him, and nipped him smartly on the leg. The man gave a howl and went up the steps as quickly as he had come down!

'Good dog, Scamper,' said Peter, pleased. 'Gosh, I'm glad you trailed us tonight! What a long walk you've had, old fellow! You're a jolly good friend!'

For about an hour nothing happened. What were the men doing? Having a meal? Looking for the pictures? Nobody could guess. They all felt very thankful that Scamper was there to protect them.

'We wouldn't have had a chance without him!' said Peter. Then he stiffened as he heard a distant noise. 'Listen – something's going on! Hark at that shouting and yelling!'

They listened – and Scamper suddenly gave a delighted whine and tore up the stone steps at top speed.

'Hey, come back!' yelled Peter – but Scamper took no notice.

'Let's go and see what's happening,' said Peter, and

started up the steps. 'There can't be anyone guarding us now, if Scamper shot away like that.'

They all went cautiously up the steps – and, as Peter said, there was no one on guard at the top. But outside the castle there was certainly *something* going on! Shouts and yells and the sound of feet stamping about – what a to-do! Scamper was in the midst of it, barking and nipping whenever he had a chance! Quick, Peter – where's your torch?

Twenty

Safe home again !

PETER shone his torch on to the shouting mob – and
nearly dropped it in surprise. 'DAD! How did *you* get
here! And *Matt*! I say, look – there's Dad and Matt
and Gardener – and they've caught all three of the
men !'

The torches shone on the six men and the excited
dog. There was no sign of the woman – she had fled
away while she had the chance !

'Now then – you just come along quietly,' said Matt's deep voice. The big shepherd was having the time of his life! He could handle bulls and cows and horses and rams and goodness knows what – and he had no difficulty at all in handling two or three frightened men, especially with Peter's father and the hefty gardener to help.

'Dad! Oh Dad! How did you know we wanted help – we weren't able to signal!' cried Peter, as his father neatly pinioned his man's arms behind him.

'Hallo, Peter – so you're all right!' said his father. 'We're just taking these men down to their van to lock them in and Matt will drive them down to the police-station. I'm sure the police will give them a bed to-night! We found their van parked up the lane, ready to take them off again – with the pictures too, I suppose! We saw your bikes somewhere down the lane as well!'

'Oh *Dad*! I can't believe you're here!' said Peter, full of thankfulness. 'I suppose Janet told you where we were. Can we do anything to help you with these fellows?'

'No – but you might look around for those pictures,' said his father. 'They're too valuable to be left in the damp and cold. These fellows won't tell us where they are.'

'Perhaps that woman took them,' suggested Matt, marching the tall man away in front of him. 'She scuttled off like a rabbit.'

'No – she didn't take them,' said Peter. '*I* know where they are! I'll get them!'

He and the others raced down the hill with their
torches to find where the rolled-up pictures had gone.
Now – where were they? Surely that woman hadn't
found them? No – there they were, lying where they
had rolled, safe and sound, spread all about the hillside!

'Good!' said Peter, and pounced on them. Soon he
and the boys had gathered them all, and ran back to
where the men were now being bundled into their own
van. They stared angrily when they saw the rolls of
canvases carried by the boys.

Matt drove away in the van, with the three angry,
frightened men locked inside. Peter's father and Gardener went to the car in which they had driven up.

'You boys will come down on your bikes, won't you?'
Peter's father shouted. 'What about Scamper?'

'Oh take him in the car, Dad, if you will,' said Peter,
lifting up the excited dog. 'He walked all the way here,
dear old fellow – he must be tired now!'

Scamper was thankful to go back in the car. Peter's
father carefully put the precious canvases out of his
reach, and away they went down the hill, following the
van.

What a joyful meeting the Seven had in Peter's
playroom, as soon as they arrived back. The girls and
Peter's mother gave them a great welcome and could
hardly wait to hear their news – and how eagerly they
listened to the four boys' exciting story.

'Oh *what* a time you had!' said Janet, her eyes shining. 'Oh, I *wish* I'd been with you! Whatever will Susie
and Binkie say when they hear all this? By the way, did
you find our telescope in the castle? I suppose the men
had hidden it somewhere there?'

'No – we didn't find the telescope!' said Jack. 'Blow!
We ought to have asked those men where it was – our
marvellous telescope that brought us this exciting adventure!'

'Here's Dad back again,' said Peter, hearing the
front door open, and Scamper's loud barking as he too
came in, and rushed up the stairs. Peter opened the
playroom door, and Scamper jumped up at him in
joy.

'Dad! We're all up here, Mother too!' called Peter.
'Oh Dad – THANK you for coming to our rescue! We
couldn't even give the signal for help – so we'd all be

down in those miserable dungeons still, if you hadn't rescued us. Oh Dad – wasn't it exciting!'

'Sir,' said Jack, anxiously, 'did the men say anything about my telescope? We're pretty sure they stole it because they knew we were watching the castle through it.'

'Oh yes – they've admitted that they stole it,' said Peter's father. 'But I'm sorry to have to tell you that they didn't take it up to the castle – they simply threw it away into the river.'

'Oh my goodness!' said Jack, looking very down in the dumps. 'That's a blow. It was such a *wonderful* telescope – I'll never, never have another like it.'

'You will, old chap!' said Peter's father. 'There's a reward offered for those pictures – a pretty good one too – and as it will go to the Secret Seven of course, I'm sure that at their next meeting they will agree to buying you a *magnificent* telescope, Jack – and there will be enough money over for the Seven to save for a very good Christmas, as well – you certainly deserve it!'

'And Scamper, you shall have the *biggest* bone we can buy you!' said Janet, patting the spaniel's silky head. 'Oh I'm longing for our next Secret Seven meeting – we'll have such plans to make!'

You will, Janet! How we'd like to listen in and hear your excited voices, planning how to spend that reward – a fine new telescope for Jack and Susie – a bone for Scamper – a lovely Christmas for everyone. And I'm sure we can all guess what your *next* password will be – PICTURES! Are we right, Peter?